(1880–1949) was born in Northumberland, the daughter of a ship-broker. She was educated at Gateshead High School and Penrhos College, Colwyn Bay, Wales. In 1902, after her marriage to a solicitor, J. A. H. Daniell, she went to live in Bristol, which was to become the setting of most of her novels. Her first, *A Corn of Wheat,* was published in 1910, followed by *Yonder* (1912), and *Moor Fires* (1916).

During the First World War Emily Young worked in a munitions factory, and as a groom in a local stables. However, after her husband's death at Ypres in 1917 she left Bristol for London, going to live with a married man, Ralph Henderson, Head Master of Alleyn's School in Dulwich. She continued to write. *The Misses Mallett*, published originally as *The Bridge Dividing*, appeared in 1922, preceding her most successful novel, *William* (1925). Then came *The Vicar's Daughter* (1928), *Miss Mole* (1930) – winning the James Tait Black Memorial Prize, *Jenny Wren* (1932), *The Curate's Wife* (1934) and *Celia* (1937). She lived with the Henderson's in South London until Ralph Henderson's retirement at the time of the Second World War when he and E. H. Young went, alone, to live in Bradford-on-Avon, Wiltshire. Here Emily Young wrote two children's books, *Caravan Island* (1940) and *River Holiday* (1942), and one further novel, *Chatterton Square*, published in 1947, two years before her death from lung cancer at the age of sixty-nine.

Virago publishes *The Misses Mallett, Miss Mole, Jenny Wren, The Curate's Wife, Chatterton Square* and *William.*

VIRAGO
MODERN
CLASSIC

NUMBER

292

E. H. YOUNG

WILLIAM

WITH A NEW INTRODUCTION BY
JOHN BAYLEY

Published by VIRAGO PRESS Limited 1988,
Centro House, 20–23 Mandela Street, London NW1 0HQ.

First published in Great Britain by Jonathan Cape Ltd. 1925
Copyright E. H. Young 1925

Introduction Copyright © John Bayley 1988

British Library Cataloguing in Publication Data

Young, E. H. (Emily Hilda), *1880–1949*
William. — (Virago modern classics).
I. Title
823′.912[F]

ISBN 0–86068–855–0

Printed in Finland by Werner Söderström OY

Introduction

In one sense the novel, as a literary form, grows ever more sophisticated, more complex, and more uninhibited. We may feel that today it can say what it likes and do what it likes. That is why the novels of a generation or two ago, even those that impressed many readers when they first appeared, may now seem naive in their preoccupations and artless in their narrative manner. Yet to discriminating readers who love good novels this may be a positive aid to discernment, as well as a source of charm. There is no better way of getting the true flavour of the past – particularly the immediate past – than by rediscovering novels that might seem *passé*.

Nor is that the only consideration. The great classic novelists – Dickens say, or Tolstoy, or George Eliot, do not seem to belong to the past in this sense, because the pressure of creation in them is so great that it animates them into a sort of perpetual presentness, human and material. Dickens's Mrs Gamp, or Tolstoy's Countess Rostova, are with us all the time, and as we read the book the same seems true of the conditions under which they live. But this presentness is not true of the more ordinary characters created in the past by the lesser novelists. They really do inhabit their time, conform to its conventions, are agitated by its problems and debates. And as the narrator of L. P. Hartley's novel, *The Go-Between*, observed: 'The past is a foreign country: they do things differently there.' A novel of our own time can only summon up the past in a highly stylised and artificial way, which may be effective in terms of its own art, but cannot give us the real thing.

And in spite of current literary theory a sense of the real thing is still very important to discriminating readers. They can be aware of it in all sorts of ways. For example in the relationship between the plot and the novelist's consciousness, and the way readers get on terms with the novelist's personality. The plot can have the odd effect of making readers get to know the novelist in the more or less formal sense in which they get to know people in life: intimacy is not immediate but comes by degrees. The conventions of intercourse are maintained by the plot of such a novel in much the same way as they are by the normal conditions of social existence. One of the possible drawbacks of the modern novel is that it takes such an intimacy too much for granted. Readers can be fatigued or repelled by the novelist's excessive openness, and lack of ordinary good manners. The novelist's disregard of fictional convention can be as irksome and off-putting as such a disregard in daily behaviour.

The modern novel, in fact, stands to lose as much as it gains from its own way of doing things. It may even make us prefer to read its predecessors. And certainly when we open or reopen the pages of E. H. Young's novels we have a most agreeable sense of meeting the author on civilised terms; not in any way that seems old-fashioned, but as if a normal privacy and propriety were being respected on the surface, while at the same time we can wonder and speculate – and in time find out – what lies beneath. The author and her novels have a lot in them; and extended acquaintance keeps bringing fresh rewards. The modern novel may impress us, or seem excitingly fresh and challenging in its approach, but it also runs the risk of seeming two-dimensional – of expending all its effects at one go, of making its point all too clear. This has always been a risk with the more sensational kinds of fiction – Tolstoy remarked on the kind of novel where 'you see too soon what the writer would be at, and you are bored with it' – but modernist techniques in fiction have exaggerated the danger that the reader may undergo the purely literary impact of a novel without getting to know the novelist, or wishing to do so.

Our relationship with Jane Austen, or with Conrad or with D. H. Lawrence or with Virginia Woolf, to name but a few, is not like this. We do get to know them, and as we sense the complexity of the relation between what Lawrence called 'the teller' and 'the tale' we become on terms of increasing friendship and intimacy with the teller, sometimes altering our opinion about him or her, just as we might over a period of acquaintance in life. If we get to know E. H. Young's novels our relation with them, and with her, will be definitely of this kind. The simplest and most obvious definition of a classic body of fiction is one that some readers, whether many or few, will have introduced to them or discover for themselves afresh in each generation. For some it will be a unique experience which they will hand on to the next. E. H. Young is likely to be a novelist whose works will continue to be handed on in this way; but physical availability is always an important factor, and Virago Modern Classics have done admirable work in reissuing novels of the class to which hers belong.

E. H. Young shares with Barbara Pym in our time an unmistakable but at the same time indefinable literary personality. Both women as novelists have a mixture of openness and reserve, a quiet sense of fantasy, and a sense of humour which is no part of their professional equipment, as it is with some novelists, but which can emerge in spontaneous and sometimes disconcerting ways. They are, as it were, secretly amused by their own sense of things, and readers can share this or not as they like. Take this small exchange from *Miss Mole*, a novel E. H. Young published five years after the success of *William*, which appeared in 1925. Hannah Mole is a woman of around forty, who has knocked about a good deal as a governess and companion; and whose character, as a part of her destiny, grows gradually more and more familiar to the reader. She is talking to a widow called Mrs Gibson.

'But you had a husband,' she said.

'Well, of course, dear. And I was a good wife to him. Those are his own words.'

'I was wondering,' Hannah said, 'if the best wives are the ones who are not married.'

'Oh, my dear, I don't hold with that kind of thing!'

But Hannah was trying to find proofs for her theory that non-realisation was the highest good.

'I don't mean what you mean,' she said.

'I'm glad of that,' said Mrs Gibson.

In both tone and topic there is a similarity here with a conversation in Barbara Pym's novel, *Excellent Women*.

'You could consider marrying an excellent woman?' I asked in amazement. 'But they are not for marrying.'

'You're surely not suggesting they are for the other things?' he said, smiling.

That had certainly not occurred to me, and I was annoyed to find myself embarrassed.

'They are for being unmarried.' I said. 'And by that I mean a positive rather than a negative state.'

'Poor things, aren't they allowed to have the normal feelings then?'

'Oh yes, but nothing can be done about them.'

Both Hannah Mole and Barbara Pym's Mildred Lathbury are 'excellent women'; and both writers have a gently sardonic and not at all sentimental view of what that role entails. Both reveal that the 'excellence' of women is a far more complex and more humorous affair than might be supposed.

William is a very different novel from *Miss Mole*, but both share the same kind of density, the richness of social and family background, and the psychological depth which goes with mastery in bringing these things to life. It is a family novel, and like all really good examples of the family novel portrays its members in a state of unemphasised mutual vigilance, bordering on hostility, as if biology required them to ignore each other, and at the same time made such an attitude impossible. In E. H. Young's portrayal of the Nesbitt family there is more than a hint of the large, asynchronic dynasties in the novels of Ivy Compton-Burnett, although the Nesbitts are firmly situated in time – the first decade of our century – and in place – the city of Radstowe, with its downs and bridge and harbour.

Radstowe is Bristol, the setting for almost all E. H. Young's novels. Herself born in the north, a member of a fairly extensive clan – her father was a Northumberland ship-broker – she came to Bristol on her marriage at the age of twenty-two to a local solicitor. That was in 1902, and before the war she had already published two novels set in the locality and society with which she had become familiar. Her husband John Daniell was killed at Ypres, and after the war she left Bristol, going to live in South London with one of his closest friends, Ralph Henderson, who was headmaster of Alleyn's School. They had been close for some years during her husband's lifetime, and it seems reasonable to suppose they had been lovers as well. Henderson was a married man, living with and caring for his wife with no physical relationship; and Mrs Daniell, as she was always known, made the household an effective *menage á trois*, even though she had a separate flat of her own on the premises.

Such a situation is itself like a novel. We have no means of knowing what Mrs Henderson thought of the situation, though she appears to have been quite content with it, the two women getting on well. But a school is a hotbed of gossip, and headmaster and novelist must have shown remarkable nerve and discretion in maintaining an appearance of respectability. Perhaps the known oddness of Henderson's wife and the quiet popularity of Mrs Daniell were saving factors. When Henderson retired, and after his wife's death, the couple retired to Bradford-on-Avon, and there E. H. Young wrote her last books, two for children, and a final and memorable novel about Radstowe, *Chatterton Square*. She died in 1949.

A gift for diplomacy in everyday life is no doubt a rare and useful endowment for the novelist. William Nesbitt, the eponymous head of the family, is well aware of it, and well aware on whose shoulders falls the main burden of keeping the peace and oiling the wheels.

> William Nesbitt stretched out his short legs and his face looked tired. It had been a long day and social relationships were more difficult than business ones. He marvelled at the endurance of women whose lives were a tangled mass of human complications, but women were tough: Providence had seen to that.

In terms of an always undemonstrative control of narration and consciousness, the presentation of William is a masterpiece. There is nothing either specially masculine or feminine about the way he lives, thinks, and is; but the family side of him is naturally more in evidence than his life as a man of business, although his prosperity as the owner of a fleet of local passenger boats is entirely convincing, and we see him at work in his office, and at the ceremony on board one of his new little steamers. But his function in the novel is as a husband, and as the father of a grown-up and variegated family, to whose lives and problems he is deeply and helplessly committed. He is not an actively benevolent man and he has no wish to appear as a tower of strength, but his family depend on him for moral support more than they are aware, or wish to be aware.

It seems likely that William has much in common with E. H. Young's father, and that his wife resembles her mother in some degree. But no doubt she drew on literature too: there is a suggestion of the Rostov family in *War and Peace,* while William has some of the dispassion of Mr Bennet in *Pride and Prejudice,* whose affection for his daughters is itself a form of inner irony and novelist's detachment. The most effective though concealed contrast in the novel is between William's way of caring about his family, and the immediate and atavistic reactions of his wife, reactions she can no more help than stop breathing. The idea that her daughter Lydia is not getting on well with her husband up in London is enough to make Mrs Nesbitt react like a tigress with her cubs; and this domestic instinct finds its natural ally and support in the social proprieties. In her quiet way E. H. Young demonstrates brilliantly how convention and mother-love go together, making it impossible for Mrs Nesbitt, in her station and age, to look with any sort of neutrality on the question of her daughter abandoning her marriage. The reader today may well find some irony in this, for a modern *mère de famille* would be animated just as much by her maternal feelings, while relating them to a completely different social code. Toleration can be as tyrannical as the rigid old concepts that Mrs Nesbitt clings to.

William Nesbitt does not have his wife's gut reactions, and the novelist shows us with her usual unobtrusive skill both why he is able to take a more 'civilised' view of his daughter's behaviour, and also why their different reactions to that behaviour go a long way towards estranging him from his wife. Marital harmony, even the affections of intimacy, are dependent in the Young world on the saving powers of mutual ignorance. Marriage may require an unconscious respect for one's partner's resources of incomprehension: it may be no use trying to make it work on shared understanding and rational debate. William and his wife have been happy while their children grew up because each pursued separately their own way of doing things and looking at things, and their spheres of interest did not collide. The novel reveals an area of marriage which the form had hardly explored before: the kind of unresolvable difficulties which may arise late in life between a husband and wife who have previously got along very well. George Eliot might well have turned her attention to it, if she had lived to write further novels – she had already shown her grasp of the issues involved in her account of the marriage of Lydgate and Rosamond in *Middlemarch*

– and E. H. Young, as it happens, was born in the year
George Eliot died. Hardy too, in his last novel, *The Well-
Beloved*, had stressed with bitter irony the increasing
estrangement that was likely to take place in marriage
between two partners who had started out with the same
views and ideals. He portrays as a secondary character
'the once intellectual, emancipated Mrs Pine-Avon',

> now retrograded to the petty and timid mental position of her
> mother and grandmother . . . She was another illustration of the rule
> that succeeding generations of women are seldom marked by cumu-
> lating progress, their advance as girls being lost in their recession as
> matrons, so that they move up and down the stream of mental
> development like flotsam in a tidal estuary. And this perhaps not by
> reason of their faults as individuals but of their misfortune as child-
> rearers.

The image of the tidal river is rather apposite to *William*,
with the sense that novel keeps before the reader of the
port and town of Radstowe. But of course E. H. Young
does not deploy the powerful direct perceptions and
arguments that go with the novel as George Eliot and
Hardy practised it. Like the animal who bears the revealing name of her own Miss Mole she prefers to work
quietly under the surface of her story, not emphasising
the directions she takes, and their significance. By her
method such matters can be left to suggest themselves to
the reader who takes a real interest; and besides, she has
no intention of making a tragedy out of these matters,
or even a 'socially meaningful' drama. The relations of
William and his wife recover, more or less, from their
difficulties, which have not after all been so very great:
in the words of a Barbara Pym heroine 'life is not really
as bad as all that'.

It is more a question of moments for both novelists;
moments good and bad, trivial moments but revealing
ones. Because his wife suddenly feels a violent and
destructive irritation with William it does not mean that
their daily relations are poisoned: merely that marriage
is necessarily like that. An inattentive reader, now or

when the novel first appeared, might well feel it to be a family comedy or even idyll, with alarms and adventures to help the plot along, and a satisfactorily happy ending. Such a reader would not be wrong, and there were very many of them when the novel first appeared in 1925, for it was an immediate and long-lived success, but there is a great deal more to it than the standard ingredients of a modest bestseller. Like many subtle novels it can have things both ways: catering to the mild appetite for trouble of a large audience, and probing much deeper down for the benefit of the thoughtful few. By experience and reflection, only known to us indirectly through the medium of her novels, E. H. Young as Mrs Daniell clearly knew a lot about marriage, and about the ways in which women have to bear its chief burdens. She is even-handed in the way she shows to us the thoughts and being of Mr and Mrs Nesbitt, but the detachment proper to the novelist means that it is more convenient for her to see matters through William's eyes than through those of his wife.

The book has its weakness, more apparent now than when it first appeared, but this weakness is itself a source of interest, particularly to those readers who have seen how other novelists have come to handle such things. William's favourite daughter, Lydia, married to a lawyer in London, is the most important character in the novel after the elder Nesbitts themselves, yet she remains a rather too 'poetic' conception who never quite comes physically to life. This is due to the role she has to play, a role possibly suggested by that of Soames Forsyte's wife Irene in Galsworthy's *A Man of Property*, which had appeared some years earlier, and which would recur in thoughtful novels of the twenties and thirties like some of those by Hugh Walpole. The role is that of the young wife who is suffering from some kind of unspecified discontent, and who is childless. William regards his daughter's childlessness as entirely her own affair, and perhaps a state of affairs that she prefers, but

Mrs Nesbitt feels about it the older mother's almost automatic response; and she is worried, too, about Lydia's relation with her men friends. This may reflect a situation in the novelist's personal life – she was also childless – but it is one she has difficulty in realising in terms of the life of the novel, elsewhere so subtle and abundant. Is Oliver, Lydia's husband, possibly homosexual, or is he simply not man enough for her – does she need a more aggressive and demanding partner? Or is Oliver simply a new-style 'tolerant' and comprehending husband? In any event the man Lydia gets, Henry Wyatt, is no more embodied as a character than is Oliver himself: Lydia, and her 'problem', have a disembodying effect in the novel on anyone in her personal life.

Nonetheless, that problem remains of very real interest, and Lydia herself a very real figure when seen through the eyes of her own family, particularly those of her father and of her sister Dora. Basically as intelligent and sensitive as her sister, Dora has settled for a vulgar husband with whom she has nothing in common, and a big family to whom she is devoted. She is kept going by mother love, and by loyalty, not love, for her spouse. Her personality is beautifully there, in the novel, as are those of the other younger Nesbitts and their wives or husbands, particularly the deplorable Mabel, with her virtuously penny-pinching ways and fierce pride in her three priggish little boys. Mabel is regarded by her parents with something of the same puzzlement with which the elder Rostovs, in *War and Peace*, regard their daughter Vera. She is, inexplicably, not 'one of us': a situation common enough in big families, but which it takes great talent to delineate with the humour and perception of E. H. Young.

'She isn't like the rest of us. She's rather coarse', the youngest daughter, Janet, finally admits about Mabel. The family's comments on each other are one of the pleasures of this novel, and particularly those of Dora and her father on Lydia. Janet's own problems, and their eventual solution, are done with great tact and understanding. The presentation of the Nesbitt family alone shows E. H. Young to be a remarkable novelist, and her other novels show her full range to be wider even than that. Every true addict of the novel will want to make, or remake, her acquaintance; and for those meeting her books for the first time *William* is certainly the one to start with.

John Bayley, Oxford, 1987

WILLIAM

Chapter 1

WHEN William Nesbitt stepped out of the old, gabled house in which he carried on his business, he was faced with a view of one of his own steamboats moored alongside the wharf across the road. She was an old boat, one of his first purchases when he left the sea and started ship-owning for himself, but she was still good for some years of easy service up and down the Channel and she was as spick-and-span as any in the fleet. The Nesbitt pleasure-boats, to say nothing of the Nesbitt cargo-steamers and tugs, were a source of pride to the city and of great profit to their owner, and William Nesbitt, walking across the road with a slight and never-to-be-lost roll in his gait, was gratified by the sight of the ship's fresh white paint, lately given in preparation of the summer season's cruising.

But with the happy thought that thousands of his fellow citizens would soon benefit by trips in sound boats, at cheap fares, and so augment his own income, there was mingled some tolerant amusement and some distaste for the class of persons who, armed with musical instruments and paper bags of refreshments, would board his steamers in the consciousness of adventure. These people outraged William Nesbitt's sense of beauty, but at the moment they were absent: the old boat had the dignity of desertion against a background of fields and trees, and William Nesbitt stood on the wharf, taking in, with unfailing enjoyment, this happy, haphazard intertwining of countryside and city.

Straight before him he could see meadows mounting to the horizon; to his left he had the ordered confusion of river, docks, factories, ships and little bridges; while to his right, dizzily high up, there swung the famous suspension bridge of Radstowe. Under it and on between high

5

cliffs the river flowed up or down with the tide, a sinuous waterway to the sea. William Nesbitt had no yearnings for the sea: he had had enough of it in his youth, but the thought of it was always with him and would have been with him even if his business had not compelled him to constant communication with it; and the fact that it lay down there beyond the river and out of sight, was like the presence of a woman, still beautiful, whom he loved no longer with desire, but with knowledge, understanding and satisaction. He breathed more deeply and happily because of it.

He looked at his watch. It was five minutes past six and time for him to be starting homewards. It was the last day of April and the trees were green. There was no lack of them in this which had once been the fashionable part of Radstowe and now was half business district and half slum. On the steep ascent from the river to the heights of Upper Radstowe they were everywhere: there was an avenue of them in a wide square where dirty children played on the pavements and slatternly women stood in the doorways of panelled halls: they towered above tiny houses, they looked over the high brick walls of gardens, now overgrown and decorated with the drying garments of the poor; and William Nesbitt, toiling up a narrow, tortuous lane, renewed his sensation of climbing through a wood where half the trees were houses and half the houses trees.

He walked slowly, for he was elderly, but easily, for his short figure was spare, and, as he went, his very bright, dark eyes under grey brows looked up at the houses behind the lane's restricting walls, at the trees against the blue sky, at the buds trying to gleam among the hawthorn leaves. Once he stooped to examine a little iron gate loose on its hinges. It ought to be put to rights: he liked to see things in good repair, and he hesitated as though inclined to speak to the householder about this neglect. It was not his business, however, and with an odd lift of the left eyebrow, which was one of his tricks, he marched on.

The lane led directly into a street of shops and these he

6

passed slowly, comparing values and prices, particularly of fruit and vegetables, and receiving the greetings of the shopkeepers at their doors. In his grey spring suit, with a faded flower in his buttonhole, a soft grey hat on his head, a trim grey moustache revealing more than it hid of his mouth, he had the appearance of a man perfectly successful in some dry-goods business; only that slight roll in his walk betrayed the sailor and nothing, to the casual observer, betrayed the poet, the poet who, at sea, had made verses for his wife, written in ink now faded on paper now worn at the folds, and preserved by her in the bottom of her jewel-case; the poet who wrote no more but kept romance in his heart like a hidden treasure. There was romance, too, for him in the old houses beyond the shops, in the wide green with its elms newly-dressed for spring, in the hoot of a steamer in the river, far below and out of sight; and there was romance, streaked with irony, in the narrow road where his own low, white house, sheltered by a sweep of garden, showed its wide front behind the trees. He nodded to the proprietor of the mews next door.

'You haven't had your clock mended yet,' he said, glancing at the dial, with the hands pointing at three minutes to ten, above the coach-house door, and he shook his head deprecatingly, secretly glad that the work had not been done, for those hands had pointed at that very spot when, many years ago, he had first wandered down the road and told his wife that one day she should live in that white house, and she, with a pretty, trustful disdain for the difficulties of such an attainment, had merely said, 'It's too near the mews.'

'D'you think so,' he had said. 'I like it.' And indeed it was part of the charm of Upper Radstowe, and Kate Nesbitt, too, came to recognize it, that fine old houses should keep company with poor ones, that little alleys should lead unexpectedly to wide gateways, and that sounds of labour should mingle with those of pleasure.

On that Sunday afternoon long ago, after a walk from their humble home on the other side of Radstowe, Kate and

7

William Nesbitt, with Walter in the perambulator and Mabel holding her father's hand, had stood by the gate of the white house and looked into the garden, as though they had been the rightful heirs. Not a word of doubt passed their lips but, to the unexpressed astonishment of Kate, William walked up to the front door and rang the bell.

'I had to take a peep inside,' he explained when he returned. 'The hall's panelled in white. It will suit us nicely. I just asked if Mr. Bodger lived there. He doesn't, it seems. As a matter of fact, I know who does and I should think he'll just last as long as we want him to – about fifteen years, Kate.'

'Fifteen years,' she mused. 'Mabel will be eighteen.'

'Perhaps sooner than that,' he calculated, and, as it turned out, Mabel was only seventeen when William Nesbitt bought the house. Neither he nor Kate had ever expressed satisfaction at that deed accomplished: on his part it would have seemed vainglorious; on hers it might have hinted surprise at his success, but they both loved the house, and for him, it was not only a home but a shrine for memories, and in particular for the memory of a swift, thin figure topped by a little ardent head, the figure of his daughter Lydia, now absent in the body but always present in his thoughts. She was a bad correspondent and though, on this evening, he looked on the hall table for a letter from her among the others waiting for him, he did not expect to find one. Why should the child bother to write to her old father? Besides, written or spoken communication was not necessary between them: they had never mentioned their sure friendship, but it was there. She had been a naughty child, but she had never asked his pardon for any of her offences, and he would have been hurt if she had. He understood her sins and her sorrows, and as he went up the stairs, thickly carpeted, he prayed that she might have no more of either, and knew that his prayer was vain. She had to suffer and make others suffer too, and he found a strange, painful exaltation in the thought, but his face was cheerful

8

as he entered the big bedroom where his wife lay resting on the sofa before she dressed for dinner.

'Well, Kate?' He kissed her. She was stout but comely. Her dark hair was hardly touched with grey, and her eyes were of a warm brown; but this evening, as he immediately noticed, they had the opaque appearance which came to them when she was troubled. 'Tired?' he asked.

'Yes, William. It's the third Monday, you know. I sometimes think I shall have to give it up.'

'So I should. A lot of old women chattering and making ugly shirts. Much better buy 'em and have done with it.'

'It would be easier,' she said with slight severity, 'but not better.'

'Now, Kate, confess you like the talking and tell me what's the matter.'

He moved about the room, changing his clothes, fixing his tie, scanning himself in the glass, as though he were entirely concentrated on what he did; and she, raising herself to a sitting posture, looked at the carpet.

'I met Dora on my way to the sewing-meeting,' she said.

'Dora is always a pleasant sight,' he remarked, apparently considering whether or not he should shave his chin: he was very particular about his appearance.

'Yes,' Mrs. Nesbitt agreed, but with less than her usual enthusiasm. 'She had been lunching with Violet after shopping all the morning –'

'All the morning? What on earth could she be buying?' he asked, and he moved from the looking-glass, having decided to let his chin alone until the morning.

Mrs. Nesbitt looked patient and did not answer his question. 'And she was going to fetch Susan from school. She does too much. Why can't she send the children to that nice little school near home? The children could run to and fro quite safely alone, but she says it isn't good enough, and they have to be taken and fetched right over the Downs twice a day, and Nurse has the babies to see to. I think it's very foolish. She looks tired.'

'Healthy exercise won't hurt Dora. She's getting fat.'

9

He cast a quick glance at his wife, now seated before the dressing-table and slowly arranging her hair, but he was busy with his own hair brushes when he said, 'I dare say Herbert wearies her.'

'Herbert? William! Could anybody be more devoted? – What do you mean?'

'Nothing, my dear. It's a way husbands have.' He lifted his eyebrows. 'You and I are quite exceptional, you know.'

Through the mirror, Mrs. Nesbitt looked at him with an almost inimical glance. She combined with the certainty of their mutual affection and loyalty, a feeling of occasional bewilderment, as though this man, at the centre of his being, were a stranger to her; and she was irritated by his unfailing poise, the good-humour of the disconcerting remarks he dropped so lightly.

'Herbert adores Dora,' she said.

'Obviously.'

'Well, then – '

'Quite so, my dear. Don't take any notice of me. I get these moments.'

She had an impulse to beg him not to frighten her, but she restrained it and said calmly, 'Dora has heard from Lydia.'

It was his turn to restrain himself. 'Ah! the minx –' he murmured.

'She is going to stay with her.'

'Lydia with Dora?'

'No, Dora with Lydia. I don't think she ought to go, leaving Herbert and the children.'

'I suppose you told her so?'

'I did drop a hint and I shall speak to her again. And Lydia wants Janet, too. I think Janet ought to go. It would do her good. The child's too quiet.'

'And is she going?'

'I haven't spoken to her yet. And, William – '

'Yes?'

'I'm worried.'

'Oh!' he exclaimed, triumphant in his premonition.

'Well, let's have it.'

'It's that Mrs. Miller.'

'Worthy woman,' he said.

'Oh, very,' Mrs. Nesbitt agreed bitingly. 'The whole family's worthy. Those ugly daughters of hers – She's jealous of our girls because they're all married – except Janet – and all good-looking, and she's jealous of my position.'

'What is that, my dear?' he asked mildly.

'Well, William – ' It was impossible to put it into words.

'Mr. Miller has never been anything but something in the museum, looking after stuffed birds and things, and he never will be. He looks like a stuffed bird himself – they all do.'

'He's a very learned man.'

'Then I'm glad you're not. He never looks clean and I don't suppose he is.'

'I've no doubt he considers himself vastly my superior and I believe he is. He has a lot of letters after his name.'

'I'd rather have a comfortable home,' Mrs. Nesbitt said without humour.

'But what's Mrs. Miller's offence? Just looking like a stuffed bird?'

'She was rude about Lydia.'

Arrayed in his neat evening clothes, William Nesbitt watched his wife putting on the rings which were his gifts, and he was aware of the slight stiffening of his body.

'Well?' he said easily.

'Well,' Mrs. Nesbitt repeated in another tone. 'I was asking about Ethel – you remember her, William, she married a curate and she's the only one who ever will marry.'

'Oh, the girl with the pig-tail.' He remembered her well enough, a hoydenish girl; Lydia's friend at the High School, heavy on her feet while Lydia was light, noisy while Lydia was quiet, thickset and rosy against Lydia's slimness and pallor, but with a great appreciation of Lydia's sense of fun. It had been a strange alliance and often, on a Saturday afternoon, the two had returned together after hockey or cricket matches to make a hearty tea enlivened by the ready laughter of the girl with the thick fair pig-tail reaching to her waist. He would find them giggling behind doors, rushing up and down the stairs, or wandering round the garden with arms linked together, and he would wonder at Lydia's forbearance with Ethel's dull good-nature, until he decided that his daughter enjoyed the other's homage and perhaps respected and envied her simplicity.

'Yes, I remember Ethel,' he said, with his mind on those good days when Lydia was in the house.

'And Mrs. Miller actually hinted that Lydia had deserted her. Ridiculous, with Ethel somewhere in the Midlands and Lydia in London, and their lives so different. And then she said Ethel was a great help in her husband's work, as if Lydia were useless in Oliver's.'

'I imagine she is,' William Nesbitt said.

'William! Your own daughter! But anyhow, the woman had no business to say it, as if she thought something.'

'My dear, what could she think?'

'Nothing,' of course,' Mrs. Nesbitt said promptly.

'Well, then – '

'I'm afraid I lost my temper,' Mrs. Nesbitt said meekly. 'It was undignified. I said something about parsons choosing their wives for use and nothing else. . . . That woman always has irritated me.'

'It's a pity to make an enemy,' he said slowly.

'I don't mind about that, but I'm sorry I let her see I was annoyed. How could she hurt us?'

'You never know. Things pop up unexpectedly. Life's a long road. It looks safe enough: you jog along, with nice trim hedges at each side and fields all buttercups and daisies, and suddenly you come to a dark place where there's a man with a gun.'

'You talk a great deal of nonsense, William.'

'Yes, Kate, but it's never wise to make an enemy. Besides – ' but he decided to say nothing of the moral aspect of the affair. 'Shall we go down?' he said.

'Why are you looking at me like that?' she asked.

'I was thinking how pretty you are. None of the girls can hold a candle to you.'

Oh, William, absurd,' she said, pleased but restive under his puzzling regard.

With her arm in his they went down the broad staircase into the white-panelled hall. A great bowl of daffodils, the work of Janet's eyes and hands, was like a globe of light against the wall, and on the dining-table more daffodils made Janet's golden hair look pale.

William Nesbitt glanced at his daughter and at the flowers. 'Very nice,' he remarked.

She made the smallest possible gesture. 'One has to do something,' she said.

He glanced at her again. She seemed impassive, but he was aware of a great reserve of strength under her fragile air and he felt a pang. She was not happy, and Mrs. Nesbitt conscious, too, of something uneasy in the atmosphere, said cheerfully:

'Janet, dear, you must go and stay with Lydia. You will like that. It will do you good.'

'Is Dora going?' Janet asked.

'Your mother says not, my dear, so that's settled.'

'It will be disappointing for Lydia.'

'Not at all. She will have you. Why didn't she ask Herbert if she wanted Dora? I shouldn't object to that.'

'Tell her so, Kate, tell her so. Lydia will put it right, no doubt.'

The eyes of Mrs. Nesbitt, with their opaque look of defence, rested on her husband and then closed for a second. 'It will be nice for Janet to go, nice for Janet and nice for Lydia.'

'But I'm not going,' Janet said.

'Not going? My dear child, why not?'

'Because I don't want to.'

'So that's settled, too,' William Nesbitt said, 'and so

13

much the better for us.' He looked at Janet and gave her a little nod. 'I don't want to keep you, but I should miss you.'

She looked back at him with a faint, not quite comprehensible smile, as though she hardly believed him yet was grateful for his tribute.

'Oh, Janet will think better of it,' Mrs. Nesbitt said, and between the father and daughter another smile passed.

Chapter 2

WILLIAM NESBITT slept lightly but well; his wife more
soundly for short periods, and often she waked during the
night and keeping very still, for she knew that a slight
movement would rouse her husband in the neighbouring
bed, she lay and planned the meals for the next day and
thought about her children and their domestic affairs, of
her grandchildren and their little ailments, and, aware
though she was of her many blessings, there came to her
sometimes in the darkness small gusts of fear lest harm
should come to any member of the family. There was
Lydia in London and susceptible to colds, living in a house
which was certainly damp, neglecting her health and, Mrs.
Nesbitt feared, her household. Lydia had no sound ideas
about nourishing food and Oliver was long-suffering. She
was gay, too, parties, theatres, people in and out – he spoilt
her, and Mrs. Nesbitt sighed secretly. Then there were
Walter and Violet. Like Lydia and Oliver they had no
children, and Mrs. Nesbitt distrusted childless marriages;
they meant trouble or led to it. The largeness of her
daughter-in-law's wardrobe was annoying to Mrs. Nesbitt;
her high-heeled shoes, her silk stockings, her innumerable
hats were out of proportion to Walter's income, she felt
sure, and it was equally annoying that Mabel's stockings
were always of black wool and thick at that. Mabel was
not so poor as she made out. John Partridge was doing very
well in the timber trade, so William assured her, and it was
ridiculous for Mabel to look like a poor relation. And
Janet, the youngest, still at home, who ought to have been
happy enough, without cares, gave Mrs. Nesbitt a faint
feeling of discomfort. What did the child want? The
others had all been married, or at least engaged, at her age,
but Janet seemed to despise young men. It was not natural.

15

Mrs. Nesbitt sighed again, but her thoughts, turned more happily to Dora, – Dora with a big house, plenty of servants, five delightful children, and an adoring husband, for even William had to admit that Herbert adored her, and it was nonsense to pretend that Dora might sometimes weary of him; yet life seemed very complicated to Mrs. Nesbitt when she lay awake at night, and though her worries were so small that they could hardly be expressed, they were there, like tiny clouds threatening the sun.

The coming of the dawn gave her a sense of security and she slept, to be waked by hearing a knock at the door, the sound of William answering alertly, the clink of teacups, and his voice saying cheerfully, 'Kate, tea.' Then she raised herself slowly and rather laboriously and took her cup. Her hair was bound in a short, thick plait which followed rigidly the movements of her head: her cheeks were youthfully rosy against the pillows and William Nesbitt appreciated her freshness though he did not mention it. She was modest, and even in their young days he had considered his compliments before he made them: fully dressed she was receptive enough, but he knew she would be faintly shocked if he spoke of her natural charms. For her part, she accepted the healthy sight of William in his pink and white pyjamas as a matter of course, and found in it the same reasonable pleasure as she found in the sunny bedroom, the songs of the birds in the garden and the trees visible from her comfortable bed.

They drank their tea slowly: there was no hurry, for they were called early and breakfast was not ready until half-past eight. She looked at the tree-tops and said in her deliberate fashion. 'William, I have been thinking.'

'An excellent habit.'

'I don't know,' she said with the acuteness which always startled him. 'But still I have been thinking – about Lydia.'

He waited, looking at the twin peaks made by his feet under the bed-clothes.

'I wish she needn't live in London. I wish she could live in Radstowe.'

'My dear, we're surrounded by children. Surely we can spare one to enliven other spheres. And how do you propose that they should live in Radstowe? Or do you want Lydia to leave Oliver in London?'

'Don't be silly, William.'

'Then how is he to support her? He has an excellent appointment in the Civil Service, so perhaps he might get into a post office here.'

Mrs. Nesbitt understood that this was intended as a joke, but she did not smile. 'He's a lawyer, William.'

'He is, my dear.'

'And there are lawyers in Radstowe.'

'Many,' he agreed.

'And I thought you might buy him a partnership. Yes, it may seem funny to you, William, but I'm never happy about her, she catches cold so easily and that house is damp.'

'Tell the truth, Kate, tell the truth. What's your real reason?'

'I want her near me. I want to know what's happening.'

'I can tell you, my dear. She gets up five minutes before breakfast and comes down late, when Oliver has nearly finished his.'

'And eats nothing herself,' Mrs. Nesbitt murmured.

'All she needs. She's much stronger than you think.'

'Surely I ought to know better than you, William.'

'I don't see why.'

'A mother – '

'Yes, my dear, but a father has his perceptions.' Mrs. Nesbitt with a sublime movement of her head, smiled wisely. 'And she sits about in uncomfortable corners, perhaps on the stairs, and reads and forgets to order the dinner, and tries a new way of doing her hair, and somebody comes to tea and she sits on the floor and smokes and listens.'

'Listens?'

'Of course. She doesn't talk much herself.'

'I don't know what she should listen to.'

'The sort of thing she wouldn't hear in Radstowe, I

17

imagine. And then Oliver comes home and there's a meal for him, after all, because that girl – what's she called? – Maria – has had an inspiration about cutlets. And Lydia tells Oliver what the visitor, or visitors, if you'd rather, Kate, what they said and did and how they looked, and he's very much amused. They spend their evening in reading, or dancing – '

'Oliver doesn't like dancing.'

'Well, he looks at her, which is far better, as Paul says.'

'Paul?'

'The saint, my dear. Or somebody else comes in and there's more sitting on the floor and a good deal of nonsense talked, no doubt. That's what she's doing, Kate.'

He poured himself another cup of tea and through the sound he heard her saying softly, 'It's not enough.'

He chose to ignore that remark and added lightly, 'And anyhow I can't afford to make such handsome presents to my sons-in-law, specially when they don't want them.'

'She's different from the others,' Mrs. Nesbitt said faintly, and William Nesbitt pictured Lydia vividly, yet more as a spirit than a body, something bright and swift, with strange advances and retreats which had to be divined. He said cheerfully: 'They're all different from each other, thank God.'

'William, don't!'

'What's the matter?'

'Well – "God" – just anyhow like that.'

'Keep Him for church, eh?' His left eyebrow went as high as it could. He did not look at his wife. He knew what expression she was wearing, yet even she had her surprises for him. Life was interesting, a great adventure enlivened by countless minor episodes. It was difficult to believe that anybody could find it dull. Every personality was more or less of an excitement to him – Kate, Janet, Lydia, the captains of his ships, the clerks in his office, the ships themselves, the very gulls swooping for garbage in the river, cutting the air with wings like swords.

'There's the trial trip of the new boat, the week after next, Kate. We must have a family party.'

'Then Dora certainly can't go to London.'

'My dear, with Mabel and John and Walter and Violet and Janet and you and Herbert – '

'I'd rather Herbert didn't come without Dora.'

'But I thought she wasn't to go to London.'

'Oh, William, you know as well as I do that she'll do as she likes.'

He chuckled. 'Yes, I know it.'

'They all do as they like. When I was a girl – '

'Now, Kate, you were married to me and ordering me about when you were much younger than Janet. You've had your own way since you were twenty. You know nothing about it.'

'Nonsense, William. I was always ready to take advice. Of course the children are good children – '

'Wonderful children,' he agreed heartily and, turning her head slowly, with the short, rigid plait following meekly, she looked at him with almost the effect of a blind person trying to see.

'Well,' she said coldly, as though in spite at a suspected irony, 'if you want Mabel to go to the trial trip you will have to give her a new dress, or she'll wear an old coat and say she can't afford to be sick in anything else.'

'A sailor's daughter! But she's a timber merchant's wife. Extraordinary how the trade suits him. He's a wooden sort of fellow. You were never sick, Kate, never, nor afraid, when you came for a voyage with me.'

She was pleased, but she said sensibly, 'It would have been absurd.' And he, with a hand on his heart, trolled out, 'A sailor's wife a sailor's star should be,' before he leapt out of bed, donned a dressing-gown of bright silk and went to his bath.

Mrs. Nesbitt sighed. It was a habit imbued by a craving for a perfection of existence which she knew was unattainable. She had nearly everything she wanted: she had money in plenty and she was too wise a woman to despise it; a husband who, but for that trick of saying disturbing things in a cheerful manner, was practically faultless; children who were, yes, they were wonderful, good to look at, affectionate, sound in health and sounder still in soul, children to be trusted; grandchildren who had not had time to develop unattractive qualities, though Mrs. Nesbitt, who was a truthful woman, had to admit that Mabel's boys erred on the side of excessive virtue; but what could be expected of them, named as they were after three of John's political heroes, Cromwell, Hampden, and Gladstone? It had given them a bad start in life and prejudiced people against them. But they were clever, they poked their sharp little noses into everything with a genuine desire for discovery and information, though Mrs. Nesbitt would rather they had climbed trees and risked their necks. Mabel was fussy and fond of taking their temperatures, and for this Mrs. Nesbitt had the scorn of a woman whose own children had thrived under a wholesome amount of neglect. It was only with her increasing years that motherhood had become for her what it already was for her daughters, a constant absorption and care.

Times had changed: nowadays wives seemed to put their children before their husbands because the children were not responsible for their entrance into the world, an argument too intimate and far-reaching for Mrs. Nesbitt's taste. But there it was. Moreover, she had seen Dora when Herbert was suffering from a severe attack of pneumonia, and again when one of the twins had a mild one of influenza, and the contrast in her two states of mind had made an impression on Mrs. Nesbitt. She had never spoken of it, she tried not to think of it, but William's tiresome remark about Herbert had revived that impression, and the idea of a marriage which was not perfectly happy in her own immediate family, shocked and horrified her. Such things did not happen to people like herself, and she was more than ever convinced that Dora ought not to go to London, for if William were right it was yielding to temptation, and if he were wrong there was no cause for it.

Mrs. Nesbitt, propped on her pillows, had a momentary relief in deciding that, in any case, she was powerless, but it was only momentary. She had to face facts and the fact she determined to face was that Herbert and Dora understood each other.

'Why,' she exclaimed, when William returned glowing from his bath, 'I've never heard them use a cross word to each other.'

'John and Mabel?'

She retreated at once. 'Any of them,' she said and, rather clumsily, she got out of bed, a squat figure in a short nightgown which was ruffled at the neck and wrists with embroidered frills.

'No, they have your self-control, Kate,' he said, and he took a clean shirt out of a drawer. 'See how you bear with me.'

Arrayed now in a stiff quilted dressing-gown, she stood on her small, square feet like an eastern idol and her smile was mysterious, delighting him with that quality, and though he was conscious of his deep and abiding love for her, he realized at that moment how much more thrilling their life together would have been if she had deliberately exercised some subtlety. The subtlety was there, useful on occasions, a weapon for the defence of her children, but never, alas, for the attack of her own charms. She would have considered such a proceeding immodest and unnecessary, and the desire for it was, perhaps, ridiculous in a man of his years, but he knew that, varied as his life had been and interesting as he had made it, he had missed something coloured, scented, and dangerous, something which Lydia offered to Oliver, or perhaps withheld.

'Well?' he said, looking up from his struggle with his cuff-links.

'You are a good husband, William,' she said.

'Thank you, my dear.' Screened by his shirt, he made a comic grimace. That was her verdict, but he wondered what obscure dissatisfaction lurked in the soul of this woman, who in spite of companionship, confidences and children shared, was still to some extent a stranger. He remained with his head hidden, his arms half in his sleeves, and he heard her pleasant voice saying, 'Let me help you, dear.'

'Thank you, Kate.' He emerged and kissed her heartily on her fresh cheek.

From below there came the cheerful morning sound of the gardener wheeling a barrow and, from the street beyond, the clip-clop of a horse's hoofs. The sun shone on the young green of the trees, the hawthorn buds, the tulips growing straight and tall from the circular lawn before the house, and he had a moment's pride that it was his own labour, resource, and courage which had procured this home for Kate. At sea, he had dreamed of such a home for her, and here it was: she was secured against poverty or straits, the horror of which he had never spoken but which had haunted his young days, and now he was hardly conscious of relief. It had crept on him slowly and he had missed the joy to which he had looked forward. He supposed that was the way with life, and what he had gained was a mellow content streaked with curiosity, undefined anticipation, a readiness to accept ills if they had to come. And that readiness was, perhaps, the chief difference between him and his wife; she would resent them, quietly, as she had taken her good fortune, but with bitterness.

Well, he thought, as he went into the garden to get his buttonhole for the day, she shall have no trouble if I can help it. But how could he help it? He saw their children and their children's children as so many by-roads on their own highway of life and from all those roads there lurked the possibility of assault. He saw Mabel as a dusty path, Walter as a plain country road with neat, low hedges and fields beyond, Dora as a lane rich with flowers on the banks and overshadowed by splendid trees, and Lydia came to him like a winding footway across a stormy moor, Janet like a stiled path across a meadow, and all those roads were capable of producing tramps, highwaymen, snakes,

22

and pitfalls. He shook his head in amused dismay. 'One's own fault for having children,' he said.

In the dining-room his youngest daughter sat behind the coffee-pot.

'I've a letter from Lydia,' she said.

'Persuasions?' he asked.

'Oh, yes.'

Mrs. Nesbitt rustled in. 'A letter from Lydia? Janet, you ought to go.'

'Mother, why don't you go yourself?'

'She hasn't asked me, and there's Father.'

'I can look after him.'

'Yes, Janet can look after me.'

'But there's the trial trip. Besides,' – she had a vision of Lydia's spare bedroom – 'I don't want to go.'

'Neither do I,' Janet said.

Chapter 3

No, the remembrance of Lydia's spare bedroom was not inviting. It was furnished with taste, but in Mrs. Nesbitt's opinion, without comfort, and even a glowing fire had not made it feel warm. She had suffered from cold during the whole of the week she had once spent there. She was used to thick carpets, warming to the eye as well as to the feet, and from her first entrance into the house with its drab floor coverings and sober Persian rugs, its elegant, severe furniture, she had been chilled. Lydia liked colour, but she liked it in patches, in a brilliant arrangement of flowers, in a heap of cushions, and her mother was convinced that she had fires in the house merely for the sake of their appearance. In the drawing-room on the first floor, a large room shaded in summer-time by an acacia tree, there stood on a mahogany pedestal a great metal bowl filled with flowers, blues and purples, pinks and yellows, massed together in a kind of riot: there were two or three chairs, a big, low settee, a slim-legged table, and Mrs. Nesbitt could remember nothing else. The books Lydia happened to be reading were scattered on the settee or on the floor: there were always flowers in the bowl, but otherwise the room had, for Mrs. Nesbitt, the effect of a desert. The only room where she had felt comparatively happy was a little back one where Oliver sometimes worked and Lydia left her letters unanswered and was supposed to keep the household accounts, for it was so small that Mrs. Nesbitt could feel it was really furnished. She was not surprised, but she was irritated, when William told her he admired the house. 'It expresses Lydia,' he said, and she answered sharply, 'I should be sorry to think my daughter was like that – practically, well, practically undressed.'

Mrs. Nesbitt much preferred the house of Dora, a

pseudo-Gothic castle looking over the river as if to guard it. There was no Gothic discomfort inside: it had the soft hangings, the pretty, tender colours, the deep arm-chairs that Mrs. Nesbitt loved: it was what she called a home, but Herbert was a rich man, the head of an engineering business started by his father, and Dora could have anything she wanted.

It was Mrs. Nesbitt's belief that Mabel was in the same happy position, but preferred grievances to possessions. She lived in a modern villa, kept scrupulously neat by herself and a bony servant whose face was a plain warning that she would stand no nonsense, and the chair covers, the table-cloths and the curtains were all of a useful shade of green, warranted not to fade and of a material likely to last for years. Mrs. Nesbitt seldom went to that house, because Mabel was always busy, cooking, mending, cleaning the boys' suits with a piece of flannel soaked in benzine, turning something inside out to make it into something else and suggesting that these exertions were necessary to the poor. She had no time for what Mrs. Nesbitt called a comfortable chat: her chief pleasures, though they were labelled duties, were finding bargains at sales and entertaining the ministers who came to preach at the chapel of which John Partridge was a deacon and a sturdy pillar.

Just as seldom did Mrs. Nesbitt honour her son's flat. If Lydia's house was bare, the flat was overcrowded. It was full of knick-knacks, photographs in silver frames, spindle-legged chairs, pictures and magazines, and the frivolities of this furnishing, combined with the excessive powdering of Violet's face, vaguely suggested impropriety.

No, it was in Dora's house that Mrs. Nesbitt felt she had a second home: she would drive over the Downs on fine afternoons and spend hours talking to Dora and the children, hearing about the servants and doing the fine crochet work which eventually adorned table-cloths, doilies and toilet-sets to be sold at the church bazaar. And now Dora had gone off to London in spite of the trial trip and her

25

mother's advice, while Janet, who might conscientiously have taken a holiday, remained at home, silent, as though patiently bored, deft and dutiful. She gave Mrs. Nesbitt an uneasy feeling of being in the presence of a mystery, yet what did the child want? If she were suffering from dullness why did she refuse the opportunity of gaiety with a devoted sister? Lydia had adored Janet from her baby-hood. As a little girl, she had spent her weekly penny in sweets for Janet, she had told her stories by the hour to-gether, and though it was true that Janet had never cared for sweets and Lydia liked telling stories, the devotion was none the less sincere. But Janet had always accepted these attentions quietly and she had repulsed caresses with the same dignified determination with which she had refused Lydia's invitation. What did she want? Mrs. Nesbitt re-peated. What Mrs. Nesbitt herself desired was a letter from Dora, but Dora, who usually wrote long letters in a sprawling hand when she was separated from her mother, had sent no more than a post card to announce her arrival, and it was not until the day of the trial trip and just as Mrs. Nesbitt was getting into the carriage to drive to the docks, that a letter came. There was no time to read it and she put it in her handbag.

'I shall want my spectacles, Janet,' she said.

'Spectacles?'

'Yes, spectacles,' Mrs. Nesbitt replied. 'On my dressing-table, or on the writing-desk, or perhaps I left them by the telephone. Fetch them, dear, quickly, or we shall be late and Father will be annoyed.'

She was a little flustered: her arrangements had been up-set. Early that morning, Mabel had sent Cromwell on a bicycle to ask if he and his brothers might accompany her on the trial trip.

'We shall have to ask Grandfather,' Mrs. Nesbitt said. 'Why didn't Mother think of it before?'

'Mother has been so busy,' Cromwell said, and, with a fall of her soft hands to her ample sides, Mrs. Nesbitt went slowly to the telephone.

'Grandfather says he can't have you all being sick on his nice clean deck,' she reported.

Cromwell said solemnly that he didn't think they would be. 'Mother's going to give us some sea-sick medicine before we start, and anyhow we'd lean over the side. Mother said if Aunt Dora's children were going, she didn't see why we shouldn't.'

'Your cousins are not going,' Mrs. Nesbitt said severely.

'In case they get drowned,' Janet added.

'Nonsense, Janet. People don't get drowned out of Grandfather's boats. What an idea to give him. But tell Mother there won't be room for you boys at luncheon. You'll have to stay in a corner somewhere, quietly.'

'Mother says she wouldn't let us have the luncheon, because it would upset us. We're going to have dry biscuits in our pockets and face the wind.'

'Very well. You must be here at twelve o'clock and we can drive down together.'

'Mother says Hampden and I can go on our bicycles if there won't be room.'

Mrs. Nesbitt eyed her grandson. 'You're all very thin.'

'That's because we're growing, Mother says.'

'You're all very thin,' Mrs. Nesbitt repeated, 'but even so, I don't see how we're all to fit into the carriage, so ask Mother to bring Gladstone, and you and Hampden can meet us at the office. But be careful of the traffic. Mind the tram-lines. And ask Mother to be punctual. I shall not wait for her after twelve o'clock.'

'Thank you, Grandmother,' Cromwell said sedately, and he put on the overcoat which he had cautiously removed on entering.

'An overcoat on a day like this!' Janet exclaimed. 'The sun's quite hot.'

'But it's an east wind, and Mother says east winds are treacherous.'

'Then you'll need some cotton-wool on the boat,' she said. 'Lots of it. Those children,' she added, when Cromwell had disappeared, 'are all medicine and mufflers.'

'It's not their fault,' Mrs. Nesbitt sighed. 'And when Mabel was a girl she was as careless as anybody. It must be John.'

'It's maternity,' Janet said coolly.

'Motherhood,' Mrs. Nesbitt corrected suavely, preferring that word, especially on the lips of a girl.

'There's a difference,' Janet said.

'Well, you're hardly a judge, dear. Wait until you have children of your own.'

Immediately, Janet walked out of the room and, with the passing of her slim figure crowned with pale gold, Mrs. Nesbitt thought, 'Now, she's offended. She doesn't like being set right. She's very self-willed. They all are, but if I don't say what I think I shall just be a dummy. I'm not going to let myself drift into that.' Her dark eyes, bright but opaque, hardened a little and she wondered if everybody had their pleasures slightly soured. Mabel was annoying with her fussiness and grievances; Janet was unnaturally reserved, and there came to her the conviction that no one in the world could truly understand anybody else. William kept nothing from her except the meaning of his words; the children were all she could expect children to be, yet there was not one of them who did not prick her somewhere with a tiny dart.

It had been different when they were all young and at school. She had felt then that they were her own, but perhaps she had been mistaken, perhaps she had not known their secret selves, and she remembered, for the first time for years, how she had once found Lydia crying in the nursery and had not been able to find out what her trouble was. It seemed to her that what she had missed then might be evading her still. She had given birth to five bodies and she would always be a stranger to their souls. This was a terrible thought and it would have been more terrible still if she had known that it was William's too.

Altogether it was an upsetting morning. Mabel arrived five minutes late, with a large and shabby leather bag in her hand. She was out of breath, she wanted warm milk for

Gladstone, she was voluble with explanations of her unpunctuality. Then, just as Gladstone finished his milk and the postman brought Dora's letter, Mrs. Nesbitt recognized the enormity of the leather bag.

'You can't take that, dear,' she said.

'I had to bring their sweaters, Mother, and the sea-sick cure.'

'But that bag! Janet, she must have my nice new case. Father would be angry if he saw that shabby bag.'

'I haven't anything better,' Mabel said stubbornly. She was handsome, with a lot of curling black hair under a hat a little askew and her clothes had the appearance of having been borrowed from some one else.

Janet asked calmly, 'Do you want the sea-sick cure all over your new case?'

'The cork's perfectly tight, Janet.'

'Yes, dear, I'm sure it is. Run and get the case, Janet. And my spectacles.' She might find a moment in which she could read that letter. 'Now I do hope we're ready at last. Let us get into the carriage. Gladstone, sit by Aunt Janet. I hope the boys will be careful on their bicycles.'

'Of course, Mother.' Mabel resented the idea that they could fail in any virtue. 'They ride splendidly. Cromwell is most cautious and they both have such good nerves – nerves of iron.'

'They don't look as if they have,' Mrs. Nesbitt said, appreciating the flowering trees at the gate. 'Isn't the hawthorn lovely, this year?'

'Yes, lovely,' Mabel conceded. 'They're sensitive, Mother, but they have such control over their nerves. That's how it is.'

'Have I good nerves, Mother?' Gladstone asked.

'Yes, dear, of course.'

'Sit still and don't kick me,' Janet said.

'He likes to see everything,' Mabel explained.

'He doesn't see with his feet,' Janet replied, and Mabel began very pointedly to talk to her mother who, as though Mabel had to be propitiated, treated her with a studied

29

courtesy and consideration, a manner which led Mabel to believe that she was the favourite daughter but produced a faint smile on Janet's lips; she knew that her mother was making amends for the secret irritation she felt.

Gladstone, a little awed by the severity of his pretty aunt, was silent for a few minutes and he contented himself with peering over the side of the carriage to watch the revolutions of the back wheel. Mrs. Nesbitt and Mabel talked amiably and Janet watched the progress of the spring. The flowering trees, for which Upper Radstowe was famous, were alight with yellow, blushing with pink, fainting under heavy blossoms of pure white, and the elms on the old green were lifting proud green heads to the sun and stretching out brilliant arms to catch the breeze. The streets had the hard, clear look given by the east wind, and the sound of footsteps, of voices, the hoofs of horses, the horns of motor-cars, were all challenging or triumphant; but the smile left Janet's lips as though beauty saddened her, and Mrs. Nesbitt, turning from Mabel to admire her youngest daughter, said suddenly, 'Are you tired, dear?'

Janet, startled, answered clearly, 'No, I'm never tired.'

'You're lucky,' Mabel exclaimed, 'and yet you look far more delicate than I do. I often wish I had not so much colour. One gets no sympathy.'

'What for, dear?' Mrs. Nesbitt purred pleasantly, and Janet said, 'We're all made of iron, every one of us.'

'Some of us have to pretend we are,' Mabel resignedly remarked.

'It comes to the same thing,' Janet murmured, and Mrs. Nesbitt, fearful that the pleasure of the day was to be spoilt by fruitless argument, plunged into happy questions about Mabel's boys.

They were getting on splendidly at school: Cromwell was top of his form and Hampden was second of his only because his rival was two years older.

'Oh, there's Aunt Violet,' Gladstone called out suddenly. 'What a white face she has.'

'He notices everything,' Mabel said in a proud aside.

'I'm afraid she will be late,' Mrs. Nesbitt complained, after waving her hand to the gaily-dressed lady on the pavement, 'and there's no room for her in the carriage. Ah, she's getting into a bus.'

'And what thin legs she has – thinner than yours, Mother.'

'Her stockings are thinner,' Mabel said.

Ignoring this little pleasantry, Mrs. Nesbitt consoled herself. 'After all, she may be there before us.'

'But the bus doesn't go to Grandfather's office, Grandmother.'

'He knows all the bus routes,' Mabel marvelled.

'No, dear, she will have to change into a tram and then she will have a little way to walk.'

'She won't hesitate to take a cab,' Mabel assured her mother. 'I saw her in one yesterday. I was carrying a heavy basket, but she just nodded and went on.'

'You shouldn't carry such heavy loads, dear. I always send an order to the tradespeople once a week and trouble no more about them.'

'I have to get things when they're cheap, you see. I can't afford to waste money. To-day, fish was twopence a pound cheaper in the city than anywhere else.'

'But you wear out your shoes,' Janet said.

'And your strength,' Mrs. Nesbitt added kindly.

'I can't think of that,' she replied and Mrs. Nesbitt controlled the sigh which was the natural comment. She said, 'Look, Gladstone, at that little boy bowling a hoop. It's running away from him down the hill. Hobbs has put the brake on.

'Cromwell could ride down it, couldn't he, Mother?'

'Yes, easily, dear.'

'Could Hampden?'

'Yes.'

'Could I?'

'Yes, dear, if you had a bicycle. Do up your coat, Gladstone. The wind is cold.'

They had left the streets of shops and occasional omnibuses, a street where business activity tried hard to overcome the leisured habits of an older world and the sluggish softness of the climate, a street where the Nesbitt's modest carriage, drawn by a sober, well-fed horse, was known to every passer-by, and Mrs. Nesbitt herself was recognized by the shopkeepers as a housekeeper hard to please but punctual in payment, a customer well worth the keeping. The careful Hobbs had put on the brake, for the hill was steep, meandering between old walled gardens in which chestnut trees had spread their branches over the road, making it dark and cool like a roofed passage between the streets.

'Do up your coat, Gladstone,' Mabel repeated, but Gladstone was watching the gambols of a little group of children who disturbed the sheltered peace.

'They'll get run over if they're not careful,' he said. 'Oh, there's one hanging on behind the carriage. Oh, isn't he naughty? Why doesn't Hobbs whip him?'

'Don't be a spiteful little beast,' Janet said; and he, shocked by this harshness, remained silent all the way through the streets which, slipping suddenly or gradually downwards, brought the family party to the docks.

Chapter 4

WILLIAM NESBITT was standing at the front door of the low white building which had the appearance of a farm-house gone astray. It pleased his humour to conduct his business in the old place with its low ceilings, its rather defective fireplaces, its delicate mouldings round the chimney-pieces, and he had been secretly thrilled when he had discovered some old panelling under many coats of paint in his private room. The defects of the fireplaces had been overcome by a system of central heating, for William Nesbitt, like many men who have suffered hardships in youth, had developed a love of luxury, while the love of beauty which had always been strong in him was satisfied now, not by the terrible beauty of the sea and thoughts of the serene beauty of the land, but by the actual sight of meadows, trees, flowers, fair faces, the sound of women's voices, the consciousness that beauty existed everywhere for the eyes that sought it. He stood at the door, and the quizzical lift of his eyebrow seemed to be repeated in the gables of the house.

On the other side of the wide road, the new steamer was moored to the quay. She was gay with flags and spotless with white paint. Behind her the fields rose slowly and a little to the right, the tree-covered cliff grew steep on either side of the water and held, poised lightly like a thread, the bridge on which people and carts seemed to pass with a miraculous ease of balance. The house behind him was white and green; the gulls, swooping here and there, had the sharp whiteness of fresh snow, and the blue of the sky, the red of a roof beyond the water were caught again by the fluttering flags. The sun shone and William Nesbitt was happy, yet prepared for unhappiness if it should come. This attitude of preparation was a habit with him: he had spent his life in foreseeing and averting the mischances of

33

the sea and of commercial enterprise: he was on continual guard. Moreover, he had always paid his debts and he felt that he was on the debit side with life. He had been fortunate, perhaps too fortunate: there must be a sum chalked up against him somewhere.

'We shall be wrecked to-day in the Channel,' he told himself with a chuckle, and his eyebrow went a little higher, but, when he gave some coppers to a ragged little girl who put out her tongue at him as he stood there, it was not in propitiation to the fates: he liked giving and he liked little girls and he was rather attracted by gratuitous defiance. 'Now what did she do that for?' he wondered as she ran off with her spoil. 'Couldn't bear the look of me, I suppose.' Yes, life was interesting. Why should the child have put out her tongue? Was it an uncontrollable impulse of dislike? Was it envy of his good clothes? Was it a declaration of her own unassisted worth? No, he probably simply looked an old fool, standing there so pleased with himself, and the child had seen it and been compelled to mock him. Women had penetration, they had impulses, and men, with all their superior power of organization and magnitude of output, were nothing to them: they had a subtlety, apparently useless but potent. He liked the sound of that word. 'Potent,' he repeated.

But they were not punctual. He looked at his watch: five minutes late already. But Kate was an exception to the unpunctual rule: it must be Mabel's fault, and the thought of that daughter for whom his love was of a beneficial but not sympathetic kind, gave him a sudden longing for Lydia. She was not beautiful, yet she expressed beauty for him: she was not eloquent, yet for him she was like poetry: she was not often witty, yet, in her company, his humour was satisfied: he was conscious, then, of a keener sense of virtue which, for him, excused her faults, though it did not obscure them. Without effort, she could charm into intense devotion, but she did not blind her adorers and she did not want to blind them.

At that moment he had so intense a vision of her that he

34

could hardly believe in the reality of his own carriage approaching at a steady pace, and when he did believe it he was slightly appalled at the prosaic aspect of the family group. That was Mabel's fault again. He foresaw that the big, flat hat she was wearing, skewered with pins, would presently be tearing at her hair when they met the breeze in the Channel.

'Six minutes late,' he said, opening the carriage door.

'How nice the steamer looks,' Mrs. Nesbitt said tactfully. Standing up in the carriage, Mabel gasped, 'Have the boys come?'

'No, – give me your hand, Kate – we shan't wait for them.'

'But they may have had an accident.'

'Well, my dear, you must go and pick up the bits. I'm too busy.' He led the way upstairs and heard Mabel's anxious voice behind him asking, 'Is John here?'

'Yes, in my room.'

'Oh, tell him to come down, Father,' she begged, but at that moment a ringing of bicycle bells was heard, and then two pedalling figures, arrayed in long overcoats, appeared.

'You're very late,' Gladstone said reproachfully, 'and I think Grandfather is rather cross.'

'I couldn't find my muffler,' Hampden explained.

'Oh, Hampden, I told you I had it in my bag.' With an adjusting pull at his collar and a straightening grab at Cromwell's cap, she bade them put their bicycles in the passage.

'Grandfather won't like that,' Gladstone prophesied. 'He's so neat.'

'Well,' – Mabel was flustered – 'I don't know what to do.' Janet had gone upstairs, and she, the eldest daughter, was left behind; but a clerk, hearing sounds of distress, came to the rescue and removed the difficulties.

The sober panels of Mr. Nesbitt's room held, as in a solid old box, the bodies and the voices of the invited guests, and Mabel made her entry, happily unaware of the crookedness of her hat, and in all the pride of her possession of three sons who were too tall for their ages. She gave a general smile, as though certain of a welcome, but nobody seemed to notice her arrival, and she was irritated that her John, that pattern of a husband and a father, who had chosen to equip himself for the trip in knickerbockers and leggings, had attached himself as usual to Janet, who was his secret ideal of a young girl. Mabel was not jealous of these attentions, but she looked at Janet's daintiness, at Violet's gay worldliness with resentment. Janet had no cares, Violet had no children, they had the leisure and the money to be well-dressed and, glancing from Violet's shining narrow shoes to her own thick ones, bought for long service, she made a mental calculation of the difference in cost of the two pairs.

With some display of those shining shoes, Violet was talking to the grave commodore of Mr. Nesbitt's little fleet, and the commodore's wife with tightly-gloved, folded hands, was occupied in the difficult task of being reasonably respectful to Mrs. Nesbitt and upholding her own position. Walter Nesbitt, the only son of the house and junior partner in the firm, leaned easily against the panelled wall, realized Mabel's presence and nodded casually.

'You'll be sea-sick,' he told the boys.

'No, we won't,' they chorused firmly, their three sharp noses slightly pink with determination, and Mabel added, 'We've all made up our minds not to be ill.'

Attention was thus called to the Partridge family and Mabel thrust forward her sons to be introduced to the captain and his wife, but before this could be properly done William Nesbitt signalled for the party to move. He gave his arm to the captain's wife, the captain followed in support of Mrs. Nesbitt, and down the stairs the little procession went, joined at the door by the head clerks of the various departments and watched across the road by a scattering of idlers and ironically cheered by a group of small boys.

'This is very ridiculous,' Violet murmured.

36

'We've got to bear it,' Janet said stoically.

'What on earth did John want to dress himself up like that for?' Walter inquired. 'He looks like a farmer at a fair.'

Violet excused him. 'I suppose he hasn't a yachting cap, but he's done his best.'

'And look at Mabel.' Walter's irritation with the Partridge family was a permanent one. 'Look at her feet. Horrible!'

'Hush! she'll hear you.'

'I wish she would. She ought to be ashamed of herself. Well, I hope they'll all be jolly sea-sick. There's a good strong breeze.'

Under it, the flags were fluttering gaily, the sun shone valiantly, the steamer gave gently to the movement of the water, and Gladstone, on the gangway, was heard in an eager desire to go home. The resourceful John, anxious that his father-in-law should not be distressed by these shrill cries, promptly took his son to see the engines.

'If Gladstone's mind is occupied,' Mabel explained to the captain's wife, 'he won't be ill. He's very scientific; they all are, and he likes working things out, and of course the mind does control the body.'

'Oh yes,' said the captain's wife vaguely. 'He seems a nice little boy, I'm sure.'

This was not quite satisfactory as a response, but Mabel's own mind was already having some difficulty with her body and she settled herself in a deck-chair, covered herself with a rug and prepared to suffer. She closed her eyes, but now and then she opened them and saw happier people walking about the deck, heard them talking, laughing, envied them their ease and yet had a consoling pride in her greater sensibility; and as the steamer moved down the river, her engines throbbing and the siren shrieking, the whole proceeding became vague and troubled, like the dream of a feverish invalid. The figures of her parents, impressed on her closed eyelids, grew monstrous, faded, and returned distorted. She had an indifferent sort of hope

37

that the boys would not fall overboard and she heard her mother's voice saying, 'Are you comfortable, dear? Warm enough? You've chosen a cold corner.'

'I must face the wind,' Mabel murmured, and Mrs. Nesbitt went away.

'Mabel ought not to have come,' she told her husband.

His eyes were everywhere; on the captain, the officers, the fluttering flags, the flying gulls, the people on the dock side, and he felt the movements of the steamer as though they were his own. He was proud of this sentient thing whose life he had created; he wished all Radstowe were on the river banks to see her, and when he looked up at the cliffs and saw people standing at their edge, he felt they must be there because his ship was steaming out to sea for the first time. Looking back, he saw the suspension bridge like a thread stretched over the abyss and, looking forward, he saw the narrow river, a grey stream going between grey, high rocks which were masked with trees or scarred with the red wounds of quarried stone. Slowly the rocks and trees gave way to meadows, lush and green, and through them the water went sinuously, unhurried, sure of its end.

'She ought not to have come,' Mrs. Nesbitt repeated.

'This is like old times, Kate,' he said.

'Mabel is ridiculous. She has taken her hat off, like a tripper. And I've had a letter from Dora, William. It's in my bag.'

'I came up this river in the old *Chiltern*, three months after we were married. D'you remember, Kate? You were waiting for me at the dock side.'

'Yes, William.'

'Good days those.'

'These are better.'

'I don't know.'

'Oh, William! All the children!'

'They're not ours now,' he said.

'You don't mean that, dear.'

'You know best, Kate. We'll have luncheon when we're fairly in the Channel.'

'Dora's letter – I thought I might go into the cabin for a few minutes – '

'My dear, the boat's yours. Do as you like.'

'Just to read it, William. Lydia – '

'Lydia? What's the matter with her?'

'Nothing of course, but Dora will tell me everything. She writes good letters.' She looked at her husband. He was thinking of the ship, and she went away with a sense of excessive isolation.

She sat down on a velvet-covered couch in the ladies' cabin. There was a slight smell of oil, of paint, of upholstery, but Mrs. Nesbitt was used to that mingled odour. She had an affection for it as the olfactory symbol of her early days with William and his success in life, and across her feeling of loneliness there came a memory of sweetness, like a waft of flower scent borne on a wind. She remembered her first voyage with him, her pride in his skill, his pride in her courage: dark nights when she stood with him on deck and faced a future in which the only lights were youth and confidence. They had been poor then: disaster would have left them penniless; yet it seemed to her as she sat in one of William's own ships, with the comfortable possession of many safely invested thousands, of children suitably married, that now only did she know the meaning of care.

Why should she feel like that? Nothing had happened to disturb her serenity except the little quarrel with the impotent Mrs. Miller and nothing, she thought with dignity, should make her reveal trouble if it came; but she had an uneasy feeling of suspense like the one which sometimes kept her wakeful at nights. With all these children and grandchildren, how could she hope to escape the common lot? With Lydia in London, Lydia who seemed to hold in her nature some element of disturbance, how could her mother be at rest? She had never been afraid of a storm at sea; she had been perfectly calm when the children had scarlet fever and William paced the house in an agony of alarm; but now, when her future was assured, when the children were established, she felt as though life were too much for her: it was complicated and her nature craved for simplicity and clearness. To-day, she was irritated by Mabel's assumption of poverty, by John's knickerbockers and leggings, by Janet's cool aloofness, and she was hurt by her own capacity for finding faults in her children. And here, in the bag on her lap, she had Dora's letter and she did not want to read it. She did not want to be disturbed and she knew she must be, for that letter would contain news of Lydia. She wished she had not brought her spectacles; yet, sooner or later, the letter had to be read, and courageously she put her thumb under the envelope's flap.

At that moment there appeared from an inner sanctum, the stewardess, a neat, elderly woman, promoted from one of the older ships, and it was Mrs. Nesbitt's pleasant duty to be gracious to the old servant of the firm; it was proper to inquire after her health, the concerns of her family and her opinion of the ship; and when that was done and the woman had retired, Mrs. Nesbitt proceeded with the further duty of reading Dora's letter. There was no enclosure from Lydia and Mrs. Nesbitt sighed. It would be easier to read a letter from her because it would tell her nothing she did not want to know, and she realized fully that there were times when ignorance was bliss. Yet what she dreaded she could not have put into words: she had a vague conviction that Lydia was constantly doing things which were not possible in Radstowe, meeting the kind of people who did not live in Radstowe, wearing clothes at which Radstowe would have been astonished, and catching the kind of colds subsequent to these activities.

Dora's expansive handwriting covered several sheets of notepaper and Mrs. Nesbitt, longing to skip and know the worst, braced herself to read slowly. Then she folded the letter and returned it to her bag and remained sitting there, very still.

Lydia and Dora were having a gay time and though Dora had no right to leave her husband and Mrs. Nesbitt definitely disapproved of the desertion, she liked to think of the girls together, buying clothes, going to theatres, laughing inordinately at jokes which no one else could understand. All that was very well, but Mrs. Nesbitt hoped that Oliver was allowed to share the jokes, she hoped Lydia would explain them, though really, even when explained they were not always successful with anybody else, and she hoped more fervently that Oliver was getting enough to eat. She did not like these picnic meals described so humorously by Dora, these unexpected droppings in and sudden rushings out; but she was not a narrow-minded woman; she knew that times had changed and she had sense enough to see, though she could still regret, that it was impossible to get perfection in children. Dora came near to it when she was safe at home, and Lydia, well, Lydia was wonderful in her own way, and as Dora said, you could not expect people who understood literature to take a vivid interest in food.

Mrs. Nesbitt was being reasonable with herself, schooling herself into acceptance, but her body stiffened in its still-ness, her dark, bright eyes had their unseeing effect. She was angry, for what, after all, did Lydia know about litera-ture? Why should she help people with their work while Oliver was out and Dora had an afternoon nap? Mrs. Nes-bitt hoped she had her nap in the drawing-room and not on her bed. In that bare room there was at least a sofa and it could accommodate Dora while the other two sat, she supposed, on the hard chairs or the floor. Lydia had a habit of sitting on the floor. Mrs. Nesbitt had no opinion of people who wrote books and read them to married ladies and accepted criticism with equanimity, and she had a clear picture of Dora, sleepy and funny and occasionally bored; Lydia bright and brilliant, showing off a little; and that Henry Wyatt wasting his time with women. She liked men of business, of regular habits, of early rising, and she was sure that Mr. Wyatt got up from a hot bed at eleven o'clock in the morning. His was not the only name mentioned by Dora in her letter, but it occurred more often than any other: there was also a man who painted, but apparently Lydia did not hold his brushes; and a woman who sang, but there was no record of Lydia's assistance with her scales, and Mrs. Nesbitt stirred from her immobility to frame with her lips the word 'dangerous.'

She realized that it was her duty to go on deck: she had never neglected to do her duty towards William, she had tried to help him, she had tried to spare him unnecessary worry: she would continue to do so.

Chapter 5

PERHAPS it was the consciousness that he was to be spared
which gave Mrs. Nesbitt a feeling of superiority, that secret
feeling which is the stay of wives, when she saw her husband
at the head of the luncheon table, and at the end of the meal,
the little speech he made, neat and humorous, fell rather
flatly on her ears. There he was, capable man of affairs,
possessor of ships, employer of men: he was clever, he dealt
lightly with many things mysterious to her, but he did not
know everything. With her own anxiety concealed in her
heart, she almost despised his gaiety and his innocence of the
fact that, for the first time in her life, she meant to deceive
him: she was going to drop Dora's letter overboard, so that
no one else should ever see it: it was an act which forced
the insignificant into importance; it was a confession of
fear, but something stronger than mere reason compelled
her to it. And knowing well enough that her William had
his reserves, an amazing enjoyment in cryptic speech and
deliberately puzzling her, she felt not only justified in deception but happy in it. She had a new conviction that she
belonged to herself, and she did not suspect that in this
she was temporarily adopting the permanent attitude of
her daughters.

She sat there, dignified and pleasant, forgetful neither
that her husband was host nor that he was the head of the
family and the firm. Outwardly, it was a successful luncheon and only Mrs. Nesbitt seemed to remember that
Mabel was still prone in her deck-chair, a prey to such
horrible sensations that she would have accepted shipwreck gladly. Even John ate heartily and afterwards
smoked a good cigar, but while the men remained below and
Janet and Violet tidied their hair and the captain's wife

found relaxation in conversing with the stewardess, Mrs. Nesbitt sought her recumbent daughter.

The boys, nibbling biscuits, were grouped round her for safety.

'Mother won't have any medicine,' Gladstone announced.

'Quite right,' Mrs. Nesbitt said cheerfully.

'But she made us have it,' he persisted, 'and we haven't been sick and she hasn't had it and she is.'

'Now, Gladstone,' his grandmother said reprovingly, 'don't criticize your elders.'

Mabel made an effort. 'It isn't criticism, it's logic.'

'Oh, logic – ' Mrs. Nesbitt murmured vaguely. 'I don't know anything about that. I'm sorry you feel so ill, dear. We've had a very nice luncheon.'

Mabel lifted a feeble hand. 'Don't talk about it.'

Mrs. Nesbitt turned her back on the little group and, fumbling in her bag, looked down at the water. Weighted with a few copper coins, Dora's letter dropped heavily overboard and as she let it fall Mrs. Nesbitt again looked solicitously at Mabel. 'Would you like another rug, dear?' she asked with a sweetness which sounded, even to herself, somewhat excessive, and proved to be useless as a piece of guile, for Cromwell cried out anxiously, 'Oh, Grandmother, you've dropped something in the sea.'

'Only some paper,' Mrs. Nesbitt answered calmly.

'Paper floats,' Cromwell retorted solemnly. 'Doesn't it, Mother? Paper floats.'

'Well, isn't it floating?'

'No, it sank at once. I saw it.'

'Oh, did you?' Mrs. Nesbitt could afford to be good-humoured, but the natural woman in her desired to chastise the child.

'Paper is lighter than water, that's why it floats, isn't it, Mother?'

Determined never to discourage her children in their mental activities, Mabel roused herself enough to open her eyes and shut them again in assent. 'And then when it gets wet and heavy, it sinks. Doesn't it, Mother?' There was no answer, but Cromwell, sure of his facts, said kindly, 'You see, Grandmother?'

'Yes, I see.'

'But it couldn't have got wet so quickly. It went down with a flop. Didn't it, Mother?'

'Your mother wasn't looking and I don't care one way or the other.'

'Well, I'll ask Father.'

Mrs. Nesbitt took a rather malicious pleasure in informing her daughter that John was in the saloon smoking cigars.

'Couldn't we go and peep?' Hampden asked.

'Grandfather doesn't like peeping children.'

'I want to see the engines again,' Gladstone cried.

'Throw some biscuits to the gulls and watch how they catch them,' Mrs. Nesbitt suggested.

'Wouldn't it be waste, Mother?'

'Don't worry your mother, child. Do as I tell you.'

'I wish,' Mabel said weakly, when they had obeyed, 'I do wish you wouldn't snub them when they're interested.'

'Snub them?' Mrs. Nesbitt was indignant. 'They have to be kept in order.'

'They're very good children,' Mabel moaned.

'They won't always be good,' Mrs. Nesbitt retorted with a curious bitterness.

To probe the secret meanings of another's speech, though natural to her when her own interests were concerned, was at the moment beyond Mabel and she merely groaned, 'Oh, when will this awful boat turn round?'

'You ought to have stayed at home, dear.'

'I'm the eldest daughter,' Mabel protested.

'Nobody would think so,' Mrs. Nesbitt said, but whether to placate or to annoy was uncertain even to herself. 'You look very young, dear.' She considered her daughter. Her features were regular, her hair abundant, dark and crisp and, subdued by sea-sickness, she looked pathetic and attractive, as though she had never married John Partridge and borne him three intelligent sons. 'Very young,' she repeated.

Mabel was only half pleased. 'It isn't because I haven't suffered.'

'You will have to suffer more,' Mrs. Nesbitt said sternly. This assumption of superiority was ridiculous. Mrs. Nesbitt had borne five children herself and thought nothing of it, and if she had never been sea-sick it was because such weakness had not suggested itself to a sailor's wife. Suffered! Rubbish! Mrs. Nesbitt walked away. She was out of patience with Mabel and ashamed of her lying there for every one to see, and in her own bosom there were troubles like small creeping snakes. She could not look at Cromwell without remembering her deception and without wishing he were a different kind of boy, a noisy creature such as Walter had been; she could not look at Janet, so fair and slim, without wondering why she never seemed quite happy: she could not look at the worthy Partridge without vexation that he should have dressed himself up like a countryman; nor at William without a feeling of triumphant guilt; nor at Violet and Walter without fearing that a childless marriage would not remain successful.

And Lydia's marriage was also childless. If there had been children, she would have had no time for sitting on the floor and flirting with novelists, for flirting Mrs. Nesbitt decided it must be. With a strong belief in the influence of women, she could still set limits to it and she did not see how a daughter of hers could be fit to criticize the work of an author of published books. She had, too, a respect for achievement, and though she did not doubt that those published books were in some way undesirable, for she was greatly prejudiced against Mr. Henry Wyatt, the fact remained that they were published and perhaps paid for. The flirtation was wicked, the criticism was presumptuous, but she had destroyed the letter and if Dora were discreet and Oliver firm, this trouble might pass.

Yes, it might pass, but never, in the thought of Lydia, could there be peace and, convinced of this, Mrs. Nesbitt wondered why she should so greatly love that daughter, love her and fail to understand her. If Mrs. Nesbitt had been given to expressing thoughts in imagery, she would have compared Lydia to a dragon-fly, bright and elusive, and Mrs. Nesbitt had a nature to which that insect was not congenial. She was bound to admire in its presence but, in its absence, to find fault with its mode of life. And then, steadying herself and showing a perfectly serene face to her husband's guests, she tried to believe she was making a great fuss about nothing. Lydia was gay, original, and daring, and nothing except age, and perhaps not that, would change her.

By the time Mabel had her wish and the steamer made for home. Mrs. Nesbitt almost wished she had not destroyed the letter: she had exaggerated facts, but perhaps it was just as well and certainly she kept her pleasure in having a secret, at last, from that little capable man who saw everything in the ship but had not seen into all the recesses of her heart. Now he was down in the engine-room, now on the bridge, and when she thought he was settled there for at least ten minutes, he was on deck again, talking to the boys and ignoring Mabel. He was always restless and it was from him that Lydia had inherited what Mrs. Nesbitt called her fidgets and her way of making jokes which people could not understand.

But William had always been faithful and if she could have suspected him of caring, even vaguely, for another woman, she felt she would have died of horror. She had his poems and though she never read them now they were as precious as they had been when they reached her in a flimsy envelope with a foreign stamp. Unfaithfulness did occur, as she knew from the newspapers, but not in respectable circles like her own, and though she was far from accusing Lydia of such sin, she feared that she played with fire, following the habits of the people with whom she associated. Had not Dora said that Lydia was having a little dinner-party for Mr. Wyatt and the woman to whom he had once been engaged? If these two, after plighting

47

and breaking troth, could meet at a friend's table without so much as a comment, what else might they not do? Mrs. Nesbitt thought again longingly of a legal partnership in Radstowe, but she thought of it now without hope. Moreover, she knew that she could no longer press for it without betraying her own fears. She might pretend she had lost the letter but her crystallized fears would shine in every word she said. 'It is always a mistake to do wrong,' she decided; nevertheless, she turned to William with a placid face when he stood by her side and told her he was pleased with the ship.

'Of course, William,' she said, 'for you,' and she accented the word, 'you never make a mistake.'

He glanced at her in search of some hidden meaning, but he could not find it: his wife was gazing at the blue hills of Wales and the white caps on the sparkling water.

'It has been a successful trial trip, dear,' she said.

It was nearly over. With a triumphant hoot from the whistle, they entered the river and the morning's scene of the high cliffs giving way to gentleness, to lush meadows where flocks and herds were grazing, was now reversed into one of impending rocks, of approaching sternness, of entrance into some grimly-guarded place. The flats were left behind, the river walls rose higher and higher, the sun shone less brightly and the gay little ship steamed more carefully, for the tide was going out. The muddy banks were appearing beyond the water and the gulls, which had swooped above the outgoing steamer like a white sail gone adrift in a wind and shattered into ribbons, were now quarrelling and screaming for the refuse on the mud.

Mrs. Nesbitt shivered a little. Fortunately there was to be tea for the company in William's office.

Mr. and Mrs. Nesbitt went home in the carriage together. The Partridges returned by bicycles and tramcars and though William Nesbitt offered to provide a cab for the shattered Mabel, she was invigorated by hot tea to the heroism of refusal.

'I suppose she thought I might forget to pay for it,' he said.

'Nonsense, William; it's just her independence. They're all as independent as they can be. Look at Janet – going off like that with Violet and Walter.'

'How did she go? I noticed nothing unusual.'

'She said just she was going.'

'Well, Kate, it's not a very desperate adventure, and Janet – '

'Well?' she asked, dreading some disquieting remark.

He smiled at her frankly and it was still more disquieting that he did not make it. 'For my part, Kate, I'm never dull in your company. We can do without her, can't we?'

Mrs. Nesbitt said, 'Oh, yes, William, of course,' and she said it heartily lest there should be a pause wherein he might refer to what must be forgotten, and while she went on to talk of the trial trip with an unnatural volubility, her mind was really occupied with a little scene which took place in the office when all but the family had departed. Dora was mentioned and Mrs. Nesbitt had not welcomed that beloved name for William had said at once, 'Ah, yes, Kate, you said you had a letter from her. May I see it now?'

She fumbled in her bag, looked up and round her and exclaimed, 'It isn't here!' Everybody made suggestions, looked on the floor, looked on the desk, but it was Mrs. Nesbitt who said firmly, 'I must have lost it.' Then Cromwell, that bright boy, cried shrilly, 'Oh, Grandmother, that must have been the paper that went oveboard. I saw it drop and then it sank. It sank,' he repeated, looking round to find the proper astonishment at this phenomenon, 'and paper doesn't sink.'

'Oh, nonsense, Cromwell,' Mrs. Nesbitt said too sharply and, meeting her husband's eyes, she saw a little twinkle play over their dark depths.

'It seems then that the letter is lost,' he said. 'If the stewardess finds it she will return it. But no doubt you have it off by heart.'

49

'It was a very long letter,' Mrs. Nesbitt said, and immediately regretted that remark. 'At least, Dora's writing is so large, but I can tell you all the news,' and she gave herself gladly to the task.

Now, in the carriage, she was anxious to avoid a subject towards which even the most innocent remark seemed to trend, but the necessary dexterity was not natural to her, and when William had helped her to alight and said kindly, 'You're tired, Kate,' she pressed his hand in gratitude, but again she had to regret her spontaneity, for he looked at her with an odd tenderness, saying, 'We're too old, surely, to start mental gymnastics now, though of course they have always had a charm for me.'

She had no answer ready, for she was only quick by chance, and it was not until she was half-way up the stairs that she was struck by a second implication in his speech: she had not been giving him, all these years, what he wanted. A hot flush ran over her body and she stood for a moment, holding to the rail of the banisters: her lips trembled, for she was indeed very tired, too tired and too old, she thought with bitter humour, to start playing hide-and-seek successfully with her husband. Yet that was what he wanted, what, no doubt, he had missed in a long life with her. She was angry with him for having found a lack in her and then, when circumstances drove her to supply it, for seeing through the game so readily and criticizing it so gently. But he had not seen everything and Dora's letter was at the bottom of the sea.

She went on slowly to her room, oppressed by the consciousness of a barrier between her and William and determined to do nothing to throw it down. She had her own stubbornness but she felt that she was permanently saddened, and the absence of Janet from the dinner-table was like a deliberate desertion.

'This,' said William with his hateful aptness, 'is what it will be like when she is married.'

'But perhaps she won't be married.'

'My dear, you'd never survive the disgrace.'

'Mrs. Miller would be able to crow over me then.'

'Ah, don't mention her,' he said, raising a hand.

'Why not?' Mrs. Nesbitt asked calmly. 'You're thinking of our little quarrel? I had forgotten it.'

'I don't like quarrels,' he said quickly, 'and if you died of the disgrace, Kate, there would just be Janet and me and that would be far worse.'

'One of us will have to go first,' she said sensibly.

'I'm mean enough to hope it will be me.'

'Really, William?' She could not help smiling. The barrier seemed to have fallen down. 'I wish we could arrange to go together.'

'Well, perhaps we could. I'll think it out. The evening papers would give us a poster to ourselves – "Tragedy of a lifelong affection."'

'Don't, William,' she said. 'It would be very unpleasant for the children.'

Chapter 6

SHE was startled by the sound of Dora's voice through the telephone and a dozen fears chased themselves through her mind before she said calmly, 'Yes, dear, what is it? Are you speaking from London?'

'No, I'm at home. Herbert sent for me. Patience is in bed. It's nothing – only a cold – but he got fussy.'

Mrs. Nesbitt did not like that word. 'He was quite right to send for you and you are glad to be at home,' she said in the most final of her tones.

'Oh, I don't know. It was quite unnecessary, and I missed a party.'

'But Herbert must be pleased.'

'Oh, yes; he's pleased.'

'I'm sure he is. Will you come and see me to-morrow?'

'I'll come to-night.'

'No, no, child; stay with Herbert.'

'Herbert can come too.'

'But he doesn't like going out in the evenings. Of course I shall be glad to see you, dear, but Herbert – '

'Oh, Mother, don't be tiresome about Herbert.'

Mrs. Nesbitt put back the receiver. If this were the influence of Lydia and London, she did not like it. In Lydia that impatience would have been natural enough, but she did not want to see Dora developing the quality. She had an unconscious appreciation, like an artistic sense, of the fitness of things and she knew that Dora, rebellious and hasty, would be like the work of a master spoiled by a bungling hand. She could understand poor Dora's disappointment, but if poor Herbert had been suffering from anxiety, it was right that his wife should return to reassure him. Wives had not only to put up with such demands but to welcome them. For her own part she was, as she admitted, absurdly excited at the prospect of seeing one daughter and learning more than she was told of the other; for though she might not be so clever as William, she considered herself a good deal cleverer than Dora. Her voice needed control when she told William that Dora had come home.

'Has Lydia turned her out?'

'The greatest friends!' she exclaimed.

'You never know,' he said smoothly, 'but certainly it would be more likely to be the other way about. Herbert has prejudices.'

'You are hard on Herbert. It's only because Patience has a bad cold.'

'Ah, that's Herbert too. He's a fussy fellow. I shouldn't wonder, though, if he exposed the child to give him an excuse to send for Dora. He doesn't like Lydia, you know.'

'Doesn't like Lydia? Why shouldn't he? And how do you know?'

'Observation, Kate.'

'I don't believe it. Everybody loves Lydia. And as to exposing the child – You get strange ideas, William.'

'Yes, all sorts of ideas. Men who run big businesses have these flights of fancy; they need them.'

'I know – but really, William – '

'Perhaps,' he went on thoughtfully, 'he picked the child out of bed to see the sunset, teaching her to appreciate beauty, you know, and letting the wind blow over her while he did it; or perhaps – oh, I can think of lots of things he might have done.'

'I'm sometimes rather glad,' Mrs. Nesbitt said with unnatural humility as she picked up her crochet, 'that I am not clever.'

'It is awkward now and then,' he admitted, 'and I should not say these things to anybody else.'

'I doubt that,' she broke in.

'But to the wife of my bosom' – Mrs. Nesbitt fidgeted at this expression – 'to the wife of my bosom,' he repeated with increased pomp, 'I can say all.'

53

'But do you?' she asked sharply and felt she had scored a point.

She sat on the sofa and crocheted with the slowness of all her movements, and now and then she looked at the clock. At the approach of Dora she could tell herself that she had been foolish and old-fashioned in her fears: she had made a great ado about nothing and set William thinking, or at least, for she had her own acuteness, she had let him see the drift of her own thoughts and that, too, was foolish. She gave his back, as he stood looking out of the window, an affectionately ironical glance. She was not so stupid as he believed, but really, what did he believe? He probably knew as much about her as she knew about him, no more nor less, and the knowledge had carried them safely through forty years of married life.

'The garden's looking very nice, dear, isn't it?' she said.

'Is it? Yes, it is. I wasn't looking at it.'

'You have been standing there for ten minutes.'

'Yes, Kate, thinking deep thoughts, wishing,' her hands lay still in her lap, 'wishing I'd gone in for bigger ships, somewhere else. I might have been a great gun now in the shipping world. You can't do much here, with this muddy brook of a river. But I don't know. The place got into my bones the first time I saw it. The fact is I'm not a mere seaman. That river – I ought to have hated it at sight, but I loved it and the cliffs and the old town. It was like coming home. Sentiment got the better of me, and it is better to be happy here, perhaps. Funny how one's ideas change. Once I thought that to own a single little tramp in the Channel would be glory and now I'm not content with dozens. Twopenny-halfpenny little ships, mine, but sound. I've always seen to that and I've never skimped anywhere. Still, I might have done bigger things.'

'You've done wonders, William.' Her loyalty was aroused. 'Wonders. Without a penny you didn't earn, without influence. I'm proud of you.'

'Thank you, Kate. That's enough reward. I hope you'll never be ashamed of me.'

'I don't think I shall be, dear,' she said confidently.

'Oh, you never know,' he said.

With that remark he spoilt this pleasant little passage, but Mrs. Nesbitt had not time to indulge her annoyance, for there was the sound of an arrival in the hall, and as she lifted herself from the sofa, Dora opened the door. She was tall and, in spite of a tendency to stoutness, she had an air of youth due to the soft contours of her face, the engaging sweetness of her smile, and a simplicity of manner which nothing ever changed. The sight of her beauty was soothing to Mrs. Nesbitt, her greeting was a reassurance. Behind her was Herbert and Mrs. Nesbitt kissed him with an affection increased by her knowledge that the rest of the family gave him very little. He, too, was tall, his hair was a little longer than that of most men, his evening coat had the embellishment of a velvet collar, his whole appearance was touched with little studied differences. On his chin he wore a small imperial which had the most distant relationship to John Partridge's beard: like his hair, it was of an auburn colour, but so dark that it looked almost black. This, it said plainly, was not the result of laziness in the matter of shaving, nor of gratitude to a providence which had provided men with hair, but an indication of the character of the man, a hint that though he might have been forced by circumstances into the business of an engineer, he was by nature attached to higher things: he had, in fact, a collection of miniatures and was on the committee of the Radstowe Academy of Arts.

'Well, dear,' Mrs. Nesbitt said, 'what about Patience?'

'It's only a feverish cold.'

Herbert made a gesture. 'And I have brought Dora back.'

'But you were anxious,' Mrs. Nesbitt said soothingly, 'and she is glad to be back.'

Dora said nothing to that. Her expression was amiably detached and, throwing herself on to the sofa with an accompanying backward fling of her wrap, she said, 'Herbert has bought a car at last. We came in it.'

'Oh, how nice, dear,' Mrs. Nesbitt exclaimed; but William Nesbitt's shoulders went up. 'That's why he brought you back,' he said.

'Why of course he wanted Dora to see it. Quite natural, and I hope it always will be so, but I'm sure Herbert didn't want to spoil Dora's holiday.'

'I want her to go back next week,' he said. 'I wish you would, darling. I should be happier.'

'But one of the other children might be ill then,' Dora said smilingly, and her father eyed her with an awakened interest.

'Yes, I think you had better stay at home now you are safely back,' Mrs. Nesbitt decided. 'William, don't you want to see the car?'

'They're all one to me,' he answered.

'But you would like to see it.'

'Of course you know best, Kate. Come along, Herbert. They want to get rid of us, and I'll try to be intelligent.'

'And now, dear,' Mrs. Nesbitt said, studying her crochet pattern, 'how is Lydia?'

'Furious.'

'Furious?'

'Yes, with Patience and Herbert and telegrams.'

'But that's absurd.'

'Yes, she is absurd.'

'How?' Mrs. Nesbitt demanded.

'For being furious.'

'Oh,' Mrs. Nesbitt wondered if, after all, she were cleverer than Dora, 'she doesn't understand how a mother feels.'

'Lydia understands perfectly well how everybody feels,' Dora said with some warmth.

'Oh, I don't know about that,' Mrs. Nesbitt returned with slightly-tightened lips. 'Of course, it was disappointing for both of you, but you have had a nice time together, and it was your duty to come back. I'm very glad you didn't let her persuade you into stopping.'

'She didn't try to persuade me,' Dora said quietly, but she could not bring herself to repeat Lydia's words, she knew that Lydia would not like her mother to know how vehemently she had exclaimed, 'If it were my child who were ill, I'd hire an aeroplane to get to her.'

'I'm glad of that,' Mrs. Nesbitt said with an irritating satisfaction. 'Lydia will miss you, but she seems to have plenty of friends,' and as Dora, thinking of her sister, made no response, she added casually, 'rather odd friends, perhaps, but I suppose she likes them.'

'They're not odd: they're interesting. There's not one who doesn't look much more ordinary than Herbert – '

'Herbert is a distinguished-looking man.'

'But they really are what Herbert looks like.'

Mrs. Nesbitt felt slightly lost. There was here some implication of reproach, but Dora's face was serene.

'Novelists and people,' Mrs. Nesbitt murmured.

'Mr. Wyatt,' Dora said, 'is rather like a prize-fighter.'

'Oh, dear!' This, in spite of the exclamation, was satisfactory. 'And Oliver is so handsome.'

'He's a dear.'

'He spoils Lydia.'

'Yes, she makes him.'

'You mean he doesn't want to?'

'He can't help it. No one can.'

'No one else has the right.'

Dora laughed. 'It's rather spoiling to have people always on your doorstep.'

'If they stayed there it wouldn't matter.'

Dora laughed again. 'Why shouldn't Lydia have her amusements?'

'She ought to find them in her own home.'

'But that's just what she is doing. She doesn't leave them outside.'

Mrs. Nesbitt was now quite certain that she was not cleverer than Dora, and her annoyance overcame her prudence. 'I don't think it's proper for men to call on Lydia when Oliver is out.'

'There are women, too, you know,' Dora said smoothly.

'Of course.' Mrs. Nesbitt was all surprise and innocence. 'But still, Lydia should spend more time on her house.

57

Why doesn't she polish her furniture? I'm sure there's plenty of bare wood. There's very little else. Of course there are women. Lydia likes them. There's the one who used to be engaged to that Mr. Wyatt.'

'Oh, yes, – Sylvia. She sings.'

'I don't think she ought to meet her old lover at Lydia's house. I wonder she cares to.'

'She doesn't mind a bit. I dare say she likes it.'

'How can she? All these divorces – '

'But they were not married.'

'They meant to be.'

'If it comes to that, I was engaged to Jim before I met Herbert.'

'But you don't see poor Jim now.'

'No, I wish I did.'

'Dora! Poor fellow!'

'That's why I want to see him – partly.'

'I don't understand it,' Mrs. Nesbitt said. 'I do not understand it.'

'Well, Mother dear, don't worry.'

'I am not worrying,' Mrs. Nesbitt answered firmly, 'but I don't like that kind of thing and I'm quite sure Oliver can't approve.'

'Oh, Oliver!'

'Well?' Mrs. Nesbitt was ready to defend him.

'I don't think he's quite the man you imagine,' Dora said, and Mrs. Nesbitt, with a new trouble facing her, said with a difficult steadiness, 'You don't mean, dear, that he's not a nice man?'

'Oliver? Oh, he's nice,' Dora said. 'Very nice.'

'Well, then,' Mrs. Nesbitt said finally, but covertly she looked keenly at her daughter. Dora was leaning back with her eyes shut: there was no pucker on her brows: she seemed serene enough, but Mrs. Nesbitt was beginning to distrust Dora's serenity. Yes, life was difficult and people were mysterious. Mrs. Nesbitt sighed audibly and with the downward breath she heard Dora saying, 'Lydia likes excitement and she's not afraid of anybody.'

'Why should she be, indeed? Neither am I.'

'Oh, I am,' Dora said. 'I didn't know what they were talking about half the time and now and then I went to sleep. They all seem to have read all the books in the world.'

'Books are not everything,' Mrs. Nesbitt said.

'No, and if Lydia hasn't read a book or if she doesn't understand something, she says so at once. That's what I call not being afraid. There was so much I didn't understand that I kept quiet. They would have had to begin at the beginning with me. But it was very amusing. People who do things.'

'Do things! I don't call writing books doing things. I call men like your father and Herbert the really important people.'

'Oh, well, they weren't all writing books.'

'Only that Mr. Wyatt?'

'There was a poet, rather a dreadful young man. Lydia teases him. There's safety in numbers, Mother dear.'

'Safety? What nonsense! As if there could be any danger. Don't put ideas into my head, Dora. And what about Lydia's colds and her underclothes?'

'They are the same as usual. A good deal of one and very little of the other.'

'That house is damp.'

'Yes, it is. If you leave a pair of shoes in the basement. they're green when you get them out.'

'She ought not to live there. I shall speak to Father about it, and when Oliver comes down I shall speak to him. I suppose they are both coming for my birthday?'

'Oh, of course,' Dora said.

Chapter 7

Mrs. Nesbitt's birthday was at the end of June and as a
festival it was kept even more religiously than Christmas
itself. From the days when William had made an effort to
afford the flowers and strawberries with which he honoured
the occasion to these more spacious days when a jewelled
ring or brooch was attached to his little bouquet, her birthday had a peculiar significance. Her children's gifts,
gradually developing from clumsily-made needlebooks and
pin-cushions to more elaborate presents, continued to be the
work of their own hands; for Mrs. Nesbitt valued nothing
else, and her daughters were busy at embroidery for weeks
before the event, and her grandchildren were reproducing
replicas of the original little offerings which were still kept
locked away with William's poems.

It had to be fine on Mrs. Nesbitt's birthday: it always was
fine, and so there was always tea for Nesbitts, Partridges,
Johnstones, and Stones, under the spreading willow in the
garden. Since Lydia's marriage and departure to London,
there had been the added excitement of her arrival on the
eve of the great day. No engagement could stand in the
way of that visit and even Oliver kept a few days of his
ample yearly leave for Upper Radstowe and Mrs. Nesbitt's
birthday, and latterly it had become as much Lydia's
festival as her own.

Lydia's bedroom was adorned with the flowers Lydia
loved best: the meals were arranged for Lydia's palate, and
though Mrs. Nesbitt disapproved of the things she liked to
eat, flimsy puddings, unlimited fruit, and very little honest,
solid food, she was supplied with all she wanted. Mrs.
Nesbitt reminded the cook that Miss Lydia liked hot
rolls and grapes for breakfast: the cook remembered that
Miss Lydia liked cider cup of a particularly intricate kind:

the parlour-maid brought out the old green dessert service which only Lydia liked, and the housemaid took pains to make Lydia's bed in a certain way, with the under sheet as tight as a drum and one small, soft pillow for her head, The name of Lydia echoed through the house and Janet, who never mentioned it, but was sent on many errands in her service, found her father standing at the bedroom door and jingling the money in his pockets.

'I was just having a look round,' he said apologetically. 'She likes roses, Janet.'

'She is going to have them,' Janet replied without enthusiasm.

He went away thoughtfully. He was sorry he had been caught in that act and, as though in expiation of a crime, he retired to the drawing-room instead of standing, as he wished to do, in a welcoming attitude on the front steps. His wife was there before the train was due at the station.

'I advise a chair,' he said as he passed through the hall. 'You have at least half an hour to wait.'

'Not as long as that, surely. You'd better stay here too, William.'

'Plenty of time, Kate, plenty of time,' he said and went back to his self-imposed punishment in the drawing-room, while his wife told herself that there was no love like a mother's.

An effect of her anxieties about Lydia was to expect a change in her and she was almost disappointed to find there was none. As the carriage turned in at the gate Lydia lifted a hand in greeting, a characteristic gesture, and Mrs. Nesbitt, gasping a loyal 'William!' ran down the steps.

'Just the same, dear,' she murmured, embracing her daughter and noting her thinness, her pale skin, the dark, smooth hair crowned with a tiny hat.

'Why, yes,' Lydia said, with amusement as she submitted herself to her mother's clasp. Mrs. Nesbitt tactfully freed her quickly and took Oliver's kiss with a pretty dignity which had something girlish in it.

61

'Where's William?' Lydia demanded as she patted the horse.

'She always pats the horse,' Mrs. Nesbitt thought with satisfaction. 'Father meant to be at the door, dear, I know.'

'I'll go and find him,' Lydia said.

She had less beauty and less height than any other member of the family but she had elegance and grace, and the uncompromising way in which she presented herself and such physical attributes as Nature had given her had an audacity which deceived the eye into content. She ran up the steps and in the cool hall which smelt of roses she met her father and gave him both her hands; while to Janet, passing by on some errand, she called out gaily, 'Hello, Jane! Why weren't you on the doorstep either?'

'Oh!' The white figure stopped. There were flowers in her hands. 'I was just going to put these on the table.' They did not kiss each other and in the dimness of the hall Janet's eyes looked large and grave.

'It's sweet to see you,' Lydia almost pleaded. 'Oh, here's Oliver.'

William Nesbitt, who had moved into the doorway of the drawing-room, saw Oliver take Janet squarely by the shoulders from behind and drop a kiss on the top of her fair head, for though she was tall, he seemed to tower above her. She put her flower-filled hands together with a convulsive movement which narrowed her shoulders and allowed them to slip out of his grasp. 'How are you, Oliver?' she said quietly, and went on.

He looked at Lydia. 'Oughtn't I to have done that?'

'It seems not,' she said. 'Never mind. Come upstairs.'

At awkward moments, William Nesbitt had a habit of humming hymn tunes, and now he returned to the hall and walked there, to and fro, to the accompaniment of 'Lead, kindly Light.' He liked the hymn and though he had not chosen it at that moment for the words' sake, they had an application. He was puzzled by the little scene he had witnessed and he wished he could see and hear what was passing between Lydia and Oliver upstairs, he wished his code made it possible for him to listen at their door; but he knew that the capacities of his imagination compensated, in some measure, for the tiresome restrictions of his morality, and if imagination sometimes led him astray, he could correct it by observation, so he let his thoughts wander from Janet who, in her quiet way, had disappeared, to Lydia who was upstairs in her old bedroom where the windows were all wide open and the fresh breeze was blowing out the curtains. On the table and the window-sill there were bowls of roses and sweet-peas.

'How clean everything is,' she said. 'Don't you love the garden?'

He had his coat and waistcoat off and her glance took in, with appreciation, the slenderness of his hips. 'Yes, it's a good garden.'

'Lovely smells! Why do we live in dirty London? You have to buy the smells there – all the nice ones. These come clean from over the hills and far away – for nothing, nothing but a sniff.' She leaned far out of the window. 'Jasmine. It will smell better by bedtime. Glorious roses this year – the ones like dark blood. Oh, they've put some in this bowl. That's Janet.' She lifted her arms slowly and took off her hat. 'Janet seemed odd to-night.'

'Yes.' There was a noisy washing of his hands going on. 'I oughtn't to have kissed her, but I never thought about it.'

'Ah, perhaps that was too obvious. You ought to think before you kiss. You do with me. But then, Janet is odd. She doesn't like being touched. I haven't kissed her for years.' She sat down in front of the dressing-table and her thin arms hung at her sides. 'When she was little – I really am disastrously plain, but it's better than being like everybody else – when she was little and I told her stories, she always stood about three feet away and stared at me. I wanted her to sit on my knee and be cuddled.' She shook down her hair. It was very long and soft and perfectly straight. 'But she didn't reciprocate. She doesn't, you

63

know. She's one of my failures. She was my only chance to cuddle anybody and I missed it. I believe it's been my ruin. Oh, isn't it hot? I wish there were a swimming bath in the garden. I think I'll go and have a cold bath.'

'You'll be late for dinner.'

'I shall be ready in ten minutes. When I come back I'll tell you what you're going to have to eat.'

She returned to find him sitting on the window-seat with one of Janet's roses in his coat. 'Oh, would you?' she asked quickly, with her eyes on it.

'A peace offering,' he explained. 'Why not?'

'No reason at all. Well, you're going to have white soup, fried sole, boiled chicken, and the cream pudding that mother thinks I like. She has a hopeless memory for her family's puddings and she'll be miserable all the evening because I won't eat any.'

'Then do eat some.'

'She'll be much more miserable if I'm sick. Fasten me up, please.' Her red silk dress, lower in the neck than Mrs. Nesbitt would approve and still lower in the back, fitted her arms and body closely. 'You have very fumbling fingers and you're blowing down my neck.'

'Agitation,' he muttered.

'Ah, if it were that – ' she said and, as he grunted with relief at the end of his task, she turned and stretched her hands up to his shoulders. 'Thank you,' she said. 'Look at me, Oliver, this is me. Look at the me.'

He nodded. 'Charming, but I've seen it before.'

'Not quite this one. Be quick, or you'll lose it altogether, irrevocably.'

'You are the most delightful person in the world,' he said.

She nodded in her turn. 'That will do. Thank you, again. But do you realize that it's never quite, quite the same person as it was before.'

'Yes, I've learnt that, but it's the solid substratum that I appreciate.'

'I wonder. Are you ready? Let us go down. Arm in arm, to please mother.'

'Not at all. To please me.'

So linked, they crossed the landing and never noticed Janet who was standing just within her own bedroom door. She watched them as they went gaily down the stairs, the red tail of Lydia's dress curving after them, silky, narrow and obsequious. Janet followed the train and, stepping where it had been, she felt she put her feet in blood. She shivered a little and went out at the front door which stood wide open and then, holding her upturned palms to the evening sky, she walked for a minute on the darkening grass where, a few weeks ago, the daffodils had shone. 'I shall spoil my shoes,' she thought, 'but the grass is clean.'

It was very peaceful in the garden: there were people passing in the road, but they could not be seen and the sound of their footsteps was that of summer, unmistakable, softer than in winter, as though the gathered dust were smothering their fall. Janet strolled round the side of the house and wished the real darkness of night had come, when the flowers would all be of one colour: now she could distinguish pink roses from red, and white sweet-peas from yellow ones, and the trees which made a thick shelter all round the garden still kept their green, hardly less vivid than in daytime. She had a longing for the coming of a black sky without a star and the solemn companionship of the night and, instead, she found her father pacing the gravel path in front of the drawing-room windows.

'Two minds and but a single thought,' he said.

'I can't believe that,' she answered with her obscure smile.

'Perhaps not,' he agreed at once. 'Perhaps there never was such a coincidence. It must be nearly dinner-time. "A garden is a lovesome thing, God wot," but sometimes there's not room enough in it.'

She knew he was trying to probe her and she resisted him lightly. 'I'm sure it's a very large garden for Rasdtowe,' she remarked simply and, ignoring that, he said, 'Come in to dinner. That's the gong. You're not really obtuse, my dear.'

65

'I can't say you're not curious,' she retorted.

'Curious? What an idea! What should I be curious about, child?'

'You said yourself that I was not obtuse,' she replied, but she was sorry she had begun to fence with him for, sooner or later, he would be sure to get through her guard.

They entered the dining-room by the long windows and the dinner proceeded as Lydia had prophesied. There were the soup, the sole, the chicken, and the pudding.

'Your favourite pudding, Lydia.'

'Mother dear, I hate it. Don't kick me, Oliver. It's wicked to deceive one's parents, isn't it, William?'

'Janet,' Mrs. Nesbitt said in distress, 'why didn't you remind me about the pudding?'

'You didn't ask me, Mother.'

'But you have such a memory, dear, and you ought to have asked me what I had ordered.'

'Oh, don't blame Jane,' Lydia begged. 'What does it matter whether I eat pudding or not? And why should Jane have to remember such dull things?'

'I remember everything,' Janet said, 'without the slightest difficulty.'

'And you didn't care,' Lydia said, leaning over the table. 'Quite right, too. You don't like me to be pampered, do you?' Her eyes were very bright and the curve of her mouth half pleaded and half disdained her pleading.

'I don't mind in the least,' Janet said, smiling a little, and Lydia, smiling back, her arms stretched over the table in a manner of which her mother could not approve, drummed the cloth lightly and nervously with her fingers. William Nesbitt, eating his cream pudding, watched his daughters and thought they were well-matched for a fight, the one cool and steady, the other brilliant and brave; but he had not yet discovered if their struggle were merely one of opposing personalities or caused by something more intense.

Mrs. Nesbitt was still thinking about the pudding. 'But you must have something to eat, Lydia,' she cried. 'Mary, ask Cook if there's anything Mrs. Stone would like. Next year I will do better, dear.'

'Oh, next year – ' Lydia withdrew her arms and over-turned a salt-cellar. 'I hate people to talk about the future and I've spilt the salt.'

'Mary will wipe it up,' Mrs. Nesbitt said sensibly.

'Not till I've made the sign of the cross and thrown some over my left shoulder. There!' She looked at her father defiantly, who said with a shrug, 'Oh, I'm superstitious myself.'

'And I will eat Lydia's share of the pudding,' Oliver said.

The windows were wide open and the smell of the roses came on gentle breaths across the room. William Nesbitt peeled an apple for his wife: Janet sat straight, her hands folded on her lap, her eyes watching Oliver's long fingers manipulating his fruit, dipping into his bowl, and touching his napkin with slow precision. Now and then he spoke to her, not quite naturally, remembering her repulse, and she answered quietly, with a lack of animation which had no dullness in it. On the other side of the table Lydia sat, watching each of the other four in turn, missing nothing, smiling her tilted smile, answering her mother's questions with patience and trying to tease her father. Suddenly she dropped back in her chair as though she were tired.

'Is Dora coming to-night?'

'Yes, dear, after dinner. And to-morrow everybody is coming,' Mrs. Nesbitt said happily. 'All the children to tea and all the grown-ups to tea and dinner; and the day after that Dora has invited us there.'

'We're going home the day after to-morrow.'

'Going home?' Mrs. Nesbitt repeated.

'We have a party in the evening.'

'Oh, but Lydia – '

'It's rather a special party, isn't it, Oliver? I've got a new dress for it. No, Mother, we can't miss it. We've accepted the invitation.'

'But why did you accept it, dear? The very day after my birthday. I thought you would stay for a week, at least. Oliver, can't you stay? You could send a telegram.'

67

'No, no, Kate,' her husband put in quickly, 'you can't break engagements like that.'

'But Lydia goes to lots of parties. I'm disappointed, dear. Why is this one so special?'

'Lots of famous people,' Lydia said. 'Actors and actresses – ' Mrs. Nesbitt clicked with her tongue – 'and artists and people.'

'Writers?' Mrs. Nesbitt asked.

'Yes.' Lydia looked at Oliver and smiled frankly. 'Writers, and a poet who is going to recite his latest poem. That's really why I want to go. We expect that to be funny.'

'Poor chap,' Oliver said. 'They're only going to make fun of him.'

'Aren't you going?' Mrs. Nesbitt asked.

'Yes, but I shan't make fun. I shall hide somewhere and blush in secret. It's Sylvia and Henry and Lydia who are going to laugh.'

'And who,' Mrs. Nesbitt asked in her coldest manner, 'is Henry?'

'Henry Wyatt. He's a writer. Poor Henry, if he knew you hadn't heard of him. He was at Oxford with Oliver.'

'Oh, was he?' Mrs. Nesbitt said, and her husband heard a note of relief in her tones. 'All the same,' she went on, 'I think it's very unkind to laugh at the poor young man.'

'Horrid, isn't it?' Oliver agreed.

'Henry won't laugh,' Lydia said very quickly; 'you know he won't, Oliver,' and suddenly she realized that her mother was looking at her fixedly, that her father was deliberately not looking at her and that Janet was looking at Oliver and, glancing at each one of them herself, her head held very high, she said challengingly, 'He is too much of a workman to sneer at other people.' And then, more lightly, 'It's only Sylvia and me, typical cats, who will laugh.'

'And I don't suppose you will let the young man know,' Mrs. Nesbitt said soothingly.

'No, he won't know,' Lydia said. 'He has his own convictions about himself – like the rest of us.'

Chapter 8

MRS. NESBITT lay awake that night and her thoughts went
round and round. She was terribly disappointed that Lydia
was going home so soon and hurt that she should have
sacrificed her mother for a mere party and the doubtful
pleasure of laughing at a poet, a pleasure of which Oliver
disapproved, though Mrs. Nesbitt had to admit that he had
not disapproved strongly enough. Of course poets deserved
to be laughed at, but that was no excuse for Lydia's desertion of the family. 'I'm afraid she is very selfish,' Mrs.
Nesbitt thought, 'and Oliver lets her do as she likes.' For
the first time she felt a little doubtful about Oliver and she
remembered how Dora had said that he was not quite the
man her mother thought him. She had always thought him
practically perfect: his quiet manners charmed her and
secretly he was her favourite son-in-law. His only fault in
her eyes was his over-indulgence of Lydia, but there might,
she realized, be other faults of which she did not know, and
suddenly she thought gratefully of John Partridge who was
solid and respectable and altogether lacking in mystery:
she felt that Mabel's life might be inglorious, but it was safe,
while Lydia moved in an atmosphere of uncertainty and
danger. Why had she mentioned actors and artists and not
writers? Why had she said so earnestly that Henry would not
laugh? Why did she wear such very striking dresses? And
if she wore them with so very little bodice and then went
into the garden at night, it was only natural that she should
catch cold. She would be coughing in the morning. Mrs.
Nesbitt, without a word, had put some lozenges near
Lydia's bed and hoped she would take the hint, but her
hope was feeble. Lydia would only eat them if she liked
them.

Mrs. Nesbitt's bed felt very hot and she turned on her

other side, carefully, so that William should not be disturbed and, feeling as if there were an iron band round her head, she reviewed the events of the evening. There had been the pudding, but that was nothing. What worried her was the thought of the party and that Henry, though, in the matter of Henry, it was a consolation to know that he was Oliver's friend. And Mrs. Nesbitt was worried by Lydia's clothes, by her way, inherited from William, of saying things incompletely under a show of frankness. After dinner, she and Dora had spent a long time in the hammocks on the lawn, talking in low tones, while Oliver and Herbert and Janet stayed in the drawing-room as though they were not wanted, and once, quite distinctly, as Mrs. Nesbitt stood by the window, she heard Lydia exclaim, 'But Henry says – ' What did Henry say and why did Lydia quote him? It was all very agitating and, though Mrs. Nesbitt was a woman of much self-control, she gripped the sheet and longed to wake William and tell him all about it, but that would be selfish as well as useless for William would only say something disconcerting, something odd, and ask to be allowed to sleep again.

Her amazement was as intense as her pain when she heard him saying quietly, 'Why don't you go to sleep, Kate? There are limits to what we can do, you know. They have to work things out for themselves.'

She held her breath so that its escape should not betray her. 'I didn't know you were awake, William.'

'I wasn't, until a few minutes ago. Go to sleep, my dear. We can't have them just as we want them, fortunately, perhaps.'

She said nothing. To have spoken would have been to say too much and she was almost afraid of him: his perspicacity was alarming. Could he read her thoughts in the dark and did he see as much as she did and understand more? This also was disturbing and, half irritated, she waited for him to speak again.

'If you don't go to asleep, Kate, how will you adorn the present which is now lying in my collar drawer?'

70

'What is it, William?' she whispered.

'I shall not tell you.'

'But it's long past midnight and my birthday has come.'

'You're not allowed to see your presents till breakfast-time, Kate. Shut your eyes at once,' and Mrs. Nesbitt, lulled by his tones and the comfort of his comradeship, actually did sleep soon.

The birthday morning broke as it always did: the sun shone, the birds sang and the flowers bloomed with the special brightness they kept for that day. There were parcels on Mrs. Nesbitt's plate and when she was seated before them, William entered from the garden with his little posy of freshly-picked flowers and his little packet dangling from it. Here was another ring for Kate's plump finger and when she reproached him gaily, he said, lifting his shoulders and his eyebrows, 'You must have a few decent trinkets to leave your daughters when you die.'

'But I don't want to die yet,' she exclaimed. 'Not while I have you, William, and the children to care for.'

She kissed them all: she marvelled at the delicacy of Janet's handiwork, she privately thought that the sofa rug which Lydia had made for her was too gorgeous in colouring, but she was eloquent about its warmth and softness: the cut-glass bottle from Oliver contained her favourite scent.

'I do love my birthday,' she said simply. 'Now we must have some breakfast. Is that a letter for you, Lydia?'

'Not exactly a letter,' Lydia said, folding up a long printed slip. 'It's a proof.'

'A photograph?'

Lydia laughed. 'The true artist doesn't photograph, he interprets.'

'I don't know what you mean, dear.'

'If you're going to correct that,' Oliver said, 'be careful about the spelling.'

'He certainly can't spell,' Lydia replied, 'but fortunately I can.'

71

Here was that Henry cropping up again and Mrs. Nesbitt felt a sudden diminution in her appetite.

William Nesbitt did not go to the office and when he had read the paper he spent the morning in wandering restlessly about the garden and the house. He looked at the flowers, he talked to the gardener, he thought of his business and spoke to Walter through the telephone. The figure of Janet in a pale cotton dress passed quietly to and fro. In one of the hammocks Lydia lay, a bright cushion behind her head, a pencil in one hand and in the other a long strip of paper. Near her, Oliver sat smoking, and now and then their voices or their laughter came murmuring or ringing across the lawn.

'I'm sure they seem very happy,' Mrs. Nesbitt said. 'Let me have the telephone, dear. I want to speak to the fishmonger. I think we really ought to have a whole salmon, don't you?'

'Get half a dozen, Kate.'

He took her place at the window. Lydia's hammock was swaying gently: her face turned towards Oliver, was seen in profile, the points of her slippers were a little higher than her head, and as she laughed clearly, Mrs. Nesbitt paused before she attacked the fishmonger and said, 'I like to hear her laugh.'

'Yes,' William agreed. He could see Janet at a little distance among the sweet-peas, her busy hands filling the basket on her arm, her pale head burnished by the sunshine. She made a pretty picture and, at Lydia's laugh, she, too, paused for an instant and looked at her sister. The hand holding the pencil was stretched towards Oliver, who took it, held it, and put his lips to it.

'Dear me,' William exclaimed.

'What is it, William?'

'Only Oliver – demonstrating.'

'Doing what?'

'Kissing Lydia's hand.'

'Oh!' Mrs. Nesbit smiled. 'How charming!' A warmth of happiness flowed over her.

72

'And Janet is picking sweet-peas. She's rather like one herself – slim, elusive – '

'Dear child.'

'Yes.' William Nesbitt, tapping a tooth with a finger-nail, continued to look at Janet. He had not spoken the strict truth for she was no longer picking the flowers. She had dropped her basket and she was standing rigidly and staring at the two who dallied and laughed together, and William Nesbitt, with a slight cough and a certain vagueness in his movements, went out of the room, while Mrs. Nesbitt began her negotiations about the salmon. Her heart was lighter than it had been for days. The children were out there in the sunlight, laughing together, picking flowers, kissing hands: they were young and happy: it was all very delightful and, in a few hours' time, the whole family would be united in the garden to do their mother honour.

That assembly was complete at four o'clock in the afternoon. Herbert's new car came puffing up the drive and emitted its crowded contents. There were Dora and Herbert, with a suit-case containing their evening clothes: there were the twins, Maurice and Mary, there were Sarah, Patience, and Catherine, and they all carried parcels, tied with ribbon. A moment later Mabel, John, and the boys arrived on foot, with faces flushed and more parcels, tied with string. They had brought no suit-case for Mabel's summer dress would do duty for the evening and John, with his happy knack for clothes, had combined the negligent and the festive in a way which would have occurred to no one else.

The greetings, the thrustings of presents into Mrs. Nesbitt's lap, as she sat in a big chair on the lawn, the thanks and the kisses were hardly begun when Walter and Violet strolled into the garden. They were not hot for they had not had far to walk, and Violet's airy garments and her prettily-aided complexion gave her a cool and fragile look.

'And now we're all here,' Mrs. Nesbitt said contentedly. 'Thank you for all your lovely presents, darlings.' Her knees were encumbered with two needlebooks, one pin-cushion, one mat, two pictures, a fretwork paperknife, and a painted napkin ring. 'All so beautifully done and all so useful. Now let us have tea.'

Lydia immediately got into a hammock. 'I can eat here, but I'm afraid I can't pour out. Dora can do that.'

'Nonsense. I'm going to sit in the hammock with you.'

'You'll break it, my dear girl.'

'Now, now, I won't have the hammock broken,' William Nesbitt interfered quickly.

'Janet likes pouring out,' Mrs. Nesbitt said calmly.

'Then she can't be human,' Lydia said. 'I'll do it for you, Jane. I'll do it. It's a ghastly job. Oh, very well, don't say I haven't tried to be unselfish.'

'It only causes a great deal of confusion when you do, dear,' Mrs. Nesbitt said, so simply that everybody laughed.

The birthday cake, wreathed with flowers, stood on the table under the willow, and surrounding the cake were plates of wholesome bread and butter, home-made scones, sugared biscuits, biscuits in the shapes of every animal in the Zoo, jugs of milk, dishes of heaped strawberries and bowls of clotted cream, eyed with suspicion by the mothers, and when everybody had decided that the grass was not damp and when, through excess of caution, the children had all been provided with cushions or little stools, and carrying them from place to place on the lawn, had each at last chosen a suitable spot, the noise of voices subsided a little and it became possible to distinguish John Partridge's rich bass from Herbert's flutey tones.

'Oh, Lydia,' Mabel begged, 'don't swing that hammock. It reminds me of the trial trip.'

'There wasn't so much to eat at the trial-trip,' Hampden informed the company, and to Sarah he said triumphantly, 'You weren't allowed to go.'

Sarah pouted. 'I didn't want to go.'

John was heard to say oratorically, 'In the present state of the money-market – labour unrest – '

'Have you made your strawberry jam yet, Mabel?' Mrs.

Nesbitt asked, and Mabel, looking noble, answered, 'I was up till ten o'clock last night, finishing it.'

'I never make jam,' Violet laughed.

'But, you see, you haven't any children to think of.'

'Tact, tact,' Lydia murmured to Dora, and then, more loudly, 'Did you like your brown dress?'

'Yes, it's very nice, but I think the sleeves – '

Oliver, talking to Walter, said, 'You can begin on Exmoor and walk all round the coast.'

Janet, deft and silent, was replenishing cups and mugs.

'Isn't it time we had some strawberries?' Mrs. Nesbitt asked.

Dora's attention was temporarily withdrawn from the subject of clothes while she saw that her children were not over-indulged with fruit, and then she returned to her chair, with her easy, swinging movements, saying, 'But I've come to the conclusion that it's waste of money and temper to buy cheap things. Of course you can wear anything because you're such a lovely shape, but with my figure – '

Mabel dipped her strawberries into sugar and cream and listened to her sisters. Was Lydia a lovely shape? She had never noticed it and she was amazed that Dora should decry her own figure. She certainly was getting fat and Mabel measured her own body with her eyes and glanced again at Dora's.

'Oh, you're thin enough, Mabel,' Lydia said.

'I haven't time to get fat,' she replied, and Lydia said cheerfully, 'That's a mercy, isn't it?' and returned to the absorbing topic of clothes.

Mabel liked clothes herself, though she was not successful with them, but as she listened it seemed to her that the lives of these two were full of gaiety and frivolity, while her own was one of hard work and carefulness. She knew her own way was better, but she was envious, not only of their easier paths but of something indefinite, some assurance of manner, perhaps some capacity for pleasure. Then, looking at her three tall boys, she recovered herself: each one was

75

cleverer than all Dora's children put together and Gladstone who was younger than Maurice, was two inches taller. As though surprised, she remarked on this to Dora.

'Ah, but Maurice is a twin,' Dora said. 'You can't expect a twin to be very big, and anyhow he's strong.'

To Lydia it was plain that Mabel was hesitating between the values of height and strength, that when she had made her choice, she would claim the superiority for Gladstone, and then it appeared that she intended to claim both.

'Gladstone's very wiry too, and I do like tall men.'

'Oh, so do I,' Dora said amiably. 'Maurice is rather a tub, bless him,' and Mabel, looking at Maurice appraisingly, was dimly aware that Dora had come off best in that small encounter. She had implied that whatever Maurice seemed to other people, he was her son and satisfactory to her. It was rather wonderful to admit faults in that easy way, assuming the essential value of the faulty, and again Mabel was envious, but though Dora's was a strong position it was impossible to Mabel. She could not give an inch lest some one should take an ell of disparagement, and she gazed, not so much lovingly as eagerly, at her sons.

'She doesn't really love,' Lydia said in a low aside, 'she grabs.'

'Oh, yes, that's it,' Dora replied with the indignation of her own maternal passion, and Mabel, unaware of these comments, said impressively, 'These are the first strawberries I have eaten this year.'

The remark fell blankly: no one intended to encourage commiseration and Mrs. Nesbitt, with a subtle effect of deafness, said, 'And now we'll tell Mary to clear away and you can have your game.'

It was the family tradition to play hide-and-seek when tea was over. Cromwell, as the eldest grandchild, had to shut his eyes with his face on Mrs. Nesbitt's knee and count twenty in a loud voice.

'And don't peep,' Hampden warned his brother.

The game had to be explained to Catherine, the bounds

had to be fixed and in the midst of this discussion wherein the children were silent and the grown-up people voluble, and William Nesbitt insisted that his lettuces should not be trampled into the dust nor his pea-sticks broken, Mabel created a diversion, saying, 'Oh, John, have you asked Herbert about the Sunday-school treat? We thought you might be willing to lend your garden, Herbert.'

'A Sunday-school treat in my garden?' He looked horrified.

'Oh, awful!' Dora said quickly. 'We shall have to think about it.'

'But we're very anxious to settle it,' Mabel persisted. 'There's a deacons' meeting to-morrow and John has undertaken to arrange about the treat, because he's so good at organization.'

Herbert swept back his hair and frowned at the grass, and Mrs. Nesbitt, foreseeing family awkwardness, said, 'That reminds me, Lydia. I met Mrs. Miller the other day and we were talking about Ethel. Do you ever write to her, dear?'

'Never.'

'I rather think she's hurt.'

'Ethel hurt? I don't believe it.'

'Send her a card at Christmas,' William Nesbitt suggested.

'But why?' Lydia asked.

'Old friends.'

'If you'll choose it for me, William – church bells and a wreath of holly.'

'But what about the treat?' Mabel asked. 'There are only about two hundred children and I don't think they would do any harm.'

Herbert looked up. 'Two hundred? And thousands of oranges and buns.' He was deeply in earnest and he looked annoyed when Lydia laughed gaily. 'No, really, I can't.'

'And I should think a field would be much more suitable,' Mrs. Nesbitt said.

'They're tired of fields.'

77

'I'll pay for the hire of a field for you and I'll pay for the buns.'

'I'm sure that's very generous,' Mrs. Nesbitt said. 'Now what about the game? The children are waiting.'

'The buns are promised already,' Mabel said and she looked at John in exasperation at his silence and in pride at her own persistence.

'Then the oranges. The field and the oranges and the lemonade, but I can't let them spoil my garden. I'll even hire a donkey for them,' he added without humour.

'But consider the donkey!' Lydia cried. 'I think the deacons ought to act as donkeys.'

Mrs. Nesbitt said, 'Hush, dear, hush,' and Janet, joining in unwontedly, said very softly, 'Can they help it?'

'Oh, Jane, you darling! Now if that's settled, do let us start. I must tuck my skirt up.'

'Not too high, dear,' Mrs. Nesbitt begged.

'And don't break the cucumber frames,' William added hastily.

Chapter 9

MABEL did not play at hide-and-seek. She was thin and strong, but as though all her joints had been screwed up too tightly, she had a stiffness of body which did not accommodate itself to exercise, and she sat by her mother's side and asked for sympathy in the matter of the school treat.

'Well, dear,' Mrs. Nesbitt said, 'I know you want to do your best for the Sunday school, but gardens – ' she looked round at her own, so bright with flowers and children, 'there's something sacred about gardens. I wouldn't allow the Sunday school to come here, so I can feel with Herbert. And after all, half of those children are in no need of a treat. They are people comfortably off, like yourselves.'

'Like us! I have a constant struggle to make both ends meet.'

'Then, Mabel,' Mrs. Nesbitt said quietly, 'all I can say is that John doesn't give you enough money. I know he has it, Father knows he has it: he has seen the balance-sheets.'

'It's a very uncertain business,' Mabel said.

'My dear, you never seem to be happy unless you are miserable,' Mrs. Nesbitt replied with a touch of sharpness and Mabel, looking resentful, returned to the safer subject of the treat.

'There are lots of poor children in the Sunday school.'

'Then they will be delighted with a field, dear.'

'Dora and Herbert are so selfish.'

'Selfish? I don't know. It takes all sorts of people to make a world,' she quoted the words with which William sometimes admonished her.

Through the drawing-room window Mrs. Nesbitt had a glimpse of his head. 'Father finds doing nothing very tiring,' she said.

'I'm thankful to sit still,' Mabel sighed.

Mrs. Nesbitt's eyes roved over the garden, the bright flower-beds, the sheltering trees, the long white house with roses and jasmine growing up the walls. 'Yes, gardens are very precious,' she said softly.

For some time Cromwell had been conducting his search in a cautious and scientific manner. He made ever-widening circles of exploration and tiptoed swiftly back to Mrs. Nesbitt's chair, until Oliver's voice was heard from some hiding-place, saying, 'You must take some risks, Cromwell. Be a sportsman.'

'But I want to catch them all, don't I, Mother?'

'Of course you do, dear.'

Behind the bushes and among the sweet-peas and half-hidden by the tree trunks, forms could be seen moving, peeping stealthily and retreating; and soon, with a flashing swiftness, Janet and Lydia, from different sides of the garden, rushed across the lawn and simultaneously reached the goal, Janet tall and straight and bright, like a messenger from the gods, Lydia lithe and small, flushed and dishevelled. United in this success, they laughed together, panting a little.

'Aha!' Lydia cried. 'Your old aunts can beat you yet.' She sank down on the grass. 'I do love this game. Let's play it after dinner in the dark. And here comes Sarah. Quick! Sarah, quick! Ah, he's caught you! Never mind, you'll have to catch us next time. And here's Dora. Sarah, look at Mummy! Oh, how funny, oh dear, how funny!' For Dora, with her skirts held up, her sturdy legs displayed, a suspender flapping at her calf, her expression one of comic determination, was leaping over flower-beds as quickly as her breathlessness and girth would let her. 'Oh, I'm too fat,' she gasped as Cromwell clutched her. Mrs. Nesbitt was laughing heartily, William Nesbitt had risen and was looking out of the window, Mabel made stealthy signs regarding the suspender. 'I know. It's broken.' Dora's hair was loose, her colour high. 'But I nearly did it.'

Lydia had a pain in her side. 'I wish you could have seen yourself!'

'I know my legs are frightful.'

'Hush!' Mrs. Nesbitt said.

'What we really ought to have is a jumping competition.'

'No, no,' Mrs. Nesbitt begged. 'This is quite enough.'

'What could I do to get my legs thinner?'

'Nothing,' Lydia said. 'They're too short from the knee. Janet and I have the only decent ones in the family.'

'Lydia dear, the boys will hear you.'

'They must know we have legs, Mother, and they've seen Dora's!'

The children were all caught now. Violet strolled into the goal while Cromwell's back was turned, he succeeded in catching Walter, and Oliver dropped unexpectedly from the tree he had climbed. There remained only Herbert, and John Partridge. They were not to be found and after repeated calls, Herbert appeared with the oil-can he had been using on the car and John emerged from the green-house: he was interested in tomatoes.

'It isn't fair!' Cromwell cried in tears.

'John, you've hurt his feelings.'

'Herbert, how could you?'

The men looked foolish and promised to play properly next time.

'I'm afraid you're both thoroughly grown up,' Lydia said sadly.

'One more game and then it will be time to go home,' Mrs. Nesbitt ordained.

When the children had gone, a drowsy peace fell on the company. The little quarrel between the Partridges and Johnstones was ignored: Mrs. Nesbitt and Mabel talked principally about jam: Oliver, Dora, and Lydia made a little group of friends at ease in each other's company: John tried to beguile Janet into conversation and his well-turned sentences boomed forth like surf on a shingled beach.

Suddenly Lydia started up. 'Oh, heavens, I've forgotten

to post a letter! I want a long envelope. Has anybody got a long envelope? William, have you?'

'Yes, in my desk. The stamps are there too,' he added dryly.

'And now, who's coming to the pillar-box? No, Oliver, you I have always with me. Dora?'

'I can't move.'

'Jane, I haven't seen you for a second. Come with me, there's a dear.' She looked down tenderly at her sister. 'I promise not to ask you why you wouldn't come and stay with me.' William Nesbitt moved in his chair and tried to conceal his watchfulness. 'No reproaches is my motto,' Lydia said, and Janet, smiling gravely, rose and walked with her across the lawn.

'They are so fond of each other,' Mrs. Nesbitt explained. Nobody spoke. William Nesbitt looked at Oliver, whose eyes were half shut over his pipe. 'The stories Lydia used to tell her!'

'She has always been good at that,' Oliver said.

'Oh, Oliver, I didn't mean untruths.'

'The idea had not occurred to me,' he said coldly. 'I've never known her tell a lie in her life.'

'Of course not,' Mrs. Nesbitt remarked calmly and William Nesbitt raised his eyebrows patiently.

'I sometimes wish she would.'

'Oliver! What do you mean?' Mrs. Nesbitt protested.

'I don't know. Nothing.' He regretted his remark. He saw Mabel staring at him, but not really interested, Dora smiled tolerantly, Herbert looking at his nails, John looking profound, Mrs. Nesbitt looking virtuous.

'Lydia could tell us if she were here,' her father said.

Oliver gave a hardly perceptible nod. William Nesbitt was an understanding man and his son-in-law felt a spasm of gratitude, perhaps a sense of security, in his presence. 'But we won't ask her,' Mrs. Nesbitt said. She distrusted these probings. 'I think it must be time to go and dress.'

Walter and Violet went away, promising to be back in time for dinner and Mabel, looking after them, asked, 'What does Violet do with herself all day?'

'She looks after Walter.' That, Mrs. Nesbitt implied, was a career in itself.

William Nesbitt was left alone in the garden. The air was cool and the leaves of the trees fluttered a little and turned themselves, as though in hope of rain. Swifts were flying, swooping, hovering, darting past each other dexterously, and William Nesbitt, following the intricacies of their flight, wondered how much of it was careless joy and how much design. From the house there came muffled sounds of footsteps and voices, punctuated by perfect stillness. Through one of the open windows he could see John Partridge in his shirt sleeves, tidying himself for the evening meal, and William Nesbitt was glad when he retired: he was a prosaic vision.

At the next window, Lydia appeared for a second, put out a hand and pulled a spray of jasmine. William Nesbitt smiled. What a gift she had for doing pretty things! All that day, she had said nothing worth saying, done nothing worth doing, beyond the mere movements of her body, which had a daring grace, yet in her presence there was the constant expectation, never fulfilled, of something which would thrill, and in the very thought of her he touched romance, he saw poetry and felt the unreasoning joy which Kate had never given him. Kate had been practical always, even in young love, and, sitting there, looking at the white walls which enclosed his family, he felt a bitterness of loss. He had missed ecstasy. That hand taking the jasmine, which would soon be cast aside, was like a memory of what he had never had, and for a moment he envied Oliver, and then he pitied him, for Oliver, no more than himself, had ever grasped that beauty, desired and out of reach. No man could ever seize it though for a moment he might touch it, or, seizing it, he would find it lost for ever. But the tragedy was hers, the real tragedy was hers. Under her gaiety, William Nesbitt divined unrest: under that unrest, a longing for stability, and under the longing there was the essential incapacity for peace.

William Nesbitt stretched out his short legs and his face

looked tired. It had been a long day and social relation-
ships were more difficult than business ones. He marvelled
at the endurance of women whose lives were a tangled mass
of human complications, but women were tough: Providence had seen to that. Yet, as though in contradiction of
this belief, Janet, appearing at that moment from the
dining-room, looked like a spirit, so slight and fair was she
in her white gown. She stood for a moment with her hands
clasped before her, separated them with a decisive gesture
of resignation or despair, and advanced across the lawn.

'Oh, I didn't see you,' she said.

'This is a big chair and I am a small man. What a fuss
these birds are making, aren't they? Having a game of
hide-and-seek of their own, I suppose. I wonder if they
were laughing at you all, this afternoon: clumsy, they must
have thought you. Still, you can run pretty fast, Janet. It
was a dead heat between you and Lydia, wasn't it?'

'Yes, but we weren't running against each other.' She
began to pick up the cushions, the books and papers scattered on the grass.

'Can't Mary do this?' he asked.

'Oh, no. One must do something.'

'True,' he said, remembering that he had heard her use
those words before, 'but I ought to get up and help you
and I don't want to. I'm tired.'

'Are you?' With a bright cushion in her arms, she paused
and looked at him until, urged by the sympathy which felt
like a taut band between them, she sighed out, 'So am I.'
Her lips trembled, and he looked away.

'You mustn't run so hard another time.'

'No, it's no good, is it?'

'True again. You seem to be a wise young woman.'

'Wise!' She dropped the cushion and he remembered
how she had dropped the basket in the morning. 'Wise!
I'm a perfect fool. Surely you know that,' and she left him
as though his ignorance made her indignant.

84

Chapter 10

'AFTER all, it has been a happy day,' Mrs. Nesbitt said as she got into bed.

'After all what?'

This was one of those moments in which Mrs. Nesbitt felt a violent irritation with her husband, but she did not betray herself and, gazing at the shadows on the ceiling, she replied, 'I was afraid there was going to be unpleasantness about the Sunday-school treat.'

'There was.'

'But very little.'

'And I don't think it matters, but when one thinks of families one is positively terrified. Yet people continue to have them.'

'When Mabel was born – '

'She was a pretty baby.'

'She's a pretty woman, though she wants a new tooth – have you noticed it, Kate? – in the upper jaw, left-hand side. I suppose she'd say she couldn't afford it.'

'I had to speak rather sharply to her to-day about that kind of thing.'

'Did you?' He chuckled. 'You have more pluck than I have. I'm afraid of them all. I was going to say that when she was born we never suspected the Sunday-school treat, did we?'

'How could we?'

'No, we couldn't be expected to think of that.'

'You really are absurd, William.'

'Yes, my dear, but I blame myself. I ought to have known there was a small John Partridge growing up somewhere to a beard and a frock-coat.'

'He looked most unsuitable to-night,' Mrs. Nesbitt murmured.

'I nearly asked him to say grace. Lucky I didn't, but I felt awed, somehow. In his night-shirt which, fortunately, I have never seen, he must look like an apostle. I wonder what Mabel thinks of him then.'

'She must be used to it by this time. And if she loves him why should you blame yourself?'

'For having a daughter who can.'

'Then we oughtn't to have had any children at all.'

'That's what I'm leading up to.'

'Well, it's too late to worry about it now,' Mrs. Nesbitt said sensibly, 'and think how miserable we should be without them.'

'That's not the point. But to have produced a wife for John Partridge! It shocks me, Kate. Talk of sacrificing the first-born! We're no better than the heathen.'

'William,' she said seriously, 'you are very talkative to-night.'

'It's not the champagne, Kate, if you are thinking of that. I did no more than drink your health, dear, in a bumper. But it's the sight of all these young people for whom we are responsible that's gone to my head. I didn't like to think of Mabel going home to John's flannel night-shirt – '

'Pyjamas, I think,' Mrs. Nesbitt corrected gently.

'The garment may be bifurcated or it may not, but morally it's a night-shirt. And I didn't like to think of Dora returning in that handsome car to the ancestral pile.'

'I really can't see anything painful in that.'

'With Herbert,' he added suavely.

'I've told you before that you are very hard on Herbert. And there are all those dear children asleep in their nice beds.'

'They will grow up too, and Dora will have a birthday and see the shortcomings of their husbands. It's endless. We've begun something that we can't stop.'

'I don't want to stop it, William. Won't you get cold, sitting on the end of the bed like that? Do get in, or put something round you. I like to think of our grandchildren and great-grandchildren going on and on when we are dead.'

'Yes, that's a queer idea, isn't it? I wonder what it's like to be dead.'

'We can't tell, so it's no good guessing.'

'Dora's too good for Herbert. She's a big woman, really, but she shrinks herself as tailors shrink cloth to fit it for the weather. Self-protection – she has that strongly – and she's loyal.'

'She chose to marry him.'

'Ah, yes, the people we choose to marry! Don't shoot, Kate. You and I are exceptions – I've told you that before.'

She turned on him her queer, unseeing gaze and said calmly, 'I think you are making yourself unhappy about nothing.'

'Did I say I was unhappy? Do I look it? I'm simply trying to see the results of my own acts, a thing no one can do until, as you say, it is too late. So I shall go to sleep. Shall I put out the light?'

'Wait a minute. Yes, put it out.' Through the darkness, her voice came almost timidly. 'But the others, William.'

'There are so many of them.'

'You don't feel sorry for any of the others?'

'If you mean Lydia, my dear – '

'There's Walter, too.'

'Oh, Walter's happy – likes his business, likes his play-acting and his dancing, likes his golf and his Violet. And Lydia is in possession of herself.'

There came a silence and she tried to search his mind as she could feel that he was searching hers. She thought she heard him control a breath, but she could not be sure of that.

'And you are not worried about her?'

'Are you, my dear?'

'Sometimes I'm worried about them all. They go out into the world – But we still have Janet safe.' William Nesbitt turned over on his side. 'William, did you hear what I said? We still have Janet safe.'

'Janet? Oh, yes, she's still here. Good-night, Kate.'

'Good-night, William. I've had a happy day, but I wish Lydia were not going to-morrow. I shall have to speak to her about that house. It's dreadfully damp.'

'Well, don't tell her I'll buy her another because I won't.'

She answered in a gentle voice, 'You talk like that, but you would do anything in the world for her.'

It appeared, however, that Lydia wanted nothing done. She liked her house and could forgive its dampness and Oliver liked it, too.

'Oh, if Oliver likes it –' Mrs. Nesbitt had an innate respect for husbands.

'He does have likes and dislikes, you know. He even likes me.'

'Why of course, dear.'

'Oh, it's hard work, but he pretends it's easy and makes me feel comfortable about it. Dora is like that, too. She accepts me as I am.' She looked at Janet with the softened expression which was the accompaniment of all her dealings with that sister. 'Jane doesn't. Jane sits in judgment. You always did, Jane. It's in your character and I accept it as part of you, for I'm easy, too. And it's good practice for the last day. I shan't feel as awkward as some of the sinners, because I'm used to being arraigned.'

Janet, lifting her fair head, answered with painful slowness, 'I don't mean to do it.'

'That's what I say.' Lydia spoke gaily. 'You can't help it. And now I think we ought to start. Where's Oliver? Good-bye, Mother, I don't know when I shall see you again.'

Mrs. Nesbitt kept back her tears. 'No, we never know, my child, but it won't be long, I hope. Be careful to-night, at the party. Mind you wrap up well. Oliver, see that she wraps up well. Would you like my Indian shawl, dear, or my Spanish lace? Janet, run and get them for her.'

'No, no. I've a gorgeous new cloak, yellow, with a fur collar. Good-bye, Jane.'

'Good-bye,' Janet said. They stood, separated by the

88

table, looking at each other. Janet held her sewing in her hands and Lydia played with the clasp of the little bag she carried.

'I hope you're not extravagant, Lydia,' Mrs. Nesbitt ventured, thinking of the cloak.

'Yes, I am – very. Tell William he ought to make me a bigger allowance than the others, because I didn't get my fair share of good looks.'

'Beauty is only skin deep, dear,' Mrs. Nesbitt said.

'It depends on the skin and mine's so thin that I'm sure my ugliness goes to the bone.'

'You talk a great deal of nonsense, dear, like Father. And you ought to be starting.'

Oliver kissed his mother-in-law and to Janet he bowed with a slightly exaggerated formality: this was his reply to her rebuff, and Lydia, seeing the sudden pain in her eyes, hastily dropped her own.

'Jane,' she said, 'just for once, in case there's a railway accident, and although you won't like it, I'm going to kiss you.' For Janet's ear alone, she whispered a faint 'Forgive.'

'That's right,' Mrs. Nesbitt said heartily. 'I like you girls to kiss each other. I like to see affection.' Janet stood very still, like a white statue touched with gold. 'Family love –' Mrs. Nesbitt began vaguely, and stopped.

'And I shall see Father at the station,' Lydia said, lingering for a moment in the hall. She sighed. 'How cool it is and how sweet it smells.'

'Lydia dear, couldn't you change your mind?'

'No,' she said slowly. 'I'd like to stay – yes, I would, Jane – but I promised I would be there.'

'But that sort of promise –' Mrs. Nesbitt began, and Lydia, radiant and amused, interrupted swiftly. 'How do you know what sort of promise it was?' She paused with her foot on the carriage step and looked at her mother and sister standing in the doorway. Her mother's eyes, bright with the tears she refused to shed, were on her, but Janet's, Lydia saw, rested on Oliver.

'Get in, Lydia,' he said.

89

'Good-bye, Jane,' Lydia said again without looking at her, and Janet's voice came quietly, 'Good-bye.'

Mrs. Nesbitt and Janet watched the carriage out of sight.

'I don't believe she wanted to go at all,' Mrs. Nesbitt said. 'I don't believe – ' but Janet had gone into the house.

Mrs. Nesbitt followed her into the dining-room and saw her standing by the window. Something tense and rigid in her attitude startled Mrs. Nesbitt and convinced her that the child was suffering. She was struck, too, by the frequency with which she was offered a view of her youngest daughter's back. It was possible that she was crying and wished to hide her face, but she could not be crying every time she turned that part of her body to her mother. 'She's very reserved,' she thought. 'It isn't natural,' and she sighed.

'The house seems terribly quiet,' she said aloud, and as she got no answer she said kindly, 'I'm afraid it's rather dull and lonely for you here, dear. You will miss Lydia.'

'No, I shall not miss her,' Janet said.

Mrs. Nesbitt felt indignant but, wisely, she said nothing. If Janet were not depressed by her sister's departure, why did her back look so unhappy? She sighed again, but she had her household duties to fulfil and she went towards the kitchen, thankful for the alleviation of an interview with the cook.

Chapter 11

THIS was at the end of June and it was in September that Mrs. Nesbitt learnt to look back at her past happiness and see that it had been almost perfect. The little frets and worries which had oppressed her had been no more than summer waves, breaking with hardly a sound on a sandy shore; and suddenly a storm had risen, not with splendour, not with a call to fight the elements and emerge gloriously beaten or gloriously victorious, salt on the face and mighty wind in the soul, but one that rose with a dull, threatening rumble and a lowering of clouds which hung and would not break. They hung, ponderous, black, immovable, edged with angry colours, and the world was darkened.

The first rumble was heard in August, when Janet announced her intention of going for a walking tour on Dartmoor with a friend. Mrs. Nesbitt was at first amused by an idea which would give way under humorous treatment, and then aghast at Janet's determination. The friend was a capable young woman who, Mrs. Nesbitt believed, had something to do with factories and fortunately spent most of her time in traversing the country on that business; she had a firm chin, wore sensible clothes and clipped her speech, and on the rare occasions when she and Mrs. Nesbitt met, she showed no pretty deference to her elder. Now, under the provocation of the walking tour, Mrs. Nesbitt saw that anything in Janet which she had ever found unsatisfactory could be traced to the influence of this Marion.

Mrs. Nesbitt had never felt herself so greatly at a loss as she was in face of Janet's stubbornness. Dora and Mabel had both taken their families to the seaside and she could not bring herself to discuss her daughter with Violet, while William, as usual, took a tolerant view of the proposal: he seemed indifferent to the folly of an expedition in which two girls without a permanent address, with packs on their backs and unprotected save for walking-sticks, were liable to insult, to tramps, to murder and rapine, to death in bogs, to pneumonia, to broken legs. How could Mrs. Nesbitt sleep at night in ignorance of where her daughter's fair head was resting? How could she and William take a holiday together in constant expectation of a telegram calling them to Janet's aid or inquest? And yet, in retrospect, how mild a trouble this appeared! In August it had the proportions of tragedy. Hitherto Janet had meekly accompanied her parents on their holidays and Mrs. Nesbitt could see no circumstances, except marriage, which should change this suitable arrangement.

'But if you don't want to come away with me and Father, dear,' she conceded nobly, 'why not get rooms near Dora?'

'Because I don't want to see a single member of the family. Who else do I ever see?'

'Who could be better?' Mrs. Nesbitt retorted. 'Dora and the children – bathing – cricket on the sands – And I should think you would get very tired of Marion, such a mannish sort of girl. I don't know what you have in common.'

'Nothing,' Janet said.

'Well then.'

'I want an antidote.'

Mrs. Nesbitt was silent, but she decided to look up the exact meaning of that word.

'I can't think why you don't want me to do as I like for once.'

'For once! My dear child! You know I think of nothing but your good. I say nothing about mine – but I don't see how Father and I can have our trip to Scotland with you wandering about those moors, and he needs a change.'

'It will be your fault if he doesn't have it. He won't be anxious.'

'Of course he will.'

'He won't. I asked him. He said it was better to die in a bog than never to have seen one.'

'Father is always saying things like that, and if you have really made up your mind, I can say no more, but I think you are acting selfishly.'

'Very well, I am acting selfishly, but why do you expect me to give up everything?'

Mrs. Nesbitt was genuinely astonished. 'What have you ever had to give up?'

'Oh, nothing, I suppose,' and, as usual, Janet went and looked out of the window, presenting her back to her mother. 'Nothing I ought to have had, no doubt.'

'I should think not,' Mrs. Nesbitt said indignantly. 'You must do as you like, Janet.'

'There is so little I like,' Janet quietly replied, and Mrs. Nesbitt went upstairs and shed a few difficult and angry tears. The project itself had now lessened in importance and terror: it was Janet's attitude which had become formidable in its obstinacy and disquieting in its bitterness. The holiday would pass and, by good fortune, without mishap, but Janet's strangeness would remain. 'What does the child want?' Mrs. Nesbitt asked herself again, and she began to find relief in the prospect of Janet's departure, but the relief was only temporary.

'What does the child want?' she asked of William.

'Something we can't give her. Let her find her own meat.'

'Meat?' Mrs. Nesbitt queried.

'Spiritual food, my dear.'

'She never goes to church,' Mrs. Nesbitt remarked.

'I suppose she has conscientious scruples. Must have.' And as though to himself, he murmured, 'There's the sin of covetousness –'

Mrs. Nesbitt's ears were sharp enough. 'They none of them have that fault, William, except, perhaps, Mabel,' she protested.

'Oh, there are lots of sins, Kate, lots of sins. I was just taking them in order. Theft, murder –'

'Don't go on, William,' she warned him sternly.

93

'I thought you might find the one about honouring parents somewhat applicable,' he said mildly.

He was incapable, she thought, of taking any matter really seriously.

Janet started on her expedition with a coldly cheerful good-bye from her mother and not a single inquiry about underclothes: this was the measure of her disgrace: but her father saw her off at the station.

'If you break your leg, or lose your money, or come back with a cold, the strategic position is lost and my reputation ruined. I count on your success.' Then he commended her to the care of the athletic young woman, who bore tolerantly with this parental fussiness.

Standing with his hat in his hand until the oval of Janet's face had vanished, he had his eyebrows at their highest elevation. The girls made, it seemed to him, an incongruous pair, but he thought he knew why Janet had insisted on a holiday with that particular companion: she was aware of a disease for which she craved – he found her own word – an antidote. It was not in his power to give it, but he sent a bashful blessing after the departing train and felt the burden of his fatherhood heavy on him.

Mr. and Mrs. Nesbitt did not have their trip to Scotland: he saw that she did not want to go and suggested a postponement until October. She agreed to that and as she went about the empty house, with all her chilren, except Walter, far away, she learnt how much Janet's quiet presence had meant to her. It had been, in some strange way, a guarantee of peacefulness and security, and though she had no definite ideas about the influence of beauty, she found the house less bright, the garden less serene, without the shape of Janet moving here and there, and life, without the neighbourhood of that personality, duller than it had ever been, so that though she could not forgive Janet she counted the days till her return.

Each day there came a post card from her with a few words written in the space left by the picture of old cottages, moorland ponies and rocks; once a week Mabel sent a letter describing the success of the Partridge holiday, the progress of the boys in swimming, the ardour with which Cromwell sought for fossils, found and labelled them; twice or three times a week, Dora wrote and hoped her mother was not feeling lonely; and at last Lydia was happily inspired to remember her parents. The postscript contained the only news. It informed Mrs. Nesbitt baldly, callously, as she thought, that Oliver had gone away alone, to walk on Dartmoor.

'William!' Mrs. Nesbitt said in a voice which made the word a groan. She had given him the letter.

'My dear?'

'Without Lydia!'

'Yes, on Dartmoor,' William Nesbitt said, looking fixedly at the letter.

'Dartmoor – why, I didn't think of that at first, but he may meet Janet. That would be delightful.' This thought conquered the other. 'If they had Oliver with them, I should feel safe.'

'Would you, Kate?'

'Yes, I shall write to Lydia and tell her Janet is there too.'

'Doesn't she know?'

Mrs. Nesbitt's expression changed. 'I didn't tell her. I discussed it with nobody. How could I?'

'Oh well, Dartmoor's a big place,' William Nesbitt said cheerfully.

'Big!' Mrs. Nesbitt pictured it as a boundless desert.

'But if Lydia knows where Oliver is and we know where Janet is going – '

'No, no, Kate. I shouldn't interfere. Never wise to interfere. Oliver evidently wants to be alone.'

The pain returned to Mrs. Nesbitt's breast. 'But why, William? Why?'

' "And nine times to the boy I said, 'Why, William, tell me why?' " ' William Nesbitt quoted gaily. 'I don't know, my dear, but it's his business. And Janet has gone off with that masculine young person and that's her business. They're old enough to look after themselves.'

95

'But are they wise enough?'

'Are we any wiser than they? If Lydia prefers London to bogs – '

'I'm sure her own house is no drier,' Mrs. Nesbitt interrupted bitterly, but her husband continued his thought.

'That's her business.'

'But it would be so nice for Janet and Oliver to meet, nice for them both, and you see, William, Marion is there, and that would make it perfectly suitable. I think I'll just write to Lydia – '

'Now, Kate, I won't have it,' he said sternly.

She sat, silenced for a moment, trying to discover the motives which she would not ask him to explain. 'William, you don't think – do you think Oliver and Lydia have quarrelled?'

'No, my dear, I don't.'

'Then, why – '

With some asperity he answered, 'I've told you, Kate, we can't have them as we want them. We're lucky to have them as they are. And why on earth shouldn't Oliver have a few days to himself if he wants them? Try not to be limited in your ideas, Kate.'

'I am very unhappy,' she said simply.

He laughed at her, patted her shoulder, kissed her, and went off to the office, debonair, waving his hat at the gate as though there were no such thing as trouble. She did not understand how he could take things so lightly, but she did not see the slackening of his pace and the drooping of his shoulders when he turned into the street. Clean and trim in his grey suit, a flower in his coat, he passed the mews with a nod to the proprietor, who always set his watch by the punctual gentleman's appearance. But to-day the man thought, 'He's not looking so well. Getting old like the rest of us,' and as though William Nesbitt were conscious of that criticism, he straightened himself and walked more briskly. There was no use in betraying himself. He had a great belief in the moral effect of a brave exterior and under his breath he hummed the air of a song. He was a man of action and he felt in himself the power to set things right, but he knew there existed forces too vehement to be stayed by his energy. He walked on, humming his tune, but when he reached the Roman Catholic church, which he passed twice a day, he did a thing astonishing to himself. He entered the church and remained for a few minutes in that dim place where candles burned before the tawdry images of saints.

Mrs. Nesbitt was not a woman of action, but she had no conception of her limitations. She had her fixed ideas of conduct. Husbands and wives, she firmly believed, did not separate, could not separate, even for a holiday, unless the relationship were faulty: it was unnatural that they should. It followed, therefore, that Lydia and Oliver were unhappy, and to be unhappy in marriage was a sin. This was the worst moment her life had known. Her big, pleasant house, with the sun flooding the rooms, was dark to her and very lonely. She thought of Janet and that girl tramping the moors, and Janet's transgression passed into nothingness: she shone for her mother as a thing of light and innocence: she thought of Oliver wandering alone, and she thought of Lydia in London, in August, without her husband. What was she doing? What people rang her bell? What did they think of such a situation and what advantage did they take of it? Mrs. Nesbitt had a vision of Lydia sitting in that bare drawing-room, all her alertness gone and with tears staining her cheeks; and then she had another, vaguer, blurred, in which Lydia was going to theatres, going to parties, laughing, defiant, indiscreet.

Mrs. Nesbitt could not endure the company of her thoughts and speculations and, going hastily to her husband's desk, she took the time-table and turned the pages with shaking fingers. Then she rang the bell. She would be out all day and dinner must be postponed until eight o'clock. Mr. Nesbitt was to be told that she would be at home in time for that.

Chapter 12

WHAT scenes of revelry or distress Mrs. Nesbitt expected to find in Lydia's house, she did not exactly formulate, but she was a little disconcerted when Maria, that respectable servant, opened the door wide and smiled a welcome. The normal aspect of the little white house, the cool quiet of its interior, contrasted with her own heat and hurry, made her excursion seem ridiculous, and her legs shook as she followed Maria up the stairs. She was ashamed of her panic and hardly knew how to account for this sudden visitation, but Lydia, who liked people to deal easily with her, did, in these matters, as she would be done by and, rising from the low chair in which she sat reading by the window, she showed only a reasonable quantity of surprise.

'Why, Mother!'

'Yes, dear. How nice and cool it is here. The journey was so hot.'

Removing Mrs. Nesbitt's wrap, Lydia said pleasantly, 'What a pretty hat.'

'Do you like it? Father went with me to choose it.'

'But you ought to wear it a little, just a little farther over your forehead. That's better. Have you brought William with you?'

'No, dear.'

'You've run away from him. Oh, Mother!'

Mrs. Nesbitt blushed. This looked remarkably like a turning of the tables and she said almost timidly: 'The house was so lonely, I couldn't bear it, and I just made up my mind to come and see you. Janet's away, you know.'

'Is she?'

'Yes, in Devonshire, with Marion. Surely I told you?' She added nervously, 'On Dartmoor.'

'Dartmoor? No, you didn't tell me. And Oliver's there too.' There was no embarrassment in this reference.

'It would be nice if they met, dear, wouldn't it?'

'Would Janet like it?'

'Janet? She's very fond of Oliver.'

'Oh, yes, everybody's fond of him. That's how he goes through the world,' and though this sounded like a complaint, Mrs. Nesbitt was not quite sure that Lydia meant it so. 'But Marion's with Janet,' Lydia went on, 'so Oliver might feel he wasn't wanted.'

'Of course I shouldn't suggest it, dear, if Marion were not there,' Mrs. Nesbitt said seriously.

Lydia laughed. 'I hadn't thought of that.'

'No, dear,' Mrs. Nesbitt murmured. 'You're so unconventional.'

'I don't know,' Lydia murmured back. 'It's hard work and I'm lazy. Now I must go and speak to Maria about luncheon. Sit here by the window and get cool.'

Mrs. Nesbitt obediently sat. She was glad to be alone for a moment. She told herself that her legs were shaking because the stairs to Lydia's drawing-room were numerous and steep, but they could not be blamed for the shaking of her hands. She wished she were at home again, for Lydia's eyes were very bright, reminding Mrs. Nesbitt of William's, and there was a queer control about her manner which made her mother feel uneasy. Lydia was the mistress of the situation, and Mrs. Nesbitt felt like a truant child who would be grateful for no worse punishment than a mild chiding.

But Lydia's first remark when she returned was uttered gaily. 'And now tell me why you have deserted Father?'

The weakness of Mrs. Nesbitt's position forced her to meet her daughter's humour. 'He doesn't know,' she said mysteriously. 'He went to the office and I was left alone, and suddenly I decided to come, just for a few hours. I shall be back as soon as he is and I don't think,' this was meant and Lydia received it as a hint, 'I don't think I shall tell him anything about it.'

99

'This is a very bad example for me,' Lydia said, and her little flame of brightness seemed to waver.

'Ah, my dear, I'm not afraid of that,' Mrs. Nesbitt said, fitting the belief to her desire. 'And now tell me about Oliver. Is he better?'

'Better?' He's perfectly well, I believe.'

'But I thought – you told me, dear, that he had gone away.'

'So he has, to Dartmoor, like Janet.'

'Yes, like Janet,' Mrs. Nesbitt repeated, and they looked at each other, each for a moment forgetting her guard, but their thoughts did not really travel together for, to Mrs. Nesbitt all was uncertain, and to Lydia most was clear.

'I do wish they could meet,' Mrs. Nesbitt said, 'but Father told me I was not to interfere.'

'Oh, did he?' Lydia stretched out her hand and seized a branch of the acacia. She picked a leaf and held it to her cheek. 'William is generally right. Let us leave it to chance. Oliver wanted solitude.'

'And he knew you would not be lonely, with all your friends around you. He knew you would be cared for,' Mrs. Nesbitt announced firmly.

'No, all my friends are away. I'm in retreat, like a nun. It's good for the soul.'

'I don't find it so,' Mrs. Nesbitt said, 'but then I never did approve of nuns. Their clothes look so unhealthy, dabbing in the dust, and so hot. Well, dear, you may think being alone is good for you, but I'm sure it's dull, so I hope you are not sorry to see your mother.'

'I'm very glad. There's the gong. You mustn't expect much to eat.'

Yes, Lydia was the mistress of the situation, and Mrs. Nesbitt felt resentment against William, mixed with a longing for his presence, because he had bequeathed his quickness of apprehension to this daughter. There was no doubt that Lydia knew why this sudden visit had been paid her and she was behaving, Mrs. Nesbitt had to own, with tact. She was also very amusing at luncheon. It was impossible not to laugh, though Mrs. Nesbitt felt it was disloyal, at her description of the Partridge family in the sea, all excessively decent in their bathing-dresses and anxious about the temperature of the water, but when the flush caused by these exertions had faded from Lydia's cheeks, her face looked more tired and more set than before.

'I don't think you are very well, dear,' Mrs. Nesbitt said.

'I'm always well,' Lydia answered lightly.

'Tired, then.'

'Oh, I'm always tired.'

'I wish you would take things more easily,' Mrs. Nesbitt sighed.

'I take them as I find them,' Lydia replied.

Mrs. Nesbitt sighed again, silently: it had always been impossible to reach the fastnesses of Lydia's mind and it was no use trying, but she said, 'Well, I should like a little rest on your sofa and you can lie on your bed and perhaps go to sleep.'

'Oh, thank you very much, Mrs. Nesbitt, but I'm going to sit in this chair and read.'

Mrs. Nesbitt laughed. This was more normal. 'Very well, dear. It's nice to be with you. What is your book?'

'Henry Wyatt's new novel. It's very good.'

'Has it just been published?'

'Yes. I read it in proof of course,' – those two words stabbed themselves into Mrs. Nesbitt's breast, – 'but it's better than I thought.'

'So he let you read it before it was published?'

Mrs. Nesbitt saw her daughter look very much like William, whimsical and puzzled. 'Yes he – let me,' she said.

'Well, I think I'll close my eyes,' Mrs. Nesbitt said, and she kept them shut for some time, but she could hear Lydia turning the pages. Suddenly she said, 'I wish you'd lend me that book, dear, when you've finished with it. I should like to read a book by a friend of yours.'

'You must buy a copy, Mother, and increase the sales.'

'Oh, I don't know that I want to go as far as that,' Mrs.

Nesbitt murmured and, guilefully, she added, 'How much did your copy cost, dear?'

'It was given to me,' Lydia said.

'Oh, then, of course, it's valuable. I'll see if I can get it from the library.'

'You ought to help struggling authors.'

'Is Mr. Wyatt struggling'?

'Well, no,' Lydia laughed. 'It's the other people who struggle, I suppose.'

Mrs. Nesbitt wrestling with this remark, replied cleverly, 'If it's a difficult book I shan't be able to read it. I like simple, pleasant stories, I'm afraid.'

'Go to sleep, Mother,' Lydia said, and Mrs. Nesbitt immediately opened her eyes. Lydia was reading placidly, her lips half curved into a smile. The hand which was not holding the book hung limply and it looked very white and thin. It was the left hand and Mrs. Nesbitt, staring hard, perceived that there was no ring on the sacred finger. Her own wedding ring had been embedded firmly for many years; it had never been moved since William put it on her finger, and the absence of Lydia's ring shocked her into stiffness.

'Lydia,' she said, in a voice deepened by distress, 'where is your wedding ring?'

Lydia, apparently detaching her eyes with difficulty from the book, raised and looked at her hand. 'I don't know. Somewhere in my room, I suppose.'

'But, my dear –'

'I hate rings,' she said. 'It's too large for me, or too small, anyhow.' She spread all her fingers. 'Uncomfortable, anyhow, so I took it off.'

'Then I should have it made comfortable,' Mrs. Nesbitt said severely.

Lydia made no response and Mrs. Nesbitt again shut her eyes and the stiffness of her body gradually relaxed into a horrible sensation of inward shaking. She longed ardently for William and her own home and wished she had never ventured forth.

'Lydia,' she said, 'I think I'll go back by the earlier train. It's slow, but it gets to Radstowe sooner.'

Lydia smiled but she did not look up. 'You know you'll tell William you have been here. You won't be able to help it when you see him, so why not wait? Then you can have tea comfortably.'

Mrs. Nesbitt was dumb and, conscious of her impotence and her fatigue, she lay very still until drowsiness stole over her. She was dropping into a deep well of blessed oblivion when the ringing of a bell roused her.

'That's the front door,' Lydia said, 'and Maria is dressing.' She dropped her book and ran out of the room.

In the quickest action of her life, Mrs. Nesbitt left the sofa, rushed to Lydia's book in a hurry which shook the furniture and turned to the fly-leaf. She saw there no strange writing, no dubious inscription, but the words, *Lydia Stone,* in Oliver's thin, clear hand. At the same moment she heard a man's voice and approaching foot-steps and she just had time to replace the book, though in doing so she lost Lydia's place in it, and look out of the window before the door was opened. She braced herself to meet Lydia's clever friend.

'Mother,' Lydia said, 'here is a friend of mine,' and, turning, Mrs. Nesbitt faced her husband.

She gasped, and at the same time she saw that Lydia's eyes were on the book which had been left open and was now shut. 'William, whatever have you come for?'

He kissed her. 'We always think alike, Kate. I had a sudden fancy for a jaunt.'

'You might have told me.'

'My dear, you might have told me! I never heard of such a thing. You've caught the family fever for running off. I suppose we were in the same train but I had some business to do in the city and then I remembered I had a daughter!'

They both looked at that daughter who was smiling with some humour but not, Mrs. Nesbitt felt, with the kind obviously called for by this amusing coincidence and, feel-ing so uncomfortable, she had to strain the drollness of the situation. She laughed. 'It really is very funny, William,' and William, too, smiled, remembering how he had left his wife that morning with her little cry of woe in his ears, 'I am very unhappy!'

'Yes, very funny,' he echoed.

'And Lydia pretended I had run away from you,' Mrs. Nesbitt went on, and still Lydia smiled, standing before the empty fireplace with her hands behind her.

'Well, here we are, reunited,' William Nesbitt said.

'And I'm glad I shall have you with me in the train,' Mrs. Nesbitt said, feeling that it was really time for Lydia to speak. 'I don't like travelling alone.'

'Then don't do it again, my dear.'

'Still it has turned out very well,' Mrs. Nesbitt said vaguely, and suddenly Lydia gave a little laugh, not mirthful, almost discordant.

Mrs. Nesbitt sat down on the sofa. She could truthfully have repeated her morning's cry and have told her husband and her daughter that she was unhappy. Lydia's laughter sounded mocking and unkind, yet her face was a little pitiful in its brightness. Behind her the flowers in the big bowl, snapdragons of every hue, stood like a banner, a symbol of beauty and courage, and the dull red of her frock was matched by the unusual colour in her cheeks. For a few seconds, which seemed a long, long time, while she looked at her daughter and glanced from her to William who was standing with his hands in his pockets, jingling the money there, Mrs. Nesbitt felt herself adrift in a sea of circumstance of which she had not the chart. She had embarked on a little adventure which seemed to promise shipwreck and yet where was the danger? The acacia tree cast a pale green shade into the room where the flowers, the books, the elegant furniture, the presence of husband and daughter ought to have promised peace, yet it was like the calm before a storm.

But there was no storm, for William said lightly, 'I have an idea. Shall we stay till the late train and take Lydia out to dinner somewhere? She knows all the places – somewhere really gay where there's a band.'

'Oh, no, William,' Mrs. Nesbitt said. 'I couldn't go in these clothes.'

Lydia said nothing but that hard laughter had not left any impression on her face. She looked pleasant but she was leaving it all to them. This, her attitude implied, was their own game and they must play it as they chose. Her parents both knew that she knew it was her letter which had brought them there, not to spy, for she would never do them that injustice, but in their anxiety for her happiness. She saw through them as they saw through each other and she did not mind their knowing it.

'No,' Mrs. Nesbitt said, 'we ought to go home. There might be news from Janet.'

'There has been news from Janet every day,' William Nesbitt remarked, 'but your mother lives in expectation of disaster.'

'Yes,' Lydia said quietly, 'I think it is a pity.'

It was difficult to find a safe subject for conversation, everything seemed to have a double meaning or to hold a hint, and it was a relief to see Maria with the tea tray, a greater relief to know that the cab was at the door.

Mrs. Nesbitt kissed her daughter with a tenderness which seemed to ask for pardon: William patted Lydia's shoulder.

'Good-bye, William dear,' she said, 'and next time you think of coming, let me know, because I might be out.'

She stood on the pavement as they went away, a small straight figure, gently defiant, perhaps; certainly lonely.

Chapter 13

'She always loved you better than me,' was Mrs. Nesbitt's first remark.

'Did she say so?' he asked absently, a stupid question. He was feeling poignantly that he had lost something precious, and wondering if he could recover it. He had, in a manner, broken that pact of understanding which, unacknowledged, had existed between him and Lydia; yet perhaps it was merely bent, not broken; perhaps it was even strong enough to resist altogether the first foolishly obvious act of his whole relationship with her. He had done exactly what Kate had done and he was angry, for Kate's dealings with Lydia had always been tenebrous but not subtle, and he had prided himself on his superiority, he realized now how greatly. Nevertheless, if he had lost one thing, he had gained another: he had increased his secret store with a new memory of Lydia, of Lydia stiffened and controlled by hard thought into dignity. She had been for him a wisp of colour, a line of verse, the personification of the beauty he had craved for, and now she had added to these aspects that of a woman, troubled but not fretted, and with romance still clinging about her as, to his mind, it would cling for ever. He wished he could live long enough to see her through all her phases, in middle life, in old age, even in death when surely she would look more animate than any other corpse, yet when he tried to trace a future for her, he saw her always solitary as she had seemed when she stood before the hearth with her hands behind her, like some lovely flower incapable of bearing fruit, admired but never touched, and he longed to tell her that for at least one human being she had fulfilled a purpose.

'Even when she was a little girl,' Mrs. Nesbitt continued.

'Bad taste, Kate,'

'You don't mean that, William,' she said sharply. Her

106

unhappiness was now a muddle of painful feelings. She could hardly distinguish what she dreaded from what she saw, and things as they apparently were from what she imagined them to be; she did not know whether the worst or nothing at all were happening, whether she had been entirely mistaken or altogether right. Her head ached, there was a lump of discomfort in her throat and a horrible sensation of dread in her stomach, and this combination of mental and physical distress sought relief in attacking William, who looked as if he were going to whistle but did not do it. 'Everybody has spoilt Lydia all her life,' she added, meaning to hurt him.

'You suggest,' he asked smoothly, 'that we were continuing the process this afternoon? It didn't seem like it. I think we came out of it rather badly, Kate. Honours with Lydia! But I, at least, had business in the city.'

'Ah, I have no business,' Mrs. Nesbitt said, 'except looking after you and the children and none of you will let me. Look at Janet.'

'I wish I could.'

She caught a breath. 'Then you are anxious about her, too?'

'Not a bit, but she's pleasant to look at. Thank Heaven all our children are comely.'

'They are,' Mrs. Nesbitt said, taking the credit.

'So are you, Kate. I like that hat.'

Slightly mollified, Mrs. Nesbitt touched it to make sure it was in the position recommended by Lydia.

'When I married you, you were wearing a bonnet.'

'Yes, a little white straw with daisies on it.'

'And now you have grown up into hats.'

'It will soon be bonnets again,' she sighed.

'Well, my dear, you adorn everything you wear. Don't you think, instead of going to Scotland in the autumn, we might have a week or two in town? It's a stirring place. We could go to the theatres, see the sights, be gay dogs for once in our lives, hover round Buckingham Palace and see the King and Queen.'

'They're always in Scotland in the autumn.'

'Ah, then, I suppose we must go there too.'

'You want to be near Lydia,' she accused him, and with a burst of passion she added, 'but she doesn't want us. You could see, this afternoon, she didn't want us.

'Intensity of pleasure, perhaps. We must have been rather overwhelming.'

'I don't understand her, and she says Oliver is quite well.'

'I'm glad to hear that.'

Mrs. Nesbitt sank into her corner. It was no use trying to talk to William. She had meant to say something about the wedding ring but now she took an angry pleasure in silence.

She was glad of that later on, as the days passed and nothing happened. Laden with fossils and pressed seaweed, the Partridges came home, not being able, as Mabel informed her mother, to afford so long a holiday as the Johnstones; but the Johnstones returned in a hurry, after discovering imperfections in the drains of the house they had rented. Janet arrived with the soles of her shoes in holes and only sixpence in her pocket, a doubly terrible plight. She might have caught cold and what would have happened if she had needed sixpence halfpenny?

'That was the fun of it,' Janet said.

'Tramps, then, must be happy,' Mrs. Nesbitt said dryly, and abruptly she asked, 'Did you meet Oliver?'

'Yes.' Janet concealed her surprise. 'We did.'

'You never mentioned it, dear.'

'How did you know he was there?'

'Lydia told me,' and as an afterthought she added weightily, 'Of course.'

Janet, with her back turned to her mother, said slowly, 'We met him on the road one day and stayed for the night at the same inn.'

'And then he left you?'

'Yes.'

'I don't think he ought to have done that.'

'We didn't ask him to stay with us.'

'Your own brother-in-law, dear!'

'He isn't Marion's brother-in-law.'

108

'Didn't she like him?'

'We didn't discuss him.'

'Oh!' said Mrs. Nesbitt severely. 'And what was his news of Lydia?'

'News! Nothing.'

'Didn't he speak of her?'

'Oh, yes, he spoke of her,' and with the faintest tinge of mockery, Janet added, 'Of course.'

'Well, you have had your holiday, dear, and I hope it has done you good!' Mrs. Nesbitt's tone indicated that with that piece of nonsense over, Janet would be expected to behave reasonably, but it was now September, the time ordained for Mrs. Nesbitt's suffering and Janet had another shock in store. She took it out, displayed it, and met with expostulation and horror. Mrs. Nesbitt turned to her husband for support and comfort and received neither. Life was treating her hardly, but the thought of Dora, providentially driven home by drains, was like a cool hand on her aching head. The serene presence of Dora in a setting of luxury and leisure had often soothed Mrs. Nesbitt's minor ills. It was useless to visit Mabel at any time. She was always in a hurry, making cakes or jam, or just about to set out for a committee meeting, and though, in this case, Mabel would be sure to find time to condemn her sister, that was not exactly what Mrs. Nesbitt wanted. So she sent for the carriage and drove to the pseudo-Gothic castle on the edge of the cliff which broke away sheer and grey from the green downs.

The way was familiar but always charming to Mrs. Nesbitt. It went down the narrow road in which her own house stood, past the playing fields of Radstowe School, and so widened into the junction of four roads, dazzlingly white in the sunlight. On the left, parallel to the road she had descended, there was a mounting avenue of old elms and beyond them a grassy space studded with hawthorn bushes which screened the gorge where the sluggish river ran. Straight ahead, the downs started abruptly from the road, showing at their edge the limestone bones of their spreading body and through these a steep way had been cut. Trees overhung it, casting a deep shade, but at the top the downs stretched like a great green table, yellowed here and there by the sun. There were trees and bushes on it, but they looked minute in that great expanse of openness and above it the sky seemed to spread for ever, behind, over the clustered city, to the right, over the newest suburb of Radstowe, and to the left, over the gorge, the trees and the Channel to the hills of Wales.

The highest tower of the pseudo-Gothic castle was in sight and, as the carriage followed the road close to the cliff edge, the blue sky began to peep through the fretted copings of Dora's home. On the other side of the gorge, the slope was thickly covered with trees and among them was every shade of green from the darkness of firs to the gleam of the silver birches, while, here and there, a patch of tarnished leaves preluded autumn. The river, deeply set, was out of Mrs. Nesbitt's sight, but far off the Channel shone like a thin silver blade, a sharp weapon laid there in defiance of adventures against the hills.

It was all so beautiful that Mrs. Nesbitt felt a keen resentment against those human circumstances which interfered with the enjoyment of it, yet she did not actually think of her trouble: it disturbed her constantly, but through it she was aware of the fairness of the day, the cries of children playing in the grass, the splendid passing of a horse and rider, the thud of hoofs, the creaking of leather and jingling of steel. This was the scene of many a happy hour spent with her children. With the baby in the perambulator and the others on foot, she had often brought her work and sewed placidly under the trees, while the children played. Clearest in her mind were days of early summer when the hawthorns seemed, by some happy miracle, to have recalled the vanished snow and showered their green with it; and mild days of autumn with brown and golden leaves lying so deep on the ground that the children's little legs were almost hidden in the fallen glory.

Those had been happy years, with William safely retired

from the sea, so that she could lie in bed at night and hear, without a tremor, the wind howling and the rain beating against the walls, with William's schemes going well, their income increasing year by year, the children healthy and good. She had worked hard, sewing, cooking, mending, harder than Mabel, though Mrs. Nesbitt had taken it for granted: it was her business to be economical with the money produced by William's energy and brain: it had been an equal partnership, and at night, when the children were all in bed, she sat, always sewing, and listened to William who never failed to tell her all he had done and meant to do, while he paced the carpet, a few steps forward and back, as he had once paced the bridge of his ship.

At ten o'lcock she folded up her sewing and went to bed, followed by the sound of William turning the key and pushing home the bolt of the front door, and then his quick step on the stairs. He always caught her before she reached her door, for even then she was slow of movement, and together they went to look at the children. The light from the landing dimly showed each relaxed form, a hand thrown outside the sheet, a head slipped from its pillow, the tousled hair. Of them all, only Lydia ever waked and it was rarely that she slept through their visit. She would open her eyes, start up, and fling herself violently on her other side; but Janet, who had been a perfect baby, never moved, seeming to control herself even in sleep; Janet, who was now proving herself a rebellious daughter.

Tears started in Mrs. Nesbitt's eyes at the thought. Those days had gone: that sense of inner peace in a life of outward struggle had vanished; even the sure companionship of William had become less certain. He had had his odd ways then, his turns of speech, his ridiculous notions, but he and she had never disagreed. Now, the development of their children had brought out vagaries in his character, perhaps in her own, but in that latter supposition she was wrong: she had not changed at all, and she was bound to suffer for her stability.

Chapter 14

THE oak gates, gothically carved, were open and the carriage left the open downs, the spread of sky and the distant view of sea and hills for a beautiful and sheltered garden. In it there were noble trees which had calmly watched the building of the house and taken kindly to the presence of the small human beings who now played in the shade where once smaller, wilder creatures had sported, but part of the ground had been ruthlessly cleared of wood and Herbert had improved the place, neglected by its former owner, into the most delightful garden in all Radstowe. He had an instinct for acquiring fine possessions and if, for some people, the house itself had a comic aspect, he was successful in his wife, his children, his rose garden, his water garden, and his miniature orchard. The designing of the garage had cost him some anxiety. Should it be gothic to match the house or modern to match the car? He had finally built it of grey stone, without loop-holes or turrets, and planted quickly-growing creepers to hide defects. The result was pleasing to Mrs. Nesbitt's eyes but, handsome as the whole place was, she preferred, with untrained but natural taste, her own low white house with its pleasant, unpretentious garden.

In the house Herbert's effort after consistency had been defeated by his wife's love of comfort, and in the pretty drawing-room Mrs. Nesbitt waited for her daughter. If there was a fault to be found in that room, it was the number of photographs of the children. They hung on the walls and stood on the tables, a record of each child from babyhood to the present day, and even Mrs. Nesbitt found them excessive. Otherwise the room was exactly to her liking: there were deep arm-chairs and sofas, soft cushions, pale curtains at the mullioned windows, a thick carpet, everything, in fact, that was not mediaeval but that was luxurious and gay.

Mrs. Nesbitt was kept waiting for some time. This was unusual. The welcome in that house was wont to be immediate as well as sincere, but nothing in Mrs. Nesbitt's world was as it should be, and when, at last, Dora appeared, she was pale and there was darkness under her eyes.

'You're tired, dear,' Mrs. Nesbitt said at once.

On a nearer view, Mrs. Nesbitt saw that Dora's eyelids were red. She had been crying. Now, why should Dora cry and why could not her mother ask her why she cried?

'You have been worrying about something,' was as far as she dare go and, searching quickly for the reason she could not demand, she asked, 'Have you heard from Lydia?'

'Not a word.'

'Neither have I. Not a word. She really is a little inconsiderate. You don't think there is anything the matter?'

'Mother dear, she never writes if she can help it.'

'But she ought to. We don't even know if Oliver is at home.'

'Oliver?'

'Yes, he has been for a holiday on Dartmoor, alone. Janet met him, but of course,' Mrs. Nesbitt was fond of those two words, 'of course Lydia told me he was there. I thought she might have told you too.'

'Lydia expects you to know everything without being told.'

'It worried me,' Mrs. Nesbitt confessed.

'Did it?' I think it ought to be a rule in marriage – at least one holiday a year without your family.'

'Oh, my dear, I'm afraid you had a trying time with those dreadful drains,' Mrs. Nesbitt said soothingly, but she was watchful.

'The drains kept comparatively quiet,' Dora said, and her mother had a sudden dark glimpse into a life which had seemed all brightness. She remembered William's tiresome remarks about Herbert, and the pain in her heart sharpened. Was there no happiness anywhere? Dora was lying back in her chair in a rather weary attitude, but Mrs.

Nesbitt sat very straight in hers. She was not going to give way and she said calmly, settling the matter, 'It was very annoying for you, but no harm has come of it.'

Dora smiled a little. 'No, the children have come to no harm.'

'I wish,' Mrs. Nesbitt began, 'I could say the same of Janet's holiday.'

'What is the matter?' Dora asked with an effort.

'She wants to go away and be trained as a social worker, one of those women who go to factories and interfere with the girls. That's the result of her walking tour with Marion. She says she hasn't enough to do. There's plenty to do in the house if she likes. I have told her she ought to undertake the housekeeping.'

'But you'd never let her.'

'Of course I should advise her. How is she to look after a house of her own if she doesn't learn?'

'I never learnt.'

'You married so young, dear, that I hadn't time to teach you.'

'And what about Lydia?'

'She is a very poor manager, I am afraid. But when I said all this to Janet, she said she had no intention of marrying. Absurd! How does she know? That's Marion again. She pretends to despise men. I can't see why Janet shouldn't be happy at home. Can you, dear?'

'Oh, yes, I think I can.'

Here was another blow. 'I did think you would sympathize, Dora.'

'So I do, with both of you. Let her try it.'

'Oh, she'll try it!'

'I mean willingly.'

'But I'm not willing and I don't think it's right to pretend what I don't feel. Besides, I can't do it,' she added truthfully.

'You haven't practised it, that's all,' Dora said and the sweetness of her smile, wide with a gleam of even teeth, relieved Mrs. Nesbitt of another pang.

'I'm not going to begin,' she said stoutly, little knowing that circumstances would be too strong for her. 'And it doesn't matter because Father is supporting Janet. He always wants people to do as they like.'

'Well, nobody does,' Dora said, and this time Mrs. Nesbitt was not spared, for Dora did not smile.

'Janet's going to.'

'I don't think so.'

'You mean she will change her mind?'

'No, but she won't do as she likes. 'If she does she ought to have a public monument.'

This remark was so unlike Dora's usual efforts that Mrs. Nesbitt allowed a noticeable pause before she said, 'Then if she isn't going to be happy, anywhere, why shouldn't she stay comfortably at home?'

'I don't know, Mother,' Dora answered a little impatiently, 'but I've made up my mind that, as far as I can help it, my children shall choose their own careers.'

Oh, that's a long way ahead,' Mrs. Nesbitt said. 'Make the most of them as they are, dear. This is your happiest time. It will never be the same again. While they are little they are your own.' She sighed. 'And I used so to look forward to having a grown-up daughter at home with me.'

'But we are all quite near you,' Dora protested.

'Except Lydia,' Mrs. Nesbitt reminded her.

'Yes, but it doesn't matter where Lydia is so long as she's somewhere in the world.'

'Or what she does, I suppose?' Mrs. Nesbitt suggested sharply.

'Or what she does,' Dora echoed sweetly.

'Well, dear,' there was no profit in this conversation, 'let us go and see the children. I shall tell Herbert you are not looking well.'

Dora straightened herself and looked almost fiercely at her mother. 'I am quite well. I shall be very angry if you say anything.'

Now, Mrs. Nesbitt was sure that this insistence was not

done out of consideration for Herbert's tender feelings, but rather for the sake of Dora's own pride, and she went home sadly, too sadly to notice the western sky and the gulls swooping between the cliffs, holding in their wings some of the light which was going with the sun. Dora had failed in sympathy and had, moreover, shown signs of private trouble. And from sadness Mrs. Nesbitt passed to annoyance. She had no patience with the younger generation: it asked too much: it wanted liberty, like Janet: it wanted recognition, like Mabel: it wanted perfection in marriage, like Dora. Dora was a disappointment. Perhaps William was right and Herbert might be trying at times, but forbearance was necessary in married life. Had not she herself borne with William for years and she had never once reddened her eyes over the business: she was made of sterner stuff, and she had never had the leisure in which to indulge herself with fancies. The visit from which she had expected comfort had given her less than none and she was returning to the quietly rebellious Janet without a single champion on her side.

The thought of Lydia was almost restful in comparison with what faced her, and the chance sight of Mrs. Miller, dressed in dowdy black, turning in at her rusty iron gate with a despondent skirt flapping at her heels, had the effect of arousing Mrs. Nesbitt's feelings of affection. After all, her love for her children was stronger than any trouble they could cause her, and while she realized the essential loneliness of existence and found it strange that in spite of so much love she should never feel secure, she told herself, with one of her flashes of wisdom, that love does not give security: it brings with it danger, anxiety and grief, and in that moment she saw herself honoured with the right to suffer: she was proud to do it.

These children who had been her joy were now, it seemed, and so cruelly late in life, to ruffle her peace and threaten her with sorrow, but her anger had suddenly changed to a calm readiness to bear it. And yet, her common sense retorted, what had they done? Little enough, but there was menace in the air and while she accepted that, she now saw, too, the lovely mellowness of the evening, the great trees heavy with the burden they would soon cast down, autumn flowers in the gardens and people strolling contentedly through the streets and, when she found that William was waiting for her at the door, she smiled in genuine happiness. He teased her with his funny ways but he was never satisfied without her.

He helped her from the carriage. 'You are early to-day, dear,' she said, and as she lifted her face for his kiss, she saw that something had happened. He was grave, as she had never seen him. 'What is the matter, William?' she asked tremulously.

'I have something to say to you, Kate. Let us go upstairs.'

'William, you are not ill? Then you have had bad news.'

'Yes, bad news.' He seemed to have gone grey all over except for his eyes which had taken on a deeper darkness, as though trouble had lodged there.

'Oh, William, what is it? I knew something was coming. What is it?'

'Hush!' he said sternly, but he patted the hand on his arm. 'Hush! We have to take this quietly, my dear.'

He had received at the office a letter from Lydia.

'Where is it?' Mrs. Nesbitt asked at once.

'It is not here.' He paced up and down before the sofa on the edge of which his wife was sitting, her back straight, her breath coming quickly and, in her eyes, their opaqueness illumined by her fear, a look of suffering which alarmed him. 'It is no good beating about the bush. She is leaving Oliver.'

'Leaving Oliver,' Mrs. Nesbitt said mechanically, with no intelligence in her voice, and William Nesbitt went to the window and looked out. He remembered how he had sat on the lawn on his wife's birthday and, looking up, had seen that hand, thin, white and quick, seizing the jasmine spray which it would soon cast aside. He remembered how he had told himself that no man could hold her.

'Leaving Oliver,' Mrs. Nesbitt said again, and this time

with the shrill note of pain. 'But she can't! She's married to him!'

He did not turn. The words passed over his own thoughts and then a cry, fierce and angry, startled him with its enmity.

'Has he been cruel to her?'

'She tells me she loves him very much, but she loves some one else more.'

Mrs. Nesbitt took a tottering step. She threw her hands out. 'Not that, William, not that!'

'Yes,' he said quietly.

'But it's wickedness, it's sin!'

'She does not think so.'

'And you – are you going to tell me you don't think so either?'

'I can't judge for her,' he replied. He looked at her now, with a grave kindness, but he saw a woman he did not know. She stood with her head thrown back, her hands clenched at her sides, all her softness gone. He went towards her. 'My poor girl –'

'No, no !' she cried. He seemed to her to be sharing in Lydia's sin. 'This must be stopped,' she said firmly, and he felt the pathos of her impotence, of her faith in her own authority.

'It is too late,' he said. 'Lydia,' his smile was a twisted effort, 'was not so foolish as to let us know her plans beforehand.'

'Foolish! You call it foolish – !' And then, 'You mean she has gone?'

'Yes.'

'With Henry Wyatt.'

'How do you know that?'

Her look scorned his ignorance, vaunted her own knowledge. 'I have known all the time,' she said.

In his place, she would have reproached him for his secrecy but, though he was astonished and ashamed of his own dullness, he said nothing. He was in the presence of a stranger, some one quicker than himself in this matter, some one hard and inflexible, who surely had not borne his lovely daughter. He knew that for the moment her pain was controlled by her desire for action and her need to have the facts themselves in her grasp, but her hardness against Lydia stiffened him against herself.

'And Oliver?' she asked.

'Oliver has written, too. Here is his letter.'

She read it slowly, with difficulty, for the blood had rushed to her head, making her feel giddy. The letter was written with a formality which William Nesbitt recognized as a mask and in which Mrs. Nesbitt read nothing but the fact that he asked Lydia's father to accept this decision to part as final: he might believe it had been well considered: there had been no quarrel to be made up and if Mr. Nesbitt chose to assign blame, it must be Oliver's, for he had failed to give Lydia what she wanted.

Mrs. Nesbitt read it twice and then, her bewilderment breaking her rigidity, she said from the depths, 'I don't understand.'

William Nesbitt was walking up and down again, jingling his money. 'It's youth craving for perfection. They think they can get the real thing. They need it. They see a sort of immorality in putting up with mediocrity. They don't know – how can they know? They have to be middle-aged before they learn, and then it may be too late. There's a kind of nobility in it. I find a kind of nobility in it.' He was talking to himself but, when he finished, he turned to her, impelled by the intensity of her stare. It was not a look: it was the gaze of one affected beyond retort, and he was appalled by the distance it set between them. 'Kate,' he pleaded, 'we have to try to understand them.'

'I can't.' The words came with difficulty through the obstacle of all her prejudices, beliefs and loyalties. 'Thank God, I can't! You call it nobility – ! She stood up. 'I have to dress, William.' 'It was the first time she had ever dismissed him.

'Yes.' He walked to the door. 'I don't think we need mention this to anybody. Let us wait.'

With shaking hands she removed her flowered hat, the one he had chosen. 'I don't know yet what I am going to do,' she said. She did not look at him but, as she heard the turning of the door handle, she asked, 'Where is Lydia's letter?'

'It is not here.'

'You mean I am not to see it?'

'I, too, have the right to destroy letters,' he said sternly.

He had destroyed it, but he knew the words by heart. They were precious to him. She had chosen to write to him and what she had written no one else should see. Walking in the garden, waiting for the sound of the gong and dreading the sight of his wife's new face, he recited the letter to himself:

'I am going to make you very unhappy, William dear. After much prayer to which I am not accustomed and much fasting which is an easier business, I have decided to go away from Oliver. I love him very much, in an odd way, but I think I love some one else more, some one who really needs me.

'How does one know what is right and what is wrong, William? People think that what's unpleasant must be duty. I don't believe that and neither do you, I'm sure, yet I'm choosing the unpleasant road. For me, it would be easier to stay here, but then there's Henry – it's Henry Wyatt – to think of, and Oliver doesn't want to keep me here when my real self – if I have one – belongs to some one else. How could he?

'We've talked about it all together, which seems queer, but makes the thing more wholesome. There was the alternative of leaving Oliver and living alone, but that, I think, is a cowardly way out of it, and whose money should I live on? The money of the man I had left, or the money of the man for whom I would risk nothing? No, I should only be trying to save a reputation for which I don't care twopence, except for your sake, William, and losing it in my own eyes. Oh, what a muddle!

'In ten years' time I may know what I ought to have done,

but in the meantime the living process has to proceed, and I can only act according to my present knowledge; but, oh, how I have longed for the hand of God, in illness or sudden death, to take the responsibility out of mine! But God doesn't do these things. It's so difficult to distinguish virtue from habit. Why can't we know? And yet, how much more interesting life is because we don't! The way of transgressors is hard, William.

'When you get this I shall be with Henry, and when I'm with him I get the fullness of things. But he's a difficult person, rather like a dark forest through which I have to cut my way, and I'm not going to be exactly happy, but I'm going to be alive – all over.

'And there will always be a pain in the region of my chest when I think of you. I love Henry and you and perhaps Oliver better than anybody else in the world, and don't you dare to stop loving me because I'm hurting you. But I don't believe you ever could.

'Good-bye.'

At the end of the letter she gave her address.

'The Grange, Mastover, Somerset. I'm sorry to be so near, but the house belongs to Henry, so I can't help it.'

Yes, it was a letter she would have written to no one else and through his misery there ran a streak of joy, for romance, which she personified, had come close to him in her love for him, expressed for the first time, and in his new and startling vision of her. She had set out on a great adventure, full of peril, cutting her way through a dark forest, and he trembled for her and was proud of her courage, but of the two men concerned in this affair, he saw one as a dignified dolt and the other as a selfish robber. Yet this, he knew, was a primitive way of looking at them, for if his conception of Lydia were true, she was no chattel and she had chosen her way freely. Well, he repeated it, he had said no man could hold her and Oliver had let her go. How this Henry would succeed or fail, only time could show.

He was amazed at his own detachment in considering these things. Kate would have thought it wicked, but Kate would never know, and Lydia was his own daughter: he understood her: she had written to him because she expected just this detachment from him. His pain, he realized, was not for the deed done, but for his wife, for the days and weeks and months of grief, of accusations, of reiterated horror which stretched before him: for the bandying of Lydia's name on strangers' tongues and the banishment of it from her home. Mabel would be indignant, inquisitive, consciously virtuous: Walter, gay, simple soul, would be unjudgingly puzzled: Dora would sorrow in a loyal silence, and Janet, he paused at her name, Janet, too, would be silent, but he hardly dared guess at the nature of her thoughts. Of all the family, he alone would have no sense of loss or shame. He saw what no one else could see – how she loved beauty and tried to reach it even through ugliness. Once more he remembered her hand, plucking the jasmine, but he remembered, too, how Janet had stood in the garden, cutting the sweet-peas, and how, in the evening, she had called herself a fool.

Chapter 15

MRS. NESBITT sat at the end of the table with her head tilted back in her determination to keep it up, and her eyes looked everywhere but at her husband. She hardly spoke and never to him. He was sharing Lydia's disgrace and he found it difficult to accept this treatment calmly, for he was not used to being ignored. However, he had his revenge in finding his wife singularly unattractive in her hardness, and some amusement in seeing that Janet, who had offended her mother though her mother had forgotten the fact, was blaming herself for the tenseness of the situation. But Janet was not to be deceived for long. When they rose from table Mrs. Nesbitt asked her to telephone to Dora and to Walter, asking them to come at once. 'And Mabel – how are we to send for Mabel? So foolish of them not to have the telephone. William –' This appeal was the habit of years, but she broke off. 'Their neighbours, Janet. They will run in with a message. Mabel said they would always do that in an emergency. Tell them they must take a cab.'

William Nesbitt interposed. 'Kate, this is absurd.'

Janet stood with her hands on the back of her chair and she looked from her mother to her father.

'They are my children as well as yours,' Mrs. Nesbitt said, staring at the wall, 'and I intend to have them here to-night. You need not be present if you disapprove.'

'I do disapprove, but I shall certainly be present.'

Janet, now looking down, said quietly, 'What am I to do?'

'Oblige your mother,' he answered with a gesture.

His hope was that Dora would be out to dinner, Mabel at a prayer-meeting, Walter at a dance; yet, after all, what did it matter? The sooner the discussion and the exclamations began, the sooner they would be over but, begun to-day or to-morrow or the day after, the futility of talk would last for a long time, the result of Lydia's action would endure for ever. Never again, he thought, could he feel for Kate quite the old affection. But still he did not judge his daughter. In the extraordinary isolation of that moment he sent a message to her across the river and the woods, the orchards, the hills and the plains, the gleaming ditches where the water was edged with willows, to The Grange at Mastover where she was now with Henry. His message was one of understanding, and it seemed to him that at once he had an answer of gratitude, of expectation realized. She was with this Henry whom he had never seen, the person with whom she was not to be exactly happy, but he felt that to-night she was nearer to her father than to her lover. There were memories that Henry could never share, little passages of significance on which neither had ever commented, careless words, harmonious gestures, the subtle nothings which made up their sympathy, and he felt an exaltation of suffering which would soon give place to weariness but sustained him magnificently in that moment.

Meanwhile, Janet was at the telephone and Mrs. Nesbitt sat in a high-backed chair, waiting for her family. William Nesbitt lighted a cigar and paced in front of the three white steps leading to the open door. He seemed to guard it. He was the master of the house, but his wife had taken command: he had allowed it because he did not know what words to use to her. He had lived with her for nearly forty years, not deceiving himself into the belief of perfect union, but in accord, with humour, with much happiness, and now, in the face of this first trouble, he had lost touch with her, as though his consort were only for smooth waters. This estrangement was his share of Lydia's tangle. Had she foreseen it? In her letter there was no mention of her mother. It was her father to whom she had turned, for her own comfort and his: she had left her mother out of it and he was glad.

He smoked his cigar in hurried puffs, listening for the

footsteps of those who were coming to judge his daughter. Walter was the first to arrive, bringing Violet with him.

'Is anything the matter?' he asked. 'You don't look well, sir. I thought you looked queer at the office.'

'Did you? I'm all right. Your mother will tell you all about it when the family has assembled. You'd better go in – go in. I must finish my cigar.'

'It's nothing to do with the business?'

'My dear boy, no. You and I can tackle that, I think.'

They went, puzzled and discreet, and William Nesbitt heard the opening and shutting of the drawing-room door. No, his wife would not wait for the gathering of the clans: they would get the news bit by bit and one by one. He tried to laugh, but the completeness of his failure was a revelation, interrupted by the sight of Herbert's car in the gateway. It was bitter that Herbert, whom he had never liked, should listen to the naked facts of Lydia's story. He would think of his own name, the slur on his children: he would be hard with the hardness of the weak: but there was comfort in Dora. She was loyal and he spared some pity for her who would have Herbert's intolerance to endure. How life was complicated! How difficult it was to find sufficient strength in one's own convictions!

'Go in,' he said. 'I'm acting as hall porter. A family conclave.'

Dora, big and tall and gentle, looked down at him, the small grey man, his alertness gone, his eyes sombre. Her lips moved, but she did not speak.

He nodded reassuringly. 'I shall come in presently. Go and listen to your mother.'

She stood there, saying calmly, 'Don't wait for me, Herbert. Just a minute!' And to her father, she said, 'I didn't know. Ought I to have brought Herbert?'

'Oh, yes, my dear child. Walter brought Violet and we shall soon have Mabel here with John.'

'It's Lydia, I suppose?'

'Yes – Lydia. No good putting it off, Dora. Go in.'

She went slowly and from a cab, now turning into the

125

gate, John and Mabel alighted. Her hat, as usual, was a little crooked, and William Nesbitt thought impatiently, 'I wish that girl knew how to dress herself!'

'I had a presentiment this morning,' she began breathlessly, 'that something was going to happen and I knew we shouldn't be able to go to the committee meeting to-night. I said so, didn't I, John? I get these warnings. Is Mother ill? You don't look well yourself, Father.'

'Did you think she was calling you to her death-bed? Well, it's not as bad as that.'

'It was a most important committee meeting – '

'You will find this much more interesting,' he said dryly.

'All right, John. I'll pay for the cab.'

Now, all his feelings were superseded by an intense and unfamiliar irritation and in that moment he actually hated Kate. He saw his family as a pack of hounds and Lydia as their quarry. He had been weak : he should have stopped the hunt: not that it could hurt her. She was safe enough in her hole at Mastover and safe in his heart, yet this pack in the drawing-room and his wife, sitting there like the master of the hounds, roused him to fury. He no longer stooped and if his face was still worn and grey, his eyes were not sombre, they were very bright and keen.

As he entered the drawing-room where the lights were on but the curtains undrawn, the talking ceased. Mrs. Nesbitt sat, with the effect of some one on a platform, in the high-backed chair which she usually avoided: her face was flushed, her lips compressed, and Mabel, with her hat at a still sharper angle, was sitting sympathetically near. Her hands were restless, her expression bitter but somehow satisfied, and now and then she glanced at John and jerked her chin as though to say, 'I told you so.'

William Nesbitt's glance took in the group. Walter leaned against the mantelpiece looking troubled. Dora, lying back in a big chair, her fur coat thrown open to show a bare neck on which a jewel glistened, persisted in her serenity. Herbert looked out of the window at the darkness gathering in the garden and the back of his neck expressed what, later on, Dora was to hear. John, who was planted firmly in his chair, had assumed the attitude acquired at stormy deacons' meetings, the forbearance of a Christian, the seemly gravity of a person in authority who, at the right time, would speak. Janet had disappeared and, strangely enough, William Nesbitt was immediately conscious that, of all the people in the room, Violet alone could understand his feelings. He had never cared for her: he had thought her frivolous and foolish, but now, as she looked up from her seat and smiled at him, he seemed to see her for the first time. Her smile was neither gay nor sad: it had a kind of wisdom in it, and, as he passed her, he laid his hand on her shoulder by way of thanks.

'You have all heard the news?' he asked sharply and a succession of bowed heads and sibilant monosyllables assured him of their knowledge. 'Very well. I have this to say. I will not have my daughter's action criticized in my presence. Keep your condemnations and your speculations to yourselves. I'll have none of them. Lydia's affairs are her own.'

Mabel looked at John and John spoke. 'Pardon me, Mr. Nesbitt, but we are all members of one great community and we have the right – it is our duty – we are morally bound to – to take a line.'

'Take it,' William Nesbitt said. 'Take it. It's a harmless amusement, but not in this house, please.'

Herbert swung round and Dora dropped her eyes. 'You forget, sir, that our children are involved in this ghastly business.'

'That's just it,' Mabel agreed, regretting her alliance with Herbert, but seeing no way out of it.

'An aunt who has disgraced herself – ' Herbert went on, but William Nesbitt interrupted.

'Rubbish!' he said rudely. 'Rubbish!'

'And the question is,' added Mabel, 'what are we to do?'

'Tell your children she is dead,' he advised roughly, and from Mrs. Nesbitt, who looked like a figure made of painted wood, there came a voice hard and mechanical: 'She is dead to me.'

'She is not dead to me,' Dora said melodiously.

'There shall be no communication between you,' Herbert screamed, 'not while you live in my house,' and Dora answered him with a long, full look. 'My children shall not be contaminated.'

'No, they won't be that,' William Nesbitt said.

From the low stool on which she sat with her pretty dress spread round her, Violet spoke. 'Good Lord, I should think not! How could they be?'

Herbert glared at this interference, Mabel looked resentful, but Violet went on courageously, though her voice shook a little. 'And now she must be unhappy.'

'Unhappy!' The word was Mrs. Nesbitt's, but her lips, those painted, wooden lips, hardly moved, and Mabel, turning quickly, said, 'She's not your sister, Violet.'

'No, but she's Walter's,' Violet explained with an admirable simplicity.

'And you have no children.'

The flicker of some emotion passed over Violet's face.

'She has that to be thankful for,' Herbert said bitterly.

Dora rose and pulled her coat closely round her. 'You want us to go, Father?'

'Yes, my dear. There is nothing more to say.'

'But what is to be done?' Mabel cried. 'It will be found out. The boys will find out. They're so intelligent that you can't keep anything from them. They're far too clever to be put off with lies.'

'I don't intend to tell lies to my children,' John remarked nobly.

'Your children are your own affair. My daughter is mine. I shall be obliged if you will continue this conversation in your own homes.'

'And poor Oliver,' Mabel sighed. 'Such a splendid fellow. I don't know how she could be so wicked.'

'Most of us wouldn't dare to be,' Dora said.

'Your attitude is disgraceful!' Herbert cried.

She took no notice of him. Perhaps she did not want to see how negligible had become his carefully artistic appearance, how small his head seemed on the top of his agitated neck.

The wooden image spoke again. 'Dora, I'm surprised at you. And where is Janet? Janet ought to be here, too. Go and find her, Walter.'

They were all standing now, except Mrs. Nesbitt who sat as though she had been deposited in that chair and could not move of her own will. The electric light shone garishly on pale faces, set lips, eyes darkened by trouble, anger, bewilderment.

'Go and find her, Walter,' Mrs. Nesbitt repeated.

'No, Mother,' he said, 'I'm going home. This is not our business.'

John, booming bravely, interposed. 'Surely that is subversive of all we have been taught.'

'You mean you intend to bear my sister's burden?' Walter's long animosity for the Partridge family now found a vent. 'That's very good of you, but I don't think she needs your help. If she wants a home she can come to us. Good-night, Mother. Good-night, sir. See you in the morning.'

'Good-night, my son. Good-night, my girl.' Envying them their unity he saw them to the door and lingering there until Dora passed through and kissed him, he escaped round the side of the house to the little orchard. He walked there for a time, trying to soothe the agitation of his spirit, and then he went upstairs and undressed in the darkness.

'Good-night, Kate,' he said gently, but no sound came from the other bed.

Chapter 16

WHEN Mrs. Nesbitt woke after a restless night, the sun was shining and the birds were singing as they had done on happier mornings, and Nature's indifference to her sufferings seemed positively wanton, but she had done some hard thinking while William slept, and her manner was controlled. She took her cup with a calm, 'Thank you, William,' and they sipped in silence. William himself had waked in a flippant mood and though he knew it was unwise, he could not resist saying, 'That was a pleasant party you had last night, Kate.'

She turned her head stiffly, the thick, short plait following obediently, and he found her firm regard a little disconcerting. 'You behaved very badly, William.'

He shrugged his shoulders. 'That's a matter of opinion, but if you think that wry-necked son-in-law of mine and that bearded deacon are going to dictate to me in my own house, Kate, you are mistaken. We shall have Dora leaving Herbert next, and serve him right.'

'I am not afraid of that,' Mrs. Nesbitt said with exasperating certainty.

'No, she can't leave him, poor child. She has the children to think of.'

Mrs. Nesbitt said nothing. She had found her best weapon but, after a suitably impressive pause, she spoke.

'We must see Oliver,' she said.

'To what end?'

'I ought to have said that I must see him.'

'I advise you to spare him and yourself.'

'Does he know where Lydia is?'

'Of course. You don't imagine she has run away without leaving an address?'

'I can imagine anything, but I have been told nothing.'

'You saw Oliver's letter.'

'But not hers.'

'No, not hers.'

'And you are not going to tell me where she is?'

'She makes no secret of it. She merely apologizes for being so near. I hope the infection won't be carried to Herbert's children.'

Mrs. Nesbitt's calm forsook her. 'Not in Radstowe?'

'No, Kate. Your dearest wish has not been fulfilled. Not in Radstowe. She is living in Somerset, at The Grange, Mastover. The moated grange. Let them all know so that they may avoid the county. Fortunately it is a large one and we can venture across the river without fear of meeting her.'

She ignored his gibes. 'I must write it down,' she said. Comely, if a little unwieldy, in her short night-gown, she left her bed to find her pencil and her note-book. William Nesbitt shut his eyes. After so many years, it was distressing to find himself criticizing instead of applauding her appearance, yet he did criticize it, finding something funny and undignified in it and, out of loyalty, he shut his eyes, but her voice was always charming except when bitterness took command of it and he heard it now asking, 'What did you say, William? The Moated Grange, Mastover?'

'No, no, Kate, not The Moated Grange. Grange without the moat.'

'You said The Moated Grange.'

'Yes, a quotation, and, after all, a moat is rather suitable in this connection. You must remember the mote in one's brother's eye, Kate, and the beam in one's own. Holy Writ.'

Her silence reminded him that he must learn to do without the expostulations which it had been his amusement to evoke. He would miss them, but perhaps they would return in time. Life had to go on and things would adjust themselves somehow and, in the meanwhile, it was good to think of his office, his ships, the simpler people with whom he had to deal in business, the easier problems waiting for him by the river-side and, feeling the need to be doing something, as well as the immodesty of being in a bedroom with a strange lady, he hastened to his bath, finished his dressing as inconspicuously as possible and went into the garden to get his buttonhole. To have gone to business without a flower in his coat, would have been like lowering his flag.

He found Janet in the garden. His anger of the night before had caused him to forget her and though, in his mind, he had established a little thread of sympathy or a small, deep chasm of antipathy with each member of his family in this affair of Lydia, with Janet he had neither made nor cut communication yet. He spoke to her cheerfully, saying, 'I want a little talk with you,' and though he did not look at her, he felt her stiffen. 'There's a quarter-of-an-hour before breakfast. Let us walk here. There's nothing like an autumn morning – a spring evening and an autumn morning – the end of the beginning and the beginning of the end. What about this work you want to do? Have you made your plans?'

'I am not going to do it.'

'That's a pity, isn't it?'

'It doesn't matter.'

'It matters to me that you should be happy.'

She stopped and looked down at him. Of all his children, only Lydia looked levelly into his eyes: the others had to look down into them and it made a difference: they saw another man, one they had to consider, perhaps to pity, but Lydia and he were equals: she did not wish to spare him, nor could he accept any pity from the others. He made himself as tall as he could and said, 'I want you to be happy.'

She answered in a low voice. 'How can I leave her now?'

He looked at the grass. 'You are making a mistake, Janet.'

'Oh,' she said, and her voice lifted a little, 'it's not my mistake.'

He would not be beguiled into that issue. He said, 'You

132

misunderstand your mother. She is a strong woman. **She** does not need you.'

'Then, no one does.'

'My dear, we might all say that with truth – with truth.'

'All,' she agreed, 'except Lydia.'

'Perhaps,' he answered quietly. He was acutely, painfully conscious of the beauty of the day, the freshness of the sunny morning with its hint of frost and autumn, the roses blooming with the brilliance of a last chance, the sharp notes of the birds whose singing time was over and the slim, tall figure of his daughter, with the sunshine on her fair head and a deep anger in her heart. This, he told himself, was life, this beauty and pain inextricably mingled, and Lydia gave and bore them both. Perhaps she, too, was now walking in a garden and tasting the sharp sweetness of autumn and love. Thinking of her, he said, 'There are some people – '

'Oh,' she broke in, 'it is easier for you. You can afford to be magnanimous. She is your child and you adore her. And you are an old man.'

He was startled. 'Old, am I? No, no, I'm not old, Janet. But you, you are very young, and you have the right to some good days.'

'But not the hope of them,' she said.

He had to ignore the implication and he said practically, 'Now listen to me. I will not have you sacrificing yourself to your mother. I don't believe in it. The young must live and she is less miserable than she is angry. Anger is an emotion that sustains. She does not need you and you must go.'

'But I shall stay.'

'To no purpose, then, and resentment is not a wholesome diet.'

'Ah, you are not thinking of me,' she said, speaking very quickly. 'You do not want to have Lydia blamed.'

'You wrong me there,' he answered mildly, 'but as to that I can't convince you. My dear, take the advice of a man you think old and don't let this – this affair influence you.

133

Your mother will have Mabel, I think she will find Mabel a comfort.'

'You are very cruel,' Janet said. 'You pretend she is not really suffering.'

'Suffering! Suffering!' he said impatiently. 'Who doesn't get it sooner or later? Your mother and I are getting it late, you and Lydia early.'

'Lydia!' she exclaimed.

'Yes, and more than anyone.'

'Because she has done wrong?'

'Because she doesn't know whether she has done right. And yet,' he said, giving her the full glance of his eyes, 'perhaps not more than you. I should like to remind you that you have an intelligent father,' and as she stepped back a pace, he added, 'but a discreet one. Go away, child, and find yourself. I shall be happier, if that weighs with you, knowing that you are occupied and – and distracted.'

'I don't need distraction.'

'Janet, don't tell me lies.'

'We must go in to breakfast,' she said.

'One minute more. I warn you that you will be wasted.'

'Not if I help her.'

'Very well. But I also warn you that Oliver will come in for some abuse.'

'What is that to me?' she asked defiantly.

'You know best,' he said with a light gesture. 'Now let us go in. The fresh air has made me hungry.'

'And why,' her words retained him, 'why should Oliver be abused?'

'Because he is a party to this separation.'

'To separation, perhaps – '

He shrugged his shoulders. 'Oh, my dear, if you make so much of the other thing – !'

Her face flushed. 'I know nothing about it.'

'Then don't judge. Oliver let her go. I have no doubt he could have kept her with a word.'

'But in that, wasn't he right?'

'I think so, but your mother won't. Your mother certainly will not. She will have something to say about it. You will hear a good deal about Oliver.'

'But if one knows – in one's own heart –' she stopped, for she was saying too much, yet what did it matter when this little man seemed to know everything?

'That is what I tell myself,' he said, finding relief in making this confession to her. 'I think I have told myself that at least a hundred times, but it is a faulty armour and one gets pricked, and it hurts, yes, it even hurts me who am a tough old man, Janet.' He touched his chest with a comic air of despair and self-esteem. 'And I know a lot. But you are young and you don't know much.'

'I am tough, too,' she said, 'and I know a good deal.'

He had the last word. 'But what you need is wisdom.' They entered the dining-room together.

In that philosophic way which had always been his pleasure and was now to be his consolation, he considered, behind his screening newspaper, his increased knowledge of his family. In twenty-four hours he had learnt much. He had discovered, for instance, that Violet had a heart and he meant to prosecute its acquaintance: he now decided that his surprise at his wife's hardness was inexcusable: he might have known that a woman of her stubborn and engrossing affections would be inelastic, and he was genuinely interested to see what she would do next. At the moment she was eating her breakfast with a pretence of appetite and her manner was determined and composed. He was troubled by the breach of their good fellowship, but he found piquancy in it, too. It depressed and at the same time enlivened life. Would she be able to stand alone or would the time come when she must falter and appeal to him for help?

And there was Dora who would appeal to no one, who was soft and sweet and extraordinarily firm. There would be no complaints from her, though a perspicacious parent could be sure that if she had ever loved her husband, she bore with him now for her children's sake: she despised his mind if she appreciated the material results of his devotion and even encouraged that devotion, because it was not in her nature to seek that of another. Of Mabel and John he had learnt nothing new. He despaired of any excitement from that quarter and, considering these things, he was ashamed of his anger of the night before: he had put too high a value on their condemnations. He was glad that Janet had not witnessed it, for he would have to deal carefully with her: he must teach her to trust him. Poor child, he had her secret in his keeping and for a moment he felt himself omniscient, but he controlled that dangerous feeling. He humbled himself with the thought that though he knew the pitiful fact of her imagined love and certain jealousy, he knew neither their origin nor their intensity: he was in deepest ignorance of their end and he could not direct it. He was only a father who had caused the existence of these beings, so dear and so remote. Yes, even Lydia was remote and once more he tried to picture her at The Grange in Mastover. Was she breakfasting with her lover in some sun-filled room, or was The Grange a dark, damp place, overgrown with ivy, shrouded by trees, a fit retreat for the rebels of this world? It seemed to him that some day he would have to go and see.

He rose and kissed his wife. 'Good-bye, dear.'

'Good-bye.' Most unexpectedly she followed him to the door and waited there until he turned into the road. He waved his hat, she lifted a hand in answer, and he saw her beckon to the gardener. She did not mean to leave any of her duties undone.

Chapter 17

THE day was beautiful: these days of trouble had all been golden, mellow, arched with blue, and the garden was radiant with tall dahlias, early chrysanthemums and delicate last roses, these faintly nipped by morning frost, but blooming with an added graciousness in the warmth. A heap of rubbish was burning in a corner of the garden and the smoke rose steadily in a cloud of colour, as though the spirits of all the blue and purple flowers which had gone with the summer, forget-me-nots, lupins, violets and pansies, cornflowers, sweet-peas and Canterbury bells, were rising in a final loveliness from the earth to the sun, giving back what had been given in an ecstasy of thanks and prayer for the renewal of life.

The gardener threw another handful of leaves on the fire, Janet snipped a few pale roses from the house wall, and Mrs. Nesbitt, holding up her skirt, walked round the paths, looking at the pears and the plums. She meant to make no difference in her movements nor in her expression before the world, and the world at this moment was the gardener and the servants who, after the family meeting of last night and the noise of William's angry voice, might be watching curiously for developments. Mrs. Nesbitt already regretted that hasty summoning of the children. It had been the blind act of panic, as her visit to Lydia had been, but she saw in it merely a tactical mistake. Lydia's doings were always vague to the rest of the family which would have been content to know nothing of her for months, and in the meantime – Mrs. Nesbitt's lips were very tightly pressed together, but she opened them to tell the gardener that some of the plums should be picked at once – in the meantime, much might have been done to save the situation. Even now, it was not too late. Lydia might be dead to her, but there are duties even to the dead and Mrs. Nesbitt meant to do them. It was possible that a mother's eye might discern a spark of life and, if not, the corpse must be laid out decently, buried privily, and forgotten. Forgotten! Mrs. Nesbitt's lips now trembled a little, but her husband was right when he called her a strong woman, and she had decided on her course.

This was temporarily, but not seriously interrupted by the arrival of Mabel. She carried a large basket stuffed with groceries, and Mrs. Nesbitt, doubly irritated, exclaimed, 'My dear, you look, like a pedlar!' But Mabel was as full of matter as the basket and she hardly noticed the criticism.

'I haven't slept all night,' she said.

This elicited no response, from Janet, who was sewing by the window, or from Mrs. Nesbitt, who sat bolt upright in her chair.

'Neither has John.' Mabel looked from one to the other, her hat balanced precariously on her thick hair, and seemed astonished at the lack of sympathy. 'We have been tossing about all night,' she elaborated, and Janet's laughter pealed out so gaily and it was so rare a sound, that Mrs. Nesbitt turned her head to look at her and her own mouth softened.

'I can't see anything to laugh at,' Mabel said.

'Not now,' Janet reassured her, 'but in the night – '

'Janet! Janet!' Mrs. Nesbitt said reprovingly.

Mabel jerked her head. 'John has such a sense of honour – and I don't know how you can laugh, Janet.'

'I don't often do it,' Janet said quietly.

'And now, of all times!'

'John s fault,' Janet explained.

'But what are we to do, Mother? What are we to do?' She was justified in feeling aggrieved at the normal appearance of her mother after that image of one stricken, distorted, almost horrible in change, which she and John had carried home with them. 'John says he thinks some of us ought to go and see Lydia and reason with her. He's willing to go himself – '

Mrs. Nesbitt lifted a hand. 'Leave it to me,' she said grandly.

'But people will find out, and think of John's position in the chapel! I don't think you realize how dreadful it is for all of us.'

'Realize it!' Mrs. Nesbitt said in a voice deepened by the memory of her own vigil. 'Realize it! I am her mother.'

A little silence fell in the room. Janet pushed her needle slowly, as though she feared to make a noise with the fine linen she was fashioning into garments, and Mabel, resentful, jerking her head, looked at the carpet and bit her lips, but she had a great persistence which would not long be awed and she spoke again.

'Don't you think, Mother, if we went to see her and showed her what this means to us,' a gawky, explanatory gesture of a hand in a cotton glove emphasized this remark, 'don't you think it might do some good?'

'I wish you wouldn't wear cotton gloves,' Mrs. Nesbitt said. 'Oh, Dora, is that you, dear?' Mrs. Nesbitt might have been welcoming her to a party.

Dora, immediately aware that the atmosphere was to be kept thus artificially cheerful, responded with an equal brightness. She strolled in, clad in brown, her hat made of pheasant's feathers, her soft leather gloves wrinkled over her wrists, a pretty bag dangling from her hand. There was no sign of mourning and ashes here. She kissed her mother, nodded to Mabel, smiled at Janet and dropped into a chair. 'Isn't it hot?' she said pleasantly.

Though a little bewildered by these unexpected conditions, Mabel remembered Herbert's anger and turned hopefully to Dora.

'Dora, I was just suggesting to Mother that some of us ought to go and see Lydia.'

'Oh? I expect she would be pleased.'

'Pleased? I don't know about that, but John thinks it is our duty. You see, she can't realize it, Dora. She hasn't thought about our children.'

'No, indeed,' Dora agreed.

139

Greatly encouraged, Mabel continued: 'If John and Herbert went to see her – '

Dora laughed. 'Herbert won't go. Herbert wouldn't pass her doorstep.'

'Really, Dora!' Mrs. Nesbitt expostulated.

'I can't help it, Mother. Of course, it's abominable of him – '

'Really, Dora!' Mrs. Nesbitt said again, swinging over to the other side.

'Well, don't you think so?'

'What I think is that you ought not to talk like that about your husband.'

'Truth is stronger than fiction,' Dora remarked, and Janet paused in her sewing and looked at Dora for a steady second. 'And the fiction in this case,' Dora elaborated, 'is that one's husband is always right.'

Mrs. Nesbitt, with disapproval on her face, could still think bitterly that her own husband was often wrong, but where she triumphed was in never saying so.

'John doesn't want to see Lydia, either,' Mabel said, 'but he thinks he ought to.'

'Well, let him go,' said Dora, 'but he'll have to reckon with Henry.'

'Henry!' Mrs. Nesbitt gasped and, 'Henry!' Mabel exclaimed in shocked tones.

'That is his name,' Dora remarked innocently.

'And as for reckoning with him – ' Mabel began.

'I've seen him,' Dora said, and very quickly Mabel asked, 'What is he like?'

'Very strong,' Dora said gently.

'Oh!'

'With broad shoulders and a chin.'

'Oh!'

'And I don't think,' Dora went on thoughtfully, 'I don't think John would have much chance. I think it's more than likely that Henry would be very violent.'

Janet laughed again – twice in one morning, and once more Mrs. Nesbitt turned her head to look at her.

140

'And,' Dora said, in the same, almost dreamy tones, 'if I were Henry, I should kick John hard, as hard as I could.'

'So would I,' said Janet.

It was a pity that William Nesbitt was not present at this little scene. Mrs. Nesbitt sat very still, as though only by doing so could she keep a just balance of opinion and control. Mabel, secure in her own position, was, nevertheless, in danger of oscillating on her base, engaged as she was gazing at her sisters on their own dangerous standpoints, and he would have seen Janet's as a very airy situation, though she seemed to poise herself so gaily, in spite of jealous winds and strong gusts of anger; but it was plain that jealousy and anger against Henry did not exist for her.

'So would I,' she repeated.

'Janet!' Mrs. Nesbitt cried out warningly, 'and Dora, you mustn't quarrel with your husband.'

'Quarrel?' Dora's eyebrows went up. It was strange how the children had inherited their father's tricks. 'I never quarrel with anybody.'

'Your husband is not "anybody." '

'No, just Herbert,' Dora answered mildly.

A conjunction between Mrs. Nesbitt's tongue and teeth produced a sound of irritation.

'Not,' Dora said, turning graciously to Mabel and referring to an earlier remark, 'not because John is offensive in himself.'

'I should think not,' Mabel said, 'and anyhow, moral strength always wins.'

'They say so,' Dora murmured.

'But what,' Mabel's voice rose again, 'what are we going to do?'

Mrs. Nesbitt made her grand gesture again. 'Leave it to me.'

'And what are you going to do, Mother?'

'That remains to be seen.'

'But why do anything?' Janet's clear voice questioned.

'And what's the good?' Dora added. 'I had a letter from Lydia this morning.'

'A letter!' Mabel exclaimed.

Mrs. Nesbitt held her breath, but she could not hold back from her eyes their look of eagerness, anguish and anger. Janet bent her head a little lower, but her fingers did not move.

'Yes,' Dora said. 'She sent her love to any one who wanted it.' She threw into the air an imaginary handful of that love and said, 'Catch! What, none of you? Then, I'll take it all.'

'Everything,' Mrs. Nesbitt pronounced in criticism of these suddenly strange ways of Dora as well as of Lydia's sin, 'everything, the whole world, seems to have gone wrong.'

'No,' Dora said, 'but we are seeing it, for the first time, as it is.'

'It is Lydia who has made us all miserable because she has been wicked,' Mabel said.

'Oh, wicked!' Dora exclaimed. 'How do you know she is wicked?'

Mabel's large brown eyes, of the colour and texture of brandy balls and as changeless in expression, were turned to her mother, expecting some fit reproof of this outrageous question, and as it did not come she returned to the conclusions reached in the night watches. 'John says, he thinks – '

'Oh, Mabel,' Mrs. Nesbitt snapped violently, 'I don't care what John says or thinks.'

'But here,' Mabel protested, giving up all hope of support, yet persevering without it, 'here we all sit as though nothing had happened and already people may be talking about it.'

'How can anybody know?' Mrs. Nesbitt asked, with a resumption of calm. 'Of course, if you begin telling people – '

'It isn't likely I shall do that,' Mabel said.

'Then leave it to me,' Mrs. Nesbitt said for the third

time. 'I have telegraphed for Oliver,' and in the dramatic pause which followed that statement she was not without satisfaction.

Janet dropped her work and stood looking out of the window, but no one noticed the straight tenseness of her back and the extraordinary stillness of her whole figure. Dora, with her hands clasping the arms of the big chair in which she was sunk, frowned slightly, but Mabel was eager.

'Will he be here this morning?'

'I don't know.'

'I should like to see him.'

'Why?' Mrs. Nesbitt asked superbly.

'What's that bit in the Bible,' Dora asked, 'about the eagle?'

A little irritated by this apparent irrelevance, Mrs. Nesbitt said, 'I don't know what you mean, dear.'

'I know,' Dora said. ' "Her young ones also suck up blood, and where the slain are, there is she." Mabel is the eagle.'

'But who is slain?' Mabel asked innocently. 'Oh!' She thought she saw the allusion. 'I like to help people if I can.'

'Help!' The voice was Janet's and it quivered on the word. 'You like to gloat.'

'That is what I meant,' Dora said, nodding pleasantly.

'Children, children!' Mrs. Nesbitt cried. 'Yes, everything has gone wrong. There were never any quarrels before.'

'They have always been against me,' Mabel said, 'and against John and the boys. We have both felt it.'

'Oh, no,' said Dora, still very pleasant, 'but admit you want to see how Oliver looks.'

'She shan't see,' Janet said, in that strained voice, and now Dora looked at her and saw her eyes like blue flames, her face white. 'No one shall see him.' Mrs. Nesbitt also looked, with that peculiar intensity which gave her the appearance of a person blind. 'Do you want to torture him?' Janet cried.

'Nonsense, child,' Mrs. Nesbitt said gently. 'This dreadful business has upset us all. I want to help him.'

'But you can't.'

'That remains to be seen,' Mrs. Nesbitt said again with the wonderful assurance she had gained in a night. 'Leave it to me.'

Mabel was in tears. She sought for the handle of her basket.

'Now, Mabel, don't take this seriously,' her mother said. 'Your sisters did not mean to be unkind, but really,' she turned on them all, 'I don't know what you are thinking of, behaving like this. I won't have it. I will not have it. I am ashamed of you all. When you were little I used to make you kiss and be friends.'

'I'm quite ready to kiss Mabel,' Dora said amiably, but Janet shrank against the window-frame.

'I won't kiss anybody,' she said, with so much determination that Dora broke into a laugh.

'Oh, Lydia, Lydia,' she murmured, and under cover of that sound, very sweetly uttered, Mabel picked up her basket and disappeared.

Chapter 18

MRS. NESBITT found herself confronted, that afternoon, by a tall young man with a grave, but not a tormented face. He stooped to kiss her with the courtesy which had always pleased her with its suggestion of a tribute offered, rather than a duty done and that act, so natural and so endearing slightly ruffled her great calm. His good looks, the steady brown eyes in the long face, the close-cut moustache which, now and then, he touched with tentative fingers, renewed their charm, and she had an extraordinary moment of believing that the whole miserable affair was a bad dream. She had to steady herself, look at the familiar furniture of the drawing-room, assure herself that she was awake, that the pain in her heart was still there, though it was controlled by her own will, before she could say unnecessarily, 'You had my telegram?'

'That is why I am here.'

'I sent for you because I want you to go with me tomorrow to Mastover.'

'I can't do that,' he said with decision.

'It is your duty.'

He clasped his hands which hung between his knees and shook his head, smiling a little, and Mrs. Nesbitt, flushing all over her body, revealed that flush in the dark, angry red of her face. She stared at him for a moment, convinced that he was immovable but astonished that her plan, of which she had been so sure, should miscarry at the outset, and filled with a rage so deep that it was still. Once more she had the appearance of a wooden image, heavily painted, and her stiff lips opened to let her words out slowly, as though they were regulated by some inner mechanism.

'Then I have no more to say, but perhaps,' her voice

deepened a little, 'perhaps for the first ti me I understand why Lydia left you.'

'Perhaps,' he agreed gently, 'but I don't think so. Lydia isn't sure herself, but she has gone and I will not follow her unless she sends for me.'

'Sends for you!'

'Is that worse than going uninvited?'

'Worse! There is no worse!'

'Surely,' he said persuasively. 'If we had quarrelled –'

'Quarrels can be forgiven and forgotten, but this is cold-blooded, it is indecent. I thought –' her voice faltered, 'I thought we might have helped each other.'

'I came to help you if I could,' he said, 'but I see I can do nothing.'

'Nothing,' Mrs. Nesbitt repeated from some abyss into which she had sunk.

'Because you don't understand.'

'I thank God I don't understand.'

'I don't think you should do that,' he suggested, still with the gentle tolerance she found so hard to bear.

'But what I do understand,' she said in rising tones and a sudden satisfaction, 'I do understand that Lydia could not endure your – your –'

'I know,' he interrupted, 'I know. It's difficult to express it, but I know what you mean.'

She was baffled by this willingness to interpret. Was he clever? Was he stupid? Or was this some strange form of wickedness?

'So we agree about that,' he said with another fleeting smile, 'and you see, being what I am, I shouldn't make any impression on Lydia, should I? if that is what you want me to do,' and, as though to himself, he added, 'I have always failed to impress her.'

'I want you to take her from that villain who, has carried her off,' Mrs. Nesbitt said fiercely.

'Not a villain,' Oliver replied, 'He is a friend of mine.'

'Oh, this is beyond me,' Mrs. Nesbitt cried. 'This is terrible!'

'No, not terrible. These things happen, but they are not terrible unless you make them so.'

'You have no blood in your veins,' she accused him roughly. 'How can you speak of it like this? Your own wife – '

He touched his moustache again lightly. 'You can't label Lydia like that. No one's wife. All sorts of things – ' again he parted his clasped hands – 'But not a wife.'

It occurred to Mrs. Nesbitt now that she was in the company of a harmless lunatic. Nothing in her experience had approached this sort of madness, for William had been discreetly silent about his thoughts and Mrs. Nesbitt's imagination did not fill the gaps. A wife was a wife, sin was sin, and a wronged husband should be violent. She despised her son-in-law for his mildness but she was afraid of the unknown in him.

'Then I shall go alone,' she said.

'Don't do that,' he begged her.

'I am not afraid of that man,' she said.

'Of course not.' He laughed, to her relief, quite normally. 'But you will make Lydia unhappy.'

'Lydia, Lydia! It is always Lydia. She brings this trouble on us, but it is she who has to be spared.'

'Well, why not?' he asked. 'You will suffer, too.'

'Can I suffer more?' she asked with a real tragedy.

'I don't know,' he answered, looking down.

There was a pause before she stood up, dignified and practical. 'I need not keep you any longer. I see you do not mean to help me and,' she added, with inconsistent indignation, 'you do not care for Lydia.'

'Don't care for her!' he said in a low voice. 'Oh, well – '
He smiled again.

'And I have said nothing about your part in this dreadful, dreadful business. I don't know how to speak of it at all. In my own family! In the newspapers; yes – one gets used to it, but it never seems real – as if it had happened in another world. And now –' she pressed her hands to her head in her first dismayed movement. 'And now – and you come here and smile. And even I – but there are appearances to be kept up.'

'That is what I think,' he said gravely.

'But not with me.'

'With myself,' he told her.

She made no answer. Recriminations fell strangely feeble before this man, like the effect of a great shout which comes to nothing but a whisper, hopeless, tiny, in a vast silence.

'But,' she managed to say at last, across the distance between them, 'if I bring Lydia home, will you take her back?'

'Lydia knows,' he replied.

'And am I to know nothing?'

'Why,' he said, explaining the thing to her, 'you can't tell the wind not to come in at your open window, can you?'

'She has bewitched you all,' Mrs. Nesbitt said ominously. 'Her father always spoilt her, you have spoilt her, everybody – ! And now she thinks she can do whatever she likes, whatever she likes.'

'Not quite,' he said, still in his kind and explanatory manner. 'Her conscience is her difficulty. She is more moral than most people. That,' he said after a pause and as though he murmured to the carpet, 'that is where I come in.'

'This really is madness,' Mrs. Nesbitt murmured, but she wondered if the madness could be hers, if she were suffering from delusions, or if she were really lying in bed, delirious. In bed was where she should have been, she knew, for her head was throbbing under the iron band that circled it and she felt giddy. She stood her ground firmly, but she had a sensation of swaying and when the door opened softly and Janet slipped into the room without a sound, it was surely a continuation of the things that were not really happening.

Janet stood just inside the door, like a wraith. Her widened eyes were on Oliver and in a voice attenuated, far off, she said, 'I was afraid; I was afraid – '

He put out his hand to her saying, in tones which seemed very loud, 'It's all right. I'm just going.'

'Not for a minute,' she said, and Mrs. Nesbitt, dropping into a chair, saw them both leave the room, silently, as if they were on wheels. Once more she put her hands to her head and she moaned weakly, 'Oh, my head, my head!'

When William Nesbitt returned, a few hours later, he noticed a new stillness in the house and the white panelled hall seemed cold, in spite of the golden flowers gleaming against the wood. He was tired and he felt like an exile returning, after a long time, to a place which was once a home. Then, with her strange effect of appearing from nowhere, Janet slipped into the hall and stood before him, and to him, as earlier in the day to his wife, she seemed spectral in her pale dress.

'Mother is in bed,' she said in hushed tones. 'Her head aches.'

'Only her head?' His weariness got the better of him. 'I feel it here,' he said, touching his chest. 'Well, well – '

'And there's a letter for you, on your desk.'

'From your mother?'

'No, no. It's on your desk,' she repeated and slipped away again.

He looked at the emptiness she had left. 'I don't believe, I don't believe the girl was really there,' he muttered. A sense of unreality was round him too, and he hardly expected to find the letter, but there it lay, on his desk. The light in the room was rather dim and, standing by the window, he opened the envelope. It contained a letter from Lydia to her husband, and a note from him to William Nesbitt.

'I thought you might like to see this,' he had written hastily. 'Please let me have the letter back.'

William Nesbitt handled the sheets gently and paused before he read it. Behind him, the empty room seemed to stir with the thoughts, the emotions of those who had lived there, passed in and out, laughed and wept, and somewhere in the house people who were hardly more solid moved softly, lay in bed, spread silver and glass on a white cloth, stirred the kitchen fire and looked into the oven. It was all unreal, yet how foolish to desire reality, for he did not know what it was. Down by the docks, that day, he had read and written letters, interviewed people, lost his temper and picked it up again, given money to a beggar, scolded a clerk, commiserated with another whose wife was sick, taken a great deal of trouble over things that did not matter, did not matter.

It was queer to be set down in a world where it was necessary to take action and yet to be incapable of seeing where those acts would lead. There must be some sense in it somewhere. He had never felt himself in such a fog, no, not even that night off the Scillies, years ago, when he was a young man, long before Lydia was born. He had thought then that he would never see land again, and here he was, with his feet planted on a thick carpet, holding her letter, and another fog, of diverse personalities and passions, was about him, and one of his crew was in her bed, another had mutinied and a third was wandering about like a ghost. He had to steer a course, now as then, but this was harder: he had not the knowledge. He might save himself, but if he lost his ship, his crew – His thoughts went back to the old days. They had been simple, too simple for his temper, and now that he met complications he was no more satisfied. 'Never satisfied,' he murmured and, bending a little nearer to the window, still conscious of the stirrings behind him and the quiet, darkening garden before him, he read Lydia's letter.

'I am writing this,' she began, 'in a dark little room lighted by a single candle. I feel like a deserted heroine and I try not to pine for electricity. When the setting for the scene is so perfect, it would be graceless to play my part badly.

'This house is three miles from the station and I had to

150

sit on my box while Henry looked for a means of getting here. At last we hired a trap drawn by a remarkable pony, which Henry says was drawing the same trap when he was a small boy, but I don't believe it, though certainly the pony has a knack of conserving his strength. We jogged and jogged and then I got out and walked, and then I got in again, and after a century of silence and darkness and hunger and drooping spirits, we came to the house.

'I felt we ought to have arrived in a coach-and-four with a blowing of bugles and rattling of bits and steaming of horses, a sort of triumphal declaration, but, no, we just stealthily crept and the house looked stealthy too, and rather cunning. It seemed to wink at me as though it had known all the time that Henry would bring me here. It is low and square and covered with creepers, and there is a little copse of larch trees edging the rough lawn, all dreadfully suitable.

'But the country is lovely. It nearly gives one everything one wants and you know, in my case, what a lot that is. Why, even when you cross the river from Radstowe, you feel like another creature, and here I am, in the heart of it, the queer, wild, quiet heart. From the copse gate you get into a lane with rocks sticking out of the ground like a giant's bones and it leads you to a dip where a brook crosses the road, and you have to scramble by the bank. It will be fun when there has been really heavy rain and we have to fetch the milk. There's a farm there with not only eggs and butter, but a conveniently barren woman, like me, who is willing to work for us by the day. She is also an austere person and I am rather afraid of her. When she was a girl, she worked for Henry's mother and that is why she will work for me, though really it's the reason why she shouldn't. She comes in quietly by the back door in the morning and goes out quietly in the evening, tall and gaunt and wonderfully noiseless. The whole place is hushed. Even I am hushed and I'm quite startled by the sound of my pen as I write to you.

'There is a funny old photograph of Mrs. Wyatt on the

mantelpiece, watching me over her long nose. She disapproves of me but, if she didn't, she would like me. The rooms are all full of aunts and uncles in awful frames, some of them plush, but Mrs. Wyatt is the only impressive person. The others are all thoroughly dead. I believe her ghost walks in these square rooms with the high windows – you can't see out of them properly unless you stand up – and the heavy furniture she bought when she was young. You can't imagine anything more unlike me, but I don't feel I can alter anything, not even the plush frames. It's her house, not mine. She has made her effect without an effort or a particle of taste, and when I think of my own beautiful furniture and my big bowl of flowers, I feel that it was all rather meretricious – not really me at all in the way this house is her. Her character survives, but I'm sure no daughter-in-law of mine, invading my rooms, would be conscious of my presence all the time – and a good thing, too!'

At this point, William Nesbitt paused in his reading and muttered aloud, 'What nonsense!' as though Lydia were in the room. Her presence! It depended less than anybody's on her actual body. Surely she was with him now. He felt as though he could touch her by putting out a hand, yet he did not wish to touch her, for she was closer than any physical contact could make her.

'There are three square sitting-rooms and a square kitchen; three square bedrooms and a square bathroom; and all the papers on the walls are like dingy reflections of the Brussels carpets on the floors, though you can't see much wall for pictures – depressed oil paintings in gilt frames, and family portraits, family portraits everywhere. I haven't had time to look at them all yet and they will keep me occupied for days.

'Henry's father was a scholar, as you know, and I should think very little else. There are hundreds of his books, bound in that thick, black stuff that warns you not to read them, and when you look inside you see they're all theology, or Greek, or Latin. There's a photograph of him, too – rather prim. I think he must have bored her a good deal, but I dare say she consoled herself by making fun of him all the time, saying very little but thinking a great deal. He wouldn't know. Perhaps I shall get like that with Henry, but, if so, he will know quickly enough. Yes, I should have liked Henry's mother, just as I love my own father. They ought to have married each other, though the results might have been too formidable. There might have been a worse tragedy than ours. But it isn't a tragedy, is it? Perhaps it is. I'm not sure what you feel. I'm trying to find out. Here I am with Henry, and yet I'm thinking of you all the time, trying to see why I have just slipped past something, instead of seizing it, or was it you who did the slipping?

'I hope I am telling you all the things you want to know. I shall take this letter through the copse of larches, out into the lane – there is a half-cleared wood on the other side of it – and across the brook to the pillar-box in the wall, and little creatures will rustle among the pine needles in the wood. I shall run as fast as I can, there and back, expecting something to catch me, and I shall slam the front door to shut it out. The hall is narrow and dark and the walls seem to tell you, gently but firmly, that they mean to squash you flat.

'I wonder if Maria puts flowers in my bowl. In this house, it doesn't seen to matter whether there are flowers or not. It was furnished in an unromantic age, but there is something here better than romance. Henry's mother! I see that for a little while I am going to think more of her than of myself, but when I've settled it all, when I've distinguished all the aunts from the cousins and the great-uncles from the grandfathers, what am I to do then? It will be the winter and the whole country will stand still and watch and listen. Then I think I shall have to come and see you, unless you will come here. But no, don't come here.

'You have been wonderful, Oliver, but I am not stupid. I have said I don't know what you feel and I don't, quite, about me, but I know other things, better than you, perhaps, so don't come here. But keep friendship in your heart for me, please. I wish men were not so determined to have things to themselves. I can love both you and Henry, but neither you nor he would share me. Of course not. That would be too simple. One has to pay for what one gets and make other people pay as well, and who will pay most, none of us knows. But one does not mind paying – it's part of the game. And now, good-night. I must make my journey through the wood.'

Chapter 19

THE garden was still darker when he finished reading the letter, but the movement behind him had stopped. Somehow, his own personal trouble had gone, the mere fret of unpleasantness in the household, of his wife's aloofness, Herbert's petty rage and John's moral attitude. All these were negligible compared with the words he read between Lydia's lines. She had not expected to be happy, had she not told him so? – But perhaps she had expected to be happier than she was, and his thoughts, which had winged swiftly and bravely to Mastover, now halted, wavering and uncertain. He had tried to readjust his vision of her, not only in these new surroundings, but as a woman. He could not clarify his own confusion, but he thought he detected something less direct and flashing than he had imagined in her character, and he saw her subdued, less swift, almost trapped in that dark little house muffled in creepers, Brussels carpets and heavy furniture, quietly writing a letter by the light of a single candle.

The dullness of it, the stillness, hurt him. Where was Henry while she wrote? Was he sitting in a corner, watching her vivid face shadowily illumined by the yellow flame? No, Lydia had stolen from the room where he was working, shut the door gently, stepped across the narrow passage, opened and shut another door and stood for a moment in the darkness. Her heart, he was sure, had beaten a little quickly and her hands had been pressed against it, but only for a moment before she lit the candle and sat down at the table. Once or twice she had flung out her arms and laid her head on them and then, smiling, she had resumed her writing. There would be mice in that old house and Lydia could not endure them. No doubt, for fear of them, she had wound her legs round those

155

of her chair while she wrote, but would that man come to her rescue if she screamed? A single candle! Were they as poor as all that?

He began his usual pacing and jingling before the window, curtained now by the night. He had forgotten his wife with her aching head. He felt that some idea, vague but cherished, was slipping from his grasp, and he hurried to and fro, to and fro. Lydia's fulfilment – was it to be thwarted? Yet he had always seen her thwarted when he had tried to see her future. There was nothing new in that, but in her his pride was at stake. If this great experiment failed, if she were mistaken, even nobly, it seemed as if he must lose his sure hold on life. But this, he realized, was the exaggeration of a moment in which he pictured her unhappy, solitary, pressed upon by the potency of that house and her own questionings. Never before had he pictured her in dimness: always there had been light, the sun, a clearness of atmosphere playing round her, and now he was plunged with her into a gloom without grandeur. But he became aware that, in the physical darkness of this room which, doubtless, was influencing his mind, there was a white patch near the door.

He stood still, to hear a voice asking thinly, 'What did Oliver say?'

'Oliver? Say? Oliver?' He had forgotten to ask how that envelope had appeared on his desk.

'In his letter.'

'Is that you, Janet? How long have you been there?'

'What did Oliver say?' she persisted.

He sought for the scrap of paper and gave it to her. 'Turn on the light, child. There's too much darkness here.'

'Only this?' she asked, fingering it.

'Read it,' he said with a tender brusqueness, and when she looked up, he added, 'How did it come here?'

'He brought it.'

'Brought it?'

'Mother sent for him.'

'Ah,' he said and sat down. 'Did you see him?'

She nodded, like a child, a little fearful. 'I went in because I didn't know what Mother would be saying.'

'And what was she saying?' he questioned gently, as though he feared to scare her.

'Nothing. Just staring at him.'

'And Oliver?'

She made a hardly perceptible movement with her hands and the piece of paper fell.

'You've dropped that,' he said.

'Yes, I don't want it,' she answered oddly.

'He enclosed one of Lydia's, you see,' William Nesbitt said, and while he wondered whether he should let her read it, he saw her shrink. 'No matter,' he muttered and he got up. 'What did Oliver say to you?'

'He gave me the letter for you. He said,' she hesitated, and still like a child, still fearful but obedient, she went on: 'He said, "Don't think too hardly of us, Janet." '

'And you won't, will you?'

She shook her head. 'He asked me to write to Lydia.'

'And you will?'

'I don't know.'

'If he has asked you –' William Nesbitt suggested. 'You see, he loves her, child.'

'Then why,' she asked with her first human flash, 'has he let her go?'

'Ah!' William Nesbitt said again, but this time with some inner satisfaction, for this impatience was healthy. 'Ah!' he thought, enjoying the subtleties of his own mind, 'I thought he was stupid, I believe he's generous, I begin to think he's deep,' and as though this communication with Janet were a filter, his thoughts cleared, leaving pride and defiance like dregs behind them. It was possible that Henry was Lydia's filter. A new idea! He played with it, forgetting Janet, following a long train of consequences.

'It's a mistake, child, to think in the dark. Before you came in I was fogged, fogged. Never think in the dark. Black thoughts. And unhappiness is not a tragedy. It's like a tunnel and you come out into the light, dazzled by beauty. You'll see.' He was almost gay, immersed in metaphor. Henry was Lydia's filter, that little dark house was her tunnel, but both led to clarity.

'But he ought not to have let her go,' Janet said. 'I think she must,' her voice dropped, 'despise him.'

'I wonder,' William Nesbitt said untruthfully. 'I suppose women like strong men, forceful characters.'

'Yes,' Janet agreed unsuspiciously. Her eyes, opened more widely than usual, looked beyond him, and he was hankful.

'Where I've wronged you all,' he continued, 'and your mother had her share in it, is in giving you too much strength. It's hard to find men to fit you.'

'Still,' Janet said, and he felt the pathos of her necessity to talk so openly, 'one likes to help people.'

'Yes, yes,' he said doubtfully, 'yes, the protecting instinct, but women can use that on their children. They want something else in a man. Correct me, if I'm wrong, my dear.'

'I suppose you know best,' she said, turning away wearily.

'And now I must go and see your mother. Do you think she ought to have the doctor? Better ring him up, Janet. What, he's away? Well, there must be somebody there; but wait a bit, wait a bit.'

He opened the bedroom door, inch by inch, fearing he might wake his wife, but she spoke at once.

'Is that you, William? I think something is going to burst in my head. I must have the doctor.'

'Good,' he said. 'Good, I'll send for him,' but what he really commented on was the fact of her surrender.

'I am very angry with Oliver,' Mrs. Nesbitt said in distinct tones.

'Now don't worry, Kate. Keep quiet. You can be angry with him when you feel better.'

'He came here – '

'Yes, Janet told me.'

'And he went away without saying good-bye. Janet came in and he just followed her out of the room, without a word, like ghosts.'

158

'Dear me!' William Nesbitt ejaculated. 'Like ghosts, were they?'

'Yes, William, I'm not sure that he's quite right in his head.'

'We're all mad, my dear, all mad.'

'I am not mad,' Mrs. Nesbitt protested. She tried to raise herself and fell back. 'Oh,' she moaned, 'send for the doctor, William, do!'

'I will,' he said alertly, 'I'll go now.'

'But William –'

'My dear?'

'You might kiss me.'

'I was afraid you would not like it, Kate,' he said meekly.

Alone with Janet, at dinner, he thought she had a chastened air. Still strictly virginal in her white and gold, she had lost something of her young assurance. She had always sat there between her parents, saying little, listening and judging, her movements precisely deft, her expression firm, but now her mouth had a wavering line which charmed him, so that he wished he were a young man with the chance to woo her: her hands, so apt in all they did, had a fluttering uncertainty: she was indeed like a girl expecting, and half fearing, to hear words of love, yet nothing was further from her thoughts. She was self-conscious, not under his eyes but under a new knowledge of her own mind and, in watching her, his spirit, which could never long be daunted, was marvellously refreshed.

I don't remember ever having a meal alone with you, before, Janet,' he said.

'Oh, yes. Breakfast, sometimes.'

'Breakfast isn't a meal, it's a habit, a concession, a mere condescension to one's stomach. This is different. I like it. Here's an opportunity for the feast of reason and the flow of soul. Let's take it.'

'Well,' she said, smiling, 'you begin.'

'I have been feeling sorry for you, my dear – don't be alarmed – because you can never be a father. It's a charming relationship for a man with a satisfactory daughter.

Now a mother can't feel romantic about a daughter – about a son, perhaps, I don't know, but even then, it must be different. A father is more detached, more of a stranger, and where there's strangeness there's excitement. I'm glad I'm not a mother. There's too domestic a flavour about that – aired underclothes and plenty to eat! And a daughter is always a woman and a mystery.'

She leaned forward a little. 'When you were engaged to Mother, did you talk to her like this?'

He lifted his eyebrows. 'I didn't – if that's what you mean – descant on parenthood, my dear. She wouldn't have liked it. Your mother had a great modesty. One had to be careful. And now I come to think of it, you're my first audience.'

'But surely to Lydia –'

He shook his head. 'Not even to Lydia. Lydia and I have hardly exchanged a dozen remarks in our lives. That's queer, isn't it? It's all queer, all interesting. Now, what are we to say to this doctor fellow when he comes? Tell him your mother has had a shock? No need, is there? It's rather lucky that it's not old Bunford. He's as curious as I am and he'd have ferreted something out of us. You'd better go upstairs with him and I'll see him afterwards. No, I'll go upstairs and then I'll bring him to you to get your orders. That's the best plan. Your mother seems to think you spirited Oliver away from her this afternoon and he forgot to say good-bye. Not that it matters, child, but I thought I'd better warn you.'

'Warn me? What of?'

'Only a possible scolding,' He smiled frankly. 'She seemed to be annoyed about it.'

'Somebody had to look after him,' Janet murmured.

He spread his hands. 'I know, I know. Poor fellow!'

Chapter 20

WILLIAM NESBITT left his office early the next day and wound his way slowly up the narrow path over which the trees were now hanging tired, tarnished leaves. The broad fingers of a chestnut were tipped with rust colour, a tall poplar, standing in one of the walled gardens, looked like a broom with its edges blurred by work, and through the spaces left by branch and leaf, tiny patches of sky made a blue pattern. He gave all this as much appreciation as he could spare, but he was worried about his wife: the doctor, an old young man of a dry aspect, had warned him that she must be kept quiet, have no worries, and be dieted to reduce the pressure of blood. It was all very well to give advice, but a man who looked like a nut could have no idea of the complications inherent in a large family. Kate had said, 'What nonsense! I shall get up when I like and eat what I choose,' and William Nesbitt was going home to see that she did not keep her word; but a glimpse of a terrace of old houses where Walter and Violet had their flat, inspired him to call there for a few minutes and show Violet by his unusual visit that he was grateful for her loyalty.

He had not been there since he had been invited to a family dinner-party soon after their marriage, and he kept an uncomfortable impression of overcrowding and upholstery and of the maid, closely hemmed in between chairs and walls, panting with agitation as she handed the dishes. He liked space, he liked order and dignity in a household, and soon after that party he had given Walter a bigger share of the firm's profits so that he might enlarge his boundaries if he chose, and though he had not done so, William Nesbitt felt that his responsibility in the matter was at an end. It was not his affair if they enjoyed living in a place like a bric-a-brac shop.

This afternoon, as soon as the door was opened, he knew that the little drawing-room already contained a visitor. The sound of a masculine voice was immediately audible and he wondered if he was to be plunged into another amorous affair, until, descrying a soft black hat on the hall table, he was reassured. Clergymen were privileged people and the maid, saying, 'It's only a reverend gentleman, sir,' he advanced without misgiving. But though it is wisdom to be bold, it is well to placate fortune with a realization of the latent power for mischief in the most innocent of men, and this William Nesbitt did not do. He entered without fear.

Violet's vicar, if she could be said to have one, was not Mrs. Nesbitt's vicar. This one was the incumbent of a church near the docks, a poor church, dealing as it best could with the poor and not too virtuous parish. His name was Jones and when he and William Nesbitt had been made known to one another, Violet explained the vicar's call. He was anxious to arrange a dramatic entertainment for his people, partly to raise funds for necessary repairs to the church roof, but more to provide amusement which had no connection with beer. He had been informed, here Mr. Jones himself broke in, that Mr. and Mrs. Walter Nesbitt might be able to help him: he had heard they were connected with a dramatic club.

'Good idea,' William Nesbitt said heartily. 'Keep them out of mischief.'

'Just so.' Mr. Jones leaned forward earnestly. 'These public-houses –'

'Ah, I was thinking of the members of the dramatic club. They do good by advertisement and would blush if it were not known.'

'Ha! ha!' Mr. Jones applauded the joke. 'But, seriously, this drink question is very grave.' This was his favourite topic and, starting at the canter, he was soon galloping away with it, while William Nesbitt, giving an occasional grunt of acquiescence, looked through the window, over the huddled roofs of the old city, the river and the docks, to the meadows which swept to a horizon where the spire of Easterly church stood up like a lighthouse in the sea and, down below, where the water shone, the masts and funnels of ships, moored alongside the warehouses, were like a leafless forest.

'And,' Mr. Jones was saying, 'it is as bad in the villages as in the towns. My son who is in the country, tells me the evil is very great there.'

'Dear me, dear me,' said William Nesbitt, twisting his watch-chain, and still fascinated by the sight of the shipping.

'Yes, he has been presented lately to the living of Mastover – '

William Nesbitt, losing his presence of mind, stared at the vicar in so astonished a manner that he repeated, 'Mastover, a little village in Somerset, a charming spot.'

'Yes, heard of it, heard of it,' William Nesbitt said. He glanced at Violet, but she gave no answering sign and he remembered that she did not know where Lydia had gone.

'Yes,' the vicar went on, 'a lonely little place, but welcome to my son who has had a curacy in the Midlands. He loves the West country.' And turning to Violet he said, 'Perhaps you have met him? No? But you know the Millers? Mr. Miller of the Museum? My son married his daughter Ethel.'

'No, I don't know her,' Violet said, 'but perhaps my sisters-in-law do.'

William Nesbitt said nothing. This was much worse than surprising Violet with a triangular young man: this, he thought emphatically, was the devil. Ethel Miller! Had he not told his wife it was foolish to make enemies? Mrs. Miller would be pleased when she heard the news, unless Ethel had the sense to hold her tongue. She had been fond of Lydia and she might be loyal, but it would be a severe test. She would blurt it all out before she had time to think – a great clumsy, blundering girl she had always been.

He said, stretching his legs after the acute tension they had suffered, 'Well, Violet, you must put your heads together. There's that play you did last winter – what was it? – some tomfoolery or other. And look here' – he had a contemptible but an uncontrollable impulse, – 'if there are any expenses, you can call on me. A lot of my people live down there.'

He rose and drifted towards the window, disgusted with himself, deaf to the enthusiasm of the vicar and to Violet's pretty thanks. Why had he said that? It was the blind instinct to bribe. The Nesbitts were to make a lot of money for the parson, so that the parson, in decency, must hold his peace. But, alas, the matter did not rest only with the parson. Nothing would save Lydia, he had sold himself uselessly and, filled with dismay at this unexpected revelation of himself, he looked down at the scene where he had achieved success without dishonour.

'A wonderful view,' Mr. Jones said pleasantly.

'Yes,' William Nesbitt answered. He fancied he could distinguish the grey roof of his offices: he doubted if the scene would ever seem so beautiful to him again, but once more he knew he was exaggerating. Ten to one, he would have offered that money in any case.

'Well, well,' he said when Mr. Jones had departed with renewed thanks, 'here's a pretty kettle of fish! It may interest you to know that Lydia is at Mastover.'

'Good Lord!' Violet said. 'I thought you seemed rather queer all of a sudden.'

'Think he noticed it? Perhaps not, but you know what parsons are – always ready to spread glad tidings. Yes, that Ethel girl went to school with Lydia, used to come to tea, tear up and down the stairs shrieking at Lydia's jokes, a good creature, but she's bound to talk and, unfortunately, my wife had a passage-of-arms with Ethel's mother, a few weeks ago. I knew it would lead to trouble, but I don't know that it makes much difference. A choice little piece of scandal like this would be too much of a temptation, anyhow. And my wife's ill. The doctor says she must not have any worry.'

'Good Lord!' Violet said again, and William Nesbitt thought with irritation, 'This woman has no vocabulary.'

'Well,' Violet said, 'we'll give the dramatic performance, we'll make money, we'll charm the vicar, and then – '

'Ah, yes, the same ignoble thought had occurred to me. No, my dear, we're in for a bad time, a bad time. I suppose,' he appealed, 'there's no chance of young Jones of Mastover not doing his duty and neglecting to call on his parishioners? But still, Lydia's bound to come across that girl, tramping through the lanes in thick shoes. I can't imagine her without her pigtail. It made you think of a cart-horse. There was some joke about it, too. I believe Lydia once tied it to Ethel's chair at school just when she had to go up to the mistress's desk to be told what a dunce she was, or something. She was nearly scalped, but she was a vigorous young person and I dare say the chair suffered more. Well, I must be going home.'

'I'm glad you came,' she said.

'Yes, forewarned is forearmed, I suppose. But what's the use of a pea-shooter against an elephant?'

'Oh, I didn't mean that. I meant I was glad to see you.'

'You've been very good over this business, my dear. It has been a comfort. Thank you. I'll drop in again, some day, and have a chat.'

'And we'll get on with the rehearsals.'

'Bribery and corruption! It won't do any good. Still, I always think a parson's fair game, somehow. Hate their black coats. Good-bye.'

Well, as he had told himself before, life was interesting, whatever else it might be, and he had told the truth when he said he was glad he was a father, even the father of a daughter who was to become a scandal. But he ought not to have qualified that joy. He was proud of her, whatever she did and whether she succeeded or failed. No doubt he was prejudiced, for he and she were, in some ways, akin, and he had a natural pleasure in seeing parts of himself repeated, developed or subdued in her. If he had been a woman he might have been such another, though his whimsicality would probably have saved him from the seriousness productive of an act which, in the eyes of the world, must seem light. That was the world's way! It took the thoughtless marriage of the very young for the sacred thing it could not be, and maturer love for reckless passion. But what were the springs of Lydia's action, he did not really know.

He found Dora in the morning-room, turning the leaves of a magazine.

'Mother's asleep,' she said, 'and Mabel went an hour ago. She poured a lot of eau-de-Cologne down Mother's neck.'

'What did she do that for?'

'Clumsiness. It was meant for her forehead. Since she nursed the boys through whooping-cough, she considers herself an experienced nurse and as the eldest daughter she thinks she's specially important. I don't know why. She had nothing to do with it. And, of course, she talked about Lydia. I used to think we were rather a nice family, but now I'm sure we are impossible. Everybody knows everybody else's business and nobody will be quiet.'

'Who has been worrying you?' he asked.

'I don't allow myself to be worried,' she said lightly.

'What fibs you women tell! I used,' he said, 'to think mine was a truthful family, but now I find it's full of prevaricators.'

'I never said people didn't try to worry me,' Dora replied, and quickly she added, 'Mabel was awful. I'm sick of hearing about those boys of hers. Haven't I children, too? Well, I suppose it will wear itself down. In time we shall get dulled. Time is a comfort, isn't it? You get into bed and tell yourself another day is over.'

'Is it as bad as that, poor Dora?'

'Well, I love Lydia,' she said shakily.

'I know, I know.'

And one sin, if it is a sin, doesn't make a sinner. Why, if my Meg committed every crime under the sun –'

'Quite so, but how would Herbert deal with her?'

'Herbert isn't her mother.'

'Oh, this fiction about mothers! I'm not a mother.'

'No, you're a darling. Well, it's no used talking about it. One can only say the same things over and over again, and end by keeping them to oneself.'

'The best thing to do,' he said, 'but really, if I'm not very careful, you'll see me on the Downs, one of these days, standing in a cart and talking about comparative morality. That would upset some of them more than Lydia's doings. It's worse to make a public fool of yourself than a public scandal.'

'But this needn't be public.'

'Don't deceive yourself. I begin to think God doesn't approve of matrimonial muddles, otherwise why should He have allowed that Ethel Miller to marry a man who becomes the vicar of Mastover, who happens to be the son of the vicar of St. George's, down by the docks, who happens to have involved Violet in a promise to entertain his parishioners? What do you think of that? The ways of Providence are inscrutable! But all the same, Dora,' he tapped the table with his forefinger, 'all the same, there's a reason in things. I'm not going to be daunted. If God arranges things in this awkward fashion, there must be sense in it. Otherwise –' his gesture signified chaos.

'We mustn't tell Mother.'

'No, someone else will do that. Where's Janet?'

'In the drawing-room giving tea to the doctor.'

'Giving tea to the doctor?'

'He came in just as it was ready, so, as Mother was asleep, Janet had to give him some.'

'Oh, quite right, quite right. But why aren't you there too?'

'I escaped when I heard the bell. I shall go in when they've finished and eat as much as I like at my leisure. It's queer how little impression food makes on your inside if you have to talk while you eat it and I need such a lot. But I wish they'd be quick. He has been here nearly an hour already.'

'Shall I go and rescue the child?'

'I think,' Dora said dryly, 'Janet is quite equal to rescuing herself if she wants to. Let the young things have their talk.'

'Young! He's middle-aged and desiccated! His very name's dry and powdery! "Gregory," that's his name. Gregory powder!'

'Well, anyhow, it reminds one of one's youth,' she said, with a reminiscent grimace. 'Leave them alone. I expect he is enjoying looking at Janet.'

'I dare say he is, but that's no reason why I should let him.'

'And Janet is enjoying being looked at.'

'Ah, well, that's different. That may be a good thing,' and flashing a keen glance at her, he asked, 'Would you call him an attractive man?'

'I told you I escaped when I heard the bell. I've never seen him, but I gather he must be – or very hungry. Are you afraid of losing your baby, just because she's giving the man tea? Well, I can't bear to think of my own children getting husbands and wives. It ought not to be allowed. But I'm sure Janet isn't a susceptible young person.'

'No, I wish she were,' and, as he saw a lively interest in her eyes, he added quickly, 'It's normal, it's healthy. She's too quiet.'

'Yes, she's very quiet,' Dora said slowly and he wondered how much she knew or guessed. There was a pause and then he said, 'I suppose I must go and speak to him.'

'And I must be going home. I've lost my tea and I mustn't be late for dinner.'

'No, don't be late for dinner. Keep your wheels well oiled.'

She would not respond to his allusions but, laughing a little, she kissed him and tapped his cheek lightly as though in mockery of his notions.

Chapter 21

A FEW days later, and for the second time in her life, Mrs. Nesbitt ran away from home, but as she had little hope of returning that night, she left a note for William, telling him she had gone to Mastover. She was better and, though she had failed with Oliver, she had to carry out her plan which was to deal first with Oliver, then with Lydia, and, if she failed again, she could the sooner settle into her new circumstances, adjust her life, her conversation, her expression, perhaps even her views to necessity. She could not endure uncertainty and, while she suffered from suspense and nervousness on her journey, she was conscious of immediate relief in action. She was strengthened, too, by her opinion that William had behaved with a great lack of authority, a grave indifference in this matter, and she would tell him so when he scolded her for disobeying the doctor who was not, in any case, a person to whom Mrs. Nesbitt meant to pander, a dry man, with no amenity of manner.

The journey was a slow one. Country people with bulky parcels got in and out at every station, talked of crops, of marriages and deaths, nodded and shook their heads a great deal. Few of them had many teeth, but their faces were cheerful and Mrs. Nesbitt could not believe that any one of them had ever had a trouble like her own. She watched them, for some time, from this aspect, but gradually her interest in them gave way to dislike of their proximity. She had taken a third-class ticket to be sure of company and she had too much of it. Children stood on the carriage floor and leaned against her; an old man spat: a basket, containing a supply of fish, separated her narrowly from her neighbour, and with this smell was mingled that of fusty clothes and beer. Moreover, in spite of the guard's assurances, she was afraid she was in the wrong train. It went very slowly, jogging through green meadows, orchards where the apples were yellow and crimson in the trees; others, where the fruit had all been gathered for the cider press; little houses washed with pink or cream, grey churches, a glimpse of high, black moorland, woods, and streams and ditches of sluggish water edged with willows, that strangely peaceful country which has something ineradicably wild in its heart.

In and out, out and in, went the passengers, with more bundles and more babies. Friends hailed each other on the platforms, porters recognized acquaintances, station-masters had plenty of time to chat and to answer Mrs. Nesbitt's persistent inquiries as to her destination. She had to change at a little junction and get into another train, smaller and slower than the first, with more gnarled old men whose faces were like the sticks on which they leaned, and more women laden with household stores; but at length her fellow-travellers assured the lady that this was Mastover.

She felt very lonely, and when the train had puffed out of sight it seemed as though she had lost a friend. The place was solitary. From the platform she could see a few cottages, a great expanse of meadows and, far away, the soft curve of hills. It was already the late afternoon and soon darkness would be upon her, here in an unknown land, with the unknown before her. Yet, in spite of her mission, she thought of Lydia with longing, some one she knew, some one with whom, physically at least, she would be safe. The air was chilly and she drew her fur wrap round her and searched for some sign of a habitation which might hold her daughter. It was not in sight. There were only the scattered cottages and the miles of grass and, standing there, she remembered how once she had gone to meet William at Rotterdam and had arrived in a foreign country, without a word of the language, and Mabel, a baby, in the arms of a scared young nursemaid, and found no William waiting for her. She had been cold, then, and lonely, but young and full of spirit and happy in the anticipation of seeing William after months of separation; and, presently, when she had waited miserably at the docks, he had appeared and taken her to the lodgings he had found for her, where a stove glowed warmly, a table was set for supper and his bags lay about the room in an untidy homeliness. The memory of that glowing stove and the comfort of his presence came to her now with the sweetness of a past in which there were no troubles greater than those of parting.

But the high spirit of her youth had not entirely left her: she had work to do, and she addressed the station-master who, indeed, had been looking with some curiosity at this well-dressed lady.

She wanted a carriage, she told him, to take her to The Grange. There was no carriage to be had near the station. Up at the public-house, three miles away, there was one for hire, but here there was but the trap and that was not available, and the station-master told her it would not have suited her at all – a ramshackle affair. However, the carrier's cart was just leaving and as it had some packages to deliver at The Grange, Mrs. Nesbitt could be carried with them for a shilling.

'I hope your horse is quiet,' she said with dignity to the driver when she was perched on the seat beside him.

'Quiet enough, M'm,' he replied, leaving her in doubt as to what he meant.

He was not a talkative man, but he seemed respectable. He had courteously knocked out the ashes of his pipe and now he sucked it empty until, feeling that she must propitiate the being on whom her life and safety depended, she asked him to light it again.

'I get through a deal of "bacca," ' he said with a sigh, and he dropped the reins while he attended to his pipe.

The horse went steadily, rarely breaking into a trot, for the road mounted as soon as it left the flat meadows and took to the woods. It mounted and wound its way through oaks and pines whose shade encouraged the oncoming darkness. The world was very still and the horse and cart seemed to be the only things moving in it. The man puffed slowly, the horse's hoofs beat out a sort of tune, the wheels creaked, the miscellaneous goods under the tilt stirred mysteriously, now and then, as though to ease themselves. Once, from the edge of the wood, a man emerged with a gun over his shoulder and stood to watch their passage.

'Squire's keeper,' the carter said. 'Never has a word to throw at a man – trappin' – killin' – '

Mrs. Nesbitt peered round the hood and saw the figure standing there unmoved, like one of the trees, but more sinister.

'Is it much farther?' she asked, but the carter's thoughts travelled slowly.

'Pretty near killed a poacher once, he did, with 'is own hands. He's got a grip on him – '

Mrs. Nesbitt shivered. 'Are we nearly there?'

He pointed with his whip. 'Wyatt's chimneys,' he said, and after creaking up a narrow lane, so rough that Mrs. Nesbitt with difficulty kept herself from falling on the carter, they turned sharply and stopped at a wooden gate. He helped her down, she pulled her skirt into place and, drawing a deep breath, she followed a little winding path to the door.

The door stood open. The man, carrying the parcels, called out loudly, 'Hi, Mr. Wyatt, summat for ye!' There was no sound.

'Perhaps if you knocked – ' Mrs. Nesbitt suggested timidly.

Still there was no answer. 'Must be out,' he said. 'I'll just drop the parcels inside. Good-night, M'm.'

She gave him half-a-crown because he had been civil, and stretched her ears for the friendly sound of his departing footsteps, the creaking of the cart and the clip-clop of the horse's hoofs. She heard the grinding of the brakes as the cart went down the lane.

It was almost dark. The larches stood dark and silent, the narrow hall was dark. She was afraid of staying in the garden, she was afraid of entering the house. She was afraid, too, of her errand but, stepping over the threshhold, she called tremulously, 'Lydia, are you there?' and was startled by the sound of her own voice.

Perhaps this was the wrong house – but then the carter had brought her here. Perhaps, and this was possible, Lydia was not here at all. She took a few steps forward and discerned a dull glow issuing from an open door. Someone lived here and she thought, oddly but without amusement, of the three bears. 'Who's been sitting in my chair?' she said inwardly, as she advanced.

There was a fire in the grate, a kettle on the hob, and the table was set for tea. 'Who's been eating my porridge?' came like an echo into Mrs. Nesbitt's mind. She stood in this strange room, holding her breath, and then, slowly, groping in the dim light, she made her way to the window. If no one came, though surely some one was coming, what should she do, alone in this dark house with the still country round her like a barrier, shutting her in, keeping others out? Yet was everybody out? The house was gradually becoming filled with little noises, faint stirrings, perhaps sighs. She was stiff with fear and she could not turn her head, she could only look out on the little lawn and the larch trees and wait for something to spring on her from behind. A tramp – a dog – the door was open to the oncoming night.

She forgot her angry sorrow: she actually longed for the sight of Henry Wyatt, and if he had ever wanted a hearty welcome, he had it when at last she saw him emerging from the larches. She saw him, obviously no tramp, with a gasp of inexpressible relief and a slackening of her tense muscles which was like pain. She saw him stand for an instant on the grass before he slipped back into the screen of trees, as though they had put out their hands to draw him in.

Mrs. Nesbitt's heart sank. This could not be Henry Wyatt, hiding in his own trees: this must be a burglar reconnoitring the place, one of those gentlemanly burglars of whom she had read in monthly magazines. Well, she would give him her rings: she would give him her money if he would promise not to molest her: in fact, she would be thankful for his company, but she had hardly had time to make this decision before she saw Lydia, fleet and light of foot, flash from the trees, calling, 'Henry!' in a ringing voice. The next moment her daughter was in the arms of the man, who left his hiding-place with a spring, and the nature of his embrace was so violent, so unlike anything Mrs. Nesbitt had experienced herself or even seen on the stage, that she closed her eyes in a face hot with shame. When she opened them, the two were strolling easily across the grass, and between anger and relief, the desire to expostulate and the joy of having human neighbourhood, she tottered to the door and stood in the passage.

'Lydia!' she cried out in a bleating voice.

There was a silence and, though she could not see them, Mrs. Nesbitt imagined those two arrested by her cry, guiltily abashed. Perhaps Lydia thought it was her mother's tortured spirit calling to her across the country.

'Lydia!' Mrs. Nesbitt repeated, more loudly and firmly, and Lydia entered the passage.

'Mother, is that you? I can't see you. Henry, get a light.'

She advanced and took Mrs. Nesbitt's hand. 'Come in here,' she said.

'Oh, my child,' Mrs. Nesbitt sobbed dryly. 'My child!' She suffered herself to be led into the firelit room and put into a chair, the bear's chair in which she had been afraid to sit, and Lydia knelt before the fire to stir it. Then that man entered, carrying a lamp, and Lydia, rising, said, 'Henry, this is my mother.'

He bowed gravely and she sat motionless. She would not look at him, but she was conscious of the physical power of his build, more conscious still of the moral power of his presence. She tried to ignore him, but he made her nervous and only the strength of her anger preserved her impassive dignity. She had thought it terrible enough to talk to Oliver, as though she soiled her lips in doing it, but this – this was a nightmare of incongruity, shame, and confusion: it was – she found the word – an outrage, and under it she was helpless. She had to sit there while Henry asked her courteously about her journey as though she were a welcome guest: she had to admit the absurdity of the carrier's cart: she expected and half hoped Lydia would laugh, but she had already found that her daughter was not humorously inclined on these occasions, and all she said was, 'If you had let us know, we would have met you with a cab.'

Let them know! Yes, indeed, she was helpless, a victim of the situation into which she had thrust herself.

'Lydia,' Henry said, 'aren't you going to make the tea?'

'Oh, but do warm the pot, dear,' Mrs. Nesbitt said hastily, and immediately stiffened herself after this natural outburst.

'It has been standing on the hearth for hours,' Lydia said dreamily, 'all the time we were out.'

'And you hadn't a hat on.' Once more, very angry with herself, she stiffened, but how hard it was to remember that the slim figure in the purple dress, with a bunch of scarlet berries in her belt – and how like her to have chosen that brilliant scarlet to put against the purple, – must be treated as worse than a stranger, and how could she be treated like that, when her mother meant to drink some of her tea? She could not resist it. She was tired, her head was aching again: she could not tackle this problem without support: it was her duty to drink it and, having settled that point, she could take her cup from Henry with a clear conscience.

'Oh, we don't wear hats in Mastover,' Lydia said. 'And, Mother, why will you always wear yours half an inch too far back? Last time you came to see me I had to put it right. Now, let me show you – '

'Don't touch it!' Mrs. Nesbitt said sharply, and putting down her cup with a shaking hand, she added, 'I must speak to you.'

Lydia's voice was gentle. 'Won't you have some more tea first? Then, Henry, as you haven't finished yours, Mother and I will go into the other room.' She took a candle from the mantelshelf and stood before him. 'A light, please.'

Over the flame of the match as he steadied it, she smiled at him as Mrs. Nesbitt had never seen her smile before.

Chapter 22

LYDIA put the candlestick on the round table which was draped with a drab and patterned cover. The slender flame wavered and then stood straight, leaving in darkness the book-shelves, the engravings, and the photographs of Henry's relatives: only the large oval of Mrs. Nesbitt's face and her body from the waist upwards were clear to Lydia and, from the other side of the table, Mrs. Nesbitt stared at the thin shape of her daughter, the berries in her belt, the white neck supporting her small, dark head.

'Perhaps we had better sit down,' Lydia said. Her loosely clasped hands rested on the table and she waited for her mother to speak.

Mrs. Nesbitt impatiently looked from side to side into the shadows. She could find no words. Nothing could have expressed her feelings except a growl, like a dog's, for there was no sign of shame or sorrow on Lydia's face, and only the inarticulate could have met Mrs. Nesbitt's need. Anger, disgust, but chiefly helplessness ached for an outlet and she had to sit there, trembling, under the roof of that man. If the child had wept, if she had asked for caresses, Mrs. Nesbitt would have held out her arms and wept with her, but she merely waited, patiently, almost smiling, and it occurred to Mrs. Nesbitt that, at the moment, Lydia and Oliver were very much alike.

'I have come to take you home,' she began, in the voice of her anger.

'To Radstowe?'

'Yes, and then to Oliver.' Lydia said nothing. She looked down at her hands: there was no ring on them and Mrs. Nesbitt remembered that other visit and how her hands had been ringless then.

'Can we go to-night?' Mrs. Nesbitt asked.

'No, you can't go to-night.'

'Then where,' Mrs. Nesbitt demanded, 'am I to sleep?'

'In Mrs. Wyatt's bedroom.'

'Mrs. Wyatt?' Relief flooded her, explained Lydia's attitude, ignored facts.

'Henry's mother.'

'Is she here? Here? Then how – ? Oh, Lydia, Lydia!' Tears came into Mrs. Nesbitt's eyes.

'No, no, Mother, she is dead. But there is still her room.'

The tears, two of them, fell on to Mrs. Nesbitt's cheeks: she took out her handkerchief to wipe them away before they fell into her neck, and there were no more. 'Then, to-morrow morning, we will go by the first train.'

'Mother dear – '

'No,' Mrs. Nesbitt said, 'if I had been dear to you this would not have happened. I don't know how you dare look at me, speak to me – '

'It was you,' Lydia said quietly, 'who chose to come here.'

'To save you,' Mrs. Nesbitt cried, 'if it is not too late.'

'Oh, yes, it's too late,' Lydia said. 'No one can save one except oneself.'

'And you don't want to do that,' Mrs. Nesbitt said in her low, threatening voice.

'If I knew what saving was – ' Lydia murmured.

Paying no heed to that, Mrs. Nesbitt said mournfully, 'I have tried to make excuses for you. I believe Oliver has driven you to this.'

'That isn't true,' Lydia said with her first sign of heat.

Grandly ignoring the interruption, Mrs. Nesbitt went on: 'But with all the excuses in the world, this is sin. Sin! What were you thinking of? How could you – how could you dream of such wickedness? I knew my children were self-willed, but I thought they were all good. And here are you – I don't understand it. What have I done to deserve this? The whole family – And there is Dora – '

'Dora?' Lydia asked quickly with a sudden alertness, as though the thought of Dora really touched her.

178

'She was talking of Herbert as though he is of no account,' Mrs. Nesbitt announced ponderously.

'Then,' Lydia said, 'she is talking of him as he is.'

'He is her husband. She has her duty. But what is the good of talking about duty to you?'

'None,' Lydia said. 'None at all. I wish you had not come, Mother.'

'No doubt, but you were not to be let off so easily. You have to see what you have done and if I cannot persuade you to come back with me, I can at least – But no,' she whispered to the shadows in an overwhelming sense of her impotence, 'I can't. I must go back without her, I must face everybody, I must begin again.' And suddenly, in tones near a shriek, she cried, 'You sit there and say nothing!'

'Nothing,' Lydia repeated sadly.

'And Oliver was the same, sitting, smiling, moving his hands, and then went off without saying good-bye to me!'

'When,' Lydia asked with an eagerness which was determined to be answered, 'did Oliver do that?'

'Yesterday, no, a few days ago, I don't know. I have been ill and I forget, but that does not matter to you.'

'I am sorry you have been ill,' Lydia said gently. 'But how did you happen to see Oliver?'

'I sent for him. Do you think I could sit idle, like your father, and do nothing? Shrug my shoulders, as though you were a stranger?'

'Ah, poor William,' Lydia said softly, 'and poor Oliver.' She leaned forward, smiling at the thought of them both. 'Did Oliver see William?'

'No, he did not, but he saw Janet.' That incident which had so much impressed Mrs. Nesbitt forced into volubility. 'She came into the room and they both just disappeared, without a word. He never said good-bye, but he went with her.'

Looking down at the ugly table cover, Lydia said, 'And poor Jane.'

'But not poor Mother,' Mrs. Nesbitt said. 'And Oliver smiled, as you do, and said nothing, and went away.'

'What did you want him to do?'

'To come here with me and bring you home.'

'That was asking a good deal, wasn't it?'

'I was asking, I had to ask, what any ordinary man would have done of his own accord.'

'But Oliver isn't ordinary.'

'He is mad. You are all mad, or wicked, or both. Lydia,' she begged, her lips trembling, 'think of your sisters, your little nephews and nieces, all the people we know. How am I to face them all? I shall be ashamed to leave the house. Won't you come back? No one need know. Won't you come back for my sake?'

Lydia stood up. 'If I could do that now, I shouldn't have come here at all. Do you think it's easy, this? You don't know, you simply don't know how hard it is. If I ever left Henry,' her voice softened at his name, 'it would be my own doing.'

Hardening again, Mrs. Nesbitt said, 'And then it would be too late.'

'Yes, for you, but not for me. Listen! What's that?'

It was the sound of a motor car labouring up the lane, and Mrs. Nesbitt, with prescience, said, 'It must be your father. Thank God, it is your father!'

Shutting the door on Mrs. Nesbitt, Lydia ran out into the night.

The two big eyes of the car glared into the darkness, and in the golden mist they made William Nesbitt saw his daughter, waved a hand to her and continued to count out money and talk to the driver. Then he said, 'Well, child, that's an awful road of yours. Why don't you have something done to it? All right, driver. Ten o'clock to-morrow morning. Good-night. Is your mother here? Don't flatter yourself. I've really come after her.'

'I know, but still you are here and that's what matters.'

'And nearly killed myself doing it. You must have that road seen to – rocks all over it. I can't think how your mother got here.'

'In the carrier's cart,' Lydia said. 'Put down your little

bag, William dear, and just walk with me for a few minutes along the road. I do love the night. And then you can talk to Mother while I make her bed. She wanted to go home to-night, but there's no train.'

'No, I got that car from the Junction – only way to get here – and it will take us back there to-morrow. I'm worried about your mother, Lydia. She has been ill. She ought not to have come here. And what is she doing now? Sitting by the light of a single candle?'

'Yes, how did you know that?'

'Ah, my child,' he said, 'trust your father.'

'Haven't I shown I trust you?'

'Yes, my dear. I know your words by heart.'

They walked slowly along the road. On their left was the house set in the shelter of its trees and on their right was the dark bulk of a steeply rising field. The autumn colours of the country were drenched and hidden by the night and the smell of burning wood, pungent yet delicate, crept on the still air. There were no sounds but those of their own footsteps until a dog barked and somewhere, a long way off, the whistle of a train pierced the stillness with defiance.

'What has your mother been saying to you?' he asked.

'Oh, William, not with you. I don't want to talk about it with you. Let's enjoy being together and not speaking. I wish you and I could live here for a few weeks, walking through the fields and saying nothing. I'm tired. Let me hold your hand.'

'My dear – '

'Yes, I know. We know.' And then, although she had said she did not want to talk, she began again. 'It's such a hard-worked word that it almost means nothing, but if you pretend you've never heard it before it's nice to look at and to hear. Sympathy, I mean. The thing you have, William, and Oliver.'

'And you.'

'Oh, yes, I have it, too, but I'm so steeped in myself just now – '

'I thought you were steeped in Henry's mother.'

'Now, you can't have guessed that!'

'No, Oliver let me see your letter.'

'That was nice of him. Then you know all about her. I don't know what she can have thought of my interview with my own mother. I couldn't say a word – a word. You know how you get frozen! I'm just beginning to thaw, because you're genial.'

'I'm afraid,' he said, 'I never get frozen to that extent. I can't help talking. And now I must go and talk to your mother – not an easy task, though, this time.'

'I'm sorry, William – I wish – ' but she did not say what she wished and, interpreting her silence at a venture, he said: 'But your doors are not shut.'

'Ah, if they were material doors, how easy it would be! One could kick or hammer or just acquiesce.'

'Then they are shut.'

'I haven't said so.'

'It isn't what you and I say to each other that matters, my dear. Yet I'll say this. I'm curious to see your Henry but I don't want to meet him. Is there a handy keyhole?'

He felt, through the darkness, her change of attitude. 'If you choose to come to his house – '

'Oh, I realize the weakness of my position. I shall not throw things about. But it's difficult. How can I be loyal to your mother and to you at the same time?'

'I don't know, William, but you'll find out.'

He was cheered by this assurance, but for an instant he faltered before the rigid figure of his wife. This was the woman with whom he had lived for years and the pity he felt for her was utterly detached; he saw her fixed, swollen face, her hard eyes, as though they belonged to a stranger who was in trouble and he wondered whether he loved Lydia too much or Kate too little.

'My dear,' he began and, realizing that, at the moment, the words came of mere habit, he stopped, horrified at himself and aghast at the power of circumstances. 'Sit down, Kate,' he said.

She moved her head slowly from side to side. 'Take me out of this house,' she said and she seemed to speak without moving a muscle of her face.

'You must stay until to-morrow morning,' he said gently, and then, looking round him, he said impatiently, 'What darkness!'

'It is all she deserves,' came hollowly from that wooden image barred by the table.

'Perhaps – perhaps,' he agreed. 'But how unpleasant for her visitors!'

'Visitors!' she echoed and he glanced at her as though surprised at the range of speech possessed by this mechanism which was like a caricature of Kate, yet he could not help retorting, 'What else are we? Kate, do sit down.'

'Such dreadful chairs,' she murmured. Their twisted legs, their hard seats, showed dimly in the gloom, consciously uninviting, as though they understood the situation.

'Yes, dreadful, but they can be sat on. My dear!' he exclaimed and went towards her, for she had swayed a little, 'I'm afraid you will fall. Sit there. You must go to bed. There's no train till the morning. You will have to put up with it. Now, sit still, Kate, and I'll get you to bed.'

He went into the passage and shut the door. The opposite door was outlined with light as though it were set in a gilded frame, and for a moment William Nesbitt stood staring at it. Behind it were Lydia and her lover, at his back was the room enclosing Kate and, though he tried to control his sense of humour and to encourage himself in the conventions, he was not very successful, and above his own distress, which was genuine, he had the conviction that this affair had not the faintest colouring of immorality. He saw it, stripped of all falseness, all habits of mind and all accepted safeguards, as a painful attempt after truth and beauty and as, on Lydia's part, in no sense a striving after happiness. She was not happy: she had not even the consolation of a righteous sorrow: she was groping through a darkness typified by the ill-lighted house and the still country outside, and no doubt her mother thought she was rioting in sin! He smiled: he sighed: he felt all the impatience of his superior knowledge; then, making an effort to be practical, he called loudly for Lydia.

She slipped into the passage, giving him a glimpse of a glowing fire, and stood, almost unseen, in the gilded frame. They could discern each other's pale faces and hands, and slowly their bodies became visible. They spoke in whispers and the darkness of the passage seemed to hold them in a secret pact.

'Your mother must go to bed.'

'Her room is ready. I'll show it to you.'

He followed her up the stairs. He tapped the wall. 'You ought to have a bracket here with a lamp on it. It's a good solid wall. Well-built house, I should think. And one on the landing. Awful darkness, this.'

Yes, but I like it and lamps are such messy things. I didn't come here,' he heard her laugh, 'to trim oil lamps.'

'You'll break your neck.'

Ahead of him, on the landing, her voice fluttered out, 'Oh, well, William, that would be very neat.'

He felt a dreadful pang, but when he faced her in the firelit bedroom she was smiling vividly. 'But I don't really want to break my neck,' she said, 'and get into the papers. I want to see this out. You know, it's an adventure. Light those candles, please. This is Mrs. Wyatt's bedroom. I'm sorry there's only one bed, but it's large. There's another little room, though – '

'Oh, no, my dear, not at this juncture.'

'I thought not. Well, it really is a very large bed, but they always sag in the middle, don't they? Much might be written about beds. I believe Henry was born in that one and now you and Mother are going to lie awake in it. Life is queer.'

'But interesting,' he insisted.

'Oh, interesting, yes, if one could just be a watcher. Look, I've put these photographs of Mrs. Wyatt for you to see. This one, when she's young and innocent, but wise. And this one with Henry on her knee, such an ugly baby, but she think's he's sweet. I like her long nose. She must have been a wit, and she spent nearly all her life in this house with Henry's dreary father.'

'But I suppose Henry is not dreary?'

'Not a bit,' she said, with a gesture which waved him out of consideration. 'How did she bear it? But then, she had Henry. You know,' she glanced behind her, 'I feel she's here, all the time, neither cruel nor kind, just watchful and impartial. I'm not sure that she won't drive me out of the house.'

'Well, if you should ever want an excuse,' he said slowly, 'she would be as good as anything else,' and refusing to meet her eyes which might have been indignant or, perhaps, startled, though this was not likely, he added, 'The good general always prepares his retreats.'

'Ah,' she mocked, and now he saw that her eyes were lighted by merriment and appreciation, 'how clever you are, William dear!'

'So my children are always telling me,' he retorted with satisfaction.

Chapter 23

THAT satisfaction was one of the few gleams in what he was to remember as a general darkness, a material darkness, in the house, pierced by candle flames, warmed by fire glow, relieved by the voice, the movements of his daughter, and the mental darkness of his own uncertainties and her distress – though this gloom was shot by the colour of her presence and the consciousness of the love (whether stable or instable he did not know) existing between her and Henry Wyatt. He had never felt less joy in her company, but he knew he could have felt it fully if it had not been for the other presence of his wife.

The night spent in the big bed had been like a nightmare through which he had not slept: Kate had moaned in her sleep, dragging from him in her unconsciousness the loving pity he had not been able to give her when her obduracy faced him. The width of Mrs. Wyatt's bed was no compensation for its hardness, and William Nesbitt's bones ached with the contact, his ears ached under the sounds of Kate's distress, his eyes stared into the room where, when the fire had died down, the bulky furniture made thick blots on the thinning darkness.

In the room below, there was a murmur of voices for a long time, then the sound of ascending footsteps and o doors opened and shut. Outside, owls squeaked and hooted, the trees swung together in a chant and William Nesbitt had an absurd, childish feeling of loneliness and neglect. He envied Lydia and her lover an experience he had never had and the potentialities of his youth mocked the achievement of his age. It seemed to him that Lydia's acquaintance with passion must heavily weight the scales against her griefs, but what, he asked himself, did he know of that except through her? Here she was again, showing him yet another thing he had desired and missed in life: he had seen her looking at Henry, speaking to him in a way no woman had ever used to him, and he had felt himself even now capable of inspiring and receiving such tributes. And here was Kate, who had always been good and loyal and loving, lying exhausted by her sorrow while he indulged these faithless thoughts. They were beyond her imagination and he was glad of it though her limitations were the cause of them, and he was a foolish old man, pretending he had qualities he did not possess, forgetting all his blessings, allowing himself to be depressed by conventions and frightened by owls. This was how he rebuked himself, but his real trouble lay in the future and, as though by watching he could discover and perhaps prevent the evil it might hold, he did not try to capture sleep. For Lydia's sake he kept his vigil and saw the recurring symbol of morning conquering night and responded hopefully.

It was later, when he and his wife sat silent in the motor car, stood on the platform of the little junction and again sat, still silent, in the train, that the remembered events of the last fifteen hours swept over him like a storm in which he had lost his courage and his dignity. The indignity of the situation had been forced on him and his cowardice had been concealed, but they had their effect in an inward state of irritation with himself, with Lydia's Henry and with Kate. Their departure had been made ridiculous by Kate's refusal to see her daughter again. She had remained in the bedroom, rejecting food, until the arrival of the car, when he had been obliged to clear the passage and escort her forth. It had been necessary to do this without apology or comment, but he had suffered from the absurdity of this stealthy conduct and still more from the knowledge that it must seem not only absurd, but discourteous and even vulgar to the man whose house they had invaded.

William Nesbitt's pride was injured, but he said nothing. Kate would have told him that his standard of manners was higher than that of his morals though, he consoled himself, she would not have put it quite so neatly, and his only retort would have been that he had definite ideas of the first and uncertain ones of the second. He could not accuse Henry Wyatt of sin. It seemed to him that Lydia was excuse enough, if excuse were needed, and he realized that for her the man's obvious power and intellect were a satisfaction she could not find in Oliver. Moreover, he was the unknown, like a strange country in which there was a constant element of danger: he had to be explored and that exploration would be the work of a perilous lifetime. Lydia not only liked, but positively needed excitement, and though Oliver, too, like every human being, could supply some mystery, it was the mystery of a twilight landscape, with undulating meadows, dim woods, and trickling streams, from which there might come a stealthy danger but no sudden one, a calm mystery so indecipherable that it must be at last ignored. But in this new journey there would be shocks for Lydia: her country would not offer easy travelling: she would have to force or persuade her loyalty to the acceptance of hard things; but if he knew her and read Henry aright, that loyalty would be stiffened. The harder the better, he thought: the more Henry demanded, and it was evident that he would demand much, the more she would feel her action justified. Oliver had been too soft: asking so little, he had lost all and, comparing the two men free from new prejudices, William Nesbitt had to admit that Lydia's second choice was better than her first.

He had spent an hour or two with Lydia and her lover after he had put Kate to bed. They had talked in undertones that she might not be disturbed, they had been silent without embarrassment, and he had found himself strangely at ease in his company. Henry Wyatt was the least self-conscious person he had ever met. There had been no attempt at explanation, excuse or propitiation: within the limits of courtesy, he seemed utterly indifferent to the impression he was making, and this childlikeness

– which no doubt had its drawbacks in considerable selfishness – must have a strong appeal for a woman without children, mixed as it was with a virility which offered homage while it claimed service.

These were his thoughts, but Kate's he could not divine, and though he was attentive to her in little ways, settling her comfortably in her corner of the carriage, opening or shutting windows at her wish, even commenting on the loveliness of the October morning, he found it impossible to get into closer touch with her. There was a subtle change in her face: it was composed and its hardness had a different quality: there was no bewilderment and no horror in it now, and he guessed that she had come to some decision which was immovable, though when she had made it he did not know. Perhaps, after all, she had not slept all night, perhaps she had thought he did and had tried to spare him and, responsive as he always was to tenderness, he leaned across the railway carriage and put a hand on her knee, saying kindly, 'My poor girl, you must go to bed when you get home. This has been too much for you.'

'No,' she said firmly, 'not too much. It has to be borne.'

He looked out of the window at the autumn colours, the bare fields showing a richness of dark earth, the drifts of leaves round the tree trunks, the shrivelled bracken, the stretches of heather with its purple faded, the willows, like beings enchanted into odd shapes to guard the sluggish streams, the last wild flowers of the year, the hay stacked for the winter, all gilded by a sun without warmth, and the beauty and the meaning of it all slipped over him like a blessing and a reassurance.

'All this,' he said aloud, yet to himself, 'all this comes and goes, but it endures. We have to see ourselves as part of it. Things live, droop, rot, and perish, but they return. There is no end to it all.'

'There is no end to trouble once begun,' Mrs. Nesbitt said.

'No,' he agreed placidly, 'but it may take a turning we don't expect.'

'It will,' Mrs. Nesbitt prophesied deeply. 'You are not the man I thought you, William.'

'My dear, I can well believe it.'

'But one can get used to anything.'

'I can't get used to your thinking badly of me, Kate. Try not to do that.'

'How can I help it?' she cried. 'You have never said a single word of blame.'

'How can I say what I don't feel?' he asked.

'I have known you do it very often,' she replied with the sharpness which never failed to please him, and yet to hurt him with its glimpse of what their companionship might have been if she had developed her latent wit. 'Often,' she repeated, 'but not about Lydia. Lydia has special treatment. The whole world can suffer if Lydia is spared.'

'But she isn't spared,' he said with an immense patience and then, pleadingly, he added, 'Kate, even if we are not united in this matter, let us try to appear so.'

'That is what I intend,' she said and, settling back into her corner, she shut her eyes.

This, he thought, was interesting: she was yielding, not to him but to necessity, and though the outward result might be the same, he feared their inner harmony had gone for ever: perhaps it had never really existed but circumstances had been kind and intruded no jarring notes: now they had come and the pleasant tinkle of their lives was disturbed with discord of Lydia's making, and because it was Lydia's, he found it hard to decide that it must be overcome. All she gave was good to him, his love could receive sorrow as well as joy, and though for a moment he wished he had not seen her in Mastover, preferring his imagined picture to the actual one, each added mile of distance from that scene restored his vision of her in its true proportions. He saw her, as it were, inviolable: surrounded by this or that, approached, threatened, but never touched. She held herself in safety by some strange power of her own and he could do nothing for her. It was Kate who needed him, although she did not know it, and Janet whose course he could help to steer. His optimism returned. He had wooed Kate easily enough in their youth: he would win her again now that age and trouble had made the task more difficult, and with curiosity he looked forward to developments. But a thought sprang into his head. He slapped his thigh fiercely and Kate opened her eyes. He had forgotten to warn Lydia about Ethel Miller.

'Have you killed a wasp?' Mrs. Nesbitt asked. 'They are very dangerous at this time of year.'

'I've just missed doing it, my dear.'

'Where is it?'

He looked round the carriage, at the window, under the seat. 'I can't see it,' he said. 'As a matter of fact, Kate, it was a figurative wasp. I was thinking of Mrs. Miller.'

'I can't see any likeness between them,' Mrs. Nesbitt said, 'except, perhaps, her waist. Her figure is ridiculous.'

'A wasp has a sting and, unlike the useful bee, it does not hurt itself when it uses it – probably enjoys it. So will she.'

'She would if she knew how to do it, but she doesn't.'

'I'm afraid of that woman since you offended her, Kate.'

'I am not afraid of her,' Mrs. Nesbitt replied at her most superb.

'Because you don't know that unfortunately her daughter Ethel is married to the vicar of Mastover.'

Mrs. Nesbitt's colour deepened. 'Did Lydia tell you that?'

'I'm afraid Lydia doesn't know, but she'll meet Ethel one of these days, marching about with good words and a laden basket. Yes, they'll meet and Ethel will be delighted to see her friend. I can picture her, standing four-square to all the winds that blow, for she hasn't her mother's wasp-like figure, beaming with health and joy, kissing Lydia, talking hard, asking after Oliver – '

'William,' Mrs. Nesbitt demanded, 'have you no feelings at all?'

'Too many, Kate, and still more imagination. I beg your pardon. I had to warn you that the news would spread to Mrs. Miller.'

'When did you learn this and how?'

He told her and then, seeing that she was more troubled than her pride wished him to know, he said, 'Now, Kate, don't worry. We can weather this storm, if it comes, together, as we have weathered them before now.'

'But they were not like this,' she murmured and, united in their old memories of wind and sea, she allowed him to take her hand.

'No, they were fine, and so were you, dear. You never flinched.'

'I am not flinching now, William.'

'I know that, and as we're alone in the carriage don't you think you might kiss me?'

She offered him her cheek. It was very hot and he was glad of the tremor of anxiety which ran through him at its touch.

Chapter 24

MRS. NESBITT allowed herself to be put to bed. The sight of her own home with its white paint and shining windows and the dahlias and chrysanthemums in the flower-beds, the sight of Janet's golden head and calm face, were like the peace of open spaces after the tumult of a crowd, and the longing for cool linen sheets and the comfort of her own bed swamped her determination not to give way.

'Get the doctor,' William Nesbitt said to Janet.

'I don't think it's necessary,' she replied. 'All she wants is quiet.'

'Well, that dryasdust fellow is quiet enough, isn't he? He looks as if he couldn't say boo to a goose,' and Janet, after consideration, said, 'Oh, I think he could, if a goose ever came his way.'

He looked at her, found or imagined a meaning hidden under her words and masked by her grave face, made ready with a retort and gave it up. 'Here we dally, while your mother's ill. It's a fatal habit. I'll telephone to the doctor myself.'

'I will,' Janet said, and added, 'No, perhaps you'd better.' She stood by him while he did it and he felt it odd that she, who always seemed to flit about the house like a pale moth, disappearing in the middle of a sentence or leaving everything unsaid, should hover thus beside him; but this, too, though unusual, was moth-like and he had no certainty that she would not vanish without a sound, but she still stood there when he looked up and said, 'Out. He'll get the message. I shall go to the office.'

'But if he comes – '

'My dear, you're no goose, but if he does boo you can hiss, can't you? And he may be hours. I'll just go and look at your mother and then I'll get down to the docks.'

It was only yesterday that he was there, but he felt that he had been living in an atmosphere of emotion, fighting with shadows, for a long time, and he sickened after concrete things, ships and cargoes, the river-side with its faintly stale smell, the sound of rumbling lorries, the rough voices of men, the gulls winging in from the sea.

'I must keep the pot boiling,' he said, nodding at his fair, tall daughter. She was looking at him steadily, but his imagination or his sympathy divined an uncertainty in her somewhere, a question to be asked or a doubt to be expressed. 'Well?' he said.

She made the slightest possible movement. 'I don't know,' she said vaguely.

'Neither do I, neither do I!' He apologized for his impatience with a smile. 'I've been moving in mists, but perhaps I make them.'

'I think you do,' she said severely.

'And I like them,' he confessed, 'but sometimes they are too thick, too thick. I'll tell you about Lydia when I come back.'

'I haven't asked you to,' she murmured and went away.

He walked to the office with his usual briskness. He was worried about his wife and at the thought of Lydia he felt as if dark wings spread themselves over him, yet his optimism would not be suppressed, for it was of the kind which could not help discovering good in what seemed evil; the dark wings would waver, lift, and leave a clear view of the sky and, looking upwards, he saw above him the benign blue of autumn, flawless, without a cloud, cool and beneficent, while from the earth it roofed, the trees stood up, bearing their burden of glorious decay from which more life was to spring. It was a world of blue and gold and green, with leaves falling stealthily from the branches to join their fellows heaped on the ground and children playing among them, the old and the young, the past and the future.

The day suited his mood though, indeed, he could fit his mood to any day, and moralizing with a humorous appreciation of his own platitudes, he crossed the green, picked up a tumbled child, gave her a penny and a pat, remarked on the weather to a policeman, and passed through the street of shops. He paused at the green-grocer's, felt the hearts of the lettuces to compare them with those of his own growing, hesitated over peaches, ordered some grapes for his wife and then, walking on with his slightly rolling gait, he reached the little alley where the trees looked over the walls. His footsteps, which sounded so loud and clear on a spring morning, seemed to have gathered discretion from the season and he meditated on the fact that Spring which is the brave, bold time of year, with its sharp shafts of sunlight and its bitter winds, produces sounds in sympathy, hard and shrill, while Autumn, laying on all things a gentle, reluctant hand, stifles the very cries of the streets.

He pattered down the lane, tapped the wall with his stick, felt his usual distress at the sight of the broken gate, and emerged into the old square which had once been the haunt of fashion, where the fine houses kept a look of dignity under disgrace, and the trees, dropping their leaves delicately, one by one, seemed to tell themselves to pay no heed to the squalor which surrounded them. Here William Nesbitt was assailed by a group of children, ragged and dirty, with cries of, 'Give us your flower, Mister!' and he stopped in the midst of them.

'No, no, not my flower. What'll you do with it? Well, here then – ' He took it from his coat. 'But not to-morrow, mind.' He gave it to the most impudent of the little girls. 'Put it in water. It's a rose.'

'It's a rose,' she mocked and ran away with it. He stood still for a moment, watching the scampering children, and saw his rose petals dropping in the race. 'That's finished,' he said, but he was glad he had given it to the child. He liked these ragged urchins and their wild ways, their bright eyes peering through dirt and matted locks, and he wished he felt more sympathy with his own grand-children. Mabel's boys were too clearly stamped with the

mark of their worthy father, and Dora's were too ex-
quisite, too well-behaved to rouse his interest. If Lydia
had had a child, a little girl like herself, with mystery
and mischief in her imagination to be excited and odd
withdrawings to be respected, he would have felt himself
extraordinarily rich in a relationship without too much
responsibility and with all the privileges of indulgence.
There would have been Lydia's ways to watch for, stories
of Lydia to tell, how naughty she had been at school, how
she had tied that girl's plait to the chair – Ah, those Millers!
What had possessed that tom-boy to marry a curate?

For an instant, he thought of writing to her and con-
juring her by all the plum cake she had eaten in his house
not to betray her friend, but what folly and what weakness! Like that bribing of the vicar at which he shud-
dered, it would only be another poor attempt to stem the
tide and a craven acceptance of the world's judgments,
which might be right in general, but were bound, in
particular, to be wrong. He was not ashamed of Lydia,
he told himself again, and for once he missed the pathetic
humour in his reiteration: he was proud of her, and if she
had made a mistake it was a noble one, whatsoever of the
ignoble it might involve. And suddenly, in spite of his
assurance, he felt very tired, as though he had come to the
end of his strength, and his pace slackened until he reached
the docks, where his keen eyes met those objects about
which he had no doubts. Here he was an expert and here,
under the roof of this old gabled house, he had a kingdom
in which he tried to rule justly, wronging no man, yet,
at the moment, he felt that no one could live at all without in some way injuring some one else, for each man was
taking what another wanted, whether it was women or
cargoes, love or merchandise.

These thoughts tinged his conduct throughout what
remained of the day, making him a little less alert than
usual, less quick in making decisions, less ready to be
angered at mistakes, and Walter, aware of something not
quite normal in his father, made frequent excuses for

entering his room and lingering there, talking more than his wont and racking his rather simple brain for some way of showing sympathy. William Nesbitt watched him from under his lifted eyebrows and appreciated his efforts, but a certain shyness existed between them and with Walter it was not possible to indulge in cryptic speech, so he had to flounder on alone until, at last, as they prepared to leave the office, he said, 'We're starting the rehearsals to-night, sir.'

'What? Rehearsals? Oh, for teetotal Jones. All right, my boy. Thank you. Not much good, though, except for Jones. Good-night,' and William Nesbitt took his way once more up the walled lane.

It was almost dark and he felt that he was a shadow moving among shadows, a thing that passed, leaving an impression of movement, a vagueness, a faintness, and no more. He passed a man who walked quickly; he passed a woman who shuffled wearily close to the wall, and they were only shadows, yet in the heart of each there must have been memories that hurt, hopes that sustained and anxieties that nibbled with sharp teeth, as in his own, and they were as lonely as he was to-night. He could not understand his own mood; the briskness seemed to have gone out of him and all the articles of his creed seemed worthless, and then he remembered that he had not slept last night and took courage at this physical explanation, but his thoughts went to Mastover and the dark house there and his dark, bright daughter; then to his wife who had been smitten by Lydia's swift hands, and, thinking of these two, he wound his way upwards through the familiar streets, past the old houses which satisfied his love of beauty and tradition, to that old house which he had bought because he had inherited nothing materially fine, where, in the hall, lighted only by its own white walls, it was fitting to see his other daughter hovering, shadowy, too, in her pale dress.

'Well, child, how's your mother?'

'The doctor has just gone.'

'He took his time then.'

197

'Oh, he came an hour ago, but Mother was asleep and he would not have her waked.'

'Kind of him! And how is she?'

'Very angry at your sending for him. She told him she didn't need him.'

'He wouldn't agree with that, of course.'

He saw her slim figure motionless against the open door of the drawing-room, but a little run of laughter was mixed with her speech. 'No, not exactly. He said just the usual things – rest and no worries.'

'Is that all? They don't ask much, do they?'

'And he's coming to-morrow.'

'Has he any sense, do you think?'

'Mother says he hasn't.'

'Ah, she would, but in your hour's conversation, did you discover any?'

'It wasn't as long as that,' she murmured, and now she moved as though she meant to go away, and saying, 'I can't see you, child, and I'm tired of groping,' he switched on the light.

His high spirits returned, for again he found life full of an interest that overcame its burdens, and he saw that Lydia had made him yet another gift, the chance of getting into touch with this illusive creature, this daughter who, hitherto, had been hardly more than a gracious, distant relative.

She clasped her hands and said quickly, 'About Lydia?'

'Well, what about her?'

'I wondered – Is she happy?'

'Happy? No, child, no. Love doesn't mean happiness, always.'

'No,' she said, 'but if it's real love, doesn't it?'

He spread his hand. 'Perhaps.'

She went to the foot of the stairs and as she paused with her hand on the rail, he asked, 'Have you written to her?'

She shook her head. 'Not yet.'

He looked after her as she moved upwards without haste but with perfect smoothness, and to himself he echoed her words, 'Not yet. But I think you will.'

Chapter 25

He foresaw a less pleasant and more immediate event in the arrival of Mabel that evening. She had a scent for trouble and, surely enough, she hurried in, breathlessly, after dinner. Her eyes gleamed with some kind of satisfaction when she heard that her mother was ill.

'I've walked all the way,' she said, 'but I had a feeling, as soon as I woke this morning, that something had happened to Mother.'

The look of satisfaction was explained and William Nesbitt said solemnly, 'Then you ought to have come earlier. I call this neglectful. And there are omnibuses and tramcars in Radstowe. Why not use them?'

'I thought it would be quicker if I ran.'

'Ah,' William Nesbitt said, and, closing his eyes, for a moment, he had a vision of her padding through the streets in her square-toed shoes.

'And I couldn't come any sooner because I've been so busy. I haven't had a moment to myself all day. But I'll just go upstairs and see Mother now. I dare say I can make her comfortable. I'm used to nursing.'

Janet, who sat by the fire, looked up from her sewing. 'Don't worry her,' she said calmly.

Resentful, but afraid to reproach her sister in her father's hearing, Mabel went out of the room wearing the patient expression of the misunderstood.

Janet went on with her sewing and as William Nesbitt failed to get the glance he wanted, he said angrily, 'I don't know how I begot that girl. I don't believe I did. I believe she's a changeling. What's wrong with her, Janet? Or with me? I suppose, if it came to it, I should discover some parental feeling for her, but I don't like her feet.' He looked at Janet sitting under a shaded lamp near the fire. She was less illusive now, engaged in the task of combining lace and linen, and though by seeming less mysterious she had lost some of her appeal for him, she was good to look at and he was grateful. 'It's unfair to expect charm in women, but I do,' he went on. 'Virtue's all very well, but it needs trimming and conscious virtue needs smiting. Now Mabel has gone upstairs thinking she's the only member of the family who knows how to shake a pillow.'

'I shouldn't mind that,' Janet said, 'if she could really do it, but I don't think she will have the chance to try to-night. Mother is coming downstairs.'

'But she mustn't.'

'But she will.'

'Old Dryasdust won't think much of you as a nurse if you have no authority over your patient. I shall have to go and use mine.'

'It's too late,' Janet said. 'I can hear her on the stairs.'

Mrs. Nesbitt's clear, pleasant voice, mingled with Mabel's expostulations, became audible to them both, and William Nesbitt opened the door. 'My dear Kate – '

'Nonsense, William. I've had a nice sleep and my bed must be made, so I've just slipped on my dressing-gown and come down for a little while.'

'You'll catch cold, Mother,' Mabel said. 'Come to the fire. You must have a rug over your knees.'

'I never catch cold,' Mrs. Nesbitt said in her final manner, 'and my dressing-gown is thick. Such a nice padded one and so comfortable. You ought to get one like it, dear.'

'She can't afford it,' William Nesbitt said hastily.

Mrs. Nesbitt sat down and stroked the soft fabric of the garment. 'Lined with flannel. It's such a comfort to me.'

This sudden reversion to what was more than her normal cheerfulness was almost alarming: it was overdone, and William Nesbitt watched her with a horrible suspicion that her mind was injured. Composed without stiffness she sat looking at the fire, and he was aware that Mabel, too, was watching her, hoping, under a veil of anxiety, to discover something sensational, and that Janet was pretending to notice nothing unusual. In her presence he felt an extraordinary support: he felt that he and she were leagued against the suspicions of Mabel which were not, of course, connected with her mother's mental state, but with developments in the affair of Lydia: it was evident that something had happened to change tragedy to comedy and Mabel was alert, glancing from her mother to her father and from him to Janet, and quite unable to conceal her curiosity.

Janet sewed on steadily and Mrs. Nesbitt began to talk about marrow jam and Mabel's boys. It was a pleasant family group by the fire and slowly, as his wife discussed with Mabel the values of different makes of flannel for the boy's underclothes and the rival claims of ginger and lemon as a flavouring for the jam, William Nesbitt was reassured. This was no babbling reaction from grief, but a considered plan: she had recovered her poise: it was a necessity of life to her. She had been born with a natural dignity which had existed without any outside aid when she was young and poor: it had not been spuriously exalted by the accession of wealth and position, but she could not live without it and, seeing it threatened, she had adjusted herself, he divined, to the only means which could preserve it, the calm acceptance of events.

He felt a new admiration for her, yet the suddenness of her recovery alarmed him. He had said she was a strong woman, but he had underestimated her ability: he had not suspected her of such acuteness. She was now outfacing Mabel as, no doubt, she intended to outface the world, and he feared that the effort, before it became a habit, might be too much for her. In the meantime, he became interested, as in a game. Mabel, who was no actress, was plainly seen to be edging off her mother's chosen topics of conversation in readiness to jump on to her own, but Mrs. Nesbitt had a lure which never failed to call her back. To mention Mabel's sons was to give her an opportunity of praising them, for apparently they had no defects. They did well at school, they were showing aptness at their dancing, they could play the piano and never needed to be urged to practise: they were all going to have good singing voices, their appetites were hearty because their food was wholesome and they were healthy boys, or, if truth compelled her to a statement which on first hearing implied a fault, there was a compensating reason: they were so highly strung and sensitive that any little trouble affected their stomachs immediately and yet, though they showed these evidences of what she called the artistic temperament, they were remarkably scientific in intellect.

'You remember, Mother, how Gladstone wanted to see the engines on the trial trip? They are all like that, though I think he is the most so.'

'But I call to mind,' William Nesbitt said, 'some little incident with Cromwell, too, on the same occasion, something about the relative weights of paper and water.'

'Yes,' Mrs. Nesbitt agreed calmly, 'when I lost my letter.'

He looked at her and gave her a little nod and smile, but she refused to smile back: circumstances had forced her to adopt an attitude but she would not make a jest of it with William.

Mabel, blind to the subtleties of human intercourse, was delighted with this appreciation from a grandfather who was usually noticeably lacking in it. 'It's very hard to keep up with their brains,' she confessed. 'I get quite worn out with it, but they must have intelligent sympathy.'

'What are you going to do with them?' William Nesbitt asked, jingling his money and beginning to walk about.

'Better put one of them into the timber trade. Pity to let the business go out of the family.'

'Oh, I don't know,' Mabel doubted. 'It's not worth very much.'

'Now, now, Mabel, you're not going to tell me John hasn't been a success.'

'Of course he has been a success.'

'Well, you can't have it both ways. If he's a success, the business is good: if the business is bad, he's a failure. There's a choice for you!'

In this cleft stick she struggled, hurt and helpless, until Mrs. Nesbitt said soothingly, 'Father is only teasing you, dear.'

'That's all, that's all,' he said cheerfully, 'but there's an art in good teasing. All art must be founded on truth. Think it over, Mabel. You're too fond of having things both ways.'

He went out of the room and Mabel said indignantly, 'He's very unkind to me. Of course, he hasn't forgiven me for saying what I thought about Lydia.'

'About Lydia?' Mrs. Nesbitt seemed puzzled. 'Oh, you mean the other night. Well, we all spoke hastily then, dear, and I really don't think Father minds what you said. I'm sure I don't.'

'You!' Mabel's shining brown eyes seemed to leap in their sockets. 'You were as bad as anybody.'

'As bad?' Mrs. Nesbitt repeated with dignity, and then, 'I was naturally upset,' she added slowly.

'I should think so. John can't get over it.'

'It's a pity for John to worry,' Mrs. Nesbitt said, 'and very unnecessary.'

Janet looked up for an instant and resumed her steady sewing. She had a great gift for sitting still and saying nothing, but she could not efface herself. Her very stillness had an impressive quality and Mrs. Nesbitt discovered that Mabel was signalling her opinion that Janet should be dismissed. She jerked her head in her sister's direction, lifted her eyebrows, and attempted a wink.

'What's the matter, dear?' her mother said. 'Something in your eye?'

'No, Mother.'

'You were making such funny faces.'

'I was thinking you ought to go to bed, Mother. Janet, do you think her room is ready?'

'I'm sure I don't know,' Janet said.

'I shall go upstairs at half-past nine,' Mrs. Nesbitt announced. 'That's very pretty, Janet. Let me see how you are doing it. Very nice. Isn't that beautifully done, Mabel? Janet is a good needlewoman.'

'Is it real lace?' Mabel asked.

'Of course. If I couldn't have it real, I wouldn't have it at all.'

Mabel sighed. 'I haven't time to make pretty things like that and I certainly couldn't have real lace.'

'My dear, you never could use your needle. You are a good cook, but you can't sew, and as for the lace, it's cheaper in the long run, so there's no reason why you shouldn't have it if you want it.'

'Even if John is a failure,' Janet said.

'Oh,' Mrs. Nesbitt laughed pleasantly, 'we mustn't go on with Father's joke. Mabel knows he didn't mean it. I'm sure you're very proud of John, dear, and of the boys. You ought to be very happy.'

Here again, Mabel wanted to have it both ways. To say she was happy, implied that she had no cause to complain and this was difficult to admit, but to say she was unhappy implied a lack of perfection in her family, which was worse: she took refuge in her health. 'If I were only stronger,' she suggested and, getting no encouragement here, she added, on an inspiration, 'And, of course, none of us can be happy now.'

Mrs. Nesbitt turned her head stiffly and showed her daughter a pair of exceedingly opaque eyes. 'Now?'

'Because of Lydia.'

'Oh, Mabel, you exaggerate this about Lydia! You must leave her to judge for herself. It is Oliver who is to blame.'

'Oliver?' Mabel leaned forward. 'What about Oliver?' she asked and Janet, holding her needle poised, but not using it, remembered how Dora had unexpectedly quoted from the Book of Job.

'I think he is a very strange person,' Mrs. Nesbitt said. 'I know all about it. No,' she held up a hand, 'I am not going to answer any questions. And though,' she paused and took a breath, 'I should not have done as she has done, I am not prepared to blame her.'

'But, Mother –'

The door was opened. 'It's the doctor, M'm.' Mary said. 'I've put him in the morning-room.'

'The doctor! How very annoying! Janet, go and send him away.'

'It's Miss Janet he wants to see, M'm. He has brought some medicine for you.'

'I shall go to bed at once,' Mrs. Nesbitt said. 'And, Janet, tell him I am perfectly well.' She turned to Mabel. 'Dr. Bunford has had a serious breakdown and this young man is trying, much too officiously, to take his place.'

Chapter 26

WHEN William Nesbitt left the drawing-room, he undid a roll of plans and spread them on the dining-room table. He contemplated the building of a new ship, another small steamer for trading in the Channel, and he was poring over the plans contentedly and now and then walking round the table as he thought out some point, when he heard a man's voice in the hall. He would never have denied that he was curious, and as he had a right to know who came and went in his house, he left his plans and discovered that Janet and Dr. Gregory were moving very slowly towards the front door. He stepped back into the dining-room and it was three minutes by his watch before the door was opened, another two minutes before it was shut.

In that time he thought – 'What is he doing here? The man's in love with her at first sight. I thought so. This is fortunate. Of course she's not in love with him, but it will do her good. Nothing so stimulating as admiration. And old Gregory Powder must have some sense. I wonder how old he is. I suppose he's a bachelor. We can't have any more of these triangles. I must find out. Funny that I should have had a twinge of rheumatism to-day. Better not tell Kate, though, and I'll just call on the doctor on my way to the office to-morrow. Must take these things in time and I needn't listen to his advice. And after all, I needn't mention the rheumatism. It might be useful later. Kate is excuse enough. Now I wonder if I should run him down to Janet, or praise him. Can't decide yet. What on earth are they talking about? Must be themselves. Nothing else would keep them standing in that draught. Ah, he's gone. Now, I'll just give her a minute to think it over – '

He took care not to jingle his money nor to hum his

hymn tune as he crossed the hall, and so he found Janet standing before the fire and looking into it.

'Hullo!' he said. 'Mabel gone?'

'No, she's upstairs with Mother.'

'Wasn't that John I heard?'

'It was Dr. Gregory.'

The doctor! Does he think so seriously about your mother as all that?'

'Oh, no, but he brought a sleeping draught. He made it up for her himself. She has to have it when she's in bed.'

'She won't take it. I bet you a pair of gloves she won't take it. What did she say to him?'

'She didn't see him. He didn't want to see her. He just brought the sleeping draught.'

'Why didn't you tell me he was here, child? I wanted to see him about your mother. Funny kind of husband he'll think me. I'll call on my way to business to-morrow. You know you're a very capable young woman, Janet, but you might allow me to inquire after my own wife.'

'I never thought of it, I'm afraid.'

'Oh, I know I'm only an old fool,' he grumbled, 'but it's difficult to remember it always.'

He found that she was looking at him with a searching, steady gaze and she said, 'I want to ask you something.' He braced himself for a question which would reveal her own acuteness but, with her words, he learnt that she had hardly been heeding what he said. 'Do you, like Mother, think Oliver is to blame?' she asked.

He gained a fraction of time by repeating thoughtfully, 'To blame?' and rapidly recalled his cue. 'Blame is like the blessed dew from Heaven, child, or is it the rain? It falls on the just and the unjust alike.'

'Then you don't think so?'

'Blame is the wrong word.'

'Oh,' she cried, 'don't quibble! You'd quibble for ever! You know quite well what I mean.'

He shrugged his shoulders, concealing his interest in this outburst. 'I'm coming to the conclusion,' he said deliberately, 'that the sanctity of marriage is an unholy thing. It's not fair, it's cruel, it's a prison. If marriage remains holy, it's a piece of good fortune: if it doesn't, who dare say the parties to it are wicked? There's a great deal of humbug about marriage, Janet, and a forced loyalty is the devil. And if Oliver couldn't hold Lydia by love, why should he hold her by law?'

'How do you mean he could not hold her?'

This was what he wanted and, with a silent prayer to be forgiven, he said tolerantly, 'Weak, child, weak.'

'I never thought of him as weak,' Janet said, and William Nesbitt uttered a ponderous, 'Ah!' which, though it meant nothing, was intended to imply a good deal. 'I said this evening,' he went on as he began to pace to and fro, 'that it wasn't fair to expect charm in women, and it's no fairer to expect strength in men, but you do, somehow, don't you?'

'I don't expect anything – anything!' Janet cried.

'We're told that's a very fortunate state to be in. As for me, I'm always expecting things and always getting them, so trouble must be accumulating for me somewhere.'

'Haven't you enough already?' she asked solemnly.

He stood still and showed her the full glance of his dark, bright eyes. 'No, Janet, I have not. I refuse to be troubled by the opinions of other people, for that, boiled down, is what it comes to. And suffering won't hurt Lydia.'

'Or Oliver?'

'I don't know. It isn't good for everybody. Lydia can stand it because – '

'Ah, because she's Lydia, I suppose?'

'Yes, just because of that,' he said, ignoring her bitterness. 'She can stand it. Nevertheless, you might, even you, might spare some sympathy for her.'

'Even me?' she questioned, and then, putting that aside with an unnaturally brusque gesture, 'I do,' she murmured a little embarrassed but brave, and it seemed as though she might have said something more if Mabel had not appeared.

'I've put Mother to bed,' she announced, 'and now I

must go home. I have to mend Cromwell's trousers before I go to bed. He wears his things out so quickly. He can't help it. When he's thinking, he fidgets.'

'And when he fidgets, I suppose he's thinking?'

'His brain is always at work,' Mabel said doggedly.

'I'll get you a cab,' William Nesbitt said.

'Oh, thank you, Father, that will be a great help,' and as he left the room, she asked Janet in a whisper which William Nesbitt heard, 'What did the doctor say?'

'He brought a sleeping draught,' was Janet's reply.

'Oh, dear! But what did he say?'

'She's to have it to-night.'

'But what did he say?'

'Nothing.'

'Nothing? But didn't you ask him anything?'

'No.'

'Well, but we ought to know. Of course it's Lydia who has done this. I shall write and tell her so. Don't you think I ought to tell her?'

'You can tell her Mother has been in bed all day because she was tired and now she's better – that's all.'

'Then why did you send for the doctor?'

'Because she was ill before and Father was anxious.'

'Well, it was Lydia who made her ill before and she ought to know it.'

'What does it matter?' Janet exclaimed. 'Why do you want to put the blame on anybody? It might have been any of us.'

Mabel scouted this idea, but when Janet added, 'And some day, one of your boys may do something wrong,' a look of resentful alarm came into her eyes.

'I can't imagine it.'

'Of course not – now – but you wait.'

'Then Lydia will have her example to answer for.'

'Oh, Mabel, you don't mean to say that Lydia's influence is going to be stronger than yours and John's?'

Mabel had no answer ready so she said, 'I can't understand the way you are all taking this. Even Mother. What did she mean about Oliver? Has she found something out? Has she told you?'

'I shouldn't listen,' Janet said. 'I'm sick of the whole thing, but Mother has seen Lydia –'

'Seen her? Where? When?'

'Yesterday, in Mastover, and she seems to have come back satisfied, doesn't she?'

'She saw Lydia! Did she see the man?'

Janet frowned slightly. 'I don't know.'

'Does Dora know?'

'I don't know that.'

'Well, how you can live in this house and know so little –!'

'You see, I don't like being snubbed.'

'Oh, you think Mother would snub me if I asked her?'

'I'm sure of it.'

'Well, she may tell Dora. It seems to me that she confides in Dora now, and there was a time when I knew all her troubles.'

'That was before there were any,' Janet said, but Mabel, with her curiosity aroused like a lust, missed the subtlety of this remark.

'I wonder,' she said, with her eyes fixed on Janet's, as though to drag some information from them, 'I do wonder if Mother saw the man.'

Janet frowned again. 'His name is Henry Wyatt. Why don't you go and see him yourself?'

'Could I? That's just what John wants to do and he wants Walter to go with him.'

'Walter won't go.'

'No, he takes no responsibility, and I dare say it would be better if I went myself. Do you think she would be rude to me?'

'Lydia rude? Not unless you were.'

'I'll think about it,' Mabel said, 'but I couldn't get there and back in a day, could I? I should have to stay the night.'

'If that's what you want to do, why not do it?' Janet said, a remark which startled Mabel and left her in doubt as to whether or not she ought to be affronted. William Nesbitt's entrance and announcement that the cab would be at the door in a few minutes, solved the difficulty, but during the remaining moments she felt uneasy, conscious that Janet's mind moved very quickly and, she consoled herself, rather improperly.

'Well,' William Nesbitt asked when she had gone, 'what did she worm out of you?'

'Nothing, but you're quite right.'

'Always right,' he interpolated cheerfully.

'She isn't like the rest of us. She's rather coarse.'

Chapter 27

'I SHALL go to the sewing-meeting,' Mrs. Nesbitt announced next morning when she and William were drinking their early tea. 'I shall go regularly, and to church, too.'

'Certainly, my dear,' William Nesbitt said brightly.

He did not see, but he felt, the stiff turning of her head. 'Certainly?' she echoed. 'Not at all, but I shall go, all the same.'

'Armoured in a sense of righteousness.'

'No, William.' And now, as he looked at her, he saw that her lips shook a little. 'Only in pride. I couldn't,' she sought a phrase, 'I couldn't live if I had to hang my head.'

'And you need not, Kate. There's nothing to be ashamed of in this family, except Mabel's feet. I don't know why they remind me of fish – floppy, I suppose. Now, Kate, don't think I'm callous because I mention them. I'm all sympathy, my dear, you know that.'

'Yes, you are very sympathetic,' she said slowly, 'when I do as you please. You need not think I approve of Lydia, or of you. I don't. I never shall, but I cannot let Mrs. Miller triumph over me.'

He felt a most unexpected sense of gratitude for Mrs. Miller. She had, perhaps, saved the situation. 'You are more than the equal of Mrs. Miller,' he said.

Ignoring that, she went on with her thoughts. 'I must try to put that night out of my head,' she said. 'That dreadful night – and the dark house.'

'Yes, a dark house,' he agreed and, looking at her keenly, he wondered whether she really understood that darkness shot with light, whether it would be possible to talk freely to her, but her face seemed to be shut against him and he was silent.

'I must forget that,' she said bravely, and then, with a sudden quavering of her courage, she added tremulously, 'But I don't understand it and I don't know what I'm going to say – to anybody!'

'Say nothing, Kate – or even, say exactly what you think.'

'But what do I think?' she begged him to tell her.

'I don't know, my dear.'

'Neither do I,' she cried and, out of her limitations and her bewildered pain, she exclaimed, 'He must have been cruel to her!'

'Oh, no, Kate, not cruel.'

'Yes,' she insisted. 'What else? Cruel, or unfaithful. Nothing else,' her voice sank, 'could excuse her.'

Very quietly, under the bed-clothes, William Nesbitt drew up and lowered one leg after the other. He was afraid of diverting, by a sudden movement, the favourable trend of his wife's thoughts, but he was an honest man and he shifted thus under a sense of treachery.

'Unfaithful,' she repeated, as though to test him, and he was compelled to say, 'If he had been either cruel or un-faithful, Lydia would not have left him.'

She turned towards him. 'What do you mean, William?' she asked with a grave anger.

'Something to fight for,' he explained in a murmur.

'To fight for? No one wants to fight – but one might go away. If you – ' but she could not disgrace her William and herself by the suggestion and there was a heavy pause before she said severely, 'You don't understand women. She had to find a refuge. I was always fond of Oliver, but now – I see things.'

'Let me see them, too.'

'He isn't natural. He's queer.'

'All queer, Kate.'

'I am not queer,' she protested, 'and neither are you, not really, but he – why, William, he came here and smiled, actually smiled, and then he went out of the room with

213

Janet. What could he find to say to her that he couldn't say to me?'

'I don't know, my dear. Why not ask her?'

'I can ask her nothing!' she cried. 'Nothing!' She pressed her hands against her forehead and let out a heavy sigh. 'The child must have been ill-treated,' she moaned.

'Well, let us hope she will find happiness with Henry.'

'Happiness? How can she – like that?'

'She will get gleams, Kate. We all get gleams,' he said and, to his amazement, she cried out fiercely, 'She ought to divorce him! Why should my daughter live in sin?'

'It isn't sin,' he said gently.

'That is what it is called,' she replied.

It was his turn to sigh without a sound. He had not the heart and perhaps not the desire to take this comfort of Lydia's grievance from her; it helped her; in her eyes it partly justified Lydia and himself, and the extent of his relief was the measure of his past suffering from his wife's estrangement. He thought he might be forgiven for leaving it at that for, after all, what were right and wrong? Only the Omniscient could decide. The human mind was too rough an instrument to deal fairly with such subtleties.

'We must be patient,' he said. 'And, Kate, if you worry we shall have the doctor living in this house.'

'He's trying to do that already,' she said sharply. 'He wants to make a case of me, I can see, but I shall not allow it.'

'Don't offend him, Kate. Never offend anybody. I've had a twinge of rheumatism myself, and he looks as if he might understand such dry things as bones.'

'Rheumatism, William? Why didn't you tell me?' she asked, and her anxiety, her air of being ready with liniments, of having a vast store of remedies, was strangely sweet to him.

'It's nothing, Kate. Old age. Still, I'll go and see him this morning.'

'No,' she said firmly, 'you ought to go to bed and be examined.'

'I'll ask him if he thinks that necessary,' he replied meekly.

'And of course he will.'

'You haven't much faith in human nature, Kate, but I think you're right. It's pleasant to agree with each other, isn't it?'

'It's a change,' she admitted.

'You know – ' he began and broke off.

'Well?'

'You ought to develop your sense of humour, Kate, and the expression of it.'

'I shouldn't know how to do that,' she murmured.

'No, it comes naturally when the occasion arises. Mrs. Miller may inspire you.'

'I cannot,' she said severely, 'make a jest of that.'

'No, but if you could, Kate – '

'I must go my own way, William.'

He smiled and peeped at her. 'I see, now, where the children get their character.'

'Nonsense, William, they get their wilfulness from you.'

'Have it your own way, Kate,' he said.

The events of that morning would certainly have confirmed her in that determination if she had thought of it, but the discovery that Dora was defying her husband, while one to strengthen her belief in the children's inheritance, was also one to put abstract questions from her mind. Dora's defiance was, on the surface, gentle, but that was Dora's pretty trick, and Mrs. Nesbitt knew that the rebellion was none the less serious because it was serene. Dora strolled into the house, dropped into a chair with the usual backward fling of her furs, the usual outstretching of legs, which, she said, were not strong enough to support her body, and amiably announced that she was going to Mastover.

Mrs. Nesbitt looked up from her housekeeping accounts and saying, 'Janet, remind me that I have to carry over five shillings,' she took off her spectacles and then asked if Herbert had given his consent.

'Consent?' Dora looked puzzled. 'I haven't asked for it.'

'I'm afraid he will be very angry,' Mrs. Nesbitt said, and to that Dora made no answer. She had a pleasant air of being ready for any other topic of conversation. 'Is he angry?' Mrs. Nesbitt persisted. 'You ought not to make trouble in your own home, Dora.'

'I never make trouble,' she said.

'And your husband ought to come before your sister, even a sister who – well, even before Lydia. Herbert is quite right.'

Dora laughed. 'Mother dear, I didn't say he was angry, did I?'

'No, but of course he will be. This is dreadful. First Lydia and now you.'

'But so far,' Dora protested, 'I'm only going to leave him for one night.'

'You may meet Mabel there,' said Janet from her corner. 'She is going too.'

'What on earth for?'

'Curiosity,' Janet said.

'Oh, yes, Mabel is curious,' Mrs. Nesbitt said and then, suddenly realizing facts, she cried, 'But you're not to go – any of you! It's not right! It's – it's – ' she could not find words, but at last she said slowly, 'I can't allow you all to countenance her.'

'Isn't that,' Janet asked softly, just what you mean to do yourself?'

'Janet,' Mrs. Nesbitt looked bewildered, 'Janet, you ought to know nothing about all this – a girl like you! It's terrible.'

'But isn't it what you're going to do?' Janet asked again.

Mrs. Nesbitt was silent. If she countenanced Lydia, she could not reasonably object if the rest of the family did it too, and she understood quickly that her objection was grounded on her own uncertainty. She was merely persuading herself that Lydia was not to blame because there was no other way of getting peace and keeping pride, and she saw, without thinking, that the weakness of her position

216

lay in that necessity for persuasion. Very well, then she must not admit that necessity. She settled that in a flash and she said calmly, 'I know more than anyone else. I don't approve, but I understand, and that, Janet, is what you cannot do. You are too young. And Dora has her family to think of. However, nothing I can say has any effect. You all go your own way, and now Father has rheumatism.'

Janet's clear laughter, like water falling, and Dora's rich, melodious chuckle, infectious in its gaiety, did their work and Mrs. Nesbitt laughed too, found it difficult to stop, and under this uncontrollable mirth thought it was strange that she could see a joke and felt a deep delight that she and these dear girls could share it.

She wiped her eyes. 'But seriously – '

'Don't let us be serious,' Dora begged. 'It's lovely to laugh.'

'But Father says he really has got rheumatism.'

'Oh,' Dora conceded, 'I don't mind being serious about that.'

'And he has gone to see Dr. Gregory, though I don't think he understands his business – one of those silly, fiddling old bachelors. I don't like him. Do you, Janet?'

'Like him?'

'My dear, how you have caught your father's way of repeating things.'

'One gains time,' Dora murmured, and Janet's blue glance skimmed over Dora's amused brown one. 'And now I must go,' Dora said, 'but are there any messages for Lydia?'

'No,' Mrs. Nesbitt said firmly and inconsistently, but she could not explain that she had parted from Lydia in a manner which made kind messages insulting, 'but, Dora, you might say something about her underclothes. It's a nasty damp house – she always lives in damp houses – and she ought to be wearing wool next to her skin.'

'I'll tell her so. Janet, have you a kind word for the sinner?'

'Tell her Mabel is going to see her.'

'Oh, surely something more than that!'

'I don't wish Janet to send any messages,' Mrs. Nesbitt protested. 'Janet ought to know nothing about this.'

'Give her my love,' Janet said.

'And, Dora,' Mrs. Nesbitt made a half-hearted attempt to placate her conscience, 'I beg you not to make Herbert unhappy.'

'Mother dear, when you see Herbert, please beg him not to make me unhappy.'

'Does he?' Mrs. Nesbitt demanded, all the mother in her ready to do battle.

'No more or less than I do him. You can't expect to live in perfect peace with anybody.'

'It ought to be possible,' Mrs. Nesbitt said, thinking of William, and then, with a kind of innocence, she added, 'Father has tiresome little ways, but he is always kind.'

'But Father is a jewel,' Dora said.

'My child, you're not suggesting that Herbert isn't?'

'Herbert has his tiresome little ways, too,' Dora answered good-humouredly. 'We're all in the same boat, Mother. No doubt Lydia has found that Henry has them.'

'Don't speak of him like that,' Mrs. Nesbitt said sharply.

Wilfully misunderstanding her, Dora said, 'You always encourage the tyranny of husbands.'

It took Mrs. Nesbitt a few moments to follow this and then, controlling her annoyance at Dora's suavity and Janet's superior little smile, she said severely, 'You know I did not mean that, but I object to your speaking of him as though he were a member of the family.'

'But what is he?' Dora cried.

'He is a bad man,' was Mrs. Nesbitt's reply, and here she said what she believed. Lydia might be forgiven for leaving Oliver, but Henry Wyatt could not be forgiven for inducing her to live with him and suddenly her anger against Lydia rose in a little unexpected gust. There were more ways than one of deserting a worthless husband and she had taken the wrong one. She should have come home to her family, an injured woman, but a pure one, and that thought, so obvious, but so late in reaching her, struck Mrs. Nesbitt with a sharp blow. Nothing, no excuses, no extenuations could absolve Lydia from the sin of living with that man and, in an imaginative moment, Mrs. Nesbitt saw herself going through life burdened with the secret conviction of her daughter's guilt. There was no possible way of avoiding that belief, no possible way. She thought she had found in Oliver a tiny track to happiness, but she had lost it again in this jungle of Lydia's deliberate choice. Her anger died away. It was too small an emotion. She felt herself stricken and very old, but she controlled her face and voice and repeated heavily, 'A bad man.'

Dora made a tiny gesture with her gloved hands and stooped to kiss her mother. 'It will be amusing if I meet Mabel there.'

'Nothing,' Mrs. Nesbitt said, 'can be amusing in that house.'

'But there's always happiness for me where Lydia is,' Dora replied and now it was Mrs. Nesbitt's turn to gesticulate her despair.

'It is all very well to make happiness where you are,' she said, 'but what about making unhappiness where you are not?'

'One can't do everything,' Dora sighed.

'One can do one's duty,' Mrs. Nesbitt answered and felt a pang, for she did not know that she was doing hers. She meant to uphold Lydia before the world while she condemned her in her own heart.

Chapter 28

In this connection, the world included William and her reasons for this inclusion she never clearly formulated. Her subtleties were instinctive, her actual thoughts and admissions simple. Perhaps she wished to spare him but, if so, it was a new experience and an unconscious effort, for though she had always cherished him materially, there had seldom been the need to save him mentally, and she had that sort of enmity in love, that queer antagonism which made it natural and pleasant to hurt him where he was most sensitive. More probably she wished to spare herself the ordeal of producing for inspection what she had determined to hide. She suffered mutely from the loss of a daughter whom she would never see again except as a penitent, but she was upheld by her own standards of morality. She had loved Lydia uncomfortably but romantically, and the discomfort remained while the romance and almost the consciousness of love had gone, but no outsider should abuse her daughter if she could prevent it.

She took an odd pleasure in deceiving William, who had so often misled her, and her behaviour was such that he found a new subject for rumination in human nature's adaptability for purposes of defence. Nothing imaginable could have been more rigid than his wife's attitude at Mastover: the similes of mere wood, iron, and steel were inadequate to express it, for it had been governed by a stubborn mind and now the same mind, in the face of necessity, had magically and swiftly transformed that attitude into one which, in its turn, was becoming equally rigid under a softer drapery. Thus it was that her remark when William told her that teetotal Mr. Jones had stopped the rehearsals for the dramatic performance, was no more than two words uttered tolerantly.

'Ridiculous man,' she said lightly.

It was the sincerity of the remark which struck William Nesbitt. He thought this amazing woman was actually beginning to believe in the opinions she had adopted and this led him to yet another idea – that what is our own becomes precious by the mere fact of possession.

'I suppose if one had a wooden leg, one would grow proud of it,' he said.

'Has Mr. Jones a wooden leg?'

'No, Kate, a wooden head.'

'Then, what is this about wooden legs?'

'Only my nonsense. You know what that's worth.'

'This is very confusing,' Mrs. Nesbitt said. 'I wish you wouldn't muddle me, William. What excuse did the man give?'

'Change of what he calls his mind. So you see, Lydia and Ethel have met.'

Mrs. Nesbitt lifted a hand. 'You needn't describe their meeting. You have done that once already.'

'And Ethel's husband has written to his father and his father – what a funny thing conscience is – refuses to accept help from any of the Nesbitt brood, so his church roof continues to leak and his parishioners to drink. But has Ethel written to her mother?'

'I shall find out at the sewing-meeting on Monday,' Mrs. Nesbitt said.

'My dear, don't go. Why distress yourself on account of that old woman?'

'It's the whole world,' Mrs. Nesbitt replied. 'Do you think I don't feel it every time I go into the street, into a shop. I can't take this lightly, as you do, William.'

'I don't,' he said stoutly, 'but I can't bring myself to care what a Radstowe shopkeeper thinks when I know what Lydia really is. And what difference is your outfacing Mrs. Miller going to make?'

She did not answer, but he understood, better than she did, that she had to meet her enemy, conquer, and then live more easily in the satisfaction of that victory, and towards that time she looked, not without fear but with determination. Meanwhile her relationship to him adjusted itself, and if, in his romantic or his bitter moments, he recognized that he had never been entirely satisfied, he could even then admit her qualities to be greater than he had thought, and realize that she, too, must miss in him something she had always wanted. Their comradeship had been broken for a few days and that ugly space remained as a scar in the minds of both but, in spite of that and all their dissimilarities, he knew that they could never be less than lovers and now he watched her with increasing admiration, amusement and concern. Her physical recovery had been almost too good and he was afraid for her, but going home early and anxiously on the day of the sewing-meeting, ready to succour and console, he found that she had returned in a state of complete composure.

'Was she there?' he asked at once, and in the directness of the question there was proof of his fear.

'She is always there. I asked her about Ethel.'

'Well, Kate, you took the bull by the horns!'

'Not quite by the horns. I didn't mention Lydia, but I did talk as though we had known the Wyatts, so I have laid a foundation and I'm sure there were enough photographs of that poor lady to justify me. Did you notice them?'

'I notice everything, Kate.'

'So you always say.'

He laughed inwardly. He was sure he noticed more than she did. He had seen the tenseness of Janet's body when he had given the report on his twinge of rheumatism, and her relieved slackening when she heard that the doctor did not propose to make a fuller examination. He thought to himself, 'She's afraid of that man. She's afraid of being loved. Well, I can't do anything, one way or the other,' yet his mind was fidgeting for action. On further acquaintance, he liked the dry doctor and felt an honest disappointment at the slightness of his own ailments. Janet might find a worse husband, yet why, he shrugged his shoulders, should he want her to have a husband at all? The family examples were not encouraging and if she had once fancied she loved Oliver, he was pretty sure that she felt no more than a loyal, and perhaps impatient pity for him now. He had done his best, and he believed he had done it cleverly, with little side phrases, looks, and hints, to foster that pity and that loyalty, and as the matter seemed to increase so William Nesbitt's heart had lightened: the child was trying to make amends for her amorous desertion.

He chuckled. He alone, and perhaps Lydia, knew the nature of the man: his acquiescence was strength, not weakness: he was biding his time and if it never came he would not have altogether failed, for he was nearer holding her now than he had ever been. That, however, was beyond Janet's understanding: she thought him weak and she was too young to love in spite of it, and the diversion of the doctor had come at the right moment, employing her imagination if it did nothing else. He half hoped it would do more, believing as he did that neither man nor woman could approach fulfilment without marriage, but it seemed to him that she ought to have a greater scope for choice. She was vulnerable now to wounds which might heal all too quickly, and he had an absurd fancy of the dried-up doctor, winged like Cupid and taking shots with his bow and arrow.

'Look here, child,' he said one night, 'I want to talk to you.'

She looked, obediently, but there was a flicker in the eyes which had once been so steady and so unassailable. 'I'm listening,' she said.

'Admit I was right about your mother.'

'I don't remember.'

He feigned impatience. 'Of course my words are not worth remembering, but didn't I tell you she was a strong woman and had no need of you?'

'Yes, I do remember that. It wasn't,' she added demurely, 'a kind thing to say.'

'Well, you see it's true, don't you? And this is the best

223

chance you will ever get for going away. It's the psychological moment, child, if I know your mother, though really I'm not sure that I do. It's wonderful how life is never dull. Excitements every minute!'

'What is exciting you now?' she asked.

'Good heavens! Listen to her! She's a hundred years older than I am.' He tapped with his forefinger on the table. 'What is exciting me now, among other things, is the possibility of your escape. Pack your box and go.'

Janet dropped her sewing and on it her hands fell limply. 'Where shall I go?' she asked, and behind her little smile he thought he saw a kind of wildness.

'Go and be trained, as you wish.' He jingled the coins in his pocket. 'You shall have all the money you need. Escape, child, from us old fogies, and see the world and do some work. Go and get a tight mouth and an air of authority.'

She shook her head. 'It's too late.'

'For a determined character those words don't exist. Too late! Why, it's only a few weeks ago that you suggested it.'

'Weeks!' she exclaimed in a low voice. 'Is that all? And now I don't want to go. It doesn't matter.'

He was pleased under a show of petulance, for this proved that she was no longer in need of distraction and that the pain of loving Oliver was eased. 'Resignation!' he mocked. 'Let's have none of it.'

'It isn't that,' she said. 'It's indifference. I may as well stay here.'

'Drooping, getting thin and meek and a little acid! I don't want a daughter like that, thank you, a constant reminder of the chance we didn't give you. I want you to go away.'

She looked at him sideways, smiling, with the first coquettish air he had ever seen her use. 'Wouldn't it be rather a pity,' she added, 'when you and I are just getting so friendly?'

'Oh, if you're going to begin that sort of thing! You're

taking an advantage! I won't have it! Try it on some one else, child. I'm too old a bird to be limed like that.'

'But you are limed, all the same, aren't you?' she asked softly.

'My dear,' he sat down, 'I did think I had at least one daughter who had nothing of the minx in her and I find I'm wrong. It's the first time I remember being wrong. Oh, yes, I thought the doctor would make me go to bed and punch me all over and he didn't. I was wrong there, too, and I'm glad of both mistakes. I'm glad you're a bit of a minx. It's a relief and so, after all, I think perhaps you'd better stay at home under your father's care.'

'Under your care! I think you're a very dangerous man!'

He sat straight. 'How?'

'Your brain's too busy. You're always making things up and you can't help putting your finger in the pie.'

He was startled, but he said alertly, 'Where's the particular pie?'

The faintest shadow of defence passed over her face before she said easily, 'This family is always making pies.'

'Mud ones, some people would think. But general accusations are not fair, Janet.'

'Ah,' she said, 'you can't expect me to tell you more than you tell me.'

'I'll tell you one thing and it's one you want to know.'

'You needn't. I'm not curious,' she said hastily.

'I'll tell you,' he persisted, 'why I was glad to be mistaken about the doctor. Because, child, in spite of very grave temptation, he remained an honest man.'

He was hurt by the sudden whiteness of her face. 'All the same,' she said, 'you will not drive me away. I shall stay at home.'

'Oh,' he cried, 'you think I'm cleverer than I am. Upon my word, I never thought of that. It wasn't a weapon. I simply wanted to tell you he's an honest man. You see, I like to put a good deed on record when I meet it.'

'I think you really meant a little more than that,' she said gently.

He was rather alarmed by her quickness, but he consoled himself with the thought that at least she could not have seen through his little clevernesses in regard to Oliver, or she would have resisted them. She had been dull there because, that sensitiveness being no longer very acute, she had not needed to be watchful, and in this latter business he was on the whole glad that they understood each other, though he was not sure that he intended her to understand him all the way.

Chapter 29

ON his return from Mastover, William Nesbitt had written to Lydia and had found a difficulty in addressing the envelope. He had ended by directing it to Henry Wyatt and had asked Lydia to tell him under what name the inhabitants of Mastover were to know her. No answer had come and, in spite of her casual habits, he was uneasy. That fellow, absorbed in his own affairs, might have mislaid the letter, but in any case it was odd that Lydia should not have written to a father who was patently anxious about her. She would not, he knew, insult her mother's breakfast-table with the sight of her handwriting, but the office was his own kingdom and every day he hoped to find a letter from her there.

He sat, one afternoon, at his desk, wondering if he should go and see her, when there came a loud knock at the door and Dora marched in.

'This is a comfortable chair,' he said at once.

She fell into it and heaved a sigh. 'Oh, I forgot,' she said. 'A cab's at the door and I haven't any change. Would you mind paying for it?'

'How much?'

'Only three-and-sixpence. I'll pay you back.'

'I wonder when,' he said, and rang his bell. 'And now,' he asked when the clerk had gone, 'what else can I do for you?'

He was surprised to see her lips tremble a little. 'Let me talk to you,' she said. 'I've just come from Mastover. Didn't Mother tell you I was going?'

'No, my dear, your mother doesn't tell me everything nowadays.'

'I thought she would be sure to because she was so worried about Herbert.'

'Not a word of Herbert. What's the matter with him?'

'Only angry – unless something more has happened since yesterday. I went yesterday morning.'

'Your mother is becoming inured to trouble, I suppose. But tell me about Lydia.'

'She isn't happy.'

'I know that.'

'And she looks ill.'

'Oh,' he began to walk about, 'you're not going to tell me the thing's a failure? But never mind, never mind,' he was talking to himself, 'she'll get through it. One can't help her. She had to do it. She'll find a way out.' He looked sharply at Dora. 'How ill is she? Is she coughing? Does that man look after her?'

'Henry Wyatt isn't the kind who looks after people,' Dora said. 'Besides, there's nothing to do. As a matter of fact, she was frightfully funny. I haven't laughed so much for years.'

'Did Henry Wyatt laugh too?'

'Oh, yes, when he listened. There's no doubt he appreciates her. He lives on her and she likes that, but he needs a great deal of food. It's exhausting though complimentary. Oliver was peaceful.'

'So you're regretting Oliver, are you?'

'I always have. The point is that I'm afraid Lydia is regretting him, too.'

'She always has.'

'Oh, yes, in a way, but suppose the way changes?'

He gave Dora a full stare. 'There's an extraordinary amount of brains in our family,' he said with a sort of awed satisfaction.

'Well, we do remarkably little with them,' she retorted.

He now thought it necessary to avert his gaze. He did not want her to see that he knew where her brains had failed her, yet he was coming to the conclusion that these efforts of tact were useless, since his children were at least as clever as himself.

'The fact is,' Dora went on, 'he wasn't exciting enough,

though after being jostled in a whirlpool, you might begin to think longingly of a pond. Of course you'd get tired of it again, for what seems attractive at a distance is simply dull near at hand. But it is at a distance now.'

'Did she say all this?'

'Of course not,' Dora answered with a touch of scorn. She was silent for a moment before she said, 'Lydia ought to have several husbands.'

'Well, she has two.'

'No, she ought to have no husband at all, but several lovers. She can't endure claims.'

'No one can live without acknowledging them,' he said.

'They irk her.'

'Then she must be irked,' he said sternly. 'Are you telling me that this venture is a failure?' he asked again.

'I'm telling you she isn't happy.'

He stood still and demanded fiercely, 'Are you? Am I?'

'Oh, we don't matter.'

'Thank you, my dear.'

'Well, I have the children and you have all of us. And I don't think men realize how lucky they are in having work to do. She's there, in that little house – '

He interrupted and echoed, with a difference, his wife's words, 'Oliver ought to divorce her.'

'What for?' Dora asked with a simplicity he appreciated but had no time to dwell on.

'So that she can have children, too,' he said.

Their eyes met, but they did not see each other. Between them there shone a vision of Lydia satisfied and controlled by a passion of service, a love which asked no questions and claims which could not gall her, and for Dora the vision became blurred by her own tears. She had no shame for her ready emotion for this subject, and if the thought of Lydia childless had always hurt her, the thought of Lydia so enriched was a painful delight but she shook her head and the tears fell. 'Oliver won't do that.'

'Where's all his love, then?'

'Love's a queer thing, isn't it? He might do it if she asked him, but she won't, and, after all, it would be a good deal to ask, for the sake of another man's children.'

'Lydia's children,' William Nesbitt said.

She shook her head again. 'It's not only that – not only jealousy. Children would mean that Oliver had no more chance.'

'Of what?' he asked, although he knew.

'Of getting Lydia back. Of course that's what he's hoping for, that's what he's living for.'

'Then he may as well consider himself dead.'

'I'm not so sure. This – this stillness of his is making an impression. It's noble and effective. How can she help thinking of him alone, wanting her, and comparing him with Henry who has what he wants?'

'If Henry has what he wants, Lydia is not the woman I believe her.'

He was surprised to find that Dora understood him. 'No, but she's there,' she said. 'It's a kind of conquest, and if it isn't complete, well, it's all the better. That's amusing for Lydia, but irritating, too, and there are so many times when Henry's too much absorbed to think about her.'

'Quite right, too,' William Nesbitt grunted. 'You can't expect a man to be mooning round a woman all day long.'

'But Oliver could always be absorbed in her – and dazzled, and she forgets the rest. She misses him and she's sorry for him, and I think she often wants to hit Henry because he possesses her.'

'He doesn't possess her,' William Nesbitt persisted. 'Who could?'

'You know what I mean. And he sees her faults. Oliver forgave her everything. That's partly why she left him. He forgave her for being selfish.'

'Selfish?'

'Of course she's selfish. So is Henry, so there are battles. She has to be the chief person wherever she is and she can't with him.'

'My dear Dora, I think you wrong her.'

'No, I don't. I love her just as much as you do – '

'I doubt that.'

'I'm certain of it, but I'm not blind.'

'Blind!' he ejaculated.

'Well, darling, you're rather dazzled by her, too, and that's what she likes. Henry can't be blinking all the time and she gets bored. Besides, she's fretting about Oliver. I think Henry's rather too sure of himself and some day he may find her gone. And Oliver must know she's fretting. That's what he wants. There are hard places in Oliver. He's one of those quiet people who could plot for years and then take his revenge. If she could see that she'd be safe.'

'Safe?'

'For Henry.'

William Nesbitt had been standing still for an unprecedented length of time. Even the hands in his pockets were motionless, but the muscles round his eyes were twitching. 'You are not just,' he said with all the life gone from his voice. 'You've thrown the thing down so low after all my holding of it up.' He roused himself. 'But I still hold it up. Selfish she may be and I know she has to have a stage, but she knew there would be none at Mast-over. She went because she thought Henry Wyatt needed her – '

'Oh, how foolish we are in thinking people need us,' Dora cried. 'Women will throw away their lives for a sentiment.'

William Nesbitt was silent for a moment. Perhaps he was applying this remark to the daughter who made it, but when he spoke it was of Lydia. 'Because he needed her and because she loved him. I'm sure she loved him.'

'She loves him still.'

'Yet you think she means to leave him.'

'Oh, I don't say that. I don't know. Hate is so close to love. She loves him for himself but she hates him for making her hurt Oliver. She loves him because she's alive where he is, but she hates him because he means to keep her. And she would hate him if he didn't.'

'My dear child, where did you learn all this?'

231

'I worked it all out in my own little head.'

'You have made me very unhappy,' he said. It was one of the few melancholy remarks he was ever heard to utter, and at once he modified it. 'For a moment. I believe in Lydia.'

'Oh, so do I. In the quintessence of Lydia and that's several natures in one body. She's gay and serious, careless and conscientious, lawless and lawful all together. She's in love with Henry but she's sorry for Oliver, and when women begin to be sorry for people it's dangerous. She sent her love to you. I believe she loves you better than all the Henry's and Olivers in the world.'

'Then why doesn't she write to me?' he exclaimed.

'What's the good of asking why she does or doesn't do anything? If she went back to Oliver – '

'She can't do that,' he said sharply, and with an equal sharpness Dora asked, 'Why not?'

'Impossible,' he muttered to the fire.

'Well, you'll see,' she said wearily. 'She's been spoilt all her life and she misses it.'

'Ah, it isn't only that,' William Nesbitt almost pleaded. 'She's better than that. And anyhow,' he added angrily, that man ought to spoil her, too.'

'He does, in patches, but he thinks – yes, you can see it – he thinks she has a duty to him as well.'

'And so she has. She has thrown in her lot with him – she's got to stick to it. But if she doesn't, if by any chance she doesn't, I still believe in her.'

'I know. I know.' She laid back her head and shut her eyes. 'How cosy it is here, and peaceful.'

'Yes, it's a nice room,' he said. 'Fine old fireplace. Panelled walls. I was pleased when I discovered them. Tapping, you know. I'm always tapping things. And then I got my penknife and scraped. It's a fine old house. I wish Walter had a son.'

Dora, with her eyes still shut, said sleepily: 'You must take one of Mabel's boys into the business. I won't recommend my Maurice. I think he's rather dull, bless him.'

232

Ignoring that, he asked suddenly, 'Did you sleep in Mrs. Wyatt's bedroom?'

'I lay in it.'

'Awful bed, isn't it? Did you see the photographs of her?'

'Oh, yes. Lydia talks a lot about her. Says she's afraid of her.'

'Oh, she does, does she? What on earth do they stay there for? Why don't they go abroad and sit in the sun?'

'She says it would be too pleasant. I think she feels she has to pay and Henry can work best there, but when he has finished his book they are going away for a time. But at present it's dreary and she's wearing herself out. She wouldn't talk to me and she can't talk freely, about that, to Henry. He's an impatient person and if a thing's done, what's the good of wondering whether you ought to have done it? He'd say she ought to have thought of all that before – and it would be true. But it's hard to bottle it all up and not ask for reassurances and,' Dora repeated, 'she isn't happy.'

And now William Nesbitt saw that a tear was trickling from under each of Dora's eyelids.

'Don't cry, child, don't cry,' he begged. 'Nothing to cry about. Wipe your eyes. I can't bear to see you cry. Look here, shall I come home with you and talk to Herbert? Now don't pretend he hasn't given you the devil of a time over this, because I know he has, and I won't have it.'

Dora stood up and surveyed herself in the looking-glass above the fireplace. 'All signs will be gone before I get back,' she said, dabbing her cheeks with her handkerchief. 'And I must go now. Oh, by the way, Lydia has seen Ethel Miller. They had a touching meeting.'

'And what kind of parting?' It was odd how little this seemed to matter now.

'Tearful, on Ethel's part, and open-mouthed. Lydia says the poor girl was really miserable. She began by flinging her arms round Lydia's neck and gradually retreated, walking backwards, step by step. Lydia said it was funny, but I think it must have been rather sad. Of course she had to tell her husband. Ethel's the kind who would. Well, we shall get used to it all one day. Do you think some one could order a cab for me?'

'Yes, child, yes.' He could not bear to let her go – back to the pseudo-Gothic castle and a meanly irritable husband, and it was harder to bear her unhappiness than Lydia's, because he loved her less.

Chapter 30

It was with difficulty that William Nesbitt stirred up his optimism, his supporting faith that everything was for the best. Darkness, like a cloud spreading from Mastover to Radstowe, seemed to settle over him, so that even his vivid interest in life was dimmed for a time.

Janet, whose problems might have roused him, showed no sign of their existence: she poured out his coffee at breakfast, her burnished hair like a spot of sunshine in the room; she was deft and quiet, saying very little, betraying no inward storm. And when he came back at night he would meet her crossing the hall, see her moving with her smooth swiftness up or down the stairs, or watch the tail of her dress slipping through a doorway. In a person who could sit so still, it was strange that he never turned his latchkey without the certainty of a glimpse of her moving figure and, as it was not reasonable to suppose she spent her whole day in these wanderings, he came to the conclusion that she lingered in expectation of his return. This pleased him, but it also revealed the restless state of a mind which found comfort in his, and the blankness of a day in which the arrival of her old father was an event.

The cloud lifted a little. Under it, over there in Mastover, his dark daughter must remain, and in his fanciful mind he saw her like some unhappy queen, clothed in the red and purple of her state, bewildered, angry, sorrowful, tortured by the effects of the qualities that made her, and utterly remote in the closest intimacy she allowed her subjects. But here, Janet, in her elusive fairness, was like a watery sunbeam, intangible, yet capable of having her brightness transmuted into homlier uses. She, too, though differently, had captured his imagination, and dealing with her was like playing some game in which lightness of hand was as essential as quickness of head; but what was he to do with a girl whose chief relaxation was verbal sparring with her father?

The season of evening parties was approaching, but Janet had always shown little interest in it, and though she liked dancing for its own sake and accepted invitations as a matter of course, she had gone with an air of duty and returned without enthusiasm. Now, William Nesbitt, trundling home one evening, was inspired to pay his promised call on Violet, and he told her frankly that he had come to ask a favour. 'I want you to involve Janet in a giddy whirl,' he said. 'You and Walter are always gadding about. I wish you'd take her in tow and liven her up a little. Dull for her, you know, with her mother and me.'

Violet said, 'Do you think we are going to have a chance to be gay?'

'What? You don't mean that? Rubbish!' He tried to walk about the room, but the crowded furniture prevented him. 'Don't know how you can live in this box,' he said. 'Very nice, of course – very pretty –' He went to the window where the curtains were not yet drawn and looked down at the expanse of Lower Radstowe, and for a moment he watched more and more points of light popping out through the dusk. 'Plenty of room out there,' he said. 'I beg your pardon, my dear. Rather rude, I'm afraid. It's my upbringing, I suppose. No manners but lots of space.'

'I think you have lovely manners,' Violet said.

'Do you? I'm glad of that. I shall lose them though if we're going to be insulted by a set of nobodies, but somehow, my dear, I don't think we shall be. The people in this city have very little sense – why, they let me start here without a penny in my pocket and take half their business from them – but they respect money and I happen to have made that while they were all asleep. I think my money and my house and my one-horse shay, not to mention my charming family,' and in acknowledgment of her good opinion, he made a courtly bow, 'I think all these will out-

236

weigh Lydia's trespass. They're not all so unworldly as Teetotal Jones. Besides, there's such a thing as curiosity. I should think there is!' he added, thinking of his own.

Once more he proved to be right and with that self-complacency which was forgivable because he was humorously conscious of it, he told himself that the foresight which had built up his business, the power of guessing what other people were going to do before they knew themselves, was not likely to be wrong in a little affair like this. Mrs. Nesbitt had never been ardent in paying or receiving calls, but now she found herself obliged to pay a good many in return for those she received. It was soon after the second sewing-meeting, at which Mrs. Miller had markedly avoided her, that several ladies remembered it was long since they had had a chat with Mrs. Nesbitt and, dressed in their obvious best, for Upper Radstowe made serious distinctions in such matters, they rapped with the shining knocker on Mrs. Nesbitt's beautiful front door and entered the Nesbitt stronghold, which gave no indications of wishing to stand a siege.

Though the object of these visitors was evident, they were welcomed graciously and they departed with an increased respect for their hostess and, as the only addition to their knowledge, the belief that though the rumours about Lydia Stone might be true, her mother was not outwardly affected by them. Mrs. Nesbitt had a stronger personality than most people, and if her family was not in awe of her it was because she had done her share in giving power to her children, but she could awe other people successfully. A weaker woman would have betrayed herself and given opportunities for possible spite, but her dignity and her command of the situation, which was nothing more than her strength of character, succeeded in enhancing her prestige with a spice of mystery. Whatever was said behind her back, not even a hint reached her ears. Mrs. Miller's enmity, though it existed surely enough, was of a piece with all her possessions, drab and ineffectual, and the battle which had threatened to be so tremendous had dwindled into nothing: the opposing forces had simply melted away. She had braced herself for a great encounter and she may have suffered from reaction, almost from disappointment, but to William she said, a little scornfully, 'You see, I was right. I was never afraid of Mrs. Miller.'

'I'm always afraid of everybody,' was his reply, 'and most of all of you, my dear, and you have shown me that I have cause.'

'One has to be sure of oneself,' was Mrs. Nesbitt's summing-up of her success.

'You ought to have the Victoria Cross, Kate, but as you are not eligible for that, take this,' and into her lap he flung a little packet. 'Wear it as a symbol of my love and admiration.'

She opened the box with fingers not quite steady. 'You're dreadfully extravagant, William.'

'I've told you before you must have something to leave your daughters,' he said, but this time, and he noticed it with a quick contraction near his heart, she did not tell him that she had no intention of dying yet. She was, in fact, less spirited than she had ever been. Her effort had been made and in the consciousness of her exhaustion he divined a deep resentment against Lydia who had caused it. She was never mentioned by her mother, as though she had been dead so long that even memories had faded, and in this silence his own devotion and the romantic nature of his love were increased. He had once seen all his children as so many roads on which dangers might lurk and spring, but now, for he, too, was tired, he seemed to see them in a less adventurous guise. They were like tangled skeins of colour weaving into his own wintry grey, and it was natural that the three he loved best should have their colours connected with visible aspects of the world which he loved, too.

Dora was all brown and golden with the loveliness of autumn, experienced, a little sharpened by frost but growing maturely wise; Lydia was purple and scarlet, a blend of regal, passionate colours, like a stormy sunset which does not always fulfil its promises or its threats; and Janet was pale and bright as the spring. Autumn, sunset, and spring, these came and went; they had their fruit, their promise of return, their buds and flowers, but their distresses, their storms, and clouds, and winds, were in no way evil: deeply he believed that all things worked together for good, and though he had in him little of the missionary, there were times when he longed to cry out his creed, for here was Dora, learning more quickly the lesson of tolerance which, no doubt, her life with Herbert had early begun; and there, in Mastover, where the woods by now must be almost bare, Lydia's uncertainties had preserved Janet from a mistaken bondage. The idea that he could have made another and less fair picture did not occur to him. If he had not been the man he was, he could have pointed to Kate's painful struggles, to Lydia's unhappiness, to Dora's domestic felicity marred and to his own feelings of suspense; but, as it was, while he could see all this, he looked at effects which he was determined must be good.

Every morning he went out to work, disdaining any means of locomotion but his own legs, and every evening he walked home more slowly through the darkness, with his thoughts for company, and the sights and sounds of the old city for solace. From below, as he mounted, he could hear the clang of tramcar bells and, when the tide was high, the hooting of the steamers in the river and, accustomed as he was to that sound, it never failed to quicken that necessity for adventure which had first sent him to sea and now guided his life on shore. In this safe darkness where he walked on pavements, he thought of nights at sea with the wind howling and the rain lashing him with whips: he thought of the immense loneliness of those hours and the inspiration of command. A simple life it had been, deliberately complicated, in a mental sense, by his own character; and now that life presented him with complications which were not of his own making, he could look back and wonder that he had not accepted with more gratitude those peaceful hours of physical danger and plain duty.

But he did not regret the present, and the clustered houses, beautified by night and made mysterious by the humanity they sheltered within their walls, the flat shadows of trees and leaves at his feet, swaying in time with the things they shadowed, gave him in an intenser degree the joy he had known in the wonder of the sea and stars. And often, as he walked, he returned to his old thought. Close to him were thousands of people of whom he knew nothing, but whose lives were full of problems, were important to themselves, tortured or unhappy, or more likely, streaked as his own was with pain and pleasure. The noise of their footsteps, approaching and retreating, were to him a mere echo of what to some one else was an essential sound, and he was fascinated by the thought that what was real for him was for another but an illusion, that his indifferences were the passionate desires of others; and it seemed to him that nothing but direst physical cold and hunger, and perhaps not even those, could ever take from existence its enduring charm.

Chapter 31

IN Upper Radstowe there were subscription dances for
which only those who were considered the cream of that
society could buy tickets. There was, perhaps, a good deal
of preservative in the cream, but cream it was called, and
the Nesbitts, in spite of Violet's doubts, were still admitted
to be of it, and Janet went to all the dances, a little less
unwillingly, William Nesbitt fancied, than in former years.
There were other gaieties in Upper Radstowe as well as
these, and often now, when William Nesbitt went home,
he missed Janet's hovering welcome because she was
dressing for a party. The house was very quiet and he
remembered how, when Lydia was at home, her head had
popped over the banisters before she ran downstairs to
speak to him and ran up again on her proper business. He
had never seen her move slowly: Janet's actions were quick
enough, but gave no impression of haste, while Lydia,
always in a hurry, seemed to fill the house with life, and
he had not grown accustomed to her absence. Mentally,
however, he was more than ever conscious of her, and so
sadly, that he had to make an effort to greet Kate with
cheerfulness. She sat by the drawing-room fire, languidly
doing her crochet, and he knew that though their thoughts
were different, they shared like feelings of exhaustion and
weariness and a like determination not to speak of them.

'We ought to have a holiday,' he suggested. 'Let's go
abroad for a month,' and he was relieved when she said,
'With Christmas so near? Oh, no, William. And we can't
leave Janet, coming home late at night from parties.'

He used no persuasion, for he wished to remain near
Lydia lest the time should come when she had need of him
and, in a way which was not his wife's, he had to watch
over Janet, though, for the moment, she was merely pur-

241

suing her usual quiet road, doing her little duties in the house and, as he suspected with some pleasure, pretending that her pleasures were duties too.

Christmas came and passed with a strained gaiety. There had never before been a Christmas without Lydia and the family party was an effort. It was hard for William Nesbitt to realize that no suddenly opened door would reveal her, vivid and alert, straight and slim, and the game of hide-and-seek, all over the house, which was the winter counterpart of the summer game in the garden on his wife's birthday, seemed to him to have lost all its zest. She had laughed louder, run more quickly, hidden more cleverly, and escaped capture better than anybody else: she had played the game with an earnestness which inspired the rest, and in her absence Dora only laughed and exerted herself enough to deceive the children. She hid lazily behind doors and allowed herself to be found, and William Nesbitt, lifting his eyebrows at this lassitude, was answered with a little gesture of open, empty hands.

'I can't be bothered!' Dora said.

He nodded. That was what he felt. His only pleasure was in the sight of Janet, aware of the general constraint and yet, in spite of it, revealing a new capacity for gaiety, and in the thought of the cheque he had sent Lydia for a Christmas present. He wanted her to justify the conduct which had brought this dullness to his home, but she must have the means to act freely, even if it was in the lowering of her standard. What was she doing in that little dark house, he wondered? Had she picked holly in the woods and laid it above the picture of Henry's mother? He shrugged his shoulders and went from room to room, a charming father, a genial father-in-law, a delightful grandfather who let himself be caught and kissed under the mistletoe by all the children and rewarded each with the bright new shilling which was the prize for their skill.

'Grandfather's not so quick as he used to be,' Cromwell announced. 'It was harder to catch him last year,' and Mrs. Nesbitt said severely, 'Nonsense, Cromwell. Grandfather has had rheumatism. That makes him a little slow.'

'Well,' Cromwell said, looking and feeling aggrieved, 'I said he was slow, Grandmother,' and Mrs. Nesbitt, flushing a little hoped no one had perceived the inwardness of her rebuke.

This was her only sign of consciousness that things were not as they should have been, and at night, commenting as she always did on the day, she said serenely, 'It has been a very nice Christmas.'

'Very nice,' William Nesbitt said, so heartily that she took a stealthy look at him. She knew quite well that if he had been really happy he would have mocked his own pleasure with some faintly acidulated little speech, and with a kind of jealousy, with envy and with anger, she pretended to accept his sentiment, but she lay awake in the darkness, letting loose the pain she had controlled, and whether it was outraged pride or longing which hurt her more she did not know. She could not understand why life should have dealt her such a blow and, though Lydia was the instrument, she had a dim belief that behind Lydia was some power beyond her knowledge, something which for its own purposes had made a victim of herself. She was the more resentful. Anger, as William Nesbitt had once said, was an emotion that sustained, but against the unknown it lost its force, and she could do nothing but lie there in a bewildered suffering.

And then, irritating yet comforting her, came William's voice: 'What's the matter, Kate?'

She hesitated. It was hard to make a sentence out of her confusion and dangerous to open a door from which her tortured feelings might rush. She said quietly, 'I think I am over-tired – so much to think of. I'm getting old, William.'

'You are still better-looking than your daughters.'

'Of course I don't believe that, but I like to hear you say so. I thought Janet looked very pretty to-night.'

'Is she pretty? Luminous, I should say, like a shell with a light inside it.'

'What ideas you get,' she half complained.

'Yes, a light,' he repeated. 'Lighten our darkness, O Lord.'

At that Mrs. Nesbitt said good-night severely.

He felt that the Lord was certainly lightening Janet's darkness, though the word had never really fitted her. It was a stillness, rather, and now it was being stirred, and that unacknowledged excitement which he had suspected was becoming more obvious to him. It was pleasant to see her set off in her pretty frock and gleaming slippers, amusing to imagine her aloofness puzzling and perhaps attracting her partners, and one night it occurred to him that it would be interesting to see her return. Mrs. Nesbitt insisted that some one should wait up for her, even though she was brought back in the carriage; she had an imagination equal to ideas of kidnapping or the coachman's collapsing on the box, and she could not rest without the certainty of being informed if Janet did not appear at the expected hour. It was Mary who usually waited, but when William Nesbitt had once decided that a line of action would be interesting he was not to be turned from it in spite of his wife's protest.

'Mary can do it,' she said firmly.

'But Mary has to get up early in the morning, and think, Kate, how much more useful I should be if Janet didn't come home. Telephone to the police – that sort of thing, you know. Mary would only flop about like a frightened fowl.'

'Mary is a good servant,' Mrs. Nesbitt pronounced.

'Then let us preserve her health and strength at any cost. Besides, I can work at my plans. I've a lot of notions in my head, Kate. No time at the office – people coming in and out all day asking foolish questions. I'll wait for the child. I shall like it and you can sleep in peace.'

This arrangement was made one night after Janet had started for her party and when he opened the door in answer to her gentle knock, he distinctly heard departing footsteps on the gravel. Hobbs was on the box, waiting to see his young mistress safely housed before he went to the stables, according to his orders and his own sense of fitness, and William Nesbitt said at once: 'If that's Walter, he must drive back.'

'It isn't Walter,' Janet said as she passed into the hall.

William Nesbitt stood on the step for a moment, looked at the sky, bade Hobbs good-night and locked the door. 'Wonderful moon,' he said to Janet, 'but the wind's rising and I can smell rain. I can always smell rain or snow – queer thing, that.'

'But it doesn't always snow when you smell it.'

'Now, child, don't be tart. Come in here by the fire. Egg sandwiches – I'll have one myself. Feet warm?'

'I've worn out my slippers,' she said, looking at them. 'At least, Dr. Gregory has. He treads on my toes.'

'You don't mean to tell me that man dances!'

'Well, he goes to them,' she said demurely.

'Heroic!' William Nesbitt exclaimed as though to himself. 'Heroic! This age is not degenerate, after all! The moral fibre of our ancestors, Janet, survives in the person of old Dryasdust.'

'But he doesn't dance much,' Janet said, still looking at her feet.

'How many times?'

'Six.'

'Poor toes,' he said. 'All that damage in six dances.'

'What made you wait up for me to-night?' she asked.

'Fatherly feeling. I was not suspicious. I suppose that was old Dryasdust I heard?'

'It was Dr. Gregory. He's only thirty-six?'

'Then he ought to be ashamed of looking like fifty.'

'Oh, do you think he does?'

'He looks what your father might have been if you hadn't been so lucky as you are. Does he live on nuts and eat the shells?'

'Don't you like him?'

'I know nothing about him, but six times! On your toes! And he doesn't pay for your slippers.'

'He would like to,' Janet said calmly.

'Has he told you so?'

'He has asked me to marry him.'

'To-night?'

'Oh, yes, and several times before.'

He stared at her in an astonishment caused not by this fact, which was natural enough, but by her way of speaking of it, this directness so unlike her usual vagueness; and while he stared so fiercely that he looked angry, losing his control over his manner for the first time in his dealings with her, he was thinking rapidly, and before he spoke again he had time to decide that he must preserve the impression he had plainly made on her.

'What did you say to him, if I may ask?'

She was, he could see, a little hurt at the lack of the sympathy she had looked for, but she replied in this new, practical manner, 'I told him I wasn't going to marry any one.'

'No man,' he slightly stressed the word, 'would take that for an answer.'

'No, but, you see, I told him I would marry him if marriage were possible for me.'

'Janet, are you mad?'

'Mad?' She faced him hardly, as cold as a spring wind. 'Why should you think me mad?'

'That man! My dear child,' his tone was compassionate, 'no doubt you wanted to be kind, to spare his feelings, but it wasn't wise. You should have been more final. Now he will go on hoping and you will have no peace.'

'I shall have no peace,' she added, 'no peace,' and, her voice rising a little, she added, 'because I need him.'

He felt as though they two were walking on a tight-rope, swaying, bound to fall if he spoke or drew a breath: he did not know how to keep his balance or hers; he thought they might be saved if he cried out, 'Then, child, if you love him, marry him!' and suddenly he knew he must say, as he did say, gruffly, 'Of course you can't marry him. Ridiculous! I won't consent to it.'

246

He admired the look she gave him. It was cool and almost pitying, and he thought, 'This is one of the worst moments I have ever had. She misunderstands me. She thinks I don't understand her.' It had always been his pride to show his children he could read their thoughts, and now he had to pretend to fail this daughter and he was not even sure that he was wise.

'I would marry him to-morrow,' Janet said, 'if Lydia had not taught me not to dare.'

Manfully ignoring this, he said sharply, 'You would not do it with my consent.'

She smiled a little. 'I should have to do without it. And,' she continued quietly, 'I told him I would live with him for a year and at the end of that I would marry him if we found we loved each other.'

'You told him that!'

'Yes, but of course he wouldn't have it. Surely you are not going to pretend to be shocked after all you have told me and all I have seen of marriage? It seems to me the only honest thing to do. So there's no way out.'

'What puzzles me,' he said, 'is that you should want one.' He paced up and down the room and looked keenly at the figure of his daughter as she stooped over the fire, at the white neck, the fine shoulder-blades showing through the lace of her dress, and as though from a great distance, he heard a murmur:

'He has been very unhappy.'

He checked an exclamation. Had not Dora said that pity was dangerous? Yet Janet had pitied Oliver and ceased to love him, and William Nesbitt's hopes swelled. 'Ah,' he said, 'he has been telling you the story of his life, has he? They all do that. But if you don't care enough for him to take risks, you don't care for him at all. And, in any case, you need time, for I'm not sure,' he was deliberately cruel, but he spared himself the sight of her face, 'I'm not sure that you are very constant in your loves.'

'I didn't say I loved him,' she retorted quickly, 'but one doesn't easily let go of the best.'

247

He felt a little tremor of excitement. Surely she loved him if she could say that of him, and he hesitated for a moment before he said lightly, 'I'm sorry for Dr. Gregory, but he should not have been so foolish. I suppose the poor fellow will hover round you till Bunford comes back, and then you'll forget each other. Why, you haven't eaten any sandwiches?' She stood up, and, disregarding her distant air, he said, 'I hope you will make no such suggestion to any other lover. Another man might have agreed to it. You were safe with old Dryasdust, of course, but a younger man, a – more passionate man might have taken you at your word or else insulted you.'

'No one to whom I could say that would insult me,' she said proudly.

'Well, child, don't run the risk again. Now go to bed and go to sleep. I haven't any doubt the doctor loves you – how could he help it? – but love's infectious and the second person gets it, willy-nilly, in a milder form. It seems ungrateful not to, doesn't it? but it doesn't last for ever. Go to sleep and forget him. We can't take on everybody else's pain.'

She went, without saying good-night, trailing her cloak from a slack arm, and William Nesbitt was left in profound bewilderment. What had he done? Had he lost a unique chance – for he knew their confidences were over – of helping her to the man she loved? Or had he stiffened her into a determination to marry him? This was what he had tried to do, yet, even if it succeeded, it might be a mistake. He cursed his habit of meddling and, in the very act, continued to do it, for he was wondering whether he should enlist Kate's aid in disparaging the doctor. She would disparage him thoroughly and rouse Janet into violent loyalty, but was that what he wanted and had he not done enough of that already? Why should he beguile her into any marriage? Did she really love him and who could be sure of love? But she seemed to have grown into a woman in a few hours and he was half afraid of her, more than half afraid of her capacity for some mad action. Here was

Lydia again! This was her effect. Her bright colours persisted in weaving themselves into other people's lives, and for a moment he saw any possible indiscretion of Janet as a reproach which could be levelled against her sister and which must be prevented for that reason.

Then he steadied himself. There were other aspects and he must think of Janet only, for this was her affair. He would have to go carefully, be watchful, and – he shrugged his shoulders – if possible he must be quiet. 'Irrepressible!' he sighed in criticism of himself. 'Irrepressible!' He had never meant to tell Kate of Janet's proposal to the doctor: he could imagine a good deal, but he could not imagine himself doing that, and now he decided to tell her nothing at all for a time. It was foolish to foresee trouble, but his heart was heavy as he put out the lights and went up to bed. He could bear any sorrow for his children except the sorrow of being estranged from them, but this would come right, it must come right.

He slipped quietly into bed and fell asleep in that assurance.

Chapter 32

WILLIAM NESBITT was not one of those who, waking with a dull sensation of something wrong, have to grope in sleepily-befogged minds for the cause: as soon as Mary knocked at the bedroom door he remembered clearly the incidents of the early morning, and he had to restrain his immediate desire to countermand his wife's order that Miss Janet should not be waked and to go and see if she had eloped in the darkness.

'Bless you, Kate,' he said, 'a dance is nothing to a girl. Does her good. Why shouldn't she pour out my coffee?'

'I expect she will,' Mrs. Nesbitt said. 'The children never do what I tell them. She ought to sleep. She has been looking tired lately. Of course it's no good my talking to her. She always walks out of the room if I say anything personal.'

'She's a moth,' William Nesbitt said. 'A moth, but what do moths turn into? Caterpillars, isn't it? No, that's wrong. They lay eggs and die. Well, we all do that. I don't mean children, Kate. I mean thoughts, ideas, actions. Life is a solemn business and one's almost afraid to go on with it.'

'It's a good thing we start it before we know,' she responded with unexpected sympathy.

'Still, it's interesting,' he said, and Mrs. Nesbitt looked over her teacup at the tree-tops visible from her bed. She had no intention of continuing the conversation: it would only lead to more of William's nonsense and more of her own pain and, for his part, he had so much to consider that he was willing to be silent. This business was too delicate for his meddling. 'What did he know of the heart of a girl?' he asked himself in scorn, and in a secret cranny of his mind he kept a belief that he knew more of it than Janet did. What did he know of the man to whom she had offered her freshness? He knew nothing, he answered firmly. The man might be a Bluebeard, a maniac, or a villain, but William Nesbitt, who had experience as well as insight, was convinced that Janet's lover was what he called a righteous man. He was too old for her, he persisted, fighting his certainty that no youth would ever satisfy his daughter.

'Oh, I give it up!' he exclaimed aloud.

Mrs. Nesbitt turned her head. 'What's the matter, William?'

'My dear, I'm an old fool. I'm always trying to tackle problems that are too hard for me!' And cunningly he added, 'I worked at those plans for hours last night.'

'Oh, well, William, you always succeed in what you do.'

'If I could be sure of that, Kate! The thing is not to try to do too much. "Study to be quiet and mind your own business," as Paul says.'

'You seem to know a lot about Paul,' she said, 'but I don't know where you pick it up, for you never go to church.'

'But I have a Bible at the office and what's more, I read it. There's no record of Paul's having daughters, though. A pity that. It would have been awful for the daughters, but what a help to me! A text for every day. There's more about daughters in Shakespeare. I keep him with the Bible. King Lear – he had no sense. D'you know, I think Janet's a little like Cordelia. Never struck me before. You should read "King Lear," Kate. Wonderful stuff. Wind and rain on a moor, that's how I think of it, but I can never forgive him for being so stupid about that girl of his. No perceptions. That's worse than too many, though that's dangerous. "Study to be quiet" – '

'But you never do, William.'

'I'm going to begin from to-day.'

'Then, dear, why not go and have your bath?'

He laughed, and a little smile curled Mrs. Nesbitt's straight lips.

'I think I love you best when your tongue is sharpest,' he said, and immediately her face put on its defensive look. Splashing busily, he wondered if he would ever understand that woman: she expected homage, of a discreet kind, yet at the same time she suspected it – after all these years! It was his fault, he supposed. The children did not suspect him, though they saw through him sometimes, and in truth he had seldom given them cause for suspicion. He had, perhaps, dealt better with them than with her, for between husband and wife who love each other there must always be a kind of warfare; but his heart smote him for his deception of Janet, less for the thing itself than for his fear of its miscarrying. 'Watch and pray,' he said, doubting his ability to do no more, and rubbing himself vigorously.

He was relieved to see Janet in the dining-room. She smiled politely but not quite naturally as she said good-morning, and he saw that she intended to treat him with a distant courtesy. Watching her covertly, he was sure she had not slept and his own appetite failed him. He depended more than he would have owned on the serenity of his relations with his friends, and he was near retracting all he had said for the sake of winning her again. It was hard work to be silent, to feel himself in disgrace, to meet her guarded eyes, to leave the house in the certainty that she thought he had failed her, and to return in that certainty at night. Only in the office could he rid his mind of its weight, but even the office, and he would not have it otherwise, was not entirely free from family affairs. Dora had invaded it with her troubles and now, after some days of Janet's estrangement, he had a letter from Lydia. He was afraid to open it: his hopes and his fears were in confusion, for here again he was not sure what was right and what was wrong, but telling himself that at least he could believe in the essential goodness of her intentions he slit the envelope roughly.

'William,' she wrote, 'I may pop into the office before long, so don't be out. Be sitting behind your desk with that nice face of yours when I enter, heavily veiled, pallid and mysterious. But alas, I haven't a heavy veil and you can't buy them in Mastover. However, I can manage the pallor and the mystery. I want to talk to you. I want to escape from Mastover. For a little while? For a long while?

252

I don't know. Anyhow, escape – that's the word. I'm imprisoned here, imprisoned by trees and thick walls and ugly furniture and portraits. Yes, portraits, William. You were clever to give me that hint and Mrs. Wyatt certainly has become malevolent. She watches me all the time and I'm disappointed in her. I thought she was wise and tolerant, but poor thing, the grave has narrowed her.

'Still, I'm just as much disappointed in myself. I'm no heroine. I'm a nasty, scratchy, impatient little beast who wants to show off all the time and run away if she can't. I love my own personality too much, that's what's the matter with me, and now that I'm in contact with a bigger – and in some, but not all, ways a better one – I'm restive. I'm afraid of losing myself. I can't bear to think that it may slip from me. I ought to be willing to merge myself and sometimes I think I will and then a spasm of anger comes over me, for why should I? I'm not big enough, or meek enough, or perhaps I don't love enough. I don't know. It's like bathing in the sea and leaping every minute so that a wave shan't swamp me. Exhilarating but exhausting. I wanted to bathe. I went into the water willingly, but I like to come out when I choose. And of course I can come out, but there are currents that make it hard. They draw one back. I suppose I shall end by being a fish. At the moment I'm amphibious, so be prepared to see a mermaid at your door one day.

'If I could see you for a few minutes, instead of Mrs. Wyatt looking down her long nose, what a relief! Why was I made like this? As soon as a person catches me I want to run. Yet because Oliver only cajoled I went away. I think the wonderful thing about you is that you have done neither; you have just loved me. Now, don't think Henry doesn't love me. He'll love me for ever – I've seen to that – and I'll love him for ever. He has given me more than anybody else could give – sweetness, sharpness, something like frost on flowers, and I've given him little more than a mess of moods which even he, who understands people in the abstract (see his well-known novels), can't quite make out. And then, in my mind which has nothing else to work at, there are rival claims nagging all the time. I had no business to leave Oliver and I don't want to lose myself and I can't bear to leave Henry.

'I told you I wasn't going to be happy. I think I shall go into a convent, but they'd soon turn me out. Oliver wouldn't turn me out. Oh, no, he's waiting, half expecting this, and that makes me determined to disappoint him. And yet I can't bear to think of him alone. And just because Henry expects me to stay, I want to give him a shock! So now you know what kind of daughter you have. I hope you're ashamed of me, but somehow I can't be ashamed of myself. It all sounds very wicked when it's put into words, but the truth – oh, well, I needn't try to explain anything to you. And it's really rather funny, though sad.

'So much for me, but, William dear, can't you find some nice safe husband for Jane? It's queer advice from a person whose own marriage has been so odd, but she isn't happy either, and she needs a little bullying from a trustworthy person. What a mercy she can't marry Oliver! She's not like me – she ought to be held. And if you could arrange for Herbert to disappear, finally, on some dark night, I'd thank you on my knees, but I'm afraid you won't do that, even for me. If these things could be managed, the family would be comfortably settled, all except me. And oh, William, thank you for that money. I ought to have said so long ago. Pray for the soul of your Lydia and look out for her o' Thursday or thereabouts.'

William Nesbitt read the letter again, and when he had burnt it he turned from the fire and stood for a long time looking at the river and the fields beyond. It was early February and though he could not see the thickening of the trees across the water, he knew that the brown buds were there, waiting for the green to burst through, and over the river, the bridges, the ships and houses there lay the hard, exciting look of spring. It chilled yet braced him, and his thoughts, from being troubled, became stern and cold. He had always told himself that Lydia would justify her action, and now he was determined that she should. He was almost angry with her. Was all this effort, all this pain, to be wasted for a whim? He would not have it. Yet he was secretly, though sorrowfully, glad that he was right about her. No man could hold her, but it remained for her to learn to hold herself. She had said that all he had done was to love her, and though she had said it in gratitude he remembered the words as a reproach. It was not enough. He must make her face her duty, whatever it might be, and do it.

A smile came slowly on his lips and round his eyes. He knew his own weakness, he knew he was like a lover who could see faults in an absent mistress and forget them in her presence, and when Lydia entered his office with a little flourish, a dramatic gesture, a sudden lightening of the room, he would – yes, it was true – he would be dazzled by something which was not beauty, nor wit, not virtue, though in some degree she had them all, but by the peculiar compound of qualities and defects which unfailingly charmed him. He lost, for a few minutes, his own point of view and looked beyond it at the mystery of personality. In excess, it was a danger, like great beauty or great unscrupulousness; it was dangerous to its owner and to those it touched and, like genius, it could not be crushed out of existence. No, for all Lydia might say about being swamped, she would continue to leap and swim, wearing herself out in the process, perhaps, but even in the defeat of death leaving an unforgettable memory of vitality, an emptiness never to be filled. There he was again! He was incapable of resisting her. She was not so good as Dora, so hard-working as Mabel, so fair as Janet, nor so genial as Walter, but she seemed to touch him at all points with a light and lingering finger. There was no harm in that, if he could keep his head and he meant to do it. He wrote saying that she must come on a certain day, or he would not guarantee an interview and at the same time he wrote to Oliver.

255

Chapter 33

He reminded himself that he did not intend to meddle in Janet's affairs, and for two days he held his hand, but all the time he knew what he meant to do and on the third day he called at the doctor's house on the way home. It was his consulting hour and William Nesbitt sat patiently in the waiting-room until a woman with a swollen face and an anæmic-looking girl had been called into the inner sanctum and dismissed.

When his turn came, he said at once, 'It's not rheumatism, this time, Dr. Gregory. I want to talk to you about my daughter.' A sort of spasm contracted the doctor's face and William Nesbitt thought that even in a grimace it was a good face, grave and plain but remarkably honest. 'She tells me you want to marry her. She has developed prejudices against marriage, as you know, and she's quite right in theory, but when it comes to practice in the person of one's daughter, the theories have to go to the wall. I'm perfectly inconsistent, perfectly.'

'She told me you would never consent to it.'

'That is what I told her. I deliberately scoffed at the idea of you as a husband for her because I thought it might steady her views, but I don't know that it has done much good.'

'Then you have no objection to me as a husband for her?'

'I object to all the husbands of my daughters,' William Nesbitt said irritably, 'on principle. In practice they choose for themselves and I submit of course. If the child marries you, I must be content.'

'I am glad to know that,' Dr. Gregory said and he leant forward, picked up a pen from his desk, examined it and laid it down again before he looked fully into William Nesbitt's eyes and said, 'Because she married me to-day.'

His own eyes were a clear hazel and they did not waver under William Nesbitt's stare, which was not angry, nor astonished, but extraordinarily thoughtful. He stared and then dropped back in his chair. 'Then you have me to thank for it,' he said.

'I was afraid so,' Dr. Gregory murmured.

'But you took the chance.'

'Yes, I took the chance. I'm quite aware,' he held his head in his hands, 'I'm quite aware that I have behaved badly, but the fact is I was worn out.'

'I see,' William Nesbitt said slowly. 'I see. Did you tell her that?'

'I don't know what I said, but she knew.'

'Yes. I suppose she took her chance, too. Well, you've made a great mistake, though it's my own fault.'

'I have to apologize to you, sir. It was wrong, I knew it was wrong, but I took what I could get.'

'So she said it must be now or never? Absurd! You ought to have seen through that.'

'But I tell you,' the doctor snapped, 'I was beyond seeing anything. I'm sorry.'

'Oh, don't be sorry,' William Nesbitt said mildly. 'I'm not an ordinary parent. I understand things. But yes, a great mistake.'

'I have admitted that I owe you an apology,' Gregory said wearily.

'That's true, but I wasn't thinking of that. That doesn't matter. Janet does. Where is she now?'

'In your house, I hope.'

'D'you imagine she loves you?'

'I know nothing about her!' the doctor cried angrily.

William Nesbitt jingled his money, and after a moment his new son-in-law demanded, 'Wouldn't you have done it yourself?'

'Certainly not. I never do things twice if once will do. Waste of time. You'll have to marry her again for her mother's sake, in public, and you'll have to woo her, at a disadvantage.'

'I'm not sure,' the doctor said in a low voice and slowly, 'I'm not sure that it is a disadvantage.'

William Nesbitt controlled a smile. The man knew more than he claimed, more than he realized, but would he be able to turn his knowledge to account? 'Janet a moth,' William Nesbitt said and not for the first time, but he reflected that the idea might be new to Gregory.

'A moth!' The doctor mocked the insufficiency of the word.

'Yes. But there are butterfly nets.'

'Do I,' Dr. Gregory asked with a sort of mirthless humour, 'look as if I could handle one?'

'You could learn,' William Nesbitt said gravely, and suddenly he had a sense of the absurdity of the situation, but he did not laugh. Indeed he wondered if there were not something hopelessly flippant in his constitution. He ought to have been acting the outraged father, yet he sat there amiably conversing with the offender and feeling secretly glad that the outrage had been perpetrated. It was awkward, a ticklish business, but if the doctor had any wit it might be a success. 'Yes, you could learn,' he repeated. 'In the meantime, you and Janet must put up with any inconvenience I see fit to put you to. I think I have a right to expect that.'

'I am in your hands,' Dr. Gregory said.

'I wish you were. I'm afraid you're in Janet's. And, as I said before, her mother must not know of this. There must be a wooing and a marriage.'

'I don't think she will marry me twice,' the doctor said with a painful grin.

'You've got to make her.'

'Perhaps you can tell me how,' the other said with a strained politeness.

William Nesbitt felt some impatience. A man with that mouth and those eyes could not be weak in essence: he looked, at least, as though he had conquered himself but – William Nesbitt caught at this solution with the excitement of a connoisseur in emotion – he was awed by a slip of a girl, by her virginity, her aloofness and mystery. In the eyes of that man – who had been unhappy – she was too rare to be touched or breathed upon, almost too rare for his unhallowed gaze, but not, such is the inconsistency of human nature, too rare to be bound to him with a ring. William Nesbitt liked the man for seeing her thus, but it was not a practical view to take and it was not good for Janet to be worshipped in this manner. Janet, he thought, needed a good shaking: she ought to be physically beaten, but as that also was impracticable the beating must be done morally. He decided, to his own astonishment, that the child was something of a prig and yet, pathetically enough, out of her loneliness, her sorrow at the loneliness of another, her faith in this man and her lack of faith in herself, she had resigned, defiantly, her apparent sense of superiority, and William Nesbitt felt a dreadful qualm for her while he wondered at the courage of women.

'I don't know you!' he cried out. 'I know nothing about you! I have always expected some sort of certificate of character from my sons-in-law and now it is too late. And what does Janet know?'

'All I could tell her.'

The cry became a mutter. 'That's no good. The things a woman needs to know are the one's she finds out for herself.'

'That absolves me, then,' Dr. Gregory said.

'But she ought to have had more time. Not much use, though, before marriage. It's the institution that's all wrong. Horrible,' he added in a murmur.

Dr. Gregory had the air of waiting patiently for these generalizations to cease.

'However,' William Nesbitt went on, 'the institution exists and we've got to make the best of it, and I don't suppose it will be any worse than usual in your case, if you'll take my advice. It will be, though, if – you'll excuse me – if you grovel.'

'I have no intention of grovelling,' the doctor said with some show of annoyance.

'Ah,' William Nesbitt said weightily, 'intentions – intentions! But Janet likes to make you grovel, and then she uses it against you. I propose,' he stopped to tap the desk with his long forefinger, 'I propose that you do what a young man ought to do – come to my house and court my daughter.'

'She won't allow it.'

William Nesbitt lifted his shoulders, his eyebrows, his hands, 'If that's your attitude, my advice is useless. Are you going to live in this house and let Janet live in mine? Are you never going to see her or speak to her?'

'I'm willing to wait.'

'Then, you'll wait for ever. I tell you, she's sitting at home now and curling her lip at you. Oh, don't ask me to explain it all. I understand it, of course, but it's inexplicable, all the same. All wrong – quite mad. She's a member of a mad family – not insanity, just madness. However, there it is and I'd ask you to kidnap her if it wouldn't break her mother's heart. As it is, well, can't you see for yourself? She's made you marry her and now, if you don't pursue her, she'll hate you. She's pretty near it at this moment, I should think. Come to dinner to-night. I shall tell my wife I met you and asked you to come. And I shall tell Janet I know she's – she's married to you. I shall pretend I don't mind. That will annoy her.'

'I will take your advice,' Dr. Gregory said gravely. 'And thank you for your forbearance.'

'I love my daughter,' William Nesbitt said simply. 'I believe I shall like you. I can't see anything go amiss without wanting to put it right. Must have things shipshape, even in a storm.'

He went home, wearing an expression of amusement and wonder. This was all so ridiculous that he had to believe in its reality. 'Nothing is more absurd than life,' he told the sky. He was angry with the doctor for yielding to Janet's folly: it was almost as inexcusable as running off without the formality of marriage: in a way it was worse, for it had the same selfishness sanctified by the law and it was irrevocable. He could have been very angry indeed, but he was not the man to waste his energies when he had work to do and he was too wise to condemn the doctor completely because of one misdeed, especially when it was one which had served his own turn, and though his love for Lydia was not of the kind which applauded all her judgments, he had some satisfaction in thinking that what she had advised had come to pass. Janet was married to her nice, safe husband, but there were rocks ahead and one of them was Kate, sitting by the drawing-room fire, lifting her face for his kiss.

'Just seen the doctor,' he said as he warmed his hands.

'Has he come back?'

'No, no. Not Dr. Bunford. Dr. Gregory. I've asked him in to dinner.'

'To-night?' Mrs. Nesbitt quickly called to mind what she had ordered for the meal. 'Janet, ring the bell. I must tell Mary, but really, William, I don't know why you asked him.'

'An impulse of hospitality, my dear, in spite of the havoc he has played with Janet's toes.'

'Janet's toes?' Mrs. Nesbitt looked from her husband to her daughter.

'He has been dancing on them, Kate.'

'Does he go to dances? You didn't tell me, Janet,' and she sighed at the multitude of things which Janet left untold.

William Nesbitt now glanced at the girl who returned his look with a positively inimical expression and went out of the room.

'I must go and dress,' he said and followed her. 'Look here, Janet,' he said, 'come into the morning-room. I want to speak to you. Dr. Gregory has told me what has happened – a weight off his mind, I think. No, I've no criticisms to offer. You're a woman. You can do as you please, but your mother mustn't know. She can't stand any more of these shocks.'

'Ah,' she said, 'you were more sympathetic about the other one.'

He waved that aside, though it would have been a palpable hit if what she imagined of him had been true. 'She mustn't know,' he repeated.

'No one shall know – unless you tell them,' she said coldly.

'I'm not anxious to spread the news, child. Why should I be? But Dr. Gregory is at liberty to come here as often as he chooses.'

'What for?'

'I leave that to you and him,' William Nesbitt replied.

Janet's manner at dinner slowed plainly enough that the doctor did not come for her pleasure, but he was more equal to the occasion than William Nesbitt had feared. When he looked at Janet, which was not often, he paid no homage with his eyes nor did they ask for mercy, and he showed a capacity for amusing conversation which surprised and delighted his host who liked a man who left the obvious unsaid and attributed some quickness to his hearers, and once, when Janet laughed with a spontaneity too genuine to be checked by her seething indignation, her father had difficulty in restraining signs of jubilation. If old Dryasdust could make her laugh against her will, his further task would not be too hard. That laugh, even her annoyance at it, had already broken some of her stubbornness, but the situation, he admitted, was awkward for her: on consideration it was positively appalling. She sat, facing her husband, whom she was pretending not to love, in the presence of a father who, without showing sympathy, knew her secret, and of a mother who sat at the end of the table, quite unsuspicious, a little left behind in the conversation, but preserving her air of gracious dignity. Yes, it was a humiliating position for the child, but it served her right. The glorious defiance of her stealthy marriage had been stolen from her, it had become merely foolish, and if the doctor could simulate a courteous indifference or an alarming fierceness, William Nesbitt foresaw that Janet

262

would be compelled to make advances: there was nothing else for her to do.

It was the most amusing evening he had spent for a long time and the climax came when he and Kate were in bed and the light was out.

'I shouldn't be surprised,' she said, 'if Dr. Gregory and Janet fell in love with each other.'

'Neither should I, Kate – not a bit. Everybody falls in love with our daughters.'

'Everybody is too many,' she replied in a harder voice, 'but if he's a good man – '

'I think he's good, Kate. He looks good. But I thought you didn't like him.'

'I like nobody,' she said, 'who sees me when I am ill. It's an indignity one has to suffer.'

'Don't suffer it again,' he begged, wondering what more blows were to fall on her. For a little while, exhilarated by the excitements of the evening, he had forgotten Lydia, actually forgotten her, fighting her battle in the quiet country across the river, but now, in the darkness, through which the dying fire cast gleams on the rug before the hearth and the polished legs of a chair, her trouble reached him like a physical pain. He shut his eyes, and as he sent up the inarticulate prayer which was all he could ever compass, he heard Kate's voice, the pleasant, soft voice of her best moments, saying, 'What is the matter, William?'

'Matter?' He turned on his back. 'Matter, Kate?'

'I felt – I felt as if you were unhappy.'

'It's a bewildering world,' he said.

'Don't you like him yourself?'

'Yes, I like him.'

'It will be lonely with no child in the house.'

'Well, we shall have each other, as we had in the beginning.' He struggled in a sitting posture and leaned over to kiss her.

Chapter 34

AFTER all, it was Kate who remained most surely his.
Their comradeship might break but it would always heal
again; their love, in spite of all its little rifts, perhaps
because of them, was too strong in its daily use and habit
to be destroyed, and yet they had expended on each other
far less thought than they had lavished on the children to
whom, at best, they were only old people to be dutifully
loved. He told himself that he had no right to wish for
more and was content to have it so, but he knew that his
content was founded on the fact that the statement itself
was inherently untrue, the sort of remark with which
parents serve up pity to themselves. He was more than an
old father to be kindly loved: he was a force. He repeated
it – a force. Mabel was afraid of him, Walter admired him,
Dora allowed herself to weep in his presence – and what
higher compliment could she pay him? – and if Janet was
not appreciating him at the moment it was because he had
chosen to offend her: as for Lydia, his relationship with
her had always been a special one; they were friends, and
though he had never been critical enough of her conduct,
he was going to make up for lost time. No, he might be
a nonentity some day, in his dotage, or on a sick-bed, but
on the day he had appointed for Lydia's visit he felt himself emphatically a force. And then, humorously, he confessed that even now it was hard to find a just cause for
criticism of her for she had acted honestly, and all this
valiant admonishment of himself was based on a mere fear
of lightness, a fear which was unworthy of his faith in her
and his general belief in the working together of things for
good.

He straightened himself and walked more briskly towards
his office. The pale February sky had a diffused brightness,

but the sunlight struck the tree trunks until they shone, and the paths crossing the green made bands of deep blue and purple through the grass. Birds twittered with a promise of song, and now and then William Nesbitt paused to look into a garden where snowdrops and crocuses were growing. He shared with Lydia a great love of the spring, and this seemed to him a proper day on which to meet her. Even in the dark house at Mastover there must be signs of what was coming – earlier daylight at the square windows, shafts of sunlight on the dreary portraits, a bell-like ring in every sound, and outside, on the rough lawn before the larches, spear-shaped leaves should be thrusting themselves up.

In a few hours she would leave that house and start on the tedious journey to Radstowe, and though he could not picture her leaving furtively, running down the rocky lane in fear of pursuit and trying to subdue the noise of her footsteps, he distressed himself with imaginary scenes of anger, recrimination and despair, or of a weariness which could find no expression. And again he saw her at the door, taking a temporary farewell of Henry, with a light touch on his face and a gay word. That fellow, he was sure, would not see her off at the station, too busy, too much absorbed in his own affairs. William Nesbitt was not sure that he did not deserve to lose her, and if she returned to him that night she would, in all probability, have to walk through miles of darkness alone. He knew he was working himself up into a state of dissatisfaction with Henry Wyatt in case he should find it convenient to have a grievance against him, and he began to walk more slowly, horrified at the discovery of such weakness in himself. There was no end to these personal revelations even at his age, and how much more natural and forgivable that Lydia should make discoveries, too!

This life, he thought, could only be a probation and poor human beings should not judge each other too harshly. He was sure that the God who had caused the coming and going of the seasons, the budding of green leaves and the fall of brown ones, all the wonders which accustomed eyes

265

forget to see as miracles, looked as leniently on an honest, erring soul as on a tree stunted by some mischance. And who could decide, he asked again, on what was right and what wrong? He felt a sudden distaste for his own little schemings: he could do nothing: yet, after all – his optimism sprang up again – his efforts might be part of the vast plan, though he was only a small, grey man, waddling slightly as he walked, getting old but trying not to show it, with a few snowdrops in his coat and, thank God, his eyesight as keen as ever for beauty. It was keen, too, for the shop windows and, pausing as usual at the greengrocer's, he went in and bought an armful of tulips, yellow, orange and pink. Lydia was fond of tulips: she was rather like one herself, with her straight neck and her pretty head, and walking on with his gay burden he began fancifully to compare Janet to a daffodil, Dora to a big brown chrysanthemum, bitterly sweet, and Kate to a plant of mignonette, fragrant and clean and modestly sure of itself within its limits; and these thoughts accompanied him down the narrow lane where the gate still hung on its broken hinge, and into the old square where children on their way to school gathered round him when they saw his flowers. He stopped, his eyes twitching as they did when he was troubled or amused. The children had given up trying to rob him of his button-hole, but the sight of such a bunch emboldened them.

'Now then,' he said, 'you know I don't give you flowers because you spoil them. Don't know how to treat them.' He pointed his stick at the little girl to whom he had once given a rose. 'Tulips, these are tulips. Now, if I give you one, will you take it to school and give it to your teacher to put in water?'

'Give us two, Mister!' she begged.

The demand pleased him so he gave her three, and he filled the other little hands which were held out to him. He could seldom refuse a demand on his generosity and to-day, in spite of his anxieties, he expected so much pleasure that he was glad to give some. The presence of

Lydia in trouble was better than the cheerful presence of anybody else, and while he told himself he was an old fool for feeling such excitement, he was not moved by the accusation: he did not care.

He put the rest of the tulips into a big vase and placed it where she could not fail to see it on her entrance, and when he had warned Walter that he expected Lydia in the afternoon and did not wish to be disturbed while she was with him, he added that it was not necessary to mention her visit to her mother. Walter nodded. He never asked questions, he never made trouble, he tried to avoid it when it was made by other people, and in his father's ability and wisdom he had a simple faith which prevented criticism. The least remarkable of the Nesbitts, he made up with admiration and loyalty what he lacked in originality; and he was proud of his family. He felt, though he could not explain his feeling, that, with the exception of Mabel whose dress and habits irritated his latent artistic sense, his sisters were different from and superior to the sisters of other people; they were clever in a way which produced nothing tangible but created an impression and, what was of importance to him, they knew how to wear their clothes and they had a queer sense of humour which he understood. He knew they had more character than he had himself and he gave Lydia credit for knowing what she was about. He could be trusted not only to be silent but to control his curiosity if he had any.

'He's a good fellow,' William Nesbitt thought, with regret that his appreciation went no further. A good fellow, loyal, honest, but not blessed with much brain. He would carry on the business when its founder was dead but he would never develop it, and William Nesbitt foresaw that it would become a second-rate affair and be bought cheaply by some more enterprising firm. The goodwill he had created, the ships he had built, the tradition of trust between master and men, the faith in his bond, these would go. 'And leave not a wrack behind,' he murmured. But did it matter, if the things themselves had been good? It was human to feel that it did matter, and was not one of his troubles in Lydia's affair, the fear that she, with so much to hand on to another generation and so much love to spend on it, should be frustrated? A short memory of his work, a short memory of Lydia's grace, and then – not a wrack behind. Never mind! Some things did live, they went on, though perhaps no one knew whence they came. Yes, they lived: those words for instance, and getting out the volume of Shakespeare which he kept in a drawer with his Bible, he read the passage and walked up and down his office, jingling his money in excited satisfaction.

Chapter 35

HE did not know why he should be surprised to hear Lydia talking gaily to Walter as she came up the stairs. He, no more than she, was a stealthy person, but he believed that in her circumstanes he might have been slightly furtive, and he was thankful she was not. She carried her rebel's banner bravely and if she lowered it she would do that bravely, too. He seated himself behind his desk, and for a minute or two his son and daughter continued to talk outside the door: then it opened, she shut it behind her and, still holding the handle, she faced her father saying, 'Behold me!'

He beheld her small, straight figure, dressed with her peculiar elegance. A little hat shaded her eyes, some cloak-like arrangement was flung over her shoulder, muffling the upper part of her body and revealing the slenderness of the rest. One hand was behind her back, the other, covered with a long, wrinkled glove, rested on her hip with a gallant effect which struck him as extraordinarily pathetic, for though it was early afternoon the panelled room was dim and he could not clearly see her face.

'Behold me, William!' she said again, with the faintest possible faltering in her voice, and he answered, a little gruffly, 'I can't. Too dark.' He touched a switch and rose to draw the curtains. 'That's better,' he said and, surveying her, he saw that her eyes were bright and her straight mouth tilted.

'Oh! Tulips!' she said, and crossing to his desk, she touched the petals. 'Lovely! I've been wanting tulips. Did you get them for me?'

'Well, to please you,' he said.

'Thank you. D'you know,' she laughed, 'just for a moment I thought you were angry with me.'

'Never angry,' he said.

'Of course not.'

'But sometimes,' he warned her, 'sometimes stern,'

'Really? I don't believe it.' She sat down and flung off her outer garment. 'Not with me,' she added securely.

'Not with you,' he agreed, 'but, perhaps, admonitory.'

'But not to-day.'

His eyes twitched. 'Why not to-day?'

'Because it has been such a wonderful day.'

'Spring's coming,' he said, and he watched her carefully. There was a spot of colour on each pale cheek and she was restless: he had almost forgotten how restless she was and, quite unaware of his own constant fidgeting, he deplored the habit. It had its attractions when the movements were subtle and expressive, but it suggested an activity which was not healthy. 'Can't you keep still?' he growled.

'Still! I've been sitting here like a mouse!'

'Silly simile, that,' he said. 'A mouse! You should hear them in these old walls.'

'Oh, William, do they come out? I must tuck my feet up. If there had been mice at Mastover, I should have died. But no,' she made a funny little grimace and imitated the action of a man writing, 'nothing but the scratching of Henry's pen – scratch, scratch, scratch, and when he stopped it was only to scratch his head.'

'H'm, very dull, I should imagine.'

'Dull! For me who like people and parties! And in all Mastover there were only Henry and Ethel Miller!'

'And Ethel Miller only once, I suppose?'

'Not at all, William, not at all. Do you think she could keep away from me? I knew she couldn't and I wasn't going to let her. She returned.'

'With her husband?'

'Eventually. There are depths of unsuspected guile in Ethel Miller Jones, depths. I'm sure she persuaded the simple soul that we needed his Christian influence. So we did, but what she needed was just me. It says much in my favour that women like me.'

'But the simple soul, not too much, I hope.'

'No, I saw to that. I never poach, though I always, always want to, just for fun. A form of sport, but despicable, of course. The simple soul is devoted to Ethel, though her skin always looks as if it's chapped, a healthy red, but rough. And she is devoted to the simple soul, and the simple soul likes Henry. He can't approve of him or me, but he says he realizes that – er – there may be circumstances – er – in which – er – He couldn't finish the sentence because he's both modest and puzzled, and the best of it is there are no such circumstances in our case. I've told him so, but he thinks that's my generosity. Those truthful people never believe one's telling the truth oneself, at least not when it goes against one. Funny, William! Life is interesting, isn't it? And Ethel loves me still.'

'Then I'm glad we never stinted her with plum cake.'

On a laugh Lydia continued, 'Yes, she loves me still and keeps saying, "Oh, Lydia!" just as she always did, and I love making her say it, so there we are! We shall be going to church soon. Really, it makes me feel I didn't do anything very daring after all. Times are changing.'

'I wish your mother would realize it,' he said sharply.

'Ah, she doesn't change,' Lydia said and then, caught by that sharpness in his voice, she added gently, 'I'm sorry, William, but one can't act according to one's mother, or even according to one's father. Luckily for me, you are you.'

'I never said I approved,' he said quickly.

'I don't care whether you do or not. There's not that kind of love between us. It would stand anything – wouldn't it? – anything!'

'I'm not so sure,' he said gravely.

'Well, what wouldn't it stand?'

'Nothing,' he had to admit on a cry and though she uttered a little sound of triumph, he went on, still gravely, 'But I should suffer, suffer very much if I had to think you flippant.'

'Ah, you suffer a great deal already, without saying anything about it.'

'No, I do not,' he protested.

'You're a great little man,' she murmured, 'very brave, very good –'

'Now, now, none of that,' he begged.

'Well, it's the first time, William, perhaps the only time and I apologize for being obvious.'

'Not obvious at all – just rubbish.'

'But anyhow, I'm not flippant.'

'Your letter worried me.'

'Yes.' She stood up, touched the tulips again and went to the window while he walked three paces, backwards and forwards, in front of the fire, and neither noticed how like they were to each other in this way of freeing thought by movement.

'I knew it would,' she said, 'but it helped me. So did Ethel. To think that dear, dull Ethel could help me! She's loyal.'

'So are you,' he said quickly.

'Yes, but one has to decide whom to be loyal to. I didn't know. I didn't know. It has been rather – rather trying, William. If Oliver had appeared one day looking forlorn and patient and forgiving, I think I must have gone back to him.'

'And now?'

'I'm safe now, I think.'

'Ah,' he breathed deeply, 'that's a mercy because he'll be here to-day.'

She was surprised but not startled, and at that moment he was happier than he had been since September for, in her calm readiness to meet the man, he thought he saw something sane and reasoned which was not the accepted view of such affairs, something in which sex was the least important element and, to test her, he said sharply, 'And you don't mind?'

'Yesterday I should have minded. To-day I don't. I told you it had been a wonderful day. Why is he coming here?'

272

'Well, child, in a stern mood I decided that you must make up your mind one way or the other and I thought you'd better see him. Besides, I want to speak to him myself. No, never mind why.'

'But I must know, William. You're scheming something.'

'Yes, always scheming. Tell me why to-day has been wonderful.'

'It sounds silly – but Henry looked such a baby. He's never looked like that before. He's so damnably sure of himself generally, it makes me want to hit him, and this morning, when I said good-bye, he looked like a child.'

'Did he see you off?'

'No, but he came to Radstowe by the same train. He thought I didn't see him, but of course I did, in spite of all his precautions. It was rather pathetic and it made me cry a little. He must have had a sudden panic and felt he must follow me. He hadn't a hat on and the most awful old trousers. He was like a stage conspirator, recognizable as one at once! I haven't given him a very easy time, William, and he isn't so sure of himself, or of me, as he seems, and though I would never have left him without telling him, and he might have known it, that settled any doubts of conscience I had. And it was only my conscience, not my heart. Oliver looks as if he needs me more, but he doesn't. Of course I shall always have times when I hate Henry, but I shan't leave him. He's hovering about outside now, I suppose.'

'Then he'll see Oliver.'

'Very likely.'

He was surprised at her indifference, for his own ready imagination was busy. Henry would be surprised at the coincidence, jealous, perhaps accusatory, and William Nesbitt did not want a quarrel outside his premises.

'Henry will think it odd,' he said.

'That won't do him any harm.'

'I don't know. Hadn't we better have him in?'

'Oh, no, William, I've been seeing Henry for months and

273

I want to be with you. Besides, you have to tell me what you are going to say to Oliver.'

It was his habit to walk as he talked without looking at the person he addressed, but now he stood still and fixed her steadily. 'I think he ought to divorce you,' he said, and at that she did surprise him, for she shrank back a step or two and put the desk between herself and him and from behind that barrier, with a hand at her throat, she cried in a thin voice, 'No, no, not that!'

Her eyes, widened and darkened, seemed to ask for mercy and under their gaze he lowered his own. He had seen her enraged in childhood, he had seen her weeping, but never before had he seen her frightened and the sight hurt him intolerably. He looked at the carpet and asked, 'Why are you afraid of that?'

She did not answer for a moment and when he looked up she was composed again and, bending over the desk towards him, she said, 'I don't want to hate Oliver.'

'You mean he would refuse?'

'Yes – nastily. He's an angel up to a point, but beyond that point he might be awful. I've taken care never to go beyond it because I knew.'

'You have gone a good way,' William Nesbitt muttered.

'I know, and he behaved magnificently because he's proud and because he always thinks he'll get me back. He has believed all the time that Henry will be too much for me and that I shall find him out. I haven't, though, and I never shall, but what I have found out is that I'm safe with him. He has no nice smooth ways, he was badly brought up by that mother of his, and if you were dying I don't believe he'd notice. You'd have to call his attention to the fact. But right through him there's a sort of brightness, a sort of light. And with Oliver – d'you know, William, there was always something about Oliver that frightened me? Not the kind of fear one enjoys, but something dark, somewhere. He gives me the kind of feeling I get if I'm alone in a wood.'

'But this is nonsense,' William Nesbitt protested.

'You know it isn't, William. You understand perfectly well. Things exist though we may never have seen them, and I'm not going to see Oliver in a way – in a way that would spoil him.'

'This is a new aspect of him to me,' William Nesbitt confessed.

'Ah, you're clever, but you can't know everything. But I know that. Besides, I've never asked for anything in my life and I'm not going to, and, moreover, one can't have everything in this world. One ought not to want too much. You get less, you know, in the end. And one has to pay. And then, William,' she hesitated, for the Nesbitts were loyal to each other, 'apart from that, there's Jane.'

'He has never cared for her.'

'I know, but Jane – '

'Janet's all right. That's all done with. You needn't think of that.'

'But one has to pay,' she repeated.

'My dear,' he said a little bashfully, 'I want you to have children.'

She steadied her voice with an effort. 'I've given them up, but Oliver hasn't. He never said a word, he never would, but do you think he would let me have Henry's children? That's too much to expect. No, the only baby I shall ever have is Henry and I must make the best of him. William, I forbid you to speak to Oliver about that. It would be useless and it would leave,' she touched herself, 'a stain.'

'This is your affair, child', he said. 'I will be silent.' And then, in a kind of rage, he cried out, 'But it's ridiculous!'

'Absurd,' she agreed.

'It's tragic!'

'No, I won't let it be that,' and at those words, he made with his hands a motion as though to brush away his outburst.

'You're quite right,' he said. 'Quite right. I forgot myself for a minute. We make our own tragedies. And this, I think, must be Oliver coming up the stairs.'

She went to the fireplace and laid one hand on the mantel-shelf and, keeping it there, perhaps for support but perhaps only because she had a sure instinct for a pose, she turned to face the door with her other hand hanging by her side and her lips, as William Nesbitt saw, a little parted to let out a welcome.

Chapter 36

IT was Janet who entered, stood still for an instant, and then shut the door. 'They didn't tell me there was anybody here,' she said.

'But I'm nobody,' Lydia stated. 'I'm not even sure of my own name! It's nice to see you, Jane, and what a pretty frock. Now, if only Dora were here we should be complete.'

'She'd come if you telephoned,' Janet said.

'Shall I?' Lydia stretched her hand toward the desk.

'Certainly not. There are limits. I'm very pleased to see my daughters, but these are my business hours. As you're here, you shall have some tea, but this mustn't be a pre-cedent.'

'I shan't worry you often, William. It's a long day's journey from Mastover. I don't see how I can get back to-night, and there not a house open to me in Radstowe except Walter's and I don't think there's enough room in that little flat. It would be rather fun to call on Mabel – but perhaps not. Jane, aren't you glad to see me? I wish you would be.'

'I think I am,' Janet said vaguely. 'I think I am.' With her hands in her big muff she stood over her sister's chair and looked down. 'Yes, I am,' she said quietly.

'Thank God for that,' Lydia said simply. 'It's the first time for years. Make a habit of it if you can.'

It seemed to William Nesbitt that round the figure of his youngest daughter there was a kind of mist: she moved as though she could not see her way quite clearly and she spoke without her usual crispness, like a person emerging from a dream, a dream and not a nightmare. 'That child's safe, too,' he decided. 'The doctor's a man and not a mummy,' and he rang the bell for tea.

Janet had seated herself in the other arm-chair and she

277

looked at the fire while Lydia looked at her and said, 'What
have you been doing to yourself? You look as if you had
been stealing jam and were wondering if there were any at
the corners of your mouth.'

'Not jam,' William Nesbitt said pleasantly. 'More like
quince jelly, isn't it? Something that gives you an appetite
for more?'

'I have been for a walk,' Janet said, rousing herself. 'A
long walk. There will soon be primroses.'

'Well, I don't know how people who call themselves busy
can get away in the middle of the day,' William Nesbitt
grumbled. 'I can't do it. It's bad enough to have you girls
invading my office.'

'Then she certainly has been stealing jam,' Lydia said.

'I've stolen nothing,' Janet answered emphatically. 'I've
only taken what I have been given.'

'Ah, stealing's more fun,' Lydia said, but Janet, who had
once wanted to steal what was not hers, shook her head
at the fire.

'It isn't,' she said, and William Nesbitt, who understood
the unspoken allusion, began to hum his hymn and Lydia,
who understood too, was careful to look scrupulously at
the fire in her turn.

'When I came in just now,' Janet began, and Lydia said,
'That's right, Jane. Change the subject, but you needn't
be afraid of me. I'm not curious. I'm not like William.'

'When I came in,' Janet persisted, 'there was rather an
odd-looking man at the door. He had no hat on –'

'And baggy trousers? That's Henry. He must be getting
rather cold out there. Cross, too, I should think.'

'I didn't imagine him like that. He looks good.'

There was a moment's silence after this unsolicited
testimonial to Henry Wyatt's appearance. It had been
given with perfect naturalness, and while William Nesbitt
heard it not only as an opinion for which he was grateful
but as one made by a daughter who had freed herself or
been freed to a wider womanhood in which she need no
longer consider each word before she uttered it, Lydia sat

278

with a light smile on her lips and seemed to be thinking back to all the incidents and impulses and convictions which had caused her to join her life to that of the man who, to Janet's clear eyes, looked good; and Janet, a little startled by the impressive stillness in the room, glanced from her sister to her father and back at the useful fire. Then she said calmly, 'I think you ought to ask him to come in.'

'But I'm not supposed to know he's there. And why didn't you ask your own young man to join the party, my dear?'

'What has Father been telling you?' Janet asked.

'Not a word, but you didn't go looking for primroses alone, did you? I suppose you came to confess your sins to William, as I have been doing. Well, I shall go soon and leave you with him.'

'Don't hurry, don't hurry,' William Nesbitt begged with mock politeness. 'I've no work to do. I'm thinking of starting a matrimonial and confidential bureau to employ my idle hours. Must do something'.

'Then, I advise a detective agency,' Janet said with a kind of good-humoured bitterness.

'I might combine the two,' he said.

'So he has been prying into your affairs, Jane? Well, I'm glad you have some to be pried into, and you're safe with him.'

'Safe!' Janet cried. 'He's a public danger!'

'My dear,' he said, 'there are times when dangerous expedients are the only safe ones. But I do make mistakes, and I wish I had not asked Oliver to come here to-day.'

Janet who, perhaps out of habit, had stiffened suddenly, relaxed deliberately and murmured absent-mindedly, 'Oliver? Why not?'

'William's afraid he and Henry will fight on the doorstep,' Lydia explained. 'But they won't. Here's the tea, and a telegram for William.' She stretched her feet beyond the fender. 'Pour out, please, Jane.'

Janet had already risen to clear a space on the desk for

the big tray supported by a small office boy, and as she began to handle the cups and saucers with her quiet deftness, she looked across the room at Lydia, on whose warm bright dress the firelight flickered, and asked with the sober interest of a person who no longer judged but tried to understand things, 'Do you want to see him?'

Lydia leaned forward and clasped her ankles. 'No,' she said slowly, 'I don't think I do.'

'Then why don't you go before he comes?'

'Because I hate running away. And I want some tea. Have you lost some old boat, William, and got the insurance money? You look pleased.'

'We don't lose our boats,' he said. 'We're rather particular about that.'

'Ah, it's a wonderful firm, Nesbitt and Son, isn't it? But you'd better knock wood. If Oliver doesn't come by the time we've finished tea, I'll go. That won't be running.'

'You need not hurry,' he assured her. 'He isn't coming,' and he put the telegram in the fire.

Lydia leaned forward again as the fire annihilated the flimsy paper. 'There he goes,' she said softly. 'There he goes,' and with her hand she seemed to help the upward movement of the flames. Then, turning her head swiftly, a trick for which William Nesbitt always watched with pleasure but also with the readiness of a hunter anticipating a spring, she asked, 'But what did he say?'

'Can't come. Writing.'

Apparently content with that, she turned back to her thoughts, and William Nesbitt, glancing at his other daughter, saw a look of doubt on her face, but he nodded reassuringly, well aware that he had given her cause to suspect him, even when he was innocent.

'How cosy it is here, and peaceful,' Lydia said, leaning back and balancing her cup on her lap, and her father, remembering that Dora had said that too, felt a great happiness that his children should find rest in his company, but he said modestly, 'It's a nice room.'

'It's not the room,' Lydia replied. 'It's you. Being with God must be rather like this, only more alarming. You have all the divine attributes, William, except justice. You're hopelessly prejudiced about the people you love.'

'If you think,' he said, 'that I haven't seen through you –'

She put up a lazy hand and it was odd and rather touching to see her so languid. 'Now, don't disturb me with arguments, please. Of course you see through me, just as God does, but I suppose He's grieved and you are not. We all see through each other, all the clever members of this family, Dora and Jane and you and I. That's what's so comfortable about it, no sudden shocks and disillusions and misunderstandings and bickerings. Jane was outside the fold for a little while, but she has come back. Oh, yes, Jane, you were and you have. I'm no more of a fool than you are.'

'Not so much of one,' Janet said, and she made the confession abruptly but with dignity.

'And now, farewell,' Lydia said. 'I must go. Where, I don't know. Henry hasn't a hat and probably no money.'

'Here,' William Nesbitt said, taking his hand from his pocket. 'Here you are. Better get a car and drive to Mastover. Or you can get that train, that train I got, you know, and drive from the junction. Mind that awful road, though. Tell the man to drive carefully. You ought to have that road seen to.'

'No, no, I like the steep and stony path to heaven. The primrose path of dalliance is for Jane. I hope you'll find the primroses soon, Jane. There will be plenty at Mastover in a few weeks, if you like to come.'

'I'll come and see you,' she hesitated, 'when I'm married.'

'Then get married soon. And I hope the matrimonial bureau will be a great success.'

'It is!' he cried. 'It is! Good-bye, child. Make that Henry of yours take care of you.' He was deeply moved by this parting, by his renewed confidence in her whom he should never have doubted, by the vague atmosphere of happiness surrounding Janet, by the courage of Lydia whose road was indeed rocky but worth ascending, and all three stood, a little shy and intimidated by emotion; but the Nesbitts could be trusted not to make scenes involuntarily and with a word and a laugh the tension broke. There was in them all, as he realized at that moment, something hard and something humorous which, with enjoyment of its own dexterity, could turn blows aside or receive the blows, if necessary, without showing pain.

'Now I come to think of it,' he said thoughtfully, 'you children never cried when you were hurt. Your mother saw to that.'

'I sometimes forget,' Lydia said in the same tone, 'that she has any part in us,' and at that, stung by his own disloyalty in not regretting her absence, in having forgotten her for a time, he exclaimed, 'But you must remember it!'

'I remember her,' Lydia said, 'as herself. A wall, with flowers growing on it, ivy, clinging plants, but underneath a wall.' Turning aside and picking up her gloves, she added, 'I can't scale it. I can't get through. However, I like to think of it. But you, William, you're only an old tree. I can get round you easily enough and climb into all your branches, except the very top ones, near the sky, near the stars, too fine a perch for the likes of me.'

William Nesbitt blinked. 'She's quite poetical,' he told Janet.

'I live with a literary man. Scratch, scratch, scratch. Good-bye, my friends. If you look out of the window, you'll see Henry and me going off together like the Babes in the Wood.'

'And mind you get that car,' William Nesbitt called after her gruffly.

Chapter 37

HE drew the curtains, opened the window, and found Janet at his side. They both leaned out and not far below them, for the old building was not lofty, they saw the upturned faces of the other two, pale in the oncoming darkness. With the hand which was not holding Henry's, Lydia waved, and they passed out of sight in the shadow of the house. Straightening themselves, William Nesbitt and Janet stood and listened to the footsteps, growing fainter until they were lost in the sounds of other footsteps, the rumbling of a cart, the soft swish of a boat in the river, the knocking of oars in the rowlocks and the subdued voices of two men talking near the water.

William Nesbitt drew the curtains and shut the window again. 'Time to go home,' he said. 'We'll go together, Janet.' He felt very tired and, as on that night at Mastover, he suffered from an absurd sense of desertion. She had gone with a wave of her hand, gaily, gallantly, as she did everything, and it was right that she should, but the room felt cold in spite of the fire, and his well-worn limbs slackened suddenly, as after a great strain. Things had turned out as he had hoped they would, she had kept to her path, and though he felt limp and weary now, the inner part of him was at peace if it was lonely. He went to the fire and raked out the coals, a habit he had formed when he was poor, and then, realizing that Janet stood there waiting for him, waiting also on his mood, he shrugged himself cheerfully into his overcoat, but still neither of them spoke until, as they were ascending the narrow lane where even in the twilight the trees showed their thickening branches and here and there a bud, Janet asked, 'What did Oliver really say?'

'What I told you,' he replied. 'I could see you were suspecting me.'

'Well, you have a way of – diverting things, haven't you? Aren't you sometimes afraid?'

'Yes, always. I was always afraid when I took a ship in or out of harbour, afraid of storms, wrecks, illness, mutinies, always on the watch. I was afraid when I left the sea and started here, but I have been hopeful, too. You must be willing to take risks. No good crawling into holes. And I have an interfering nature, child, as you have discovered, but,' he walked more slowly and putting out a hand he slipped it under her arm and leaned on her a little, 'but perhaps my interfering days are over. I can't get up this hill as fast as I did.'

'There is no hurry,' she said in her level voice. 'It's a lovely evening.'

'A wonderful day, Lydia called it. You haven't told me why you came to see me.'

'There's no need, is there?'

'No. A good day.' He dropped her arm so that they could go separately between the iron posts which marked the lane's top and, drawing a deep breath, he said, 'I wonder what will be the next adventure, the next act in the comedy of the Nesbitts.'

'You will find it dull if we just – just amble along, won't you?'

'No, life's never dull, so commit no indiscretions on my account. No further indiscretions,' he added weightily, but she had either a remarkable control over her tongue or a remarkable inability to loosen it and he drew nothing from her. 'Why, the sky changes every minute,' he said, referring to his earlier remark. 'On these spring evenings I always think it likes to stay light as long as it can. It must be a treat for it after the winter, like a child allowed to stay up late. And then,' they had reached the shops, 'there are the greengrocers' windows. Very attractive. I never cared about gardening. I like to see the flowers growing and the lettuces coming up, but I could never bend my back for them, yet I find it hard to pass a greengrocer. I think I'll get a bunch of grapes for your mother. She ought to eat fruit – at least so your doctor says and I suppose he's always right.'

He went in and made his purchase, leaving her to wonder at the tiredness in his voice, and when he came out she saw on his face – illumined by the lighted window – that look which becomes permanent with people much older than himself, the result of gazing backward and inward and beyond, so that passing events and objects are slightly blurred, and it was so remarkable a change in him that, moved out of her reserve, she stepped towards him, saying quickly, 'I think you're very tired. Why don't you hold my arm again?'

A little annoyed at this betrayal of himself, he gave a half shake of his head and then, anxious not to check her expansiveness, he said, 'Very well, as an equal, as a friend, not as a doddering old father,' and so, walking quickly, they passed the shops, crossed the green, empty of children at this hour but dotted here and there with the figures of lovers strolling on the paths or sitting close and still under the trees, passed the mews where an electric lamp showed the motionless hands of the disabled clock, and turned in at the gate to see the early flowers splashed with light from the windows of the house.

He took his latchkey from his pocket, but before he put it in the lock he said impressively, 'Many of the things I have wanted have come to pass, but not all. I ought not to expect them all. A man who has made his own place in the world is inclined to feel angry when he doesn't get his way, but that's a waste of energy and time. One wants perfection and forgets that the very root of imperfection is in oneself – oneself.' He turned the key and stood aside for her to enter, gave an assertive nod to assure her of the truth of his remark, and shut the door sharply.

From the drawing-room a murmur of voices was audible. He raised his eyebrows, pointed to a loaded basket on the floor and said in a whisper, 'Mabel!'

'Oh, I don't want to see her to-night,' Janet complained.

'No,' he agreed. 'She makes an unromantic finish to your day. It's the marmalade season. She will be telling your mother all about that. Creep upstairs and I'll go and applaud her labours.'

But it was evident at once that a topic more exciting than her own domestic virtues had caused Mabel's eyes to shine with an extra polish, and Mrs. Nesbitt's attitude was not the one of gentle sympathy she assumed for Mabel's benefit. She sat upright with her face flushed, and without waiting for William's kiss, she said almost fiercely, 'Mabel has seen Lydia!'

He kissed them both. 'Been to Mastover?' he asked genially.

'Certainly not,' Mabel replied.

'But I thought you and John were contemplating a visit. Your mother and I have been, Dora's been, why shouldn't you go?'

'William,' Mrs. Nesbitt said sternly, 'don't you want to know where Mabel saw Lydia?'

'If I may hazard a guess,' he said pleasantly, 'it was somewhere between the station and my office. She came to see me.'

'You knew she was coming?'

'I did, Kate.'

'And you didn't tell me!'

'My dear, what would have been the good?'

Mrs. Nesbitt stifled something like a sob. 'Everybody,' she said, 'can see my child except myself.'

He could not find it in his heart to make the obvious retort, and he turned from the sight of her pain to discover on Mabel's face an expression of disappointment, of collapse. She had been exercising the energies of a mind capable of much secretiveness on a mystery which was solved at a casual word, and she felt that her acuteness had been cheated.

'So that's very simple,' he said.

'I wonder she cares to come to Radstowe,' Mabel said.

'Ah, she's fond of her old father, fond of her mother, too. She said to-day she liked to think of you, Kate. She said you reminded her of flowers and growing things on a wall.'

Mrs. Nesbitt, raising her head stiffly, stared at him and beyond him with her opaque gaze and hardly roused herself to bid Mabel good-bye, but when he returned from seeing his daughter out, she moved her lips to ask pitifully, 'Did she, William?'

He nodded, patted her shoulder, and said loudly, as though he replied to a host of hostile critics. 'I don't say she's right, but I say she thinks she is.'

'About the flowers?' Mrs. Nesbitt murmured, and he cried, 'No, no, Kate. About Henry.'

Mrs. Nesbitt recovered herself a little and said sharply, 'I always said Oliver was to blame.'

'Let's leave blame out, Kate. We can't judge.' Shuffling his feet, for it was never easy to speak of the finest things to her, he said awkwardly, 'I like to think of what that great man said when the woman was taken in adultery. He said, "He that is without sin among you, let him first cast a stone." Clever, clever – and how quick! A great mind and a great heart. I can see all those fellows standing round, biting their nails, peeping at each other, and then slinking away. They'd find plenty to say afterwards, talking about it among themselves, but they couldn't find a word when they had to meet those eyes. Not a word. There was no word. He had said it all.'

With her hands trembling on her lap, Mrs. Nesbitt looked up like a child, and the tenderness of his own feelings reminded him that such a look on Henry had crystallized Lydia's troubled love into a sparkling clearness.

'I wish,' she said, 'I had thought of saying that to Mrs. Miller.'

'Mrs. Miller again!' he exclaimed, with a conviction that the woman whose spite he had always dreaded had, after all, done Kate some good turn.

'Yes, I met her this afternoon and she stopped me in

287

the street, so I knew she had something cruel to say to me. She said she supposed Lydia had ruined my life and now she was doing her best to ruin Ethel's. I didn't mean to tell you, William, and make things harder for you.'

'Things are not hard for me when you are kind.'

'I am not naturally kind,' she confessed with difficulty.

'I am not like you, but I did,' the words came strangely, 'I did – stick up for her. My own daughter! I said Lydia could harm no one because she's good. And then I went away because my legs were shaking. They are shaking still. And I don't know what she meant, but that is what I said. And then you came home and told me what Lydia said about the flowers – '

She paused and, fearing his honesty might be disastrous, yet realizing the necessity for it, he said, 'But beneath the flowers, Kate, she said there was a wall which she could not get through, but she was wrong there, I think.'

'Yes,' she said, 'she can get through.' She lifted and dropped her hands in despair of understanding or making him understand. 'I can't believe Lydia is right, but I can believe she is good.'

He felt an extraordinary peacefulness, as though the actual presence of that power, that pervading goodness in which he trusted, were in the room and, going rather stiffly on his knees and making a pretence to stir the fire, he offered, in that attitude, his humble thanks.

VIRAGO MODERN CLASSICS

The first Virago Modern Classic, *Frost in May* by Antonia White, was published in 1978. It launched a list dedicated to the celebration of women writers and to the rediscovery and reprinting of their works. Its aim was, and is, to demonstrate the existence of a female tradition in fiction which is both enriching and enjoyable. The Leavisite notion of the 'Great Tradition', and the narrow, academic definition of a 'classic', has meant the neglect of a large number of interesting secondary works of fiction. In calling the series 'Modern Classics' we do not necessarily mean 'great' — although this is often the case. Published with new critical and biographical introductions, books are chosen for many reasons: sometimes for their importance in literary history; sometimes because they illuminate particular aspects of womens' lives, both personal and public. They may be classics of comedy or storytelling; their interest can be historical, feminist, political or literary.

Initially the Virago Modern Classics concentrated on English novels and short stories published in the early decades of this century. As the series has grown it has broadened to include works of fiction from different centuries, different countries, cultures and literary traditions. In 1984 the Victorian Classics were launched; there are separate lists of Irish, Scottish, European, American, Australian and other English-speaking countries; there are books written by Black women, by Catholic and Jewish women, and a few relevant novels by men. There is, too, a companion series of Non-Fiction Classics constituting biography, autobiography, travel, journalism, essays, poetry, letters and diaries.

By the end of 1988 over 300 titles will have been published in these two series, many of which have been suggested by our readers.

ALSO OF INTEREST

OTHER NOVELS BY E.H. YOUNG

MISS MOLE
New Introduction by Sally Beauman

"Who would suspect her of a sense of fun and irony, of a passionate love for beauty and the power to drag it from its hidden places? Who could imagine that Miss Mole had pictured herself, at different times, as an explorer in strange lands, as a lady wrapped in luxury and delicate garments . . . ?"

Miss Hannah Mole, a farmer's daughter, has for twenty years earned her living as nursery governess or companion to a succession of difficult old women. Now aged forty, a thin, shabby figure, she returns to the lovely city of Radstowe with its hills, trees and arching suspension bridge. Here she is, if not exactly embraced, at least sheltered and employed by the pompous nonconformist minister, Reverend Corder, whose motherless daughters are sorely in need of care and good food. But even the dreariest situation can be transformed into an adventure by the indomitable Miss Mole. Blessed with wit, intelligence and the splendid capacity to call a spade a spade, she wins the affection of Ethel and of her nervous sister Ruth, transforms life at the Vicarage, and triumphs in her own entrancing way . . .

THE MISSES MALLETT
New Introduction by Sally Beauman

There are four Misses Mallett. First come Caroline and
Sophia — large and jolly spinsters with recollections of a past
glamour which sustain them as the years slip by.

Then there is Rose. Beautiful Rose with her knot of dark hair,
pale complexion and lovely grey eyes. So much younger than
her stepsisters, she calmly awaits the event — or the man —
that will take her away from their life of small social successes
in the city of Radstowe. But she is independent and fastidious:
no man, not even the eligible Francis Sales, can entirely
capture her heart.

The fourth Miss Mallett is Henrietta who arrives to share the
conventional home of her three aunts. With her Aunt Rose's
beauty and her own wilful spirit, she determines against
spinsterhood. Encountering Francis (no longer so eligible),
she falls under his spell. As Rose and Henrietta circle round
Francis they are forced to decide between sense and sensibility
— and each of them makes the perfect choice.

JENNY WREN
New Introduction by Sally Beauman

"Jenny, too, wanted pleasure, pretty clothes, laughter, admiration and love, but she would not stoop to get them. She would wait, holding herself erect, until these gifts came to her unsought."

On their father's death, Jenny and Dahlia Rendall, with their mother Louisa, move across the river to the heights of Upper Radstowe. Here they try to make a living by taking in lodgers. But their neighbours eye this all-female household with alarm and distrust — especially when a local farmer takes to calling on Louisa, now an attractive, if not entirely respectable widow. Dahlia takes it all with a pinch of salt; fastidious, conventional Jenny cannot. Embarrassed by her mother's country ways, smarting at every slight, both real and imaginary, she longs for a different life. Then Jenny falls in love with a handsome, young squire — but certain of his prejudice and a prisoner of her pride, she dares not reveal her name . . .

THE CURATE'S WIFE
New Introduction by Sally Beauman

"Life would be a much simpler matter with her will, her thoughts and her footsteps following Cecil's, but how very dull this docility would be, how bad for both of them!"

Dahlia Rendall has moved not many yards from her family home, Beulah Mount in Upper Radstowe. While her sister Jenny sojourns in the English countryside, the lovely unconventional Dahlia launches forth on what appears to be the most conventional of marriages — to a curate, the Rev. Cecil Sproat. As Cecil struggles with his sermons, Dahlia battles with domesticity, her naturally irreverent wit, and her weakness for handsome young men. And Dahlia's vision of marital perfection is at odds with Cecil's. But she has intelligence, determination and a sense of humour — all useful weapons in that age-old battle of the sexes called marriage.